An Irish Promise

An Irish Promise

Isabella Connor

Published 2014 by Choc Lit Limited
Penrose House, Crawley Drive, Camberley, Surrey GU15 2AB, UK
www.choc-lit.com

A CIP catalogue record for this book is available
from the British Library

ISBN 978-1-78189-179-7

Printed and bound by CPI Group (UK) Ltd, Croydon, CR0 4YY

To Mariana

Acknowledgements

Liv Thomas thanks …
With much love and thanks to everyone who has supported
me since I started this crazy journey. Thank you Mike, Jim,
Stuart and Claire, Christian and Gemma, and Samantha
and Nick, for spreading the word, and with special
thanks to Julie and Jamie Giles for going way beyond
the call of duty in that respect! Thank you Jo Porter for
being encouraging and constructive, and thanks Julie
Macintyre for being a great friend. My work colleagues
deserve a mention for their encouragement and for
putting up with my constant references to 'my novel' and
'Choc Lit' – Kathleen, Sandi, Ali, Rosie, Sita and Sally.

Valerie Olteanu thanks …
Linda and John, Alan, the Fab Four: Andrew, Ross, Scott,
Calum – an ocean away but so often in my thoughts;
Carol, special friend and confidante, who knows that
wine and Monty Python jokes are the only sane response
to a mad world; Adelina Suvagau, for her creativity
and enthusiasm; and Codin, 'le sens a mes demains,' for
Terrace Time, and for always knowing the answers.

We jointly thank …
Leanne Hayter and Brigid Killen for their invaluable
help with research; the lovely, if slightly mad, Di
Baker; America's Chris Evans for being just right; our
readers who inspire us to keep writing; the Tasting
Panel readers who passed this book: Jaimee, Jemma,
Susan C, Betty, Julie, Sammi, Susan P, Liz and Caroline;
and last but not least, the entire Choc Lit family for
their continued support which is second to none.

Chapter One

This was where they'd raised the devil. School bullies, playing their sick game of torment in a small village church. Terrifying a fourteen-year-old girl, then leaving her locked inside overnight with the darkness, where every sound struck fear into her heart. When morning came, the church was finally opened, but it was days before she could speak, and nightmares made her scared to sleep. And it had all been covered up. Not one of the bullies had been publicly shamed or punished.

Rachel stood in the grey stone porch of St Kilian's Church, willing herself to stop shaking. She was an adult. The bullies couldn't hurt her. However, she would do her best to make them share her pain, and by the time she'd finished here, everyone in the village would know the truth about what had happened. That was a promise – and Rachel never broke a promise.

* * *

Father Daniel Quinn heard someone struggling with the rectory gate. He really should have that faulty latch fixed, but it was such a useful early-warning system. He peered round the curtain just in time to see a young woman wrench the gate open. She was a stranger to Kilbrook. No one local would choose a white winter coat. Not practical for an Irish country village with its mud and mess. And those heels on her boots were catching now in the cobbles of the rectory path. He saw her suddenly lurch to one side, and an outstretched hand grabbed the holly tree. Her face creased in pain as the sharpness of the leaves punished her for the error.

Daniel went quickly into the narrow hallway and opened the front door. The woman was staring in dismay at the cut on her hand. A few drops of blood had spattered her coat, the colour stark against the white wool.

'Hello there!' he called, moving down the path towards her. 'That holly tree's a bully, isn't it?'

Her head jerked up at his words and she was staring at him as if she'd seen Lucifer himself. Better get her some tea or she'd be fainting on the path, and he'd have to carry her inside. The village gossips would have a field day with that.

'Come in, why don't you, and let me sort out that hand. I'm Father Daniel Quinn. Call me Daniel.'

He smiled. The benevolent, trustworthy smile he used for children and pensioners. Just in case his dog collar wasn't reassuring enough. People saw potential axe murderers everywhere these days.

* * *

The priest was bowed over Rachel's hand like some courtier in a medieval painting. Not bestowing a kiss of loyalty, though, just cleaning the scratch on her hand. Rachel looked around the kitchen. Though it had been painted and modernised, some of it was still familiar – the slate floor tiles and the pulley-operated drying rack dangling from the ceiling. As children, she and her sister had lived in the small house next door but had spent a lot of time in this room as their mother was housekeeper to Kilbrook's priest, Father Milligan.

The sudden sting of disinfectant made her gasp.

'Sorry,' Daniel murmured, and glanced up at her.

She saw kind brown eyes behind the wire-rimmed glasses. Eyes which showed no sign of recognition. That wasn't a surprise. Sometimes she didn't even recognise herself. He'd grown into quite a handsome man, his face still unlined by the pastoral cares that had weathered old Father Milligan. People would look at Daniel Quinn and see a friendly parish priest, but Rachel knew better. This man absolved other people's sins while his own festered. In an ideal world, sin should be visible for all to see, like the brand marks burned on criminals centuries ago …

'All done.'

Rachel stared down at the plaster on her hand. It was bright yellow with a cartoon chicken's face. She couldn't help but smile.

'We're out of plain,' he explained. 'The kids love these. Helps them forget their pain in no time.'

And what about my pain, my heartache? Can you take that away so easily?

He was still kneeling like a penitent next to the chair, and for a brief moment, she wanted to confess her real identity. To see the shock – and perhaps the shame – on his face. He'd claim he was just a boy then and hadn't known any better. Apologising might give him closure. Make him feel like a great weight had been lifted from him, but that was too easy. Why should he have such a short time of suffering when his actions had caused her years of trauma?

'Thanks for rescuing me,' she said. 'I'm Rachel Ford by the way.' Years ago, when they left Kilbrook for England, Rachel's mother had changed her married name of Rinaldi and reverted to her maiden name, Forde, dropping the telltale Irish final 'e'. Part of the fresh start she thought they needed. At first, Rachel had worried the name change would be disrespectful to her dead father, but she quickly got used to it. The new surname sounded solidly English. Although she'd actually been born in England, and her English accent hadn't been affected by the year spent in Ireland, Rachel hadn't wanted to stand out as different in any way at her new school. Now, back in Kilbrook, this change of identity would work to her advantage, hopefully helping her go undetected. 'I'm the art history student who wants to study the Stokeley murals in your church.'

Daniel beamed. 'Rachel! Of course! Pleased to meet you. How was your flight?'

'Fine.'

'And did you use that car rental company I recommended?'

'I did. Thanks for the advice. I was given a Toyota Corolla at a very reasonable rate. I'd have been here sooner but the traffic was bad in Galway.'

Daniel clicked his tongue sympathetically. 'Sure, and isn't it always. You take your life in your hands on those Galway roundabouts. Still, you made it, and that's what counts.'

But there were times during the drive when Rachel had been tempted to head back as fast as she could to Shannon Airport: one short flight and she'd be home safe and sound in London. It was a miracle she'd made it to Kilbrook at all, and the temptation to flee was still strong.

'This calls for some tea. I've just warmed the pot. Then I can show you the Stokeley murals before evening Mass.'

'No!' The word, spoken too loudly, echoed around the kitchen, and Daniel raised his eyebrows. 'Sorry, it's just that I'm a bit tired. I'd prefer to see the murals tomorrow.'

Rachel *was* tired, but the truth was she couldn't face going into the church today. Just standing in the porch had been bad enough. Hopefully tomorrow she'd feel stronger. And she'd go there alone. Having Daniel at her side would be too risky. What if she broke down?

'Fair enough.' Daniel busied himself at the kitchen counter. 'By the way, I've set up a job interview for you tomorrow at eleven o'clock at The Fat Pheasant restaurant. It's in the main square. You can't miss it.'

'Thanks so much, Daniel. I really appreciate it.'

'My pleasure,' he said, bringing the tea cups over to the table. 'Like I said in my email, I'm friends with the chef, Henri Breton. Quite a character. I fixed his car last week, so he owes me one. Mind, you might just be washing pots.'

'That's fine.' Rachel smiled and sipped her tea. Daniel had been helpful to a fault. Not only had he got her this interview for a temporary job, but he'd arranged accommodation with Molly Doherty, an elderly widow who sometimes took in boarders. Of course, Daniel didn't know the real reason she wanted a job in The Fat Pheasant. The restaurant was owned by Melissa Maguire – now Melissa Cole since her marriage. She was one of Kilbrook's school bullies.

Months ago, when at a particularly low ebb, Rachel had researched the bullies online. She wasn't sure why. The word 'closure' had become something of a cliché, but the need for it was very real, and was something she'd always craved. On the Kilbrook Community School's webpage, she'd seen an announcement about the latest ten-year class reunion, to be hosted in Mel's restaurant.

Of course there was no guarantee that all the bullies would turn up for the reunion, but it was a start. Rachel had decided to come to Kilbrook a few weeks ahead of time to see how they, and their lives, had turned out. There was no twisted plan of revenge in her mind – she certainly wasn't going to do anything that would get her into trouble with the police – but any opportunity that came up for payback might go some way to easing her pain.

'You've come at the right time,' Daniel was saying. 'The Winter Festival starts at the end of this week. Lots of fun. And the local theatre's putting on *A Christmas Carol* …'

He chatted on, but Rachel's thoughts were elsewhere. This adult Daniel seemed like a nice man. She hadn't expected that. It was one thing to think about revenge in the abstract, but quite another when the person had shown you a kindness and was sharing tea with you. Maybe this whole thing was going to be far harder than she had imagined.

* * *

'Have some more,' said Molly, ladling another portion of potatoes onto Rachel's plate. 'You look like you need feeding up.'

'Thanks.' Rachel was already stuffed, but she didn't want to be rude to her new landlady. They were getting on like a house on fire. Molly was thin and brittle like a twig, and she walked with a cane, but her mind was still razor-sharp. Best of all, she had lived miles away in Ballinasloe with her late husband when Rachel was here, so there was no possibility that she would be recognised.

'Daniel's been so helpful,' Rachel commented, hoping Molly would open up about the priest.

'He always is. Can't do enough for people. Best thing to happen to this village when the church brought him in as junior priest. He was sorely needed. The senior priest, Father Milligan, was losing his memory something chronic. Once he preached about Christmas at Eastertide. The children were so confused, not to mention the adults. He was long overdue for retirement.'

Rachel had read about that on St Kilian's website and was grateful the priest was now out of the picture. He probably knew her best out of all the people in Kilbrook because her mother's job had brought them into close proximity with him. If anyone was going to recognise her, Father Milligan could have been the one. Although he had always been a bit vague. Not to mention a coward. One of those who'd thought it best to hush up the bullying incident in the church. 'The unfortunate incident' was how he'd described it when Rachel's mother had demanded some kind of action. He'd likely have called World War Two a skirmish. It probably wasn't coincidence that Daniel had worked with the man who'd protected him from justice.

'They're supposed to be finding a replacement for Father Milligan,' Molly continued. 'Daniel's a junior priest and he should have a senior priest here to help him out, but it seems there's a bit of a shortage right now. Older priests are retiring and the seminaries aren't getting the same numbers of young men.' Molly tutted. 'No doubt that's because of all the scandal in the Church. I don't know what the world's coming to. Anyway, I do feel for Father Quinn sometimes, rattling around in that rectory on his own. He'd never say it, but I think sometimes he gets lonely.'

That was some consolation. Evenings alone with his guilty conscience was what he deserved. The Quinns had been a large family, though, spilling over into a second pew in the church. How could he be lonely? 'Surely he has family here in Ireland he can visit?' Rachel had been about to say 'here in Kilbrook' but had stopped herself just in time. She couldn't appear to know too much about Daniel.

Molly shook her head. 'I heard that he was born in Kilbrook, but his family all live in England now. They moved there when he was in his teens. Not enough work here for his father.'

That must have happened after the church incident. So it hadn't been business as usual for the Quinns. Maybe they'd moved not because of the job situation but to give Daniel a fresh start. Lucky him. But why had he come back to Kilbrook?

'Would you like more chicken?' asked Molly, pointing hopefully to the bowl.

'I'm full, Molly. It was great – really. You must let me make you something tomorrow as a thank you for all this.'

'Are you a good cook?'

'I can only do a few dishes really well, but wait till you taste my tiramisu.'

'Tira-me-what?'

'It's an Italian dessert. Coffee-soaked biscuits, eggs, sugar, mascarpone cheese, and a dash of Marsala wine.'

'Did your mammy teach you how to make that?'

Rachel checked herself. She'd felt so at home, she'd given too much away. There couldn't have been that many Italian families in Kilbrook. If Molly happened to mention it to some of her older friends, they might well remember the Rinaldi family who'd lived here a short while.

'I learned to cook at boarding school,' she said. 'I'm an orphan.'

Molly clucked sympathetically. 'Now that's too bad, but look how well you've done for yourself. An art student in London. It sounds so glamorous. Sure, and your parents would have been proud of you.'

Rachel thought about her mother in the hospital, dying by degrees, her liver riddled with alcohol. She'd barely known her own daughter at the end. Not that Rachel had ever visited much. There was school, summers with her cousins in Italy, and then the excitement of London. No time for a woman old before her time, filled with guilt, who spent her days sipping tea laced with vodka and trying to hide it. Rachel thought she might cry at the memory.

Perhaps Molly sensed that because she dropped the topic. 'Why don't you stack the dishwasher? Then come and join me in the sitting room and we'll see if there's something on TV. Maybe one of those reality shows where they all get angry at the one who cuts his toenails on the coffee table.'

Rachel laughed. 'Count me in.'

She cleared the plates from the table. Staying with Molly would be fine, even fun. But what would this sweet old lady think of her in a few weeks' time when the reunion – where Rachel planned to give the bullies and their protectors a piece of her mind – was over? Rachel only wanted to hurt the guilty, but the reality was that innocents might well get caught in the crossfire.

* * *

Rachel finished unpacking her clothes and sat down on the single divan. It was a pretty room, decorated in white muslin sprigged with roses. Simple and pure, like a child's room.

The house was silent. Molly was asleep in the converted bedroom next to the kitchen – the stairs were getting too much for her – so Rachel had the upper level all to herself. Such privacy was an unexpected bonus. She'd spend most of her time here concealing her real identity, so it would be a relief to have some place where she could let down her guard.

Rachel went to the window and pulled up the blinds,

staring out at the inky blackness of the night sky. She was exhausted, but sleep wouldn't come in this unfamiliar house in this all-too-familiar village. She tried phoning her cousin. The call went straight to voicemail. Sophia was either having an early night or was otherwise engaged. Perhaps it wasn't too late for Rachel to change her mind and go home. It was all so risky. She'd almost slipped up this evening with that Italian reference. And this was a village with only a few thousand people. All it took was for one person to recognise her, or to start making connections if she said the wrong thing ...

Determined to strengthen her sense of purpose, Rachel moved over to sit at the small, white dressing table. From her bag, she pulled out the battered purple diary with the faded image of a boy band on the front. She flicked the pages to an entry near the beginning and let the teenage scrawl draw her back into the past ...

1 January

Mam said I looked good for the New Year's Eve party. Well, she actually said 'cute', which I guess is okay. I couldn't believe Mel had invited ME to her New Year's Eve fancy dress party. Everyone wanted to go. Being invited meant you were someone. You belonged. Mel lives in this huge house just outside the village. Her parents are very rich. She was the one who told me to come as Minnie Mouse, and she'd be a Disney character too, and people would see we were friends. And I forced Mam to rent me a costume, using up money she didn't have. I lied to her when I got home. Said it had all been great, so she's gone to bed a bit happier, thinking everything's fine. I didn't tell her I sat on a bench in the cemetery, freezing, until after midnight. How could I tell her how terrible it really was? Me turning up at the party as Minnie Mouse when NO ONE else was wearing fancy dress. I wanted to DIE!!! Some of the kids looked embarrassed for me, but not Mel or Jay. They were laughing and Mel said I must have misunderstood. That it was easy enough to do when you're foreign. When you're a wop is what she actually said. I hate that insult. People used to call Papa that all the time. I've told everyone at school it's just my name that's Italian – I've never even been to Italy, and my mam's from Ireland! But I was born in England, and I talk different to them, so I guess I'm labelled as a foreigner. Maybe it's the price I have to pay for being new. It was just an unkind joke. I've got no bruises. Not visible ones anyway. They'll get bored with me if I don't react.

Rachel closed the diary. If she read any more she'd not be able to sleep. Already she could feel anger welling up inside her. So much for the optimism in that diary entry. The bullying had just got worse – much worse. More than any child should have to bear. And all the bullies got away with it. Protected by their parents from any kind of punishment.

Rachel pulled out the creased school photograph from the back of the diary, and looked at the pupils of Kilbrook Community School as they were at age thirteen, all their names neatly printed underneath the picture. Taking a red pen, Rachel circled Mel's head. She was in the middle of the front row – the best position, of course. She looked like a model student – hair perfectly styled, smart uniform, a serene smile on her face.

Unlike 'the wop', who was hiding in the back row. Jay Cole had pushed her into some mud on the way to school so her clothes were dirty. She'd been given hell for that when she got home. Rachel circled Jay's head next in red ink. Not surprisingly, he'd married Mel – the bullies sticking together. She'd seen a photo of them together on Mel's Facebook account. There was a photo of Daniel too – they were obviously still friends, which didn't go in his favour. His face hadn't really altered since the school photo, apart from not wearing glasses as a child. Had he changed since becoming a priest? Rachel pushed that unhelpful thought aside, and circled Daniel's head.

Finally, she circled the head of the fourth bully, Jody James – or Spook as he was known, because he was born on Halloween, and from what Rachel could remember, certainly had the devil in him. He was proving elusive. Neither he nor his family had shown up on Kilbrook's Register of Electors. And she couldn't ask around about him too much in case she set off alarm bells. Hopefully, he'd show for the upcoming Kilbrook Community School reunion.

Of course, none of the bullies would be expecting Rachel to turn up, telling everybody exactly what happened fourteen years ago. Well, they were going to get the surprise of their lives. Karma was about to come calling.

Chapter Two

As Melissa Cole turned her car into the back parking area of The Fat Pheasant, she stamped on the brakes. Henri had taken her spot again. He'd been warned about it so many times that he could only be doing it deliberately. Blatant insubordination. He might be one of the best chefs in the North-West of Ireland, but he was also a royal pain. If she didn't need him so much, she'd have sent him packing long ago.

As she was manoeuvring the car into the tight space next to the bins, her phone rang. She lost concentration momentarily and heard the scrape of metal on metal. Once again, she slammed on the brakes.

Perhaps she should just return home and go to bed. Pull the covers over her head and let everything go to hell. Who needed all this hassle? Anyone who thought running a restaurant was glamorous didn't know the half of it. Suppliers always trying to rip you off, pilfering staff, whinging customers, and pig-headed chefs. And doing it all on your own was the hardest. She'd tried to persuade Jay to give up teaching and help her out with the restaurant, but he'd refused. Said he had no head for business, but what he really meant was it was more fun flirting with teenage schoolgirls on a sports field.

The phone shrilled again. Mel snatched it from her bag and glanced at the call display. Her father. She didn't answer. He'd been on her case so much of late, checking everything was in hand for the special dinner he was planning at the restaurant with a bunch of American interior designers who wanted to purchase antiques for their clients. Why couldn't he just trust her to get the job done? Jay was lucky – his parents left him alone. They'd never interfered in his life, even at times when they really should have.

Mel grabbed her bag and got out of the car, almost gagging

because of the overwhelming stench of fish coming from somewhere. She stormed through the restaurant kitchen and into the office, where Henri was sitting in *her* chair behind *her* desk reading his post. He didn't even get up when he saw her come in. If only there could be a return to the days when masters could legally beat their serfs senseless.

He beamed his stupid crooked smile and waved a letter at her. 'We have the good news, Madame. Pierre Lévêque has accepted my invitation to come to our restaurant.'

Our restaurant? In his dreams. 'Who?'

He looked scandalised, and she thought she might punch him. 'Pierre Lévêque is a food critic *par excellence*. He writes reviews for *Le Bon Weekend* magazine. This is a great honour.'

'When's he coming?' asked Mel, still standing. No way was she sitting in Henri's chair.

Henri looked at the letter. 'Monday, the twenty-fourth.'

'But that's the day of my father's special dinner!' Mel thought she might faint.

'*Exactement*! I choose this day for a reason. We will excel and Pierre will write the good review.'

'Put him off,' she demanded.

'*Pardon*?'

About tenth on her long list of things Mel hated about Henri was his pretence that he didn't understand English. It only ever happened when she said something he didn't like. 'Tell him to come on another date,' she said slowly. 'Put. Him. Off.'

Henri got up awkwardly from the chair. He was as large as his ego. He carefully manoeuvred himself from behind the desk, and Mel was reminded of her difficulties with the car and the bins in the car park. 'Pierre Lévêque is not some naughty passenger on a bus,' he said, towering over her. 'I cannot – how you say – put him off. He will never come then. *Non*, Madame. He comes on that day, or I go.'

Just who was running this restaurant? Sometimes it felt like the tail was wagging the dog. Perhaps she could discreetly advertise and find a replacement chef.

'Anything else?' she asked, sarcastically, as he moved past her towards the door.

'Yes. The scallops are not fresh today. I throw them in the bin. I cannot create a masterpiece from – how do you say? – garbage.'

He slammed the door behind him at the same time as Mel slammed her fist on the desk.

* * *

Rachel drank the last of her cappuccino. It was average at best, and the croissant hadn't been fresh. That much hadn't changed since her day, but the décor in Gulliver's café certainly had. The plastic tables and chairs had been replaced by fancy black metal ones, and the lino had vanished in favour of the original wood. The walls were now a subtle beige, and Impressionist prints of gardens and river scenes hung on the walls. Gulliver's great advantage for Rachel, however, was that it was conveniently located in the village square, directly opposite The Fat Pheasant restaurant. Rachel was to report for her interview there in ten minutes.

The restaurant was definitely upmarket, with its mullioned windows and gleaming brass fixtures on the door. The food guides Rachel had read praised its exceptional fish dishes and said the desserts were a work of art. The key tourist websites for Ireland and this area told people The Fat Pheasant was a fine dining experience not to be missed. The restaurant had won a Michelin star last year. Mel had obviously done well for herself, but then those who walked over other people often did succeed.

For the first time since hatching her plan to return to Kilbrook, Rachel felt the smallest tremor of fear. She was taking on Mel and her wealthy family, the people who'd defeated her own family years ago. Who could crush her again very easily. She was David against their Goliath. She remembered a nun at her boarding school reading that story to them years ago. Courage and brains could defeat brute strength, she'd said. Hopefully, that was true.

'Can I get you anything else?' The waitress – who'd introduced herself earlier as Kelly – collected up the plate and empty cup from Rachel's table.

'No, thanks. I must be going. I've got an interview at The Fat Pheasant. Have you ever eaten there?'

'The Fat Peasant, we locals call it,' said Kelly, with a laugh. 'Though no peasants could afford it. They have a posh French chef, so dinner will set you back a bit. Food's grand, though. I had my twenty-first there.'

'What's the owner like?'

Kelly glanced over her shoulder, although they were alone in the café. She lowered her voice, conspiratorially. 'Well, you never heard it from me, but that Melissa Cole is a right cow. Thinks she's a cut above with her convertible and live-in nanny. Still, money doesn't always buy happiness. Her man's got a bit of a roving eye, if you know what I mean.'

The café bell jangled as a customer walked in, and the waitress excused herself. Rachel took out her purse. She'd leave a generous tip because she might need more information in the future. Always good to have someone with inside knowledge on your side.

'Morning, Finn.'

'Morning, Kelly. A double espresso, please.'

Rachel glanced over at the customer who'd sat down close by. Kelly was looking like she'd won the lottery because he'd spoken to her. The man was wearing sunglasses despite it being a dull day. Maybe he was famous – some footballer perhaps. He certainly had the physique. And that was an Australian accent, although he couldn't be just passing through because Kelly knew his name.

Rachel suddenly remembered the interview. Time to get moving. She shrugged into her coat and picked up her bag.

'Was it something I said?'

The man was smiling at her. He took his glasses off, and Rachel did a double-take. He was gorgeous with his slight stubble and sun-streaked brown hair.

She smiled back. 'I've got to go. I have a job interview.'

'Well, good luck,' he said. 'You can tell me about it when we next bump into each other. It's bound to happen. People fall over themselves in Kilbrook.'

'I'll look forward to it.' God, that sounded a bit keen, but he really was something special. That smile had almost made her knees buckle.

'Bye now.' He took out his phone and started texting.

Rachel hurried out of the café, feeling like a teenager at a One Direction concert.

* * *

The Fat Pheasant's kitchen was like a sauna. At least working here would open up Rachel's pores. Free facials as a perk.

Her arms ached as she turned the handle of the butter churner. This was part of Chef Henri's interview test – 'to see if you have strength in those leetle arms.' The other part of the test – thirty bread rolls, made from scratch – were on trays beside her, covered with cloths. Once they'd risen, she'd bake them in the kitchen's large ovens. She was on safe ground there because as a child she'd watched and helped her mother make bread many times.

An hour later, Rachel had scooped some butter into a little serving pot and set two rolls onto a plate. Henri stood there for a minute, cocking his head to the left and then the right, like a spaniel scenting game. He broke open a roll, sniffed it, and rolled a piece of the bread between his fingers. Next, he spread butter on the roll and popped it into his mouth, standing there for what seemed like an eternity after he'd swallowed.

'The butter is very nice – smooth and creamy,' declared Henri. 'For the rolls – leetle more air. Stretch the dough up like

16

this, and fold.' He demonstrated with thin air, his beefy hands moving up and down with surprising grace. 'It is not the rat you are pounding to death here. More like shaking the water off your hands.'

Rachel smiled and nodded.

'Okay, leetle Ra-shelle … now you chop the vegetables. Here. This is the knife to use. Watch me with the onion.'

She observed and copied his chopping technique, but at a much slower pace, afraid of losing a finger.

'Good,' said Henri, wiping his hands clean on a cloth. 'You have passed the test. So you will be responsible for bread, butter, vegetables. And washing the pots in the sink at the back. You can stay for the rest of the shift, yes? I will make sure you receive the money. The owner, Madame Cole, will be here later. She will give you all the details. Now chop.'

Rachel pulled a carrot onto the board and set to work. Thanks to Henri – and Daniel Quinn – she was now inside the enemy gates.

* * *

Her two hours would soon be up. The vegetables were heaped mini mountains in front of Rachel. Her co-workers had drifted in while she'd been chopping. They seemed a nice bunch – Will on fish, Calum on meat, Sam on garnish, Eddie on starters, and Colette, the pastry chef. Only Sam – a tow-haired twenty-year-old – was local, and he was too young to remember the Rinaldis.

Ten minutes later, the back door crashed open and Mel Cole walked in, sweeping between the cooking stations like royalty. Rachel saw all the chefs duck their heads and become absorbed in what they were preparing. Mel slowed and stared hard at Rachel, then moved on into the office. Had there been a glimmer of recognition in Mel's eyes? Rachel prayed not. Fourteen years was a long time and she'd changed so much. No longer the timid little goose she'd once been.

'That's the boss,' Will told her. 'From hell. Do what she says, or at least pretend to, and never answer back. She likes to lord it over us, but she knows she'd be lost without Henri. He protects us.'

So it seemed that some childhood bullies grew into adult bullies. So far, what Rachel had heard about Mel convinced her she hadn't changed, and would likely have no regrets about the trauma she'd inflicted on a young girl in her schooldays.

'Ra-shelle – will you come, please?' Henri called.

She took off her apron and walked past him into the office, where Mel sat behind the larger of two desks. Mel stared at Rachel, assessing her from the tip of her head down to her toes. An X-ray machine couldn't have been more thorough.

Rachel assessed Mel in return. No one would call her beautiful. Her eyes were too large, set too far apart, and her nose was a little crooked. She made the most of what she had, though. Perfectly cut hair, manicure, designer clothes, and just the right amount of make-up to subtly accentuate her good points.

'Father Quinn recommended you,' Mel said, 'and Henri thinks you're suitable, but if you mess up, I'll fire you on the spot. Understand?'

Rachel nodded, adopting a meek expression. Inside, she seethed at the woman's attitude.

'Two hours a day, five days a week,' Mel continued. 'Eleven-thirty to one-thirty. Seven euros an hour. We're closed Sundays, and Wednesday will be your day off. We have two big evening events coming up – my father's hosting a special dinner, and then there's a school reunion – so there'll be extra hours available if you want them. You're temporary and part-time, so there are no benefits. Karen at the front desk will sort out your wages … Now, Henri, we need to talk about this consignment of wine you've ordered. At that price, I assume they're transporting it from France by private jet.'

Henri raised his voice in angry argument, and Rachel crept

out of the office, closing the door quietly behind her. Mel hadn't changed a bit. And that meant she was as dangerous now as she'd been all those years ago.

* * *

Rachel pushed open the heavy oak door of the church with a feeling of dread and went inside. St Kilian's was gloomy in the late afternoon light. It was also empty, and she was thankful for that. She might have left if there had been people inside. It was hard enough to do this alone, but her cover story meant she should be in the chapel with the murals most days. It would arouse suspicion if she never set foot in the place.

She ignored the holy water stoup and didn't genuflect. Once, long ago, she'd believed in God, but with everything that had happened, it was no longer possible. Even the Old Testament God who'd claimed vengeance was his had let Rachel down. If you wanted revenge, you had to take care of it yourself.

Rachel shivered as she walked slowly down the carpeted nave. It felt as if the blue and red figures in the stained glass windows were watching her every move. The Gothic-style Christ on the cross in torment behind the altar seemed to mock her pain, and the vases of blood-red carnations ranged at the sides made her feel ill. Her imagination was working overtime. Chanting, black robes, darkness, screaming ...

Feeling dizzy, Rachel sank down into the nearest pew and lowered her head onto her folded arms. Breathing deeply, she tried to think about normal things to calm herself. The bus ride beside the Thames on the way to university. Walks on Clapham Common. Doing the weekly supermarket shop with Sophia. That was her real life. Did she have the strength to do this? Less than a day here and she was losing her nerve. Even now, her legs were too shaky to get her out of this wretched church. A sob escaped, and she tried to muffle the sound.

'Rachel?'

She peered up to find Daniel standing over her, and that

made everything much worse. A bully here of all places. It was like God's ultimate slap in the face.

'I'm sorry,' she whispered, and wiped at her tears with her scarf.

'Nothing to be sorry about.' He sat down in the pew alongside, leaning towards her. His expression was kind, concerned. 'Can I help?'

She shook her head. The strain was getting to her, but she couldn't live with herself if she didn't see this through.

'Would you like some tea?'

Rachel shook her head, and almost laughed. A cup of tea would be no help to her at all. A shot of morphine was what she really needed. Something to stop the images that kept replaying in her mind. Or a bottle of vodka – her mother's choice of poison.

Daniel was watching her and waiting. She'd need to give him some kind of explanation for her tears. Some other painful memory. She had plenty of those to choose from. 'It's just … I lost my mother last year. Being here made me remember the funeral service.'

Although she hadn't cried then. She'd been too numb to cry. Anyway, her mother had wanted to die. Life had been too much for her.

'That's a hard loss to take,' said Daniel. 'It must have been very painful for you.'

The expression in his eyes was one of absolute sincerity, as if he really did understand and sympathise with her pain. It was so difficult to equate the man she saw before her with the bully he'd been. Obviously he'd changed, but still that didn't excuse what he'd done. And got away with. He'd probably confessed it all to Father Milligan and got absolution.

'She'd been ill for some time, so it wasn't unexpected,' she told him, 'but sometimes memories ambush you without warning.'

He nodded, and a silence fell between them. Before coming here, Rachel had toyed with a revenge scenario that involved seducing Daniel, but she wasn't up to that. This was hardly *The Thorn Birds*, after all. But Molly had said she believed Daniel was lonely. Maybe he would be vulnerable to some subtle flirting. And then if he felt flattered, and came looking for more, she'd give him the cold shoulder. He would know pain then – the pain of rejection.

'I actually came here to thank you, Daniel. I got the job.'

'You did?' He smiled. 'That's grand.'

'Maybe I will take you up on that offer of some tea.'

* * *

'And here we have the Stokeley murals,' Daniel announced, pride in his voice, and Rachel followed him into a side chapel, where the ordinary became extraordinary.

Each of the four walls of the chapel had been painted with a huge mural of a biblical scene – the Creation of the world, the Expulsion of Adam and Eve from the Garden of Eden, the Birth of Jesus, and The Transfiguration. Rachel had seen these famous wall paintings as a child, but time had dulled the scale and the colours in her mind. Slides and photographs couldn't convey such luminous reds and blues and greens. It was like seeing the Palace of Knossos on Crete all over again, when she'd felt as if she could drown in the beauty of the bright and brilliant hues.

'They're breathtaking,' Rachel said.

She looked around and saw Daniel had sat down on the viewing bench. She joined him there, moving as close as she dared. 'I love that Gilbert Stokeley painted this village into the murals.'

'I know,' said Daniel. He pointed to the middle of the scene in front of them. 'That's the old Yarn Market doubling for the stable. It's over five hundred years old, and still standing in the main street today. Stokeley had to include it because it was the Kilbrook Merchants Guild who commissioned him.'

This was all familiar to Rachel. There wasn't much she didn't know about Stokeley, the English-born artist with the

Irish mother, who might well have died in obscurity if he hadn't been loosely connected with the famous Pre-Raphaelite artists. But she let Daniel talk.

'Molly's grandmother knew Stokeley, you know. Apparently he was always an odd fish. Only worked at night, so he ruined his eyesight, of course. Used to wear a kimono, and never touched meat. And his models were always ...'

Daniel paused, and Rachel glanced at him. Was he blushing?

'Always what?' she prompted.

He cleared his throat. 'In a state of undress.'

'Well, artists do need to be able to see the body naked in order to paint it successfully.'

Daniel murmured agreement and shuffled on the bench. Then he pointed to another part of the painting. 'There's Bracken Hill. At the top you get a grand view of Lough Corrib. And you can see a ruined castle, which they say was built by the last king of Ireland ...'

He was babbling to cover his embarrassment. She'd have to let him know that everything was okay. 'Maybe you can show me the Lough some time?'

He looked surprised. 'Well, yes, I can do that.'

'Good.' She picked up her bag. 'I've got to go. Molly will have dinner ready. Would you like to join us?'

'Alas, I have an appointment with the parish council.'

'No rest for the wicked, eh?'

He smiled, and the easy camaraderie between them gave Rachel a feeling of accomplishment.

* * *

Rachel stretched out in bed, thinking about the day and all that had happened. Now two of the bullies were well and truly in her sights. She'd work hard in the restaurant in order to be above suspicion, and then she'd see if she could create any problems there before the reunion dinner. She wasn't sure yet what to do about Daniel. The problem was that he was so likeable, which made it difficult to focus on making him suffer.

Turning on her side, Rachel pulled the diary onto the pillow and flipped to an early page, which was peppered with Mel's name. She started to read.

24 January

Detention this afternoon because I hadn't done my homework. Except I had. I spent all last night doing it and I know I did a good job. Someone took it from my bag and I swear it was that cow Mel Maguire. She 'accidentally' bumped into me this morning, and knocked my bag flying. Then she 'helped' me put my stuff back in. What was worse was that Miss Murphy didn't believe me when I said I'd done it. I've got a huge bruise on my side where Mel bumped into me – she made sure her bag caught me, hard. It felt like there was a brick in it. Maybe there was.

Some of the girls are wearing the new uniform – same colours, just more modern-looking. I'm not the only one still in last term's uniform, but I'm the only one who had a comment made. Katie Shaw asked if I'd been down in the dumps. Stupid me didn't realise what she meant, so I said I hadn't. She then fell about laughing and said, 'Oh, I thought that's where you got your uniform.' I think Mel put her up to it. Rest of the class thought it was hilarious. Obviously want to stay onside in case they're next. I keep trying to be friendly, though. I even joked about the New Year's Eve set-up to show them I've got a sense of humour and I was fine with it.

I don't know why they hate me so much. Mam asked me after dinner if I was okay because I'd come home late from school, and I nearly told her everything, but Rosie called her, and she went to her right away. As she always does. I do understand Rosie is ill, but I wish sometimes Mam would put me first. Just once.

Chapter Three

Finn MacKenzie sat in the stationary car, his hands trembling on the steering wheel. Ten minutes he'd been there, waiting for the panic to pass. He'd planned a short drive along the lough and back, but it was no use. As soon as he even thought about starting the ignition, the memories flooded back. That bend in the road, the skid, the crash ... He wasn't safe to drive. He'd not put anyone at risk.

Biting back his disappointment, Finn got out of the car and pulled up the collar of his coat to combat the wind. How did people stand this godawful Irish weather? Australia had never seemed further away. Right now he needed a shot of caffeine. He turned away from the car that sat there like a reproach and headed for the village square.

Finn liked Gulliver's Café. Not for the coffee, which was no great shakes, but because he could sit by the window and observe, unnoticed, as village life unfolded outside. He'd always been something of a people watcher – it helped him with his acting – and he was now familiar with the faces of schoolchildren, of young mothers, and of elderly men and women who seemed to typify the image of 'ye olde world' villagers. Kilbrook was like the land that time forgot.

The doorbell jangled as he walked into the café. Only a few regulars were there, and his usual table by the window was free. He sat down and peeled off his jacket. He wasn't warm by any means, but as Helen would frequently tell him, he wouldn't feel the benefit when he went back outside.

'Hi, Finn. Your usual espresso?'

He nodded as Kelly came over and wiped down the table, leaning over to give him a clear view of her cleavage. She always flirted with him. He wasn't interested, but he'd not be rude.

'How are the rehearsals going?' she asked.

'Pretty good.'

It was a small village. Most people knew by now that Finn was here to help Helen, his aunt, with the annual production of *A Christmas Carol* in the small Kilbrook theatre. Not that she needed much assistance. She'd had over thirty years of acting and directing experience in Australia before she moved back here.

'It's such a shame you're not performing,' Kelly said.

He smiled. 'Well, it's a high school show. I'm too old by a decade or more. The kids are shaping up well, though. They'll be doing six performances spaced out over two weeks. I hope you come along to one of them. I think you'll really enjoy it.' He took out his phone, hopefully a subtle hint that the conversation was over.

'I'll be there on the opening night.' Her tone was husky, and she gave him her best Hollywood smile as she went off to prepare his drink.

Finn looked at his watch. Helen was at her yoga class now, and after that she'd be checking on costumes with the various mothers who were helping out with the play. He texted her, suggesting they meet for lunch in the pub. Once he'd had his coffee, he'd go to the theatre and check the lighting programme again. Sorted. He picked up a copy of the local newspaper and immersed himself in the highs and lows of Kilbrook.

* * *

The sun was out as Rachel left Molly's house and walked towards the village square. She'd managed to sleep right through the night without waking, and the undisturbed rest made her feel more optimistic that she would be able to cope with whatever the day would bring.

First order of the morning was a coffee in Gulliver's. Molly only had instant and Rachel needed the real stuff to wake her up. Crossing the square, she glanced at The Fat Pheasant. It was Wednesday, her day off. No vegetable chopping today. Perhaps that was also helping her mood.

The Australian Adonis from yesterday was sitting at Gulliver's window table, texting away. Wearing a white T-shirt that showed off his tan and some firm biceps, he looked like a surfer straight from Bondi Beach. Sophia would have him down as someone who'd missed every branch of the ugly tree and been at the head of the queue when God gave out sex appeal.

He looked up and gave her a wave and a smile. Near perfect teeth. Now he was motioning to Rachel to come inside, and she felt a fluttering of nerves. And some guilt. She was here for revenge, not to flirt with a handsome stranger. But what harm could there be in a little distraction? It might even give her some much-needed balance while she was here.

Rachel entered the café, and the man stood up. 'Told you we'd bump into each other again. Please, come join me. Tell me how your interview went. I'm Finn, by the way.'

That spark of humour in his eyes was irresistible. She'd chat with him a little. And treat herself to a hot chocolate. It wasn't right to let Kilbrook deprive her of all fun.

* * *

Finn MacKenzie was an actor. That didn't come as a surprise. He wouldn't exactly have looked at home stacking the shelves in Tesco although he'd probably have done wonders for their sales. He was over from Sydney for a couple of months, visiting his aunt and helping her with the production of *A Christmas Carol*.

'But enough about me,' he said. 'Tell me, did you get the job?'

'I did.'

'Congratulations.' They clinked coffee cups. 'This should really be champagne. So, what is it?'

'I'm a pot washer and vegetable chopper in a restaurant,' she told him. 'Lunch service, two hours a day, except Sundays and Wednesdays.'

'I'm guessing that's not your chosen career.' As soon as the words were out, Finn groaned. 'Did I really say that out loud?' He closed his eyes, waving his hands in front of his face like a magician, and said, *'There's no place like home, there's no place like home* ... Can you still see me?'

She had to choke back her laughter. He was great fun. 'Yes, I can still see you. The spell didn't work.'

He opened his eyes again. 'Darn it. Why does it always work for Dorothy and not for me?'

'Because you don't have ruby slippers?' she suggested.

'Not that you know of! Anyway, I'm sorry. I sounded like a patronising git. I didn't mean to insult your job.'

Finn really was quite sweet. Not the brash smoothie she'd thought he might be. She hadn't taken offence at his career comment, but he was obviously afraid she had. That showed some sensitivity. 'You were right, though. It's not my chosen career. It's only a temporary job. I'm an art student, here to study the murals in St Kilian's.'

'A-ha! So you're an artist?' Finn seemed oddly excited about that.

'Not exactly. I'm an art historian. I study art, though sometimes I paint in my spare time.'

'You're just what I need!' exclaimed Finn. 'Our best artist is sick today. He was in charge of painting a replacement backdrop panel that one of the kids damaged accidentally. It's not finished yet, and tonight there are only two kids wielding paintbrushes, and they're no da Vinci's. I'm begging you – would you supervise? Give them a hand if necessary? It's less than an hour's work, I promise.'

It *was* her day off. She'd planned to see Daniel later this morning, but then she was a free agent.

'I can't pay you,' Finn continued. He'd taken her silence for reluctance. 'We've got no budget, and all the profits from these shows go to charity. But, tell you what – Saturday's the official opening of the Winter Festival – as a thank you, I'll take you to the ice rink in the park. I'm crap on skates, but it'll be a good laugh. What d'you say?'

'*Go for it, girl.*' Sophia's voice echoed in her head. She was always trying to pull Rachel away from the memories of Kilbrook, but they weren't easy to forget. Painting sets for this play might make her feel normal again for a while.

'Finn – I'd love to help out.'

* * *

Daniel had just sat down at his desk when there was a knock on the office door. All the saints give him strength. Could he not have a few moments of peace in a day?

'Come in,' he called out, hoping such self-sacrifice would bring him a few steps further up the long ladder towards salvation.

The door opened, and Rachel walked in, holding a tray covered with kitchen roll. 'I come bearing gifts.'

'It's a bit early for the Magi,' he joked.

She whipped off the kitchen roll with a flourish, revealing four cupcakes on a plate. 'Ta-da! Made them with my own fair hands. With Molly's guidance. As a thank you for all your help.'

Daniel was really touched. Anyone could buy shop cakes, but she'd gone to the trouble of baking – for him. 'They look amazing. Will you share them with me over a cup of tea?'

'Sure.'

'Why don't you have a seat?'

He put the kettle on and started rinsing two cups. One slipped out of his hands and clattered into the small sink. 'I'm all fingers and thumbs today.'

'Let me do it.'

Rachel was suddenly there at the sink, taking the cup from him. Their hands touched for the briefest of moments, and it felt like a jolt of electricity through Daniel's body.

'How do you like it?' she asked, turning to face him.

'Sorry?' He couldn't think straight, distracted by her eyes, blue as cornflowers, and the hair flowing round her face like a soft brown veil.

'Your tea. How do you like it?'

'Milk and two sugars,' Daniel managed to say, and then retreated to his desk. He picked up a letter and stared at it, unseeing. He hoped Rachel hadn't noticed his blush. What would she think of him? A priest clearly having un-priestly thoughts. He'd have to tell that to Father Dunne when he went for his monthly confession.

Seven years of seminary and training, three years at a parish over in Cheshire, and here Daniel was being swayed by a pretty face. He'd need to get his feelings under better control.

The phone rang, and Daniel answered it, relieved by the interruption. Mrs Clarkson from the flower-arranging committee wittered in his ear – could they use white carnations as well as white lilies for the First Communion? 'Of course,' he assured her, deliberately not looking at Rachel as she came close and placed his tea and a cupcake on the desk. She sat down in the chair opposite.

Putting the phone down, he tried to keep the image of Mrs Clarkson – early seventies, heavily overweight, and with severe varicose veins – at the forefront of his mind. She'd be scandalised to think her priest was eyeing up young women. He took a bite out of the cupcake and hoped he wouldn't get cream on his nose. 'This is grand. A real treat.'

Rachel smiled and sipped at her tea. 'So, Daniel, do you ever get any time off?'

'Sometimes,' he said warily. 'Why?'

'You said you'd take me to Lough Corrib.'

'Did I?' His mind was blank.

'Yesterday. When we looked at the frescos. Remember?'

What had he been thinking? There was no way he could go on a drive with Rachel. It would be even more for the gossips to get their teeth into. 'Well, I'm pretty busy at the moment.

There's a First Communion coming up and the Lantern Parade and Advent ...'

'I see.'

Rachel looked disappointed, and it was disturbing how much he savoured that. Better to be honest with her. 'Rachel, this is a small village. You're a single woman, I'm a priest. Even though it's just friendship, it wouldn't look right. Can you understand that?'

She sighed. 'Yes, I can. But surely you should be allowed to have friends – men and women. This isn't the dark ages.'

'It is here!' he told her. 'Tell you what – the Winter Festival opens this Saturday. There'll be a big outdoor party at the ice rink in the park. I'll be there. Will you come as well?'

'Safety in numbers?' she asked.

'Something like that. But it'll be fun. I'll buy you some roasted chestnuts.'

'Deal.'

They smiled at each other, and it felt good to have cleared the air. They could relax together as friends on Saturday.

* * *

Kilbrook's most popular pub, Donegan's, was full to the rafters with lunchtime trade. Gulliver's only did basic sandwiches, and The Fat Pheasant cost an arm and a leg. It seemed the pub was a good compromise for people's pockets. That suited Finn. He wasn't one for posh restaurants. In the city, they were okay. In a village like this, it was all about snobbery. Besides, Donegan's had plenty going for it, with its ornate woodwork, frosted glass, and cosy snugs that in the old days used to hide drinkers from their families or courting couples from prying eyes. Plus the beer was good quality and served cold. No bigger crime than warm beer.

He got himself a pint now and joined Helen. She'd managed to nab a table close to the fire. He just couldn't seem to get warm in this country. Even the winters in Sydney were mild. Maybe years in the sun made you soft.

Helen looked up from her soup as he approached the table, and she smiled a welcome. Her passport might say she was sixty but you'd never guess it. Yoga and cycling helped her stay rake-thin and full of energy, and she kept her mind young. Every day she did the cryptic crossword. One was half-finished now in the newspaper beside her plate. She was his aunt, his friend, his adviser, his inspiration. Everyone should have a Helen in their life.

'Sorry I'm late.' Finn kissed her cheek and sat down. 'I was checking that lighting rig and lost track of time.'

'I ordered you the same as me,' said Helen. That was a huge bowl of steaming tomato soup, with what looked like a full pound of grated cheese swimming in it. Just the ticket.

'How was the drive?' Helen asked.

Finn sighed. 'I didn't go. I did make it as far as the driver's seat, but then I couldn't do it.'

'Don't stress about it, love. When the time's right, you will.'

He hoped she was right. It was only a few months till they started shooting his new TV series in Sydney. The director might not take kindly to an actor who couldn't – wouldn't – operate a car. 'Some TV detective I'll be if the camera truck has to keep towing me around on car chases.'

'Wouldn't be the first time.'

'But I told the casting director I could drive.' Finn could feel the panic welling up inside him.

Helen patted his hand. 'I heard that young actor in the *Twilight* movie didn't have his licence at the start of filming. Didn't hinder his career one bit.'

Finn gave her a weak smile. She always did her best to reassure him, but she had worries of her own – he shouldn't be adding to them. Best change the subject now. 'I found us a volunteer to help with painting the scenery tonight. Her name's Rachel. She's an art student, here to study the Stokeley murals.'

'Really. And where did you meet *her*?'

'In Gulliver's. We had coffee together ...' He wagged a finger at her. 'And you can stop it with the knowing look, Helen. There's nothing going on between us. We just met.'

She smiled. 'If you say so, Finn.'

Time to change the subject yet again or she'd be hearing wedding bells. She was an incurable romantic. 'I was thinking we should change the lighting in the scene with Marley's ghost ...'

They chatted about the play until they finished their soup. While they were waiting for the bill, Finn tried to stifle a yawn.

'Bad night again?' asked Helen. 'Maybe you should see a doctor.'

'Another shrink? No thanks.' They'd just tell him the same thing. Guilt and grief would pass in time. That didn't help him cope with the here and now.

'No, Finn,' said Helen gently. 'Just a doctor who might prescribe something to help you relax. You can't go on being as tired as this.'

'I'm not going back on medication,' Finn insisted. 'I'll be okay. Maybe I'm still suffering a bit of jet lag.'

Who was he kidding? Certainly not Helen, but she smiled anyway. 'I'm so glad you're here, Finn. We always said we wanted to do a play together, and now we are.'

Although the circumstances were far from ideal, she was right. There was nothing like the theatre for helping him forget his troubles.

* * *

Rehearsals for *A Christmas Carol* had finished in Kilbrook's theatre, and the young actors had gone backstage to get their things. Rachel stretched and stood up from her seat in the auditorium, where she'd watched the rehearsals after she'd helped to paint the set piece. The play was shaping up well. Finn and Helen had obviously put a lot of time and effort into it, and in a little over a week, they'd have their first live audience. Those red velvet curtains would swish back, the lights would dim, and two hundred people would be applauding. This was their world – Finn and Helen. He'd said acting was now as natural for him as breathing. Rachel wondered what he'd say if he knew she was putting on her own private performance here in Kilbrook.

Just as Rachel stepped out into the centre aisle, the door at the side of the stage swung open, and thirty children rampaged down the aisle towards the exit. Rachel stood where she was, letting them flow around her.

'Show no fear,' Finn called to her from the front. 'That's when they attack.'

She smiled at him, and waited for the chaos to subside. When it did, he motioned for her to follow him.

'Come on backstage for a bit,' Finn said. 'We usually review things over some wine.'

He led her into one of the dressing rooms. His aunt, Helen, was already there, going over what still had to be done. Finn had introduced them earlier, and Rachel had taken an instant liking to her. Down-to-earth and friendly, and clearly very talented.

'Half those children have had a growth spurt,' said a woman, gazing fretfully at a pile of costumes on the table in front of her. 'I'll be letting down hems all weekend.'

'And our Scrooge is still missing cues,' complained Helen. 'Jenny lost it this evening and snapped, "Is there a line?" at him.'

Finn brought a bottle of Beaujolais over to the table and poured everyone a glass. 'Here's to Rachel,' he said. 'The set looks great. Thanks for stepping into the breach.'

They toasted her, and Rachel felt flush with her good deed for the day. 'If there's anything else to do, I'd be happy to help out.'

Helen's face lit up. 'Well, we do need a prompter for the second act. And the props have to be sorted ...'

'Be careful what you wish for,' Finn said to Rachel, with a wink.

It was good to feel wanted. And these people were all safe. They couldn't possibly have known her in the past. Finn was Australian, and Helen had only been in Kilbrook for the last few years. She could blend in with this group of creative people. Let down her guard for a while, and relax.

* * *

'She's a sweetheart, but she's always trying to feed me up ...'

Rachel was talking about Molly, the woman she was staying with, but Finn was only half-listening. Even though her lodgings were only ten minutes away from the theatre, he'd insisted on walking her home so that he'd have a chance to show her his serious side. In the café this morning, she'd seen Finn the Joker. He'd been performing for her – something he did when he was nervous. For many actors, the problem was how to drop the facade and just be themselves.

'Finn, are you listening to me?'

Rachel stopped suddenly, and he had to retrace his steps. The glow of the streetlight gave her upturned face a luminous quality, like that of an actress from the silent movie era. She was lovely. She was also waiting for an answer.

'I am listening, honest,' he told her, 'but I've been worrying that you might think I'm a lightweight.'

Better to get those feelings out there. On the other hand, his comments might make him seem totally self-absorbed. Had he just shot himself in the foot?

Rachel was quiet for a moment, watching his face. It felt like the agony of a close-up when you'd had a rough night.

'Finn, we've only just met. I don't really know you, so why would I be judging you?'

He stared down at his feet. 'You're right. It's just ... I usually joke around when I really like someone. It makes me less nervous. But it sometimes backfires because they think I can't be serious about things.' The old persona was threatening an appearance – no confidence, full of self-loathing.

'Excuse me,' a voice said, and they both had to move aside to let a late-night dog walker pass. The dog pulled back on the lead and yipped around Finn's ankles until it was yanked away again.

He made a lame joke. 'See – even dogs don't like me.'

Rachel laughed. 'More likely he's jealous of your good looks. Come on, it's getting cold.'

She headed off, and Finn followed, smiling to himself. She'd just paid him a compliment. All was not lost.

* * *

Rachel sat propped against the pillows, turning the diary over and over in her hands. She was thinking about Finn MacKenzie. He'd made it clear tonight that he was interested in her, asking if she had a boyfriend and telling her he was unattached. But was it all moving a bit too fast? How could she get close to someone when she was hiding her real identity? It would be a lie. And unfair on Finn. He'd shown her his vulnerable side, and that put a responsibility on her not to use him or hurt him. This was not the best time to start a romance. She'd have to put the brakes on and stop things with Finn before they went too far. She wasn't here for love. This diary was her reminder of that. She opened the pages and started to read.

4 February

At least there was some good news today. Gulliver's offered me a Saturday job! I've got to go and see Mrs Laferty, the manageress, tomorrow. It'll be SO cool to earn some money. Only clearing tables and some washing-up, making sandwiches, but I don't care. It's a job. I'll be able to save and buy some DECENT stuff. Mam means well but she buys what she calls 'functional' clothes. Trouble is they last forever and don't go out of fashion because they've never been in fashion. I'll save up and then go to one of the good shops in Galway. Maybe I won't be so unacceptable if I dress better.

17 February
So much for the job. I want to scream and cry. Mrs Laferty had gone to the bank and told me to keep an eye on everything. It was so good she trusted me, and it should have been okay – it's not like it gets really busy in there. They must have known she was going, or else they were just waiting for their chance – Mel and her gang. They came in and ordered stuff, then kept changing their minds until I got really confused. They settled on sandwiches – all different, of course, with just about everything in them, nothing basic – and it took me ages to make them. Mrs Laferty came back when I was still doing them, and the gang told her I'd got the order totally wrong. I heard Mel say I was useless, and they'd go to Snax at the other end of the village in future – and tell their friends to do the same. I felt terrible.

At the end of my shift, Mrs Laferty said she wouldn't be needing me anymore. That I'd done really great, but business had been slack in the café recently. She looked sad, a bit ashamed about it, and at home I found she'd given me extra money in my wages. So she felt sorry for me but wouldn't stand up to those bullies!

I couldn't eat anything at dinner. Told Mam I had a sore stomach, then went to my room. I'll tell her tomorrow about the job. Just say what Mrs Laferty told me, nothing about the bullies. I don't want any trouble. Anyway, grown-ups can't do anything to help me. I'm the one who has to take the long way round to school and hide in the toilets at the break. I can't burden Mam with this. I'm on my own.

Chapter Four

'I don't like it!' Leanne slapped the spoon down into her bowl of cereal, and milk sprayed all over the kitchen table.

'Eat it! It's good for you.' Mel stood there, hands on hips, glaring down at her mutinous daughter.

'No!'

How could a five-year-old be so bloody-minded? 'Then no skating for you on Saturday.'

Leanne absorbed the threat. Her lower lip wobbled, and then the waterworks started. Her wails were loud enough to wake the dead.

'Ilsa!' Mel shouted into the hallway. Where the bloody hell was that girl? What was the point in paying a fortune for an au pair if she was never there when you needed her? 'Ilsa!'

The door of the downstairs bathroom opened. Ilsa emerged, pocketing her mobile phone. The girl seemed to spend her whole life texting her friends back in Sweden.

'Hello? Yes?'

She was staring with that wide-eyed innocent look Mel hated so much. She'd privately christened her Dopey. 'If it's not too much to ask, could you do your job and get Leanne ready for school.'

When Ilsa came into the kitchen, Leanne deliberately cried even harder. 'Mammy shouted at me.'

Traitor. Now Mel was being branded as a bad mother. Kids certainly knew which buttons to press. No time for reconciliation, though. If Jay wasn't out the door in ten minutes, he'd be late for work. Why did the responsibility for everything seem to fall on her shoulders?

As she turned the corner at the top of the stairs, Mel heard Jay's voice. She tiptoed to the bedroom door, which was slightly ajar, and glanced inside. Jay was sitting on the bed, talking on his mobile, speaking too softly for her to hear. He was smiling. The smile he used to reserve for her.

Feeling sick, Mel backed away and took refuge in the bathroom, locking the door behind her. She sat down on the edge of the bath, processing what she'd just seen. Jay could have been talking to a friend, although he didn't have many of those, but then why would he have lowered his voice? And that secretive smile. It didn't feel right. This is what he'd reduced her to – creeping around her own house, filled with suspicion.

She had good reason to be suspicious, of course. Jay's flings stretched into double figures now, and those were only the ones she knew about. He'd made Mel the laughing stock of the village. It was one reason why she didn't socialise much. Any attractive young woman might have had an affair with her husband. Might know things about her she'd never want shared.

She'd read in a magazine once that adultery was a sickness, an addiction like drugs or gambling. The article had offered ridiculous solutions, like buying sexier bras or being more adventurous in bed. As if it were all the wife's fault.

Jay was the only man Mel had ever wanted. She'd never had another boyfriend, not even to try to make him jealous when he fooled around with other girls. She'd felt triumphant on their wedding day, assuming he'd change his ways and stay true to her. Six months later the phone calls had started. A woman's voice, asking for Jay. The calls had ended soon enough, but worse followed. Jay would come home in the early hours, smelling of unfamiliar soap.

Mel had never confronted him, too scared he'd leave. He was affectionate with Leanne – in truth, more than she was – but a child surely wasn't enough to hold a husband with a roving eye. Sometimes she thought the only reason he stayed with her was because of her money. She bought him all the gadgets he wanted, denying him nothing. She'd kept him so far, but every time a new affair started, the fear was there that the new woman would be the one who finally lured him away.

And now she was crying. Pathetic. She grabbed some toilet paper and dabbed away the mascara streaks. She didn't know how much more of Jay's affairs she could take. Maybe this time she'd have to find some courage and confront him.

* * *

Daniel pushed aside the parish accounts with a sigh. His head was throbbing – hopefully he wasn't going to get laid low by another migraine. Always the same – too many things to do and never enough funds to do them. Advent was coming up soon, and the outdoor nativity figures needed a spruce up. They could use the leftover white paint from the lychgate for Mary's veil, but he might have to raid the supply of poster paints from the catechism classes for the swaddling. The baby Jesus wrapped in a lime green blanket would surely raise eyebrows. Still, if December turned out to be as cold and overcast as November, perhaps few people would notice it in the gloom.

Daniel glanced at his watch. Almost time for his parish council meeting. When Father Milligan had been here, they'd shared the load and kept the church open most of the day – important because the murals were a tourist draw and tourists left financial contributions in the coffers. On his own, though, Daniel couldn't man the church all day, and he was reluctant to leave the deacon in charge. He was almost as old as Father Milligan, and just as forgetful.

Putting on his coat and scarf, Daniel grabbed some papers and left the office. He announced from the front that the church would be closing in ten minutes. A few tourists were wandering around, including an elderly woman who was staring hard at Christ on the cross behind the altar, as if he was a suspect in a police line-up. To his right was the Chapel of St Catherine, patron saint of wool merchants, the people whose wealth had transformed the village of Kilbrook from a blip on the road somewhere else to a thriving trade centre all those centuries ago.

The Stokeley murals were in this chapel. And so was Rachel, sitting cross-legged on the viewing bench in front of the Creation mural, scribbling something into a blue notebook. She was a left-hander. Centuries ago, the church would have been suspicious of that. Might even have burned her at the stake, perish the thought. Such loveliness going up in flames would have been a tragedy. Today, her hair was tied back with a ribbon, revealing the delicate pale skin of her neck and a mole above the line of her jumper ...

Daniel cleared his throat to distract himself from those inappropriate thoughts, and Rachel looked up from her notebook.

'How's it going?' he asked, walking over to stand next to the viewing bench. He kept his eyes glued to the fresco, but his peripheral vision saw Rachel stand up.

'Fine,' she said. 'I've been making notes about the self-portrait.'

They stood side by side looking at Kilbrook doubling as the Creation. It was a magnificent picture – horses, sheep, lambs, foxes, rabbits, pheasants, all running free and easy in a green and blue sparkling new world without any people in it. The huge bearded man at the side was God, looking out at the viewer with Gilbert Stokeley's face.

'At the time, the bishop was furious when he saw that self-portrait,' mused Daniel, 'but Stokeley refused to change it.'

'And his commissions dropped off because of that,' said Rachel. 'Perhaps he should have painted the bishop as God.'

'That's not fair. The bishop was right—'

'It was a joke, Daniel,' she said gently.

He turned and found her smiling. A sweet smile with no malice in it. He'd overreacted, and now he felt like a fool. He turned away to hide his embarrassment and moved the rope barrier across the entrance so no tourists would come in. 'I'm sorry but I have to close the church for a few hours.'

'Okay. I have to get to work anyway.' Rachel began packing her things into her rucksack. 'What are your plans?'

'A parish meeting, quick bit of lunch, a trip to the post office, and then I'm giving communion to some sick parishioners.'

'I could post something, if you like,' said Rachel, as she put on her coat. 'It's on my way.'

'If you're sure …'

'No problem.'

He handed over the letter. 'It's to thank my mother for this.' He indicated his scarf. 'She knitted it for my birthday.'

'It's your birthday!' exclaimed Rachel. 'I didn't know or I'd have gotten you a card.'

His heart did a strange flip at that, which he tried his best to ignore. 'It's not till Monday. My mother always sends gifts well ahead. She doesn't trust the post.'

Rachel looked at the address on the letter. 'She lives in England? She must miss you.'

'She does, but she's happy for me. She always wanted to have a priest in the family.' And it made up for the heartache he'd caused her when they'd lived in Kilbrook years ago.

'Sounds like it was your destiny,' said Rachel.

'Maybe.' But really it was more like his punishment.

'Was there ever anything else you wanted to be?'

Rachel asked the most unexpected questions. He had to think for a moment about an answer. 'Astronaut, footballer, explorer – but I grew out of all that. I would have quite liked to be a writer, though, or a journalist.' He hadn't thought about that in years.

'Righting the wrongs of the world? Social justice? Similar to being a priest in some ways.'

True. Apart from the celibacy, of course. The only job where you weren't allowed to have a wife. Perhaps that was a way to punish himself as well …

'Is this chapel open?' demanded one of the tourists from behind the rope barrier.

'It's closed, I'm afraid.'

'Well, how come *she's* in there?' snapped the woman, eyeing Rachel.

'She's not a tourist,' Daniel explained, as patiently as he could.

'Look, we've driven all the way from Ennis to see these murals. The website doesn't say anything about the chapel being closed.'

Daniel gave a small sigh. He'd have to update the website. Yet another thing for him to sort out. 'You can have five minutes,' he said, and pulled the barrier aside.

'Bye, Daniel,' said Rachel. 'See you tomorrow.'

She shouldered her rucksack and left, but a trace of her perfume lingered in the chapel.

* * *

Rachel set down the knife and flexed her fingers. It felt like she'd cut up enough vegetables to feed an army. She was getting quicker at it, partly because yesterday she'd practised her chopping technique on two pounds of carrots, with Molly timing her.

Rachel knocked at the open door of the office. Thankfully, Mel had gone out.

Henri, seated at his desk, looked up and beamed at her. 'Ra-shelle. Come in. Today I see you were winning the war with the vegetables.'

Even caught up in the rush of lunchtime service, Henri kept a check on everything his chefs were doing – or not doing. Rachel found it reassuring rather than intimidating. 'I practiced at home yesterday,' she told him.

'Did you? Smart girl. Tomorrow I teach you how to make crème brûlée. When you finish here, you will adore the art of cooking.'

That was unlikely. Sophia and Rachel had only a few staple recipes between them, and they microwaved ready-made meals when they were busy or tired. Still, she'd not rain on Henri's parade. Especially since she had a favour to ask.

'Henri, I wonder if you could help. It's Daniel's birthday on Monday, and I'd like to get him a cake. But the ones in Gulliver's aren't that great—'

'Gulliver's!' Henri looked like he might explode. 'A cake from Gulliver's! That would be the huge insult for my friend Daniel.'

'Well … would you be able to make one?' ventured Rachel.

Henri stood up, his girth pushing the desk so far in Rachel's direction that she had to take a step back. 'I will make the cake, Ra-shelle. And a big feast as well.'

'There's no need for that …'

Rachel had envisioned turning up at the rectory on Monday evening with the cake. Alone.

'No need!' sputtered Henri. 'In France, a priest is honoured on his birthday. We will have the party in my house.'

'But—'

'We must keep it a secret, yes? So he will have the big surprise. We will invite everyone.'

This was getting out of control. 'If you invite everyone, won't it be hard to keep it a secret?'

Henri thought about that. 'You are right. Let us invite selective persons only. I shall make the list.'

Rachel's idea of a cosy evening for two had been scuppered by Henri's kindness. She gave it one last try. 'But won't you be needed here in the restaurant on Monday evening?'

Henri shook his head. 'My chefs have been trained by me. They will cope magnificently.'

He was right. Rachel had seen them in action. They would cope. There was clearly no stopping Henri. He was now a man with a mission. All Rachel could do was buy a special gift for Daniel, and hope to corner him for a dance or two.

* * *

Daniel pushed away the plate of lamb stew, half-eaten, though there was nothing wrong with the food prepared by one of his most devoted parishioners. When Father Milligan was here, they'd been cared for by a housekeeper who seemed older than Methuselah. She'd retired along with Father Milligan, and Daniel had declined a replacement, claiming he was young and able-bodied and could take care of himself.

However, the wives of the parish councillors and the ladies of the flower-arranging committee had set up their own unofficial rota to feed him. To decline it would be seen as a slight. They'd even clean the rectory if he let them, but he wasn't above a bit of polishing and vacuuming. Plus it was a way to keep his privacy. So much of him already belonged to his congregation.

He'd been lucky to get this parish, especially as he was only in his late twenties. The number of young priests had dwindled so much of late, though, that Daniel suddenly found himself at a premium. The Church wanted to keep him and so wanted to keep him sweet. When he'd expressed his interest in coming back to Kilbrook, where he was born, his superiors had listened. Father Milligan had recommended Daniel to the bishop, and that had carried considerable weight.

Father Milligan had privately questioned Daniel about why he wanted to come back to Kilbrook. The old priest was one of the few who knew all about the church incident, so he had every right to ask. It had been hard for Daniel to put his feelings into words. He'd told Father Milligan that he felt God wanted him to atone for what he'd done, and that had been accepted. The Church knew all about self-flagellation. But the disappointing thing was that all these months on, Daniel wasn't feeling any better about his past, and perhaps that was because so few people knew the truth about what had happened all those years ago. Perhaps only then would he feel that he had been truly punished, but it would also likely mean the end of his time in Kilbrook.

Daniel wished he had someone to talk to about all this. Someone who could really understand, but being a priest was a lonely job. He was surrounded by people all day, yet in the evenings everyone went home to their families, leaving their priest alone in his kitchen, eating warmed-up food and sipping a glass of cheap Chardonnay. That was the nature of the job, of course, and in time, he'd likely cope with it better.

Loneliness was probably why Rachel was affecting him so much. Plus he couldn't exactly avoid her as she had to be in the church every day to study the murals. A daily temptation. Still, she was only here for a few weeks. It wasn't as though she'd moved in next door and would be here permanently. Getting through this would make him a stronger priest, better able to empathise with his parishioners.

Daniel went into the sitting room and opened up the heavy leather-bound Bible to find some guidance. The story of David and Bathsheba would do.

* * *

'Get me a brandy will you, love, I'm all done in.' Helen collapsed into an armchair, kicking off her shoes.

Finn poured them each a generous glass. He gulped down most of his, then stretched his long legs out on the sofa, balancing the glass on his stomach. Helen sipped at her brandy, making appreciative noises, her legs settled on the coffee table. This had been their wind-down routine when they'd shared a place in Australia. Discussing their day and their projects over a nightcap. He missed those times.

He mentally reviewed the evening's rehearsal. Moments of glory and moments of despair. 'You know that old cliché about not working with children? It's not just a cliché, is it?'

Helen smiled. 'No. They can give some wonderful performances, but they've got such short attention spans. Kids make everything wildly unpredictable.'

'Still, we'll get there. As long as they have fun, that's the main thing.'

The central heating hummed and Finn saw Helen's eyelids growing heavy. He started to brood about Rachel. She'd arrived late at the rehearsals tonight and left early. He'd managed to catch up with her before she left the theatre and asked if anything was wrong. She'd been so cool with him that it hurt. Saying she'd be too busy to help out any more with the play. A quick goodbye and that was that. Yet yesterday she had seemed so keen. What had he done wrong?

'What is it, Finn?'

Helen was watching him now. He could never hide anything from her. Nor would he lie.

'Do you think Rachel likes me?' he asked. Helen's intuition about people was always reliable.

'Do you want her to like you?'

He nodded.

'She's a bit different from your usual type, isn't she?'

Finn sat upright, frowning. 'What d'you mean?'

'Well, there's a brain there for a start ...'

Grinning, he grabbed the cushion and threatened to throw it. She put up her hand in defence and gabbled apologies. It had been a joke, but there was truth in it. He was getting bored with the girls he met through his work. Girls who usually threw themselves at him, and who he'd not exactly flinched from catching. Undemanding relationships left him with lots of energy for his acting. That's what he told himself anyway, but maybe his subconscious was telling him now he needed something more than full breasts and empty heads.

'I'm only here for a short time, though,' he said. 'And so is Rachel.'

'Passing ships have been known to collide but both sail off into the sunset.'

'That's the worst analogy I ever heard,' Finn protested. 'They'd sink.'

She laughed. 'Well, I'm tired. But I've got more experience than you in affairs of the heart, so heed my words, young one.'

Finn still wasn't convinced. 'Rachel seems to blow hot and cold. I don't know how to handle that.'

'Invite her for a drink tomorrow,' suggested Helen. 'Let her talk. And you listen. I mean, really listen. We always follow that advice when we're acting. Sometimes we're not so good at it in real life.'

'But what if she says no?'

'Give it your all. You know how I like a nice romance.'

'Shall we quickly find a man for you? How about old Miley – he's been giving you the eye. Then we can double date and you won't have to ask me a million questions when I get back.'

It wasn't that much of a joke. The caretaker of the theatre really did seem sweet on Helen. Unfortunately, he drank more than was good for him, and had a wife and seven children.

It was his aunt's turn to threaten Finn with a cushion.

Chapter Five

The church was now closed to visitors for an hour, but Daniel had allowed Rachel to work on in the chapel while he took a group of seven-year-olds through their paces for First Communion this coming Sunday.

There seemed to be a surprising amount of laughter filtering through from the church. In Rachel's time, the priest instructing them on First Communion had been so stern that nobody dared say a word, and he made more than one child cry. That clearly wasn't the way Daniel handled things.

Her curiosity got the better of her, and Rachel moved quietly out of the chapel, slipping into the pew near the back, where the children's teacher, Miss O'Hanlan, was sitting. Daniel had briefly introduced the two women earlier.

The children were clustered up at the altar rail, and Daniel stood behind.

'And then you drink,' he said. 'Now we know this is absolutely not soda pop, don't we? It's very special. What is it?'

'Blood!' shouted one of the boys excitedly.

And so it went on, Daniel patiently explaining, and answering their questions when necessary.

'He's so good with the children,' said Miss O'Hanlan. 'They love him. He'd have made a grand teacher.'

Yet another person who had only good things to say about Daniel. Molly, Henri, Miss O'Hanlan ... they all saw him regularly and knew more about the man he'd become than she did, so their opinions had to count for something. Now Rachel felt a bit shabby about her flirting. If he responded to her advances, he could lose his job. That wouldn't have seemed too high a price to pay before she came back to Kilbrook, but now she had her doubts. Anyway, if he was as good a priest as everyone seemed to think, he'd be full of remorse after the reunion. He'd punish himself.

'Right. Who wants a jelly baby?'

The session was over, and Daniel was now holding out a glass jar of coloured sweets. Little hands dived in and found the treasure. Then the children skipped happily up the side aisles to Miss O'Hanlan, who ushered them out the door. Quietness returned to St Kilian's.

Rachel walked back towards the chapel. Daniel met her at the entrance and held out the glass jar. 'Help yourself. The red ones are the best.'

She grinned and took a jelly baby, popping it into her mouth. The chewy softness took her back to childhood – far back, to when her father was still alive and would take her for walks, hoisted on his shoulders. 'You'd have made a good father, Daniel,' she said thoughtfully.

'I *am* a father in a way. To all these children.'

'I suppose so.'

This was a man devoted to his job, who did the best he could for his community, and Rachel wasn't going to mess with that. She'd drop her Mata Hari plans and turn her sights instead on Mel and Jay. And Spook – if she could track him down.

'You have a good day, Daniel.' For the first time Rachel meant it.

* * *

Rachel hurriedly pulled on her coat, not bothering to untie the ribbon from her hair. Her shift at the restaurant had just finished, and it was time to beat a hasty retreat. Mel had been in a foul mood again today, and nobody could do anything right. Henri was in the office with her now, and their raised voices echoed around the kitchen. This wasn't a workplace – it was a war zone.

'Bye,' Rachel called to the other chefs, then escaped out of the restaurant's heat and noise into the cool outside air – where she found Finn, lounging against the wall of the car park.

His face lit up with a smile when he saw her, and he walked over. 'Hi, I was hoping to catch you.'

Rachel hadn't expected that Finn would come looking for her after she'd given him the brush-off last night. Clearly he wasn't a man to take a hint. She'd have to be more direct. But how to do that without explaining why she was here, which was too much of a risk? And how to do it without hurting him?

'I wondered ... would you like to go to Donegan's for a drink this evening? It's a nice little pub – just opposite the theatre. Not as a date or anything. Just as friends.'

He looked so uncertain, so vulnerable, that Rachel didn't have the heart to refuse him. What harm could there be in one drink? And then she could find a way to tell him she was unavailable.

'Sure,' she said. 'I'll meet you there at eight.'

* * *

Jay swung out of the car park. School was over for the day. Now it was his time. A jar or two in the pub before heading home. Some TV and time with Leanne, then he'd head out for his evening run.

He was so lost in his thoughts that he drove right past the girl. Catching sight of her in the mirror, Jay stopped the car and quickly reversed. She stood there, smiling at him. Jenny O'Neill. Even shrouded in a shapeless anorak, she was still the loveliest pupil in Kilbrook Community School. How her shovel-faced culchie of a farmer father had managed to produce such a stunner was beyond Jay. It was against the laws of genetics.

He rolled down the window. 'Can I offer you a lift, Jenny?'

She ran round the front of the car and got into the passenger seat, throwing her bag in the back. 'Thanks, Mr Cole.'

'We'd better buckle you up,' Jay said, reaching across her for the seat belt. She smelled of vanilla – maybe her shampoo.

Adjusting the belt, he let his fingers trail lightly across her breasts, but she didn't look at him, just stared straight ahead.

Smiling to himself, Jay started up the car. As it purred along, he glanced at Jenny's legs. The school skirt revealed a hint of thigh, and it was too much for him. He put out a hand and gently stroked the soft skin, reaching higher ...

She smacked away his hand. 'Jay! Wait till we're clear of the houses.'

He groaned. 'You'll get a spanking for that later.'

'Promises, promises.'

They smiled at each other. She loved this fantasy of the chaste schoolgirl and the randy teacher. Personally, he'd prefer to get on with the sex as soon as possible, but a sweet sixteen-year-old was allowed her quirks.

'All clear,' said Jenny, and his hand crept back once more to her thigh as he turned off into the usual side lane with its high hedges and hidden spaces.

* * *

It was after eight, and Donegan's was just getting started. From a reasonably peaceful place at lunchtimes, it was now a hive of noisy activity, the locals drowning out the singer who didn't seem to mind, happily drinking his Guinness while the fiddler seemed quite lost in the moment. Finn could swear he was playing a different tune to what was being sung, but no one seemed to care. He returned to Rachel in one of the corner booths, with two packets of Taytos and their drinks. Only a half for him. He wanted to keep his wits about him.

'Thanks.' She sipped at her vodka tonic. 'This should be mandatory after a shift at The Fat Pheasant. The boss is a bit of a dragon.'

Finn nodded. 'I know ... I've heard people say she has a bad temper. It's a shame you have to put up with it. Can't your family help you out with some money?'

'My parents are dead.' There was regret in her voice, and

Finn wished he'd picked a safer topic. She didn't clam up, though, as he might have done. 'I have lots of relatives who've helped me out in the past, but I think there comes a time when you have to stand on your own two feet.'

He respected that. 'I felt the same way about Helen. She'd have given me the moon and the stars if I'd asked. But the day after I started drama school, I took my first modelling job. Boring work, but it gave me my own steady income. I got picked up by Calvin Klein, and I didn't have to ask for handouts any more.'

'So your face became your fortune,' Rachel commented.

Finn suddenly felt shy. Tongue-tied. Like he was sixteen again and didn't know how to talk to girls. 'My father wouldn't call that a real job,' he blurted out, just for something to say to cover his discomfort.

'Isn't he pleased you're doing what you want?'

'He's dead.'

'Oh, Finn. I'm so sorry …'

'Don't be. He was a bastard.'

Rachel looked shocked and no wonder. Too much information, too soon. He should be trying to sweep her off her feet with his charm, not make her think he came with baggage. 'Don't feel sorry for me, Rachel,' he said. 'Lots of kids have crappy parents. They don't all have someone like Helen to take care of them. I'm lucky. She's been like a mother to me.'

Another can of worms. Next thing she'd be asking about his mother, and he couldn't bear to talk about her. Even thinking about her would get him upset. He'd have to head Rachel off. 'So, tell me about you. Do you like living in London? Did you always want to study art history?'

Rachel suddenly closed her eyes and held up her hand, palm towards him. 'Finn, please …'

He stopped talking immediately and sat there in shock. What had he done wrong? She dipped her head and stared into her drink. He was on the verge of panic, not sure what to do. At that moment, he was thankful for the din of the music, the laughter, and the foot-tapping in the pub. Silence would have been unbearable.

When she finally looked up, her eyes were full of sadness.

'What is it, Rachel? Please tell me.'

'Finn, I like you, I really do—'

'Good. I like you, too.'

'But we have to end this now. Before it starts.'

Disappointment clawed at Finn's heart, and the feeling made him realise he couldn't give her up without a fight. At the very least, he needed an explanation. 'Why, Rachel? Help me understand.'

She took a big gulp of her vodka and set the glass down carefully. 'It's very complicated. I'm not in a good place right now. I'm working through some really bad stuff.'

Finn sat there, absorbing what she'd said. It would surely be the wrong thing to push for more information, however much he wanted to. All he could do was be supportive. Helen had told him to listen – to really listen. 'I hear you, Rachel, and I don't want to make things more difficult for you. If you don't want anything more, can we at least be friends?'

Her expression was doubtful. 'You could get hurt, Finn,' she whispered.

'That's my choice,' he said. 'Friends stick by each other, no matter what.'

'But what if I'm not the girl you think I am?'

Finn knew all about self-doubt. It had taken him years to suppress it, but it was still there, lurking beneath the surface. 'I'm here for you, Rachel,' he told her. 'Whatever you need, just ask.'

'That doesn't seem like much of a deal for you,' she protested.

'Hey, if this all leads to something more, I'll be delighted, I won't deny it, but I won't push. Us just being friends is fine with me. And I think maybe you need a friend right now.'

'I do.'

The atmosphere between them was highly charged. It was time to lighten the mood a bit. 'So, that's settled. Now for some ground rules. Eye contact only. No secretly checking out the other's bits. A friendly peck on the cheek is fine – anything else and the person has to pay a forfeit. Touching of the hands is allowed, but it has to be pre-approved twenty-four hours in advance. Should I draw up a contract?'

Rachel was laughing now, looking much more relaxed. 'Oh, Finn, you're a tonic.'

'One of my many talents,' he said. 'I also cook well, mix a mean cocktail, and have been known to vacuum.'

'All admirable skills. But can you ice skate?'

He frowned. 'Never tried. Why?'

'We're going to the opening of the ice rink tomorrow, remember?'

'So we are. Well, it'll be a first for me. Just promise you won't think less of me if I fall over.'

'I promise.'

He raised his beer mug. 'Here's to friendship.'

'To friendship,' she said, and chinked his glass.

It felt to Finn like they'd made it safely across a very shaky bridge.

* * *

Rachel sat at the dressing table, brushing her hair, lost in thought. The day had been one of surprises. First, her decision about Daniel. To leave him alone until he found out who she was at the reunion. Was that cowardly? Not really. It took more courage not to make him suffer. She'd keep contact with him to a minimum from now on. There was his birthday party on Monday, but that was really Henri's baby. Rachel would show up for a while but leave early.

She wasn't giving up all her plans for revenge, though. Mel was holding a special dinner next week at the restaurant for her father's clients, and she'd asked Rachel to be a waitress for the evening. She'd use it as a dry run for the reunion the week after that. But she'd have to be careful. Messing up the food in some way would reflect badly on Henri, so she couldn't do that. It would have to be something connected to the building itself. Perhaps cutting the heat somehow? Whatever she decided to do, she'd make sure Mel's dinner was a disappointment.

The other surprise of the day had been Finn, who'd come looking for her and then agreed to settle for friendship if that was all that was on offer. But could it really stay as just a friendship, or was Rachel fooling herself? The more she saw of him, the more attracted she was. Why couldn't she have met him in London? Then there would have been nothing standing between them.

No point in wishing things were different or in feeling sorry for herself. She was here, now, with a job to do. And things were only going to get more challenging. Time to toughen up. She took out the diary and started to read.

5 March

There's a school trip to the Cliffs of Moher. I've always wanted to go, and now's my chance, but I can't bear the thought of being alone on the coach, alone during the day. It should be a special time, one to look back on. A fun time with friends. They're all going, though – Jay, Mel, Spook and Daniel – so no one would risk upsetting them by including me. And that means that either the teachers will insist they do, or else I'll be stuck with a teacher for the day! No thanks. I'll pass. Mam is already excited on my behalf because she knows I've wanted to see the Cliffs. I'll have to think of a way to tell her I don't want to go. Anyway, I wouldn't put it past them to accidentally push me off.

They're making my life hell.

Chapter Six

Jay poured himself more wine and tried to tune out the dreary conversation around him. How he'd tolerated Gerald and Tessa Maguire as in-laws for five years, he'd never know. Mel had invited them for lunch today because they were going to the ice rink in the park this afternoon for the opening of the Winter Festival. Leanne was excited about it, but Jay wasn't sure he could bear another three hours of the senior Maguires. He'd prefer to go to the pub. Or maybe Jenny could escape her farm chores for an hour or so.

Gerald was talking now about the American interior designers who were coming soon to snap up whatever expensive old tat they could find for their clueless rich clients. Gerald, the leading antiques dealer in the area, would be on hand to part them from their money. God knows why he was so proud of himself. It wasn't as if he was a self-made man because he'd inherited the antiques emporium in Galway from his own father.

'Treacle pudding for dessert,' announced Mel, and headed off to the kitchen.

As soon as she was out of earshot, Gerald started on Jay. 'End of term for you soon, Jay. Smart choice to be a PE teacher. No final exams to mark. How exactly *do* you assess them? Two laps round the football pitch? A game of rounders?'

Tessa sniggered, ever the dutiful wife. Jay did appreciate the effort laughing must have cost her since she'd had more Botox in her time than he'd had hot dinners.

'Actually, they're assessed on co-ordination, teamwork, leadership skills—' Jay began, but Gerald cut him off.

'Just pass or fail them – give yourself an easy life. After all, none of them are likely to choose to make a career out of sport, are they?'

The insult to his job hit home, but Jay tried to keep his expression neutral. These snide comments when Mel wasn't around was how it had been for the past year. Ever since Gerald had spotted Jay holding hands with a blonde in a restaurant in Westport. At least, he might have spotted them holding hands. It was hard to be sure. His father-in-law had come over to the table, and Jay had truthfully been able to introduce his companion as the real estate agent who'd handled his parents' recent move to the area. Gerald had seemed fine with that at the time, but shortly after, the subtle attacks started. He clearly had his suspicions, and for a while, Jay was on tenterhooks that Mel would be told. The more time that passed, the less likely that was, but it still made any contact with Gerald uncomfortable.

Mel returned with dessert, and the conversation switched to Henri and how he'd parked in the wrong place again. Good for him. At least the chef had balls. Jay had traded his in years ago for an SUV, a Rolex, two holidays a year in the sun, and the biggest house on the block. No one could blame him for that choice. Certainly not his father with his history of poor investments. Jay had lain awake some nights, listening to his mother giving out about how they never had enough money. They'd put on a front for the neighbours, of course, but it was always there like a black cloud over everything. Probably why they were so easy on him all the time instead of doling out punishments like Spook's dad did.

It could all have been so different if Manchester United had taken him on that year after he'd finished school. It had almost happened. He'd come so close. After the trials, the coaches said he showed real talent, but that was as far as it went. They lost interest in him after he'd got himself into a nightclub brawl, so he'd eventually hitched his wagon to Mel's. God knows she deserved something for patiently waiting for him ever since they were at school, but he'd paid a high price to be at the top of the social heap. One day, though, Gerald and

Tessa Maguire would be six feet under, and all their wealth would go to their only child, Mel – and, by default, to him.

'Let's get ready and walk down to the ice rink,' said Mel, when lunch was finished.

'I'll go and help Leanne with her boots,' offered Tessa.

'No walk for me,' said Jay. Mel gave him the evil eye, but he ignored it. 'I get enough exercise during the week. I'm at no risk of a heart attack.'

'Not unless the alcohol gets you first,' Gerald responded, looking pointedly at Jay's wine glass. The man always had to have the last word.

They all trailed out, leaving Jay behind. He took out his mobile phone and started to text Jenny. Just because he had to stay shackled to Mel didn't mean he couldn't have some fun of his own.

* * *

They were both as bad as each other on skates. Standing upright was fine, but every time they glided off, within seconds Rachel would clutch at Finn's coat or he would grab her arm, and they'd collapse in an untidy heap of laughter. They were sitting on the ice now after the latest undignified fall. The other skaters whizzed past them, their blades throwing up a fine crystalline spray. Children as young as five were putting them to shame. Not that it mattered. Rachel was having the best time.

The sun shining in a blue sky took the chill off the afternoon. Music sang out from the pavilion in the centre of the ice. Around the edge of the rink, vendors were selling hot chestnuts and mulled cider to people seated at tables. There was laughter everywhere. It was an inspired start to the Winter Festival – bringing all the villagers together for some fun.

'How about a break?' suggested Finn, brushing ice from his jeans.

Rachel nodded. 'Problem is, though – how do we get off this ice? We fall down every two seconds.'

'We could crawl?'

'Not cool.'

'Beg for help?'

'From a five-year-old? No way.'

'Right then. Be brave.' Finn scrambled upright, his arms windmilling around.

Rachel clutched his legs, giggling. 'Don't leave me!' she begged.

'Up you get, Jayne Torvill.' Finn somehow managed to stay upright, and hauled Rachel safely to her feet. The park started to spin around, and she felt her skates about to slide from under her. Finn wrapped his arms around her in a bear hug.

'This is the plan,' he whispered. 'You lean into me, I lean into you. And we sashay sideways in sync to the edge.'

'Brilliant,' said Rachel, and they started stepping slowly to the side like a crazy crab out of its element.

Although Rachel could hear the noise around them, her eyes were fixed on Finn's. They were stunning. Bluey-grey. Like crystals, but not cold. They were bright and full of fun and warmth. And framed by the thickest lashes she'd ever seen. His strong arms were squeezing her tight into his lean body, and she could smell the subtle tang of his aftershave ...

'We made it,' Finn announced, all too soon. A group at a nearby table were applauding their improvised escape from the ice. Finn grinned and bowed. Then he stepped onto solid ground and lifted Rachel gently over the edge of the rink. 'Let's get these damned skates off. I see a free table over by the trees. Last one there's a wuss.'

* * *

Daniel heard Rachel's laughter peal out into the cold air. She was sitting with Helen MacKenzie's nephew, Finn, who was tossing chestnuts up in the air and catching them in his mouth.

They hadn't yet been introduced, but Daniel had seen Finn around – and overheard smitten schoolgirls giggling and talking about him. Good-looking, always in sunglasses, even though it was November. Such a poser ...

'Not skating, Danny boy? I seem to remember you were quite good.'

Mel plonked herself down opposite Daniel. Typical Mel. Not even asking if the seat was free. Though why wouldn't it be? Who, these days, wanted to socialise with a priest?

'Or does the Church not allow you to have any fun?' She gave him a sly look and then gulped down some of her mulled cider. 'God, this tastes like paint stripper. At the price they're charging, somebody's cutting corners and making a tidy profit.'

She always seemed to see the worst in people. It was depressing. When he'd returned to Kilbrook, Daniel had tried to avoid his former classmates as much as possible, but Jay had latched onto him. Came visiting at the rectory whenever he felt like it. Acted as if they were friends, when the only thing that bound them together was complicity in covering up a shameful act.

Daniel had been thinking recently about what happened in the church all those years ago. Dreaming about it, too. As he did every year. Although the memories never really left his mind, they were much worse around Halloween, the anniversary of the Ella Rinaldi incident. That hadn't even been his idea – he certainly didn't get any pleasure from tormenting the girl – but it seemed he was the only one of the group who'd felt some responsibility ... and guilt. Mel still revelled in having power to destroy people's lives if she chose to, and Jay flat out refused to discuss the bullying he'd done. They were both morally bankrupt yet didn't seem to lose any sleep over it.

'How are things going with the reunion?' he asked Mel.

'Fine. I should have upped the price per ticket, though. I'll be out of pocket when it's all over.'

'I wonder if Ella will come,' Daniel said. They'd never

talked openly about this before, although it had always been the elephant in the room.

'Don't be stupid!' Mel was staring at him as if he had two heads. 'Why should she? We showed her she wasn't welcome here. No, no – she's long gone, thank God.'

Her harsh words sickened Daniel. 'Don't you feel guilty about what we did?' he asked, but he already knew the answer.

'No, I don't. And neither should you. She had it coming to her.'

'But why? Why did we bully her?' He'd never really been convinced about the reason Mel gave. 'You said she was a ...' – he glanced quickly around him and lowered his voice – '... a wop, but I heard she was part-Irish, too. And even if she wasn't, it still wasn't a reason.'

Mel took another gulp of the cider, then emptied the rest out onto the grass. She shrugged. 'She thought she was better than the rest of us. Always had her head stuck in a book. Always doing exactly what she was told and sucking up to the teachers. Thought she was so smart. And she said Jay was thick.'

'What?'

'Jay once asked to copy her maths homework. She said he couldn't. It wouldn't be right. I told her she'd never belong here if she was going to be that stuck-up. She said she didn't want to belong if it meant doing homework for people who were too stupid or lazy to do their own. So she brought it on herself. Anyway, school was so boring. It brightened things up a bit.'

Daniel felt close to despair. They'd tormented a girl for months because she didn't agree with cheating. Because she wanted to follow the rules.

'Don't look so shocked,' said Mel. 'No one twisted your arm to make you join in.'

'Daniel!'

Leanne jumped into his lap and wrapped her mittened

hands around his neck in a hug, babbling excitedly about the ice skating. How Daniel loved this little girl. She was the best part of Mel and Jay. Yesterday, Rachel said he'd have made a good father, and Daniel felt again that small stab of regret at what he'd never have.

* * *

On her way back from the park's washroom, Rachel spotted Daniel sitting at a table playing the pat-a-cake hand clapping game with a little girl. It was hard to tell who was having more fun.

Daniel smiled as she came up to them. 'Rachel, I'd like to introduce you to my very good friend, Leanne.'

'Hello,' said Rachel to the girl. 'Are you having fun?'

'Yes,' Leanne announced, her big green eyes shining with excitement. 'Granda mostly held my hand, but I skated by myself for a bit.'

'That's great. You did better than me. I kept falling over.'

'Yes, I saw you out on the ice,' said Daniel. 'With Helen MacKenzie's nephew.'

Rachel could have sworn she detected a hint of jealousy in his voice. It would be ironic if the one day she wasn't making a play for Daniel was the day he started paying her some attention.

'Mammy, I want to skate some more,' cried Leanne. She ran over to Mel, who was talking to some people at a table nearby.

'Why is your coat open? You'll catch cold.'

Rachel stared at Mel, zipping up Leanne's parka. This adorable little girl was Mel's daughter. An innocent in all this. If Rachel took revenge on Mel and Jay, she could indirectly hurt Leanne.

Rachel said goodbye to Daniel and hurried back to Finn. At least when she was with him, she could take a break for a while from these dilemmas. And this evening she'd be at rehearsals, embroiled in Scrooge's ghosts of the past instead of her own.

* * *

'Why do we all love this story so much?' mused Rachel, watching the rehearsal of *A Christmas Carol* from a front row seat. 'An old man and three ghosts doesn't exactly sound like a winning formula.'

Helen laughed beside her. 'I know what you mean.' They were taking a short break while Finn gave some direction on the stage to the boy playing Scrooge. 'But Dickens was a clever man. He knew we all have regrets about things we did, things we didn't do. And he takes us to a scary place in this story – the end of our lives – and makes us look back.'

Helen's words made Rachel shudder a little. What did her mother see at the end of her life? 'The stuff of nightmares, really,' she commented.

'Yes,' agreed Helen. 'Except Dickens gave his readers a happy ending. One of the happiest endings in literature, I think. Scrooge gets a second chance.'

Happy endings were for fairy tales. 'Pity that doesn't happen in real life.'

'Oh, I think it does.' Helen's glasses had tipped forward down her nose, and her deep green eyes were fixed intently on Rachel. Her gaze was quite intimidating – like she could see right through you. 'Sometimes we get a wake-up call. Don't you believe people can change for the better?'

Helen wasn't making idle small talk. That was a real question and she wanted a real answer. 'I'd like to believe it,' said Rachel, 'but I haven't seen much evidence yet.' Of course, she was going to be the wake-up call for the bullies here in Kilbrook. Somehow she didn't think they'd come out of the experience as happily as Scrooge did. This wasn't fiction.

'Well, you're young,' said Helen, giving Rachel's arm a pat. 'Life might surprise you. Just take my advice and don't let opportunities pass you by. That way you have no regrets in old age.'

Rachel smiled politely, then turned her attention to the stage. Finn was on his knees, text in hand, listening to his lead actor say some lines. He was totally absorbed in the task, head tilted. As co-director, he was patient and helpful. The joker was off-duty.

'Did you and Finn have a good time at the ice rink earlier? How was he at skating?'

'About as bad as me.' Rachel turned back to Helen, whose expression radiated curiosity. 'We spent most of the time drinking cider and talking on the sidelines. He does some good impressions.'

Helen nodded. 'I know. He's famous back home for his Dame Edna Everage. He's got a real gift for making people laugh. Surprising, really ...'

That caught Rachel's attention. 'Surprising – how so?'

Helen paused and glanced down at the notes in her lap, tapping her pencil on the paper. 'Finn's not exactly what he pretends to be.'

What did that mean? Was Helen going to tell her Finn wasn't really an actor? It wouldn't be a huge lie, but Rachel preferred honesty. That was hypocritical, though. She was hardly being honest herself.

Helen started speaking again. 'He's not as confident as he likes people to think. It's all an act ... he's a very good actor. He's had it rough in the past.'

Rachel glanced at Finn again. To her, he seemed like one of life's golden people, whose looks and charm opened all doors. With so much already in their favour, a little bit of suffering would surely pass like a summer shower. Then she remembered what Finn had said yesterday. 'He did hint that he didn't get on with his father.'

Helen sighed and leaned forward, elbows on knees, face in her hands. 'His father didn't get on with many people. But apart from that, Finn's suffered losses in his life, and they've taken a toll. Perhaps he's told you about them?' Helen glanced across at Rachel. She shook her head. 'And perhaps he won't. I'm not saying he's broken. He's a fine young man, but ...'

'You're afraid he'll get hurt?'

'I try not to be a mother hen, but the odd cluck escapes sometimes.'

'He's lucky to have you,' said Rachel, and meant it. If only there'd been someone like Helen to have a protective chat with some of her ex-boyfriends. 'He speaks very highly of you.'

'Does he?' Helen's smile of affection spoke volumes about the bond she had with her nephew. 'They love him in Australia, you know. He's got a lead role in a new TV series that starts filming in February. His career over there is set to take off.'

Was there a veiled warning there? A hint not to get too attached? It was the sensible thing to do, but Rachel would be making her own choices. She decided to change the subject to something more neutral. 'Do you miss Australia?'

The older woman settled back in her seat, pushing fingers through her salt-and-pepper hair. 'I do miss it, yes. I spent thirty-five years there. Met and married Leo MacKenzie when I was fresh out of drama school. He was ten years older than me and directing a play at the Edinburgh Festival. Quite the catch. Before I knew it, I was married and acting in plays in Sydney.'

How romantic it all sounded. Rachel could imagine the younger Helen, bright and sparky, the same shoulder-length layered hair but fully brunette, catching the eye of the handsome director. And then flying off to an adventurous new life in Australia. She'd certainly grabbed opportunity when it called.

'Leo died sixteen years ago,' Helen told her, and Rachel's happy visions changed to a bleak cemetery scattered with mourners. She tried to stop her mind taking her back to both her mother's and her sister's funerals by focusing on what

Helen was saying. 'It was a hell of a blow, and I struggled until Finn came to live with me, and kept me going. Then my brother got sick – terminal cancer – so I came back here to nurse him. He passed away just over a year ago.'

'I'm so sorry, Helen … Are you settled in Kilbrook now then?'

'No, I'm going back to Australia, but there's a bit of a problem with my brother's will. I'll have to go to court soon. That's another reason Finn came over – to give me some moral support.'

Rachel was about to ask more questions when Finn called from the stage. 'Helen! We're ready for Act Two now.'

'Well, the show must go on.' Helen stood up and stretched. 'Off you go into the prompt box, Rachel.'

Finn and Rachel passed as he was coming down the side stairs – which she'd learned were called the treads – and she was heading up to the stage. He gave her a big smile and a wink, and she swore her heart fluttered.

Chapter Seven

Clutching the tray of tea and cakes, Rachel threaded her way through the café tables towards Molly. They'd had to wait a bit for a seat because everywhere in the Galway Shopping Centre was jam-packed. Rachel had thought Sunday shopping would be a more leisurely affair. Clearly not. Maybe people were getting an early start on Christmas. The crowds were nothing to Rachel, who was used to the all-hours pandemonium of London's Oxford Street, but she'd worried initially about Molly. Needlessly, it turned out. Molly was more than a match for a crush of shoppers and not above using her cane to swipe a few ankles.

'Here we go.'

Rachel set down the tray and took a seat. Molly busied herself, pouring the teas from the little individual pots.

'You must be exhausted, Molly.'

Molly waved her hand, dismissively. 'No, no, pet. I'm tougher than I look. Besides, we couldn't have Father Quinn with no presents on his birthday now, could we? That'd never do.'

Molly was excited about Daniel's surprise birthday party. She was the one who'd suggested they drive to Galway for some shopping, after she'd been to Mass and they'd finished lunch. She opened a shopping bag and plucked out some black socks. 'D'you think Father Quinn will like them? They're thermal, you know. Just the ticket for that drafty old church.'

'I'm sure he'll love them,' said Rachel.

'Those decorations cost a pretty penny,' commented Molly.

'I know. Nothing's cheap these days.' Rachel had stocked up on streamers and balloons and gilt letters to spell out, *Happy birthday, Daniel*. 'But Henri's paying for it all.'

'Now, isn't that kind? And you're decorating Henri's place tomorrow. This is what community is all about.'

Rachel smiled, but inside she couldn't help thinking about her schooldays in Kilbrook. Outsiders had been targeted and then ejected. That was definitely *not* community.

'And what are your plans tonight?' asked Molly. 'Are you seeing that nice young fellow again?'

'Finn.' Rachel nodded, noting the twinkle in Molly's eyes. Older people seemed to be incorrigible matchmakers. 'We're just going to the pub for a drink or two. I won't be back late.'

'Will he be at the party tomorrow?'

'No, he can't come. There's a rehearsal for *A Christmas Carol*.'

'That's a shame, but you know most of the people at the party will be over forty and needing their beds by nine, so you'll probably have time to see him afterwards.'

Rachel smiled. 'Maybe.'

She would really have preferred to be at the theatre with Finn tomorrow night. Now that she'd changed her mind about flirting with Daniel, the party seemed risky. What if someone recognised her? That guest list had been littered with names of older people whose names she remembered. Pity they hadn't made the party fancy dress. She could have gone in disguise.

* * *

As birthdays went, this one had been mostly uneventful. It was just after seven and choir practice had finished. Time to close up the church for the day. Daniel opened the desk drawer and picked up the birthday card. He sat there, turning it over in his hands. Rachel had given it to him that morning when she'd come to study the murals, and it was touching that she had remembered.

The card was handmade, which meant it was all the more special to him. Rachel had taken a wide-shot photo of the ice rink and the pavilion in the park at Saturday's Winter Festival opening, and she'd glued it to the front of the card. Daniel could see himself there, a tiny figure on the right of the picture, Leanne's parka a pink blur next to him. Inside the card, she'd wished him a happy birthday and signed it 'Your friend, Rachel.'

He hadn't broadcast the fact that it was his birthday. Father Milligan had warned him against it, saying people, especially the seniors, might feel obliged to buy their priests gifts, and they really needed every euro they had for themselves. However, somehow Henri had found out this was a special day – Rachel had probably told him – and he'd invited Daniel over. It would be a good way to spend the evening, in the company of a friend. And there'd be great food on offer, for sure.

He'd do his perimeter check of the outside of the church and then be on his way.

* * *

Rain was forecast for later, but Daniel had decided to walk to Henri's cottage. It wasn't far, and the evening air would clear his head. People nodded and greeted him as he passed, a few doing a double take to see their priest dressed in jeans. He felt strange without the dog collar. It had become so much a part of him. The job and the man had melded, which was how it should be, he supposed. But there was still a small part of him that sometimes rebelled against that, wanting the things he'd never have. Keeping busy was a way to quiet that part of himself, but it never quite went away.

He turned into Henri's street. The chef lived in the very last house, which was just out of range of the streetlight, but luckily the cottage was whitewashed and loomed out of the darkness. As he opened the gate, Daniel could hear the flapping in the wind of the huge French flag on a pole, which the chef had planted in the rockery in his front garden. Only the hall light was on, although Daniel could hear voices inside. Maybe Henri had company, though it could be the TV.

Daniel rang the doorbell and waited. The voices stopped and, before long, Henri swung the door open. He wore his customary green velvet smoking jacket, and he was beaming.

'Daniel, *mon ami*!' he cried, pulling him into a bone-crushing hug. 'Come in. You are cold like the icicle. We must get you a fur coat for the winter.'

Daniel laughed. 'No need for that. I'm used to this weather.' He stepped into the hallway and took off his coat. Henri's cottage always amazed him – it was neat as a pin, and filled with furniture that seemed too frail and delicate for this bear of a man.

'Come through into the salon,' urged Henri.

'Salon' was just a fancy word for sitting room, but the word didn't seem pretentious when Henri used it. They'd likely drink some brandy this evening and play backgammon. Not the worst way to spend your birthday.

Henri had disappeared into the room, which was still in darkness. Daniel hesitated in the doorway, and then the light flashed on, blinding him for a moment.

'Surprise!' various voices shouted, and then Daniel saw the room was full of people blowing party poppers and smiling.

'Happy birthday!' yelled Henri, and everyone else echoed him.

Rachel stepped forward and handed him a champagne glass. Music started playing – a cheerful Latin beat – and Daniel was pulled into the heart of the group. Kilbrook had just become a much less lonely place.

* * *

'Try some of these,' said Henri.

Daniel accepted the plate of food. He was in danger of exploding. Henri had prepared a buffet fit for a king: smoked salmon, caviar, boeuf bourguignon and platters of colourful canapés, some of which Daniel had never seen before.

He bit into the unknown delicacy Henri was tempting him with now. He tasted dates and bacon and cheese. 'This is wonderful. What is it?'

'They're called devils on horseback.' Henri threw back his

head and roared with laughter, and it seemed like the walls shook. 'Devils for a priest.'

Daniel laughed at the chef's joke. 'Thanks for all this, Henri.'

'My pleasure. But it is really Ra-shelle you should thank. She had the idea for you to have a birthday treat.'

Daniel's eyes searched for Rachel and found her talking with some of the parish councillors by the window. *She* had organised this? For him? A stranger here, yet so full of kindness. He'd always remember this night. And he'd always remember her. What a woman. She looked lovely tonight in a long-sleeved purple dress with a wide neckline.

Rachel saw him looking at her. Leaving the group, she came over and sat beside him. 'Are you enjoying yourself?' she asked.

He nodded. 'Henri told me this was your idea. Thank you so much.'

'My pleasure. And there's more.' She reached back behind the sofa to the table, which was loaded with presents, and handed him a flat package wrapped in shiny gold paper. 'I hope you like it.'

She could have given him a wooden spoon and he would have treasured it. He opened the present and found a journal, bound in calfskin leather, with blank pages of creamy parchment.

'For the writer in you,' she said. 'But you're not to use it for sermons. It's for your personal thoughts and stories.'

She'd remembered what they talked about a few days ago. That touched him even more than this wonderful party. 'I love it,' he said. 'And now can I make a request? Will you dance with me?'

She hesitated. 'Um … I'm not a great dancer.'

'Don't worry. I know how to dance. I had a life before I was priest, you know.'

Daniel took Rachel's hand and led her to the far corner,

where a young couple were already spinning around to the music.

* * *

Daniel kept Rachel up and dancing for a second song. He was good, and didn't seem at all nervous about holding her hand and spinning her around. Perhaps it was the alcohol that was loosening him up, although she hadn't seen him drink much at all. She'd barely had more than a glass of wine, mainly because she was the designated driver for Molly, but also because alcohol was a risk when you were trying to keep a secret.

The doorbell rang just then, the long buzz penetrating the beat of the music. 'Maybe it's the police,' Daniel joked. 'Come to arrest me for disorderly conduct.' He swung her round again, and she had to lean against his arm to steady herself.

'Danny boy!' a voice shouted from the living room doorway, and Rachel saw Jay Cole coming towards them. He was exactly like his Facebook picture – square jaw, piercing blue eyes, crew cut. And tall enough now to dwarf most men. The shock of seeing him again close up rooted her to the spot.

'Happy birthday!' Jay slapped Daniel on the back, and then he turned to Rachel, his eyes running up and down her body. 'And is this your birthday present? Not bad. Not bad at all.'

Daniel looked mortified, and Rachel wanted to slap Jay. With his muscles, though, she'd likely be out cold with a broken jaw in seconds. 'I'll leave you two to talk.'

Rachel made it to the bathroom and locked the door before her knees buckled and she sank to the floor in an untidy heap. Jay's greedy eyes devouring her body had been sickening. But worse than that was the fear as he'd towered over her. Jay was the most dangerous bully of the group. He'd fight his way out of any corner she tried to put him in, and he'd play dirty. Yet he was the bully she most wanted to hurt. She had no clear-cut plan of revenge for him, other than trying to sabotage Mel's restaurant, but she'd watch and wait for her chance. She'd use anything she could get on him, however small. That was a promise. And she'd have to bite back this fear of him, not sit here quivering like a victim.

* * *

Rachel worked hard to avoid Jay, but he finally cornered her in the kitchen when she went for a refill of orange juice. They were the only ones in the room, and she tried unsuccessfully to edge around him.

'We haven't been introduced. I'm Jay Cole.'

'I'm Rachel.'

'Rachel, eh?' he said, moving closer. 'You look familiar. Have we met somewhere before?'

Rachel stared up into Jay's face, trying to keep herself calm. His words had sent a shock of fear through her. Was he about to blow her cover, or was it just a chat-up line? 'I doubt we've met. I'm an art student from London. I'm here to study the Stokeley murals.'

'Lucky Daniel,' he murmured.

'Sorry?'

'Nothing.' Jay smiled, and it gave Rachel the shivers. Perhaps that was only because she knew about his bullying nature. Other women might be attracted by his air of arrogance.

He stroked Rachel's arm, and she flinched. 'If you get bored by those old murals, Rachel, come and find me weekdays after five in Donegan's – the best pub in town. Experience some real Irish hospitality.'

What a pity she didn't have the ability to vomit on cue. Time to end this. 'I know your wife. I work part-time in The Fat Pheasant.'

And like magic, he started to retreat. 'Well, nice to meet you, Rachel. I'd better get back to the birthday boy.'

He'd not bother her again tonight. Or any other night, hopefully. Although Rachel might have had success seducing

Jay, she'd never seriously considered it. Number one, because she doubted she could stomach it. And number two, because that really would have been playing with fire. Jay Cole had always been capable of anything and probably still was.

Henri bustled into the kitchen. 'Time for the cake, Ra-shelle. Go through, please, and turn off the living room lights when I'm at the door.'

She did as he asked, and the giant cake, with its elaborately decorated surface and green candles, was presented to Daniel, while the guests sang 'Happy birthday'.

The flickering candles lit up Daniel's face, but he seemed lit up from the inside, too. He was obviously happy tonight, with the company and the music and the laughter, although she could have sworn that, like her, he was trying to avoid Jay as much as possible.

* * *

It was just after nine and Molly was wilting. Rachel helped her into her coat.

'I can always call a taxi, pet, if you want to stay.'

'No, I'm ready to go, too.' There was still time for her to see Finn, if he wasn't too tired after the rehearsal. She'd spent the evening dodging questions about her family and background. Finn didn't push for information like that. That's why it was so relaxing to be with him.

'Where's Daniel?' asked Molly. 'I'd like to say goodbye.'

The last time Rachel had seen him, he was slurring his words. Jay had been plying him with alcohol all evening, obviously thinking a drunk priest would be hilarious. She'd wanted to tell him to stop, but it was Daniel's party and it wasn't fair on him to make a scene.

He wasn't in the living room. 'You sit here, Molly, and I'll find him.'

Rachel searched in vain for Daniel in the cottage, then someone mentioned they thought he'd gone outside for some air. She opened the front door and stepped out into the night, her eyes slow to adjust to the darkness of the garden. She picked her way carefully down the path, calling softly, 'Daniel?'

'Boo!'

A figure swung round the flagpole towards her, and Rachel gave a small scream. Moving back, her heel caught in a paving stone, and she tumbled down, more startled than hurt.

'Hey, it's only me. Only me.'

She recognised Daniel's voice. 'God, you scared me. Help me up.'

'What are you doing down there?'

'I just told you—' snapped Rachel, then stopped.

Daniel was weaving his way towards her, waving his arms around in a strange way. 'Come up here and talk to me.'

Rachel scrambled up. He was very drunk, his eyes glazed over. She'd have to discreetly find someone to take him home. He certainly couldn't come in the car with her and Molly.

'Hey, don't go.' Daniel pulled her close with surprising strength. 'I love you, Rachel. D'you know that?'

She almost laughed out loud at the irony. Now that she didn't want this to happen, of course it did. 'That's nice, Daniel. It's getting cold, though. Let's go inside.'

But Rachel couldn't free herself, and suddenly his lips were on hers, his kiss pushing her back with his intensity. The door opened, and music spilled out into the night. She bit hard on Daniel's lower lip, and he backed away from her with a roar of pain, falling to his knees.

'What's this then? Lover's tiff?'

Rachel swung round to see Jay standing there, leering. Thankfully, he'd closed the front door again. 'He's drunk!' she snapped. 'Thanks to you.'

'It's his birthday,' protested Jay. 'Can't a man have a bit of fun on his birthday?'

'Were you born stupid, or have you just worked really hard

at it?' said Rachel. Her anger was overcoming her fear of Jay, even though his mouth had clamped into a hard line. 'Daniel's a priest. He has a reputation to maintain. People can't see him like this.'

Although that would be revenge of sorts. To make him look foolish in the eyes of the community. But when she looked at Daniel, slumped on the path, clutching his lip, she knew she couldn't do it to him.

She turned back to Jay. 'How much have you had to drink?'

'A couple of beers. Why?'

'Have you got your car?'

Jay nodded.

'Right. You're driving him home. Now. Before anyone sees him like this. And take him inside the rectory and put him to bed. Don't leave him wandering around outside. I'll tell everyone inside that he went home, feeling unwell.'

She couldn't do it herself – go into the rectory late at night with a priest. There'd be a scandal. She'd likely no longer be welcome in Kilbrook, and she could kiss the reunion goodbye. And anyway, she doubted she'd have the strength to handle a drunken man.

'He's a grown-up,' Jay protested. 'He doesn't need me to nursemaid him.'

'No – what he needed tonight was a friend. Seems he was out of luck. I'll get Henri.'

'All right, all right,' Jay muttered under his breath, but he moved forward and hauled Daniel to his feet, stringing his arm over his shoulder. He was going to do what she'd said. 'Bossy bitch,' he muttered over his shoulder, but Rachel didn't care. She'd just confronted Jay Cole, and given him a piece of her mind. It was a heady feeling.

* * *

Finn opened the front door. Rachel was there on the doorstep in an elegant purple dress and black wrap.

'I didn't realise this would be a formal occasion,' he quipped. 'Should I go and change into my tux?'

'No need. I'll dress down if you can loan me a jumper. I'm freezing.'

'Come in,' he said. 'I'm in the living room – it's just here. Go through and make yourself at home.'

Finn dashed upstairs and rooted around in his wardrobe. Grabbing a jumper, he pounded back down the stairs. Rachel had called him ten minutes ago, and he'd suggested she come over and they could watch a movie together. Helen was out – not due back for an hour or so. Impeccable timing.

In the living room, Rachel was on the sofa, legs curled under her, high heels abandoned on the rug. She slipped on the navy jumper he handed her. It dwarfed her and made her look really cute.

Once he'd sorted them out with drinks, Finn sat down on the sofa, careful to maintain a reasonable distance between them. They'd agreed on friendship only, and he'd respect that. 'How was the party?'

'Okay.'

But her eyes were telling a different story. Finn wondered if someone had made a pass. Not unlikely, because she was beautiful.

'How were rehearsals?' she asked.

'Didn't go as smoothly without you. Some of the props got misplaced.'

'I'll be there tomorrow night, I promise. So, what film are we going to watch?'

* * *

Rachel had let Finn choose the film. That seemed only fair because she'd gatecrashed his evening. Plus she'd not be able to follow it properly. Her mind was too busy processing the events of the evening.

Jay was an idiot. Getting a priest drunk. Some friend. At

least she'd made sure no one saw Daniel in that state, and Jay would take him home and help him because he wouldn't want to risk being blamed. She wondered how Daniel would feel in the morning? Would he remember what he'd done? If not, should she tell him? Probably best not to. It would just make him feel bad. The fact that she didn't want him to feel bad came as something of a surprise.

'He's behind you!' Finn shouted at the screen, totally absorbed in the film.

She sat there, her eyes flicking to him more than to the screen. Finn was the first man Rachel had really looked at since the break-up with Andy. He was witty and talented and sensitive. And gorgeous. Why should she pass up on a chance at love because of the bullies? Hadn't they taken enough from her already? Tonight's encounter with Jay had been scary but empowering. How much stronger would she be if she had Finn's affection surrounding her like a shield? Later, when she told him her true reason for being here, he might not be very forgiving, and she'd have to live with that. But if they were close it was possible he would be more likely to understand her quest for revenge.

Rachel unfurled her legs and shifted closer to Finn on the sofa. He looked at her, startled.

'I think I need a cuddle,' she explained. 'Just a cuddle.'

He clicked his tongue and shook his head. 'Did you apply for this twenty-four hours in advance? That was the agreement regarding touching.'

She giggled. 'Can I pay a forfeit?'

'Okay. I'll decide what that is tomorrow. Come on then.'

He wrapped an arm around her shoulders and pulled her in close. She'd forgotten how good it felt to be held by a man. The warmth, the security. There was no need to go any further tonight. That would happen if it was meant to. Just being close like this was more than enough for now.

Chapter Eight

The doorbell just kept ringing, and Daniel would gladly have strangled whoever was doing it and depriving him of sleep. He threw back the bedcovers and sat quickly upright, which was a mistake because his head started throbbing with a dull, persistent pain. The doorbell rang again. Who wanted to see him at seven o'clock in the morning? That was taking things too far.

'I'm coming!' he yelled, and then grimaced as the sound of his own voice cut through him. He pulled on his bathrobe and exited the bedroom, just as his mobile started shrilling from his coat pocket in the hallway. Clutching the banister for support, Daniel went down the stairs and marched angrily to the front door, swinging it open to find Jay standing on the doorstep, his mobile phone to his ear. 'I'm here. You can hang up now.'

'Morning,' said Jay, pressing on his phone. Although he'd also been drinking last night, he looked fresh and healthy in his tracksuit and trainers. 'So, how's the birthday boy?' He peered at Daniel. 'God, you look rough. Reckon you should take the day off.'

He walked into the house, uninvited, and headed for the kitchen. Daniel followed but wished he could just go back to bed. He really wasn't up to a post-mortem about yesterday's party. At least Jay would have to leave for school soon.

In the kitchen, Daniel was dismayed to see Jay plugging in the electric juicer, and he soon had it going, the noise exactly like that of a dentist's drill – the main reason why Daniel rarely used it. Soon orange peel was scattered all over the kitchen counter. Daniel sat slumped at the kitchen table, praying it would all be over soon. Perhaps he'd follow Jay's suggestion and stay at home. The deacon could manage things today.

Jay finally brought the orange juice over and gulped his down in one go. 'Ah – that's better. Drink plenty – it'll help to soak up all that booze.'

Daniel frowned. 'I don't remember drinking that much.'

'Well, it's easy to lose track, isn't it?' said Jay, buttering some toast. 'Especially when you're not used to it. You're lucky I was there, or you might have pushed it too far with Rachel.'

Daniel almost dropped his glass of juice. 'What do you mean?'

'I came out into the garden, and you were grabbing at her. You even managed to get a kiss in. That's why you've got that swollen lip. She bit you.' Jay was smirking. 'Obviously passionate for you, Danny boy.'

Daniel put his head in his hands.

'Now, I'm sure she started it. She came on to me a bit earlier, but I headed her off. Still, the thing is – what if she tells someone?'

Daniel stared at Jay. Of all the people to witness last night, there couldn't be anyone worse.

'How long is she staying here?' asked Jay.

Daniel sighed. 'A few more weeks. Don't worry – I'll talk to her and apologise.'

'Maybe there's no need for that. Only if she brings it up. Let sleeping dogs lie, eh? And remember, it looked like she was coming on to you. Though she might not admit that.'

There was silence for a few moments.

'Anyway – your secret's safe with me.' Jay winked.

That hint of collusion turned Daniel's stomach. He hated cover-ups more than anything. 'You'd better go, Jay. I think I'm going to throw up.'

That did the trick. Jay was out the front door in double quick time. So much for friendship.

Daniel went upstairs and got back into bed, hiding his head under the covers. He would apologise to Rachel, and she might well forgive him. But in a way that wasn't the point.

He'd sinned. He'd broken his vow to the Church. To God. Just what kind of a sad excuse for a priest was he?

* * *

Rachel shivered as she cleaned her second window. Will had loaned her his puffer jacket to keep out the chill, but the wind was biting right through it. Sam looked as miserable as she felt – he was hosing down the bins, his hands almost blue with cold. Eddie was muttering curses under his breath as he tried to sweep up leaves that the wind kept scattering.

Mel had ordered them to clean up the area behind The Fat Pheasant in advance of the banquet for her father's cronies. The Bloody Banquet as the staff were now calling it. Will had dared to say to Mel that it would be dark when the guests arrived and they wouldn't be inspecting the car park. 'Everything will be perfect for next week!' Mel had shouted at him. 'And if you don't like it, you can get out!' No one risked a word after that.

Ten minutes of hell later, and Henri's creaking, rattling car turned into the car park. He'd been in Galway selecting wines for the Bloody Banquet so hadn't been there when Mel issued her instructions. He screeched on the brakes and got out, not even bothering to park. His face was a mottled pink but getting redder by the minute. 'Sam – Eddie – Ra-shelle – what are you doing out here?' he demanded.

'Mrs Cole told us to spruce up the place for next week's special dinner,' said Eddie.

'But – who is cooking?'

'Will and Calum. Colette's outside, cleaning the front windows.'

'*Merde!*' cried Henri and fired off a torrent of indignant French. '*Vous êtes chefs de cuisine et non pas femmes de ménage. Rentrez à l'instant!*'

Henri barged through the back door.

'What the hell did he say?' asked Sam, bewildered.

'We've to go back inside,' Rachel told him. 'He's pissed off with Mrs Cole.'

'I might do a runner,' Eddie said, throwing down the broom. 'It'll be World War Three in there.'

'I'm not going to miss him putting her in her place.' Sam quickly turned off the hose and went first through the door.

When Rachel and Eddie followed, there was no sign of Henri. Will and Calum were standing at their stations, heads turned towards the dining room door, mouths open.

A few moments later, Henri reappeared with a startled Colette.

'Madame Cole!' he bellowed in the direction of the closed office door. Rachel was reminded of some terrible call to battle. She half-expected the walls to shake.

The door swung open and Mel stood there in elegant fury. 'Henri – how many times have I told you not to shout like some ignorant fish seller ...' She stopped when she caught sight of Colette and the other temporarily assigned cleaners. 'Colette – Sam – did you finish the cleaning?'

Colette's mouth worked but no sounds came out.

'*Non*, Madame,' said Henri. 'They did not finish the stupid scrub-a-dub. I bring them back inside.'

Her hands on her waist, Mel stalked out into the kitchen to face her head chef. If they had holsters, this would be the showdown scene in a western. Rachel felt like ducking down behind the counter. 'How dare you!' snarled Mel. 'I'll thank you to remember who owns this restaurant. If I give an order, I expect it to be carried out.'

'Only an *imbecile* would order trained chefs to leave the kitchen and sweep up the leaves. This is a big insult. You have regular cleaning staff. Give to them the broom.'

'For your information, one of the cleaners called in sick,' said Mel, 'and the other is overworked ... and don't you dare insult me, you clueless baboon!'

There was a collective intake of breath from Rachel and the other staff members.

Henri turned and picked up a meat cleaver. Dear God. Was it about to turn into a crime scene? Rachel's heart started pounding, but Henri didn't sink the cleaver into Mel. In one quick movement, he lifted it high and brought it down on a rainbow trout, neatly severing the head from the body. 'This is you, Madame,' said Henri, pointing at the fish. 'Brain not connected to the rest of you. Why didn't you hire extra cleaning staff for this banquet for the colonials? This is what any normal and sane human being would do.'

He turned away from her, heading down the kitchen towards the back door. The staff parted for him like the Red Sea. Will was handed the cleaver.

'And where do you think you're going?' demanded Mel, her voice shrill and shaking.

'Home to bed,' said Henri, over his shoulder. 'When I wake up, maybe I will find this is all the bad dream. That I really work in a place where the chefs are respected people.'

The back door slammed behind him and there was silence. Finally Mel found her voice. 'Eddie – Sam – Colette – get to work in here. Lunch service is coming up. Rachel – you can finish the outside cleaning since you're not a trained chef. Surely Kaiser Henri can't object to that. Now get to it – all of you!'

Mel stormed back into her office, and the others commiserated with Rachel for drawing the short straw. Still – only an hour to go. And tomorrow was her day off. She'd invited Finn for a drive, and he'd accepted. She wasn't sure where to go. Galway, probably – lots to do there. It didn't really matter where they ended up. Just being in his company was enough for her.

But after her shift finished today, she needed to check on Daniel.

* * *

Rachel used her elbow to press Daniel's doorbell because her hands were clutching a pot of soup. All the curtains were closed in the rectory, and she was genuinely worried about Daniel. Earlier, at the church, the deacon had told her he'd called in sick.

It was a relief when he opened the door after her second ring. He was in jeans and a jumper that had known better days – the most informal Rachel had seen him since she arrived. His face was pale except for the slight stubble – and the swelling on his lower lip. There was a wariness in his eyes.

'Hi. I heard you weren't well.' She held up the pot. 'Thought this might help. Chicken soup. Courtesy of Molly.'

'Oh, that's kind.'

He seemed unsure what to do next, so Rachel took charge. 'Can I come in for a minute? Molly said I was to make sure you ate at least one bowl.'

Daniel's eyes raked the street outside before he stood aside and invited her in.

In the kitchen, he set out two mismatched soup plates on the table. Rachel thought she had probably eaten out of those in Father Milligan's day.

'Will you share some of this with me?'

She nodded. Although she wasn't hungry, it would give them a chance to talk.

He ladled out a portion each, and they started to eat. The soup was creamy and rich, with a delicious aftertaste of herbs. 'Nothing like homemade soup, is there?' said Rachel. 'Real comfort food.'

Daniel murmured agreement but kept his eyes fixed on the soup plate. A little bit of colour was coming back into his cheeks, which was a good sign. Rachel didn't know the best way to open up discussion about last night's events. She didn't want to torment him, just clear the air. Get things back to a kind of normal.

'Daniel—'

'Rachel—'

They'd spoken at the same time, and both cracked a smile. The tension in the room dropped a notch.

'Ladies first,' he said.

Great. There were times when gender really didn't work in your favour. Still, she was responsible for some of this. It was only right that she helped fix it.

'About last night ...' She trailed off. That had to be the worst way to start this conversation. 'I mean, about what happened at the party ... it was nothing ... please don't stress about it. Okay?'

Daniel frowned, and for a moment she wondered if he knew what she was talking about. He'd been really out of it in the garden. Had she jumped the gun?

He sighed and attempted a smile. 'That's good of you to say so, Rachel. I'm really embarrassed ...'

'Don't be! You'd had a lot to drink. You weren't thinking clearly.'

It was tempting to tell Daniel that Jay had been the one to give him most of the alcohol, but she wasn't about to put a target on her back. Jay could easily deny everything anyway. She had no real proof.

Daniel touched his swollen lip. 'Actually, I think one of us *was* thinking clearly last night.'

'God, I'm so sorry about that. Does it hurt?'

He smiled. 'I'll live. But what about us, Rachel? Are we okay? As friends, I mean. Or will this come between us?'

'I don't want it to come between us.'

'Me neither.'

'So we won't let it.'

'Deal.'

Rachel felt relieved. Things were back on track. But she'd certainly not be targeting Daniel anymore. He'd suffered enough, although he would be part of the fallout after the reunion but she couldn't help that. After last night, though, Jay was definitely still fair game.

Chapter Nine

'And it's Greg Norman coming to the eighteenth hole. The crowd waits with bated breath. Can the champion overcome the upstart Brit?'

Finn had provided a hilarious running commentary as they'd putted their way round the crazy golf. Rachel was sure it was a ploy. She hadn't been able to concentrate on her shots because she was laughing so much at his antics.

'You can hit the worst shot in the world here,' she told him. 'The eighteenth hole always captures the ball. To stop people going around again for free.'

'Hmm – let's test that, shall we?' Finn turned around and hit a terrible backwards shot. The hole swallowed up the golf ball.

'It's a draw,' she declared. 'Not bad for a beginner.'

'What's next? Croquet on the lawn?'

'I think that's enough sporting excitement for one day. I'm ready for some tea. The café's over there.'

They wandered slowly across the manicured lawns of Dunkellin Hall. The stately home itself was closed for a wedding, but the gardens were open. The car park had been a bit pricey, but the crazy golf course had more than made up for that.

Rachel took a chance and linked her arm through Finn's. He didn't resist – in fact, he pulled her in tighter to his body. Other women were giving him sidelong appreciative glances. He must get that all the time. Any girlfriend of his would probably be paranoid within a week.

'Let's say hello to the animals.' He veered towards the fence of the children's zoo, where he patted a scruffy-looking donkey, and then pointed to a pot-bellied pig. 'George Clooney used to have one of those.'

'So you like animals?'

'Love 'em. I've got a dog back in Australia. An Aussie bulldog called Butch. My cousin's looking after him.'

Rachel had never owned a pet. Just one more missed experience in her sad childhood. At boarding school there had been hamsters and rabbits, but they belonged to everyone.

In the café Rachel and Finn brought their sandwiches and tea to a table next to the window. Finn kept his coat on. Rachel knew he felt the cold easily, and that he was looking forward to getting back to Australia's warmer temperatures in January. Only a few weeks of his company and then both she and he'd be gone. Life was a bitch sometimes.

'Helen said your career's really going to take off when you go back home,' Rachel said.

'Did she?' Finn picked the tomato out of his sandwich and set it on the side of the plate. Rachel found herself mentally updating her files – doesn't like tomatoes. 'Maybe. I've got a starring role in a new police series, but you never know if these things will work out. I'm the young, reckless sidekick.'

'Typecasting?'

He grinned. 'Well, I'm young …'

'Not reckless?'

'I have been in the past.'

'For example?'

Finn gave it some thought. 'I got engaged at twenty-two. Too young to settle down, really – for me, at least. But I was in love, and I thought that way she'd stay with me. Didn't work. She dumped me for a richer, older actor.'

He'd spoken lightly enough, but there had been a flicker of disappointment in his eyes. Helen had said he often put on an act. She'd intended it as a warning, not knowing that Rachel did the same thing. Kept her secret pain close. When Andy dumped her a couple of months after her mother's death, he'd claimed she'd changed, become harder, more secretive. Which she had. So she'd had to grieve for Andy, too. A double loss. It all still felt so raw.

'So I just had casual relationships after that,' Finn continued. 'Protecting myself. But then ... when a crisis happens, you find yourself all alone.'

'Crisis?' Rachel prompted.

He gave her a long, searching look, as if he were deciding whether he was ready to unburden himself to her.

She broke the silence. 'It's okay, Finn. You don't have to tell me. Some things are hard to talk about, I know.' Her relatives rarely mentioned the Kilbrook disaster. They thought if you didn't mention something, it was as if it had never happened. How wrong they were.

'Maybe another time,' Finn said. 'I don't want to spoil this gorgeous day with gloomy talk.'

'Fair enough.' She bit back her disappointment. They'd known each other only a short time. Not many people could bare their soul to a virtual stranger.

* * *

Walking around the gardens, they saw the wedding party posing for photos on the terrace. The poor bride was shivering in her sleeveless gown.

'Perhaps I should loan her my coat,' suggested Finn, as they watched the different groups form and re-form. 'In Australia, people often get married on the beach, then have a barbie. Much more civilised.'

'They're probably off somewhere hot for their honeymoon,' said Rachel. 'They're clinging on to that thought as they shiver.'

The bride and groom had shots on their own next. The photographer called out instructions, and the couple came together for an awkward kiss. They were very young, and neither looked comfortable. There was probably a story behind it all that Rachel and Finn would never know about.

Finn sighed and shook his head. 'They'd have to do a million retakes if this were a movie. His hand's in the wrong place, she looks like she's got a double chin, and it's clear neither of them are enjoying it.'

Rachel laughed. 'I feel like I'm fifteen again, reading a girl's magazine about the best way to kiss.'

'So *that's* where girls learn how to smooch.'

'How do boys learn?'

'Well, I always like the scene in *Lady and the Tramp*. A spaghetti surprise. Al fresco becoming al frisky. Always wanted to try that, but no girl I've been with has ever ordered spaghetti in a restaurant.'

Rachel laughed. 'You can tell you're a dog lover. Oh! Now her earring's caught in his buttonhole.'

The bride was shrieking in pain now, and the photographer was flinging his hands up in despair. Finn took hold of Rachel's cold hands and pulled her round to face him. 'Let's show them how it's done.'

She looked surprised but didn't pull away. To many of his friends, kissing was just a precursor to sex, but Finn always thought of it as an enjoyable end in itself. He stroked a lock of hair away from Rachel's face. She brushed his cheek. He gently encircled her waist. She put her arms around his neck. They complemented each other's moves like dancers in a *pas de deux*. Coming closer and closer to the kiss. Their lips finally touched, tender and sensual. The world could have ended there and then, and Finn would not have cared. He was born to kiss this woman.

* * *

Everything was going well at the evening dress rehearsal for *A Christmas Carol* until Jenny O'Neill got dizzy and sank down heavily into a chair instead of waltzing around the stage as her character Belle was supposed to. Everyone around her froze.

Rachel, who was in the wings helping out with the props, hurried onstage. Jenny was very pale and shaky. There was no way she could continue. Rachel glanced at Helen in the front row and shook her head.

'Understudy for Belle!' Helen called out as Rachel led Jenny off the stage. That wasn't callous. As Finn had explained earlier, even though there was no audience present, a dress rehearsal had to be considered a live performance. If something went wrong, the show had to go on, right the way through. It was the only way to discover problems.

Rachel got Jenny to the girls' dressing room and sat her down on an old battered sofa. She fetched water and watched Jenny gulp it down, her hands trembling around the glass. Tears had smudged some of her make-up, and she looked like a sad little Columbine who'd lost her Pierrot.

'Thanks,' whispered Jenny. 'I'm really sorry ...'

'Don't be. It was hot out there on the stage with all the lights. I'm surprised more people aren't getting dizzy.'

'It's not that,' said Jenny, struggling up from the depths of the sofa. 'It's this dress.' She swung round and the Victorian crinoline skirt swished. 'They pulled the stays so tight. See.'

Rachel worked the lace-up ties a bit looser. 'How's that?'

The girl breathed in and out, and turned to face Rachel. 'Better. Thanks.' Music drifted through the door. 'I should get back on stage.'

'Why not rest here till the start of the next act?' suggested Rachel. 'It's better for the timings that way, don't you think?'

'I suppose.'

Jenny sat back down on the sofa. One hand slowly twisted a strand of her flaxen hair. She was a real beauty with her heart-shaped face and big blue eyes. However, at the start of the dress rehearsal, there had been a glow about her that was missing now. Perhaps she was coming down with something. Rachel thought she had best stay with her in case the girl had another dizzy spell.

'Is Finn your boyfriend?' asked Jenny.

Rachel smiled. Teenagers could be so direct. And at Jenny's age it was all about boys and how to catch one. Rachel and Sophia had railed endlessly about being stuck in an all-girls boarding school. 'We haven't known each other very long.'

'Would you like him to be your boyfriend?'

'We'll see.' If Rachel said more than that, the whole cast would likely know about it by tomorrow.

'I've got a boyfriend,' said Jenny.

She didn't look particularly happy about it. Maybe that's how it was these days – you had to appear blasé.

'We're going to get married.'

'When you finish school?' asked Rachel.

Jenny hesitated. 'Maybe soon. Before I finish school.'

'Oh.' In Rachel's time in Kilbrook many girls had married young. Things obviously hadn't changed much since then.

'Why do you say it like that? As if it's wrong?'

'No – it's not wrong if you love someone …'

Jenny leaned forward on the sofa, pinning Rachel with her gaze. 'But?'

'But you're very young.'

Jenny frowned. 'Age has nothing to do with love.'

This was a very tricky conversation. Rachel wished she was back in the wings with the props. 'But finishing your schooling gives you options for the future.'

'What options?' Jenny slumped back on the sofa. 'My family only think about the farm. It's all they know. Cows and milking. My dad keeps trying to teach me about it. He wants me to take over one day. To marry a bloody farmer.'

That did sound a bit bleak. 'Does your boyfriend want to be a farmer?'

'Of course not.' Jenny sounded scornful. 'He's already got a job.'

'What does he do?'

'He's a—' Jenny stopped suddenly, and she looked a bit furtive. 'He's going to have his own gym one day.'

'Could he help you go to drama school? You're very talented.'

'Do you think so?'

That was the first smile Rachel had seen during this whole

conversation. 'I do, Jenny. I heard Helen say it, too – and she should know.'

'I love acting. My dream is to perform at the Abbey Theatre in Dublin.'

'Then go for it. I'm sure Helen could help you prepare an audition for drama school.'

'That would be great.' The excitement on Jenny's face was a treat to see.

By the time she left the dressing room, Jenny's confidence seemed to have returned along with that indefinable glow which made her so watchable on stage. Hopefully she could hold on to that positive energy for the opening night. Rachel wanted the show to be a big success because Helen and Finn had put their heart and soul into helping the kids create a show they and their parents could be proud of. And she was happy to have played her own small role in this performance. It would give her one good memory to take away from Kilbrook with her.

* * *

Rachel held the auditorium door open as the kids streamed out at the end of rehearsals. Some of them said goodbye to her and she smiled. She felt a part of their play now.

'Jenny says her dress is too tight,' she told Helen once she got inside.

Helen sighed. 'Another growth spurt! Could you be a love and put it in the alterations box?'

Rachel went backstage to the girls' dressing room and took Jenny's dress off the rail. There was movement behind her, and she whirled around. Finn pulled her in close for a kiss.

'I've been wanting to do that all evening,' he murmured as they came up for air.

'The kids would have got a terrible shock if you had,' Rachel whispered.

'Let's lock the door and stay in here.'

'They'll come and find us.'

'You hide behind the rail, and I'll say you've gone back to London.'

'And how would I explain my sudden reappearance tomorrow morning?'

'You changed your mind. Women do it all the time.'

Rachel giggled. 'C'mon, Romeo. We'd better get back.'

'Just one more kiss, Juliet …'

For a moment, Rachel actually felt like Juliet, stealing illicit kisses out of sight of the grown-ups. Perhaps this was all a dream, although the man holding her close seemed real enough.

'Meet me tomorrow at Gulliver's at nine,' said Finn. 'I'll treat you to a stale croissant.'

'My hero,' Rachel said in a breathy voice and blew him a farewell kiss.

* * *

10 March

Great. I need braces. Like I'm not plain enough already. Something else I have to pretend not to be bothered about. But I am bothered. If you'd given me the choice, God, I'd have been pretty like Rosie. I'd even have put up with her rheumatic fever instead of having a face only a mother could love – as Spook so kindly put it. He can talk. He wasn't exactly at the front of the queue for looks either. No one teases him, though. Maybe because his dad is a Garda, or else they're afraid he'll sit on them. Ugly great lump! I'd ask Mam for contact lenses for my birthday, but what's the point? I know she can't afford them. I'm a freak of nature. Might as well get used to it.

Rachel closed the diary. It was too hard to concentrate. All she could think about was Finn and his passionate, insistent kisses. Jenny had asked if Finn was Rachel's boyfriend. Was he? She could feel a smile on her lips as she drifted off to sleep, and hoped she might for once dream of something other than revenge.

Chapter Ten

Mel gently placed the Limoges cup and saucer on her father's desk, away from the edge. It was part of a valuable hand-painted set, and she lived in fear of breaking a piece and incurring his wrath. He'd given them a Wedgwood dinner service as a wedding present, but it spent most of its time in the display cabinet except for special occasions. Jay was ham-fisted, and Leanne too young to be trusted with breakables.

'So, Mel, is everything prepared for next week?' Gerald steepled his fingers and gazed at her across the wide expanse of desk.

The noise from the antiques showroom outside seeped through into his office – a ringing phone, crates being hauled along the floor, someone shouting instructions. Mel often wished they could meet in a quiet café and talk without interruption, but her father always said an owner should be at his place of business as much as possible. Therein lay success.

'I picked up the menus before I came here,' she said. 'I went in person to make sure everything was okay.' She took a menu out of the box on the table, handed it to her father, and watched anxiously as he read through the list of courses. This wasn't just about the dinner for his clients. It was Gerald who had bought the restaurant for Mel, so he oversaw all important decisions about the business.

'This is excellent. Now, you will make sure that claret is decanted, won't you?'

She nodded, wishing sometimes that he didn't micromanage so much. She saw that as a sign of his lack of faith in her abilities.

'And how are things with Henri?' asked Gerald.

Mel felt her blood pressure notch up. Her father knew all about the difficulties with the temperamental Frenchman. 'We had a fight on Tuesday,' she confessed. 'I mean worse than usual. All over a bit of cleaning. He walked out, though he was back in yesterday morning, moody as ever.'

Gerald shook his head. 'It's time you replaced him.'

'What! But, Daddy, he got the restaurant a Michelin star!'

Her father leaned towards her. 'And that's good because other chefs will now be more than willing to work at The Fat Pheasant, to helm a successful restaurant. You'll be able to take your pick. Henri Breton isn't the only fish in the sea. A pity he forgot that.'

Mel stared at her father. She'd dreamed of getting rid of Henri many times but had thought Gerald would disapprove when the restaurant was doing so well. Now he was actually suggesting it. A wonderful thought, but ... 'There's still six months left to run on Henri's contract.'

'Give it to him in pay and tell him to clear out. For abandoning his post. You have witnesses to that, I'm sure. What have I always told you? Don't pity the weak or inadequate or those who oppose you. Beat them down if they get in your way.'

Mel nodded. Firing Henri would be a nightmare, of course. The crazy chef might threaten her with that blasted meat cleaver again. She'd have to leave the office door open, make sure all the other staff were close by ...

'Get an ad out soon,' Gerald suggested. 'Maybe in an English newspaper, so there's less chance of Henri seeing it. You'll have scores of replies within a week, trust me. One thing, though – don't fire him until the dinner's over.'

God forbid. Henri was insane enough to wreck the restaurant, or worse. When there were no customers around for him to try and poison, she'd give him the news he was no longer wanted. Maybe she'd ask Garda Farrell to be on hand, just in case. 'Don't worry, Daddy. I'll choose the right time. And I'll draw up the ad today.'

'That's my girl.' He was beaming with approval, and she allowed herself a rare moment of relaxation in his presence.

Gerald's mobile rang and he was soon in a discussion about a missing clock. Mel got up and pointed at her watch, mouthing 'Must go.' She blew her father a kiss and left the office. He'd given her an unexpected gift by allowing her to ditch Henri. To thank him, his special dinner next week would be spectacular, or she'd die trying.

* * *

Mel glanced out into the kitchen area. Less than an hour till lunch opening, so the staff were hard at it. Henri was circling the stations, checking and tasting. She quietly closed the office door and yanked open the filing cabinet, rummaging under E for Employees. Pulling out the advertisements folder, she flicked through till she found the one for head chef.

Back at her desk, she scanned the ad, considering what to update. Ideally, she wanted someone with Henri's cooking skills but without the lip. Someone who didn't mutter what were surely insults in French under his breath. So, an English-speaking chef – but she couldn't write that in the ad. She'd weed out the foreign applicants at interview.

Mel amended the salary figure to factor in the pay-off to Big Bear Breton. A new chef could earn a little less than Henri and still consider himself well paid. She'd use the same recruitment agency as last time. She'd fax through the ad to them next week, when her father's special dinner was safely over. Put a closing date of mid-December. Interviews in early January. With a bit of luck, she'd have a new chef in place for February. Then she could say, with the greatest of pleasure, *au revoir, Henri*.

There was a knock at the door. Mel quickly slipped the ad in between the other papers on her desk. 'Come.'

It was the new girl, Rachel, looking worried. 'There's a problem, Mrs Cole. The supplier sent green napkins. They say they don't have enough blue ones.'

The girl held up a light green napkin. Totally wrong. Mel would swing for that supplier, making a promise he couldn't fulfil. She shot up out of her chair. 'I'll have to drive to Galway to get what we need.'

And everything had been going so well. Still, it was early enough to sort out the problem. That supplier's name would be mud by the time she'd finished with him, though.

* * *

'Bring me the copy of next week's menu, Ra-shelle. On my desk, I think.'

Rachel went to the office and sifted through the mess on Henri's desk. How did the man ever find anything? There was no menu that she could see. Moving over to Mel's desk, she impatiently flicked through paper after paper: invoice, invoice, customer letter, review, bank statement, job ad ...

Rachel's fingers paused, then pulled out the advertisement. Scanning through, she realised with a shock that it was for a new head chef. The deadline for applications had been marked as mid-December. Rachel remembered the recent argument between Mel and her chef. Mel must be planning to replace Henri. Without telling him, most likely.

Henri had given Rachel this job. He'd taught her patiently how to prepare a marinade for the lamb, how to caramelise the crème brûlées with a blowtorch. She'd decanted wine under his careful eye. He'd prepared a wonderful birthday treat for Daniel. She hardly knew him, really, yet all the other chefs and kitchen workers loved him. They said it was his talent and drive that had got this restaurant its Michelin star. Now Mel was about to shaft him because he'd stood up for his chefs. Well, not if Rachel had anything to do with it.

She left the ad out, right in the middle of Mel's desk. It would be impossible to miss. Then, going back out to Henri, she told him truthfully that the menu was nowhere to be found on his desk. As she'd hoped, he headed for the office. She busied herself at the vegetable counter where she could watch through the open door.

It was heartbreaking to watch Henri finally see and pick up the ad. She could swear his hands were shaking as he read the words. He slumped down in Mel's chair, his shoulders drooped forward, his chin in his hands. An idea began to form in Rachel's mind. A way that both she and Henri could pay back Mel. Would he buy it, though? Would he be able to contain his anger and distress long enough to pull it off?

The other chefs were all busy, rattling their pans and shouting timings to each other. Rachel walked over and into the office, closing the door behind her. Henri looked up but didn't really seem to see her. She gently asked him what the matter was. '*Allez-vous bien?*'

The chef's eyes clicked back into focus at the unexpected sound of his mother tongue. He gave a sad smile. 'Ah, Ra-shelle. This is a bad world to be living in. *Très mal*. Look at this.'

He handed her the ad and she pretended to read it. She summoned up a frown. 'I don't understand. Is Mrs Cole opening another restaurant?'

'*Non, non.*' Henri shook his head. 'She is going to – how you say – give me the marching orders.'

'But she can't do that! You've done nothing wrong!' Rachel didn't need to play-act her outrage.

'For rich people, they always find the way. Maybe tomorrow she will say I am stealing from her. She will try to stick the mud on me. I must leave now before she can ruin my reputation.'

'But where will you go? What will you do?' Rachel genuinely wanted to know that he would be okay.

'I will go back to Toulouse. I am sick for home, you understand? I make good money here for two years. I think now it is time to open my own restaurant.'

Rachel felt like crying. 'And call it *Henri's* so that one day when I visit Toulouse I can find it.'

Henri smiled. 'You shall have the position of honour at the chef's table ... Now, leetle one, I must pack up the things.'

'Wait.' It was now or never. She sat down in the chair opposite him. 'Don't go like this, Henri. Then she gets what she wants, and she doesn't lose anything.'

He gestured to the kitchens. 'She will lose her head chef. Not so easy, I think, to replace me right away. Customers may go. The Michelin star may also go.'

'But you've trained the other chefs so well. They can carry on without you for a bit – not as brilliantly, but they'll get by. *She'll* get by. Henri ... there's a saying in English – don't get mad, get even. Do you know what it means?'

He nodded his big head slowly.

'Next Monday is a very important day for Mrs Cole,' Rachel continued. 'Her father wants to impress the Americans so he can take their money, and Mel wants to impress her father ... but what if the evening was not a success?' Henri's eyes were wide open now, his caterpillar eyebrows almost touching his hairline. 'What if something went wrong – with the food or the wine or the restaurant? The guests would be unhappy. Mrs Cole would be very upset. At least then if she fires you, you'll have had your revenge.'

'*La vengeance* ... revenge ... revenge ...' Henri rolled the English word around his mouth like a marble. 'Yes ... the great Cyrano de Bergerac never let an insult to his honour go unavenged, you know.' He suddenly stood up, the fire back in his eyes, and gestured to an imaginary world. 'Madame Cole will regret the day she crossed swords with Henri Breton. She will have the big lesson, eh ... *Vive la France!*'

'*Vive la France!*' echoed Rachel, wondering what exactly she had unleashed.

Chapter Eleven

Finn drew back the bedroom curtains. A weak sun was winning out over the clouds – a good omen for the play's opening night. It would be a long and busy day, but at the end of it there'd be the first-night party and Rachel. Sweet.

Downstairs he followed the aroma of fresh coffee into the kitchen and found Helen seated at the counter, tackling the crossword in the newspaper in front of her. He gave her a kiss. 'Morning. How long have you been up?'

'Ages, love. You know I don't sleep well before first nights.'

They were polar opposites in that. Finn slept like a baby the night before a performance. He'd never suffered stage fright, either. Other actors would be chucking their guts up while he was in the wings, desperate to get onstage. He'd always felt more comfortable being someone else.

'Let's start the day right.' Finn rummaged in the fridge and brought out a carton of orange juice and some champagne. This was their opening night ritual. 'You do the honours.'

Helen smiled and took the bottle. She eased off the cork with professional precision, then poured the bubbling golden liquid into the glasses he'd got from the cupboard.

Finn gave the toast. 'Here's to another great Helen MacKenzie production.'

They clinked their glasses and drank. All was right with the world.

'So what do you need me to do today?' he asked, settling down onto the stool opposite.

Helen passed him a handwritten list. 'Food and drink for the party tonight. Best go to Galway for it.'

Finn frowned. 'I can't bring all this back on the bus.'

'I know. Rachel, bless her, has agreed to take you in her car when she's finished her shift.'

Helen's butter-wouldn't-melt-in-her-mouth look didn't fool Finn. She was matchmaking – and loving every minute of it. He shook a finger at her, playfully. 'Are you by chance hearing wedding bells?'

'I live in hope,' she murmured, downing the rest of the champagne cocktail.

Finn smiled. It would be an added bonus to spend extra time with Rachel today, however mundane their task.

Helen stifled a yawn. 'I'll definitely be taking a sleeping pill tonight. I'll be dead to the world.' She gave him a knowing smile. 'So if you want to ask someone to stay over …'

'Are you trying to corrupt me, Helen? I'm shocked!'

'You forget, I was a child of the sixties. Young people today didn't discover sex, you know. I read *The Kama Sutra* …'

'I wouldn't be surprised if you wrote it, but it's too much information!' cried Finn, holding his hands up in protest.

Helen laughed. 'I know – you can't bear to think that your old aunt was once a hot-blooded girl with passion and needs.'

'Not listening!' Finn clamped his hands over his ears, but he was really trying not to laugh. These were roles he and Helen had played many times before – the square young man and the liberated older woman. Finn loved the banter he could have with Helen. She was more his friend than his aunt, though she'd not been afraid to lay down the law when he was younger. Still wasn't. Not all his girlfriends had appreciated the close, eccentric relationship he had with Helen. And because of that, they didn't last long. Passing the Helen test was critical.

* * *

Rachel checked the items in the supermarket trolley. 'We forgot the quiche.'

'And where would that be?' Finn was juggling three oranges to the delight of a watching toddler.

'In the deli section.'

'The *Delhi* section? We're having Indian food then?' he quipped, and she smiled.

In truth, Finn hadn't been much help on this shopping expedition. He picked out items at random, often the most expensive, and which Rachel discreetly put back on the shelves. He wandered aimlessly down the wrong aisles, gazing at light bulbs and batteries. It was like shopping with a child. 'How do you cope in supermarkets back home?' she asked.

'Well, mostly I eat on set or at the theatre. Hospitality tables are great.'

He needed a housekeeper, Rachel decided. Or a wife. 'You go and wait in the queue. I'll get the quiche.'

'Okay.' He wandered off in the wrong direction, away from the tills. This shopping trip could take hours, but there was no one else she'd rather be with. She was going to enjoy this evening to the full. Surely avenging angels were allowed a day off now and then.

* * *

Rachel was packing the groceries into the boot when she heard the sound of running feet. She glanced round the car and saw a boy of about ten dashing for the supermarket doors. Before he could get there, two bigger boys caught up and crashed him into the wall, where he stood, cowering. 'Finn!' she called.

He was already there. He must have moved at the speed of light. Grabbing the two boys by the scruff of their jackets, he heaved them away and placed himself in front of their victim. Rachel moved closer, fingers wrapped round her mobile in case of trouble.

'Pick on someone your own size,' said Finn. 'Or better still – don't pick on anyone at all. Get a life instead. Now, piss off!'

Rachel watched as the two boys skulked away. As they reached the safety of the supermarket corner, they shouted 'Aussie wanker!' and pelted away.

Finn turned to the other boy, who was still breathing hard, tear-tracks on his face. 'You okay, mate?'

The boy nodded, but he looked miserable.

'Does that happen a lot?' asked Finn.

No answer, but the boy's eyes told the whole story.

'Join a martial arts class,' Finn told him. 'The local library can tell you where. Because those idiots will keep coming back for more until you stand up to them. Take control, kid. Here – a donation to your first lesson.' Finn took a banknote from his pocket and pressed it into the boy's hand, then walked away to the car.

The boy stood there, first gazing at the money, then at Finn, a kind of hopeful wonder in his expression. Rachel felt tears prick her eyes. The entire incident had only taken a few minutes, yet Finn just might have changed someone's life. If only he'd been around fourteen years ago – someone with a sense of justice who would stand up for the underdog. Textbooks would likely say ignore the bullies and they'd go away. Rachel knew better. Words might not break your bones, but they could break your spirit. It was a jungle out there for young people, and they needed more than platitudes to survive it.

* * *

Gerald was bitching because they hadn't been given front row seats for the opening night of *A Christmas Carol*. 'Those seats are reserved for the cast members' families,' Mel told him. He knew that, but still made the same fuss every year.

'But we make the biggest financial contribution to this play.'

Jay sighed and closed his eyes. What did that matter? All the profits went to charity anyway. He wished they'd been able to bring Leanne – then he could have ignored his in-laws completely and focused on her. But Leanne was too young to watch a play about ghosts. Children had to be at least eight to attend.

Personally, he was bored rigid with Scrooge and his ghosts. He'd seen this play more times than he could count and could recite the lines along with the cast members, although he'd always refused to get involved in drama at school. Said it was for cissies. Jody and Daniel had wanted to audition, but Jay had set them right on that one. A real man spent his time on a sports field.

His mother-in-law's voice interrupted his thoughts. 'Excuse me, could you switch places. I can't see.'

Jay opened his eyes. The tall man in front of Tessa turned round to glare at her, but he took one look at Gerald and meekly changed seats with his shorter partner. Why was everyone so spineless around Old Man Maguire? He wasn't God, although years ago Jay had thought of him that way when he'd made the trouble around the church incident disappear. It had only been a game, but that wop girl had overreacted and her mother had caused a fuss, going to the police, and anyone else she thought would listen. Probably would have tried the local paper next if Gerald hadn't shut her up. Jay never knew exactly how he'd managed it, but of course the Maguires had influence and the Rinaldis didn't. Jay had got out of the whole fiasco by association because Mel was involved and her father protected her like a lion.

He scanned the front row and spotted Jen's mum, Susan, passing round sweets to her two younger daughters. No sign of that old ox, Sean O'Neill. Probably putting his cows to bed. Jenny was his only claim to fame and he was too blind to see it.

The lights dimmed, the curtains opened, the audience applauded. When he met Jenny tomorrow, Jay would tell her she'd given a brilliant performance and could be the next Saoirse Ronan. He'd get a lot of brownie points for that. The sex would likely be great.

* * *

The party at Helen's house was in full swing. About thirty people spilled throughout the ground-floor rooms. The actors, all schoolchildren, always had their celebration at the theatre immediately after the show. This late evening party with alcohol was for the adult volunteers and the theatre employees – people who took care of the lighting, scene changing, costumes, props, publicity, front of house, cleaning …

Helen – with Rachel and Finn's help – had done them proud, laying on pizza, chicken wings, samosas, quiche, endless bowls of salad and three different desserts. The alcohol was flowing, and Finn's iPod was blaring out a succession of soft rock. Helen didn't have to worry that the neighbours would complain about the noise because she'd invited them as well.

Finn loved first-night parties, especially when the show had gone well, as it had tonight. The few sticky moments – a wavering set, a mixed-up line, and a torn dress – were minor and would be fixed by the next performance. He opened another can of beer and took a sip, his eyes sweeping the living room. Someone at the piano was competing with the iPod, drunken fingers botching a tune. Helen was on the sofa, holding court. The people around her were enthralled by her acting stories. 'Hugh Jackman's got a great sense of humour …' Finn heard her say, as he left the room in search of Rachel.

He found her in the kitchen. She'd been cornered by Niall, the sound guy. Her eyes were glazed over. Obviously no competition for Finn's affections there. Rachel looked like a woman drowning. Time for the lifeguard. He pushed his way through the crush and tapped Niall on the shoulder. 'The iPod dock is sticking, mate. Could you take a look at it?'

Niall beamed, clearly thinking he'd go up in Rachel's estimation as a man of technology. 'Don't go anywhere,' he told her, before scuttling off.

'I can't leave you for a minute,' Finn teased. 'They're like flies round a honey pot.'

'He was enthralling me with his BMX biking record. Said he wants to take me along next time he goes.'

'And will you go?' Finn heard the trace of anxiety in his voice. Like a lovesick teenager. Not cool.

Rachel smiled. 'Nothing can compete with miniature golf.'

He relaxed. 'Let's go and dance. I'll find some slow ballads.'

'How? Niall's probably dismantling the iPod dock.'

'Then we'll dance on the landing. More private. We'll make our own music.'

'Oh, Mr Smoothie!' Rachel said. 'Lead the way, but I'm not sure if I'll manage a dance. I've had a bit too much wine.' She slipped down off the stool and swayed dangerously to the left.

Finn grabbed her arms and straightened her, saying 'I've got you.' He hoped that was true.

* * *

Finn was stationed at the front door, saying farewells to the guests. It had been a good evening, but he was desperate to get back to Rachel.

'Bye, Finn.'

'Great party!'

'Give us another impression before we go.'

Helen had made him entertain everyone with his repertoire of impersonations. Then they'd had a drunken singalong around the piano. She had more energy than an Olympic athlete. Finn had lost sight of Rachel later in the evening and hoped Niall hadn't made another move on her. No one would believe he could be so insecure. He was too good at acting a part.

Rachel wasn't among the departing guests. Must be waiting inside. Finn finally closed the door and went back to the living room, where she was curled up on the sofa, her eyes closed, her lovely chestnut hair tumbling around the cushions. A regular sleeping beauty. Helen was standing over her. 'She's dead to the world,' she said. 'We'll make her comfortable here. Then give her a good breakfast in the morning.'

While Helen went to get a blanket and pillow, Finn leaned over and gently kissed Rachel. Her lips twitched, and she gave the faintest of smiles. The evening hadn't ended as he'd planned, but Finn had the memory of the slow dancing they'd done on the landing earlier when he'd found a late-night radio station playing love songs. That and the thought of their shared kisses would keep him warm that night. And Rachel would be there when he woke up. It was enough – for now.

* * *

Rachel woke with a start to find herself alone in Helen's living room, a lamp glowing gently on the piano. She glanced at her watch. Four o'clock in the morning. She must have been asleep for hours. Someone had kindly covered her with a blanket. Probably couldn't wake her. How embarrassing.

She threw back the cover and sat up on the sofa, head in hands. If only she'd remembered what a lightweight she was when it came to alcohol, she wouldn't be feeling like death now. The party had been so much fun, though. The music, the laughter, the dancing – Finn. She smiled to herself when she remembered the long kisses they'd shared on the landing as they danced to 'Show Me Heaven'.

Suddenly, she started to cough. Her mouth was dry as sandpaper. She desperately needed water. Maybe some coffee. Getting up from the sofa, she quietly opened the living room door and tiptoed down the hallway towards the kitchen. She'd add insult to injury if she woke Helen and Finn after crashing out uninvited in their house.

Someone had left the light on in the kitchen. She pushed open the door … and screamed at the sight of a ghostly figure in the dark window. There was a sound to her left and Rachel swung round, stance wide, karate hands at the ready, like they'd taught her in self-defence class. Finn was sitting at the breakfast counter, eyes wide. They stared at each other, frozen with shock.

Finn found his voice first. 'Bruce Lee in my kitchen. That's a first. Would you like some coffee?'

Rachel dropped her hands and felt the shaky weakness after an adrenaline surge. 'Oh God, Finn, you scared the life out of me. I thought you were a ghost or something.' She collapsed onto the stool opposite him.

'Do karate chops work on ghosts?' he asked, pouring a coffee and passing it to her.

She drank the tepid liquid gratefully. The caffeine started to do its trick. Made her feel more human again. Then she had a thought. 'I've probably woken Helen with my screaming.'

Finn shook his head. 'No worries. Helen always takes a sleeping pill after the opening night. Not even an earthquake could wake her. She'll be out of it till at least nine.'

'That's a relief. Speaking of out of it … I'm so sorry I fell asleep on the sofa.'

'Why?' asked Finn. 'You were tired, you were comfortable. It's actually a compliment. You felt at home enough to relax.'

Rachel smiled. He always made everything feel okay. 'It was a great party, but why are you up so early?'

Finn sighed. 'Couldn't sleep. Haven't been sleeping well for a while. Not since …'

He paused and Rachel finished the sentence for him. 'Not since that crisis you mentioned?'

Their eyes locked, and Rachel could read the admission there. Whatever this crisis was, she wished he'd talk about it. It would be a sign that their relationship was deepening. Fun and jokes were great, but when you cared about someone, you wanted to help banish the worries that circled them in the dark hours. 'Let's take our coffee to the living room,' she suggested, holding out her hand.

A moment's hesitation then he took it, letting her lead the way out of the kitchen's bright glare.

* * *

Rachel was in Finn's arms and it felt like the most natural place to be. They were lying on a rug in front of the real fire that

Finn had lit. The aroma of fir cones drifted around the room, and the flickering flames gave a gentle glow to the darkness and cast intriguing shadows on their naked bodies.

Rachel stroked the tattoo on Finn's arm. 'What does this symbol mean?' she whispered.

'Tiger,' he told her, as he kissed her eyelids, cheeks, the tip of her nose. 'My Chinese horoscope sign. Got it in Bali.'

'Bali,' she murmured, but his kisses were making it hard for her mind to hold on to the information. His lips were moving slowly down her body. He was a man who was turned on as much by giving pleasure as he was by receiving it. Andy hadn't been as patient as this.

'You're so beautiful, Rachel.' Finn had moved back up to gaze into her eyes. Maybe that was all talk, but she needed to hear tender words. Couldn't bear for this to be just a one-night stand.

She wrapped her arms around his neck, wrapped her legs around his body, holding him to her as close as she could. As their bodies began to move together in the quiet firelight, Rachel could see beyond the nightmare her life had become to the possibility of something better.

* * *

Rachel and Finn were lying on the sofa, gazing into the dying embers of the fire. Daylight was struggling through the small gap in the curtains. They'd made love twice, and Rachel was becoming more familiar with the contours of Finn's body. Intimacy was like discovering a new country. His arms were wrapped around her, and there was no other place she'd rather be.

'Are you warm enough?' she asked, attuned now to his difficulties with this northern climate.

'Yes ma'am,' he replied, nuzzling the nape of her neck. That somehow felt even more intimate than their lovemaking.

'What would you be doing in Australia – in November?'

'Well, it's summer there now so if I wasn't working, I'd be swimming in the morning with Butch. He loves the water. Then I'd go for a coffee to Potts Point, near where I live. It's an arty community. A lot of actors hanging out between jobs. Actually, Gulliver's reminds me of a café I used to go to there ...'

His voice tailed off. Rachel felt his body tense behind her, as if he'd experienced an unpleasant memory.

'Why did you stop going there?' she asked. Silence. She turned to see his face, glimpsed an expression of such sadness. 'Finn – what is it? Tell me – please.'

'Another time. Let's not spoil the moment with my hangups. It'll keep.'

He pulled her in close, and Rachel gently stroked his hand. Finn was an enigma for sure, but he was special. Worth fighting for, and that meant trusting him. It meant honesty. She should tell him why she was here. It was a risk, but maybe not much of one. Finn wasn't from around these parts. He didn't know any of the bullies. He'd be leaving not long after her ...

The unknown factor was how he would respond to what she was doing. Revenge wouldn't change the past, but it could destroy her future. Finn might think badly of her for messing with people's lives, however much pain and suffering they'd caused – but this was who she was. She could hide that, or she could show herself, faults and all. It was a huge risk, but a relationship should be based on truth.

'Finn,' she said softly, glad that she had her back to him. 'You want to know about me, so I'll tell you my story now. About a girl who wanted so much to fit in. To be accepted. But who was rejected by everyone. And it hurt her very much ...'

There was no response. Rachel glanced round. He was asleep. No longer the joker, no longer the lover. He looked young and vulnerable. She didn't have the heart to wake him up. Her story could wait until another day.

Chapter Twelve

The rubbish bag was full to the brim by the time Rachel returned to the kitchen. She rinsed all the glasses and set them to dry on the counter. Leftovers were neatly stacked in the fridge. The only thing that remained to do was the vacuuming. She opened a couple of hall cupboards and dragged out an antiquated machine.

She heard footsteps on the stairs. Like Finn predicted, Helen had slept until after nine. Swathed in a flamboyant green silk dressing gown embroidered with huge roses, she was treading slowly, delicately, as if every step brought pain. The hair stood up around her head like she'd slept plugged into an electricity outlet. She gave Rachel a weak smile, then stared in horror at the vacuum cleaner. 'Not this morning, darling, please. I couldn't take it.'

'No problem.' Rachel pushed it back in the cupboard. 'Would you like some orange juice?'

'Lovely. And put a raw egg in it, would you?' Helen followed her through into the kitchen and sat down at the counter. 'God, I've just seen my hair in the hall mirror. I could be Jedward's mother!' She gazed around her. 'You've cleaned up, you angel.'

'Finn and I did it together,' said Rachel, handing Helen the glass of fruit juice and egg, which she downed in one, giving a little shudder.

'Where is Finn?'

'Gone to get us some breakfast from Gulliver's. He said it tastes better if we don't have to make it ourselves. He should be back soon.'

'Isn't he the best?'

'Yes, I really think he is.' The words were out before Rachel could stop them, and she felt herself blushing.

A slow smile spread across Helen's face. 'Well – there's nothing like a party for bringing people together. My Leo used to say that.'

Rachel wasn't sure she was ready to talk openly with others yet about her feelings for Finn, and Helen must have sensed that because she launched into an anecdote about a notorious party on a boat where everyone's clothes got tossed over the side.

* * *

Finn balanced the tray of three coffees in one hand like a waiter and slung the plastic bag of pastries over his shoulder. He left Gulliver's and headed homeward. It was chilly as usual, but today he didn't mind the cold. Memories of Rachel in his arms were keeping him warm. If this was a musical, he'd have burst into song. Maybe danced as well, even with the coffees. Ironic that he had to come halfway round the world to find a girl he really wanted to be with. Rachel was based in London, which wouldn't be easy, but she'd finish her post-grad studies next summer and then he might be able to persuade her to come out to Australia for a while. See if she liked it. Sydney was a hive of arts activity ...

'Hello?'

Finn stopped in his tracks and turned round, almost dropping the coffees at the sight of the man in the dog collar coming towards him.

'Morning. I'm Father Daniel Quinn.'

The priest put out his hand, and Finn looked at his own full hands, unable to reciprocate the handshake. 'Finn MacKenzie,' he mumbled.

'Yes, I know – Helen's nephew. Nice to finally meet you. I was just about to call round and congratulate Helen on a great performance last night.'

'Thanks. I'll tell her. She's not up yet.'

Daniel glanced at the coffees and the plastic bag. 'A celebration breakfast, eh?'

Finn nodded, irritated at this delay.

'Can you give Rachel a message from me?'

'Rachel?'

'Molly told me she stayed over with you.'

Was this a bit of small-town church morality? If Finn had been a dog, his hackles would have risen. 'What's the message?' he said.

'Tell her the church will be closed this morning. I can give her extra time tomorrow, though.'

'Okay.'

Finn turned to go, but Daniel hadn't finished yet. 'She's a lovely person, isn't she?'

There was something in his manner when he spoke about Rachel that wasn't quite right. Something proprietorial. 'Yes, she is.'

'Make sure you take good care of her. Bye now.'

The priest turned on his heel and walked away, and Finn stared after him. What the hell was that all about? It had almost sounded like a warning. Clearly it wasn't just Finn that Rachel had an effect on – but it was Finn she'd spent the night with. Nothing could diminish his pleasure at the memory of that, except … Had last night meant as much to her as it had to him? He knew so little about her. Not that that had ever stopped him with women before. Rachel was different, though. Somehow she'd got under his guard.

Finn set down his packages so he could unlock Helen's front door. Once inside, he could hear voices. Helen must be up. He walked down the hall and rapped on the kitchen door. 'Knock knock.'

'Who's there?' asked Helen, playing along.

'Finn.'

'Finn who?'

'Finn-k it must be time for breakfast.' He entered to groans from Helen and Rachel. 'Ladies, a feast awaits you.' He put the bag on the counter and started to dispense the goodies.

'Cinnamon croissant for you, Rachel. Helen – a tart, no pun intended. For the man of the house, a chocolate glazed doughnut. And three French vanilla coffees. No, don't thank me – I live to serve.'

* * *

Daniel raked the last of the leaves into the fire pit and stopped for a breather, sitting down on the bench in the rectory garden. The sun was out, and he turned his face towards the warming glow, eyes closed. The physical activity of the gardening had kept his brain occupied till now, but as soon as he stopped, his mind started brooding again.

Rachel and Finn MacKenzie. It was clear they were a couple now. Since the ice skating, he'd seen them a few times together, walking arm in arm along the streets of Kilbrook. Rachel seemed happy, and that was a good thing. Of course it was. She was a beautiful young woman, destined ultimately for marriage and motherhood.

Whether Finn MacKenzie was her Mr Right was not so clear. Actors were notoriously unreliable. This morning he'd still been wearing those sunglasses, so Daniel couldn't see his eyes properly – and Daniel always wanted to see people's eyes. The mirror of the soul. Finn's swaggering walk had irritated Daniel too, which was why he'd stopped him. To try to make him see how special Rachel was, and that she should be cherished. Finn hadn't taken kindly to the interruption, though. Probably dismissed Daniel as a nosy do-gooder.

He stood up and stretched his legs and then set light to the pile of leaves and watched them crackle and burn. It felt like his dreams going up in smoke. His far-fetched dreams about Rachel, and what a life with her would be like.

The smoke spiralled up into the clear blue sky, like a signal for help. And he needed help because the last few weeks had made him start to question many things. The ground had subtly shifted beneath his feet, and he didn't know what to do about it. He'd make confession as usual in Galway at the end of the month and get some spiritual guidance then. But could he last that long?

* * *

Saturday afternoon and her work shift over, Rachel was heading out to Lough Corrib, with Finn in the car beside her. Everything should have been perfect, except that he was worryingly quiet, so unlike the Finn she'd started to know. An unwelcome thought gatecrashed her mind. They'd made love – had he lost interest now the chase was over? He'd suggested this drive – maybe he thought the serenity of the lough would be the best place to tell her it was finished. But a beautiful location wouldn't soften the blow, and being dumped twice in a year would wreck what little confidence she had left.

'Look out!' yelled Finn.

Rachel swerved to avoid a rabbit, which had shot out into the road ahead. 'Good call,' she said to Finn, after she got the car back on track.

'Stop … please … stop the car.'

One glance at Finn told Rachel he wasn't fooling around. He was clawing to try to free himself from the seat belt, and his breathing was strained.

A viewing point was coming up on the right, and Rachel turned off into the deserted space. The second she killed the engine, Finn opened the door and bolted out, only coming to a stop when he reached the water's edge. He stood there, head back, gasping for breath.

Rachel was quickly by his side, and she put her hand on his shoulder. 'Are you okay, Finn?'

He nodded, breathing in a few more lungfuls of air. 'I'm fine … I'm fine.'

'You don't look fine.'

In fact, he looked terrible. His face was ashen, and his hands were trembling. It seemed like he'd had some kind of panic attack. Should she take him to a hospital? Or back home?

'I'll call Helen,' she decided, pulling out her mobile.

'No.' Finn took hold of her arm. 'It's okay. I just need to rest for a few minutes.'

Rachel put her arm through his, and they walked over to a log. Once she'd sat him down, she got them something to drink from the car.

Finn sipped at the bottled water, and slowly his hand steadied. The rhythmic sound of the waves against the stones helped Rachel's heart find a more regular beat. It was only when she was calmer that she realised how scared she'd been.

She risked a question. 'What happened back there, Finn?'

He gave a long exhale and then spoke. 'I was in a car crash in January – New Year's Day. I was lucky. Touch and go for a bit, but they pulled me through. My best friend, Ethan … he didn't make it.'

The distress in his voice made Rachel reach for his hand and clasp it tight. She could bear her own pain most of the time, but not another's. 'I'm so sorry.'

'The funeral was terrible. Unreal.'

His voice was unsteady, but Rachel didn't turn to look at him. He could probably talk more freely that way. Like closing your eyes on the psychiatrist's couch perhaps.

'I couldn't grasp that he was gone. His fiancée was devastated. She didn't blame me, but I did, even though I know it really wasn't my fault – a driver using his mobile phone came out of nowhere. I lost control of the car, and he hit the passenger side full on. I hadn't been drinking or anything, but I've never forgiven myself. I never will.'

Rachel understood. She'd feel the same way if it had happened to Sophia.

'Ethan and I had been friends for years,' said Finn. 'Kids used to pick on me because of my size, and he was the only one who stood up for me. He got me to go to a gym with him.

Get in shape, build muscle. I owe a lot of who I am today to him.'

So Finn had been bullied, too. That was hard to imagine. He was so confident now, so popular. Probably because he'd had one person in his corner. Not everyone was that lucky. No wonder he'd been angry with the bullies at the supermarket.

'I went to pieces a bit without him ... couldn't sleep, couldn't eat, couldn't work. If it hadn't been for Helen ... she flew out to help me ... even took me to a shrink ... bought Butch for me so I'd have to get up in the mornings.'

'That's good,' Rachel said, stroking his hand. 'You'll always miss Ethan, but he'd want you to go on living. To take care of yourself.'

'That's what Helen said,' he murmured. 'It's not only the grief, though. I just can't shake off the guilt. And that's why I can't drive a car. In case it happens again. I'm even nervous as a passenger. I really wanted to take *you* out today, not have you take me. I'm sorry, Rachel – you can see why I don't usually talk about this. It puts most people off.'

'Not me,' said Rachel. 'A trouble shared is a trouble halved. And you can stop right there with the alpha-male thing. It doesn't matter who drives who. It's the twenty-first century, Finn. Sexual equality.'

'I guess.' He slid his arm round her shoulder and pulled her into him. 'Thanks for listening, Rachel. You're really special.'

Being close to him reminded her of last night, and then of her earlier worry. 'You know, when you were so quiet in the car, I was scared you were going to tell me everything was over between us.'

'Hey.' He tipped her face up to look at his. 'Nothing's over. It's only just begun.'

'Last night ... was amazing,' she ventured.

His full-on smile was reassuring. 'Wasn't it, though. It's been a long time since I had ... emotional sex. Something that wasn't just physical, you know. Well, it wasn't for me anyway.'

'Or me,' she admitted. 'I'm still not sure why, though. We hardly know each other.'

'Maybe it's what they call chemistry. Or perhaps we're soulmates – if you believe in that kind of thing.'

Soulmates had a permanent ring to it. 'I didn't come to Ireland looking for any kind of attachment ...'

'Isn't that when you're most likely to find it?'

He was smiling now, looking more relaxed. The burden of guilt and grief relieved by disclosure. Would it be the same for Rachel? Now wasn't the time to mention it, though. Finn had his own sadness to bear. She wasn't going to saddle him with hers.

'Let's go for a walk,' she suggested. 'Breathe in some of this fresh country air.'

Hand in hand, they wandered along the shores of the lough, watching the fishing boats and the ever-changing colour of the water. As they talked, Rachel mentally checked off where they were compatible: beach holidays, Italian food, sci-fi movies, karaoke ... There was so much she could imagine them doing together if they were able to figure out the problem of them living at opposite ends of the planet. They weren't totally compatible, though, with Finn admitting a love of all sports, which Rachel hated, apart maybe from watching Wimbledon or drooling over David Beckham. But that was normal in a relationship. The one thing Finn didn't mention was his family, and although curious, that suited Rachel – if he didn't want to talk about them, he was unlikely to ask about hers.

Later, they skimmed stones across the lake water, and Finn won.

'Losing involves a forfeit,' Finn told her. 'You have to see how cold the water is.'

Before she had a chance to move, he'd swept her up in his arms and was heading towards the lake.

'Don't you dare, Finn!' Rachel's arms were tight around his neck. If she went in, she was taking him with her, but at the water's edge, he put her down and pulled her towards him.

'It'll have to be a different forfeit then,' he said, and he kissed her – a sweet, chaste kiss, until her tongue found his, and Rachel was reminded of the previous night's passion. She now had no power to resist Finn. That made her very vulnerable, especially since she was hiding so much from him, but there was no way she was giving him up.

* * *

In the safe haven of her bedroom, Rachel switched on her phone and flicked through the photos she'd taken of the lough. The view was stunning, and she became aware of how much she'd missed, being whisked away from Ireland before she was fully able to appreciate it. Four bullying children had ruined her perception of her mother's homeland. For years, Ireland to her meant unhappiness. Being here now, living in Kilbrook, she was seeing the beauty, the friendliness of the Irish, and of those special idiosyncrasies that made the people, and the country, so unique.

She switched to the video recording she'd made of Finn, standing on a rock and singing 'Waltzing Matilda'. It had been a memorable day. A red-letter day. Finn had trusted Rachel enough to share one of his most painful memories. It was a significant moment that she felt had moved their relationship to another level. This was not a fling for either of them, and that was both scary and wonderful at the same time. There were challenges ahead, but Rachel would face them, unafraid. Coming back to Kilbrook to take on the bullies had been the right thing to do. And once this was all behind her, she'd follow Finn wherever he wanted her to go.

Chapter Thirteen

In the bathroom, Jay started towelling his hair dry. Monday morning, yet he hadn't really felt the benefit of the weekend. The American interior designers had arrived in Galway yesterday, and Mel had insisted he go with her to Gerald's Crap and Tat Emporium to help her greet them. He'd never been so bored in his life.

He heard Mel's voice in the bedroom. He hated when she did that. Expected him to have supersonic hearing.

'Jay! Did you hear me?'

He flung the wet towel into the corner of the bathroom and kicked the cupboard door shut. 'What?' he asked, as he went back into the bedroom.

Mel was propped up in bed, flicking through the TV channels. 'I said wear your grey suit tonight. I got it dry-cleaned last week.'

Jay hated wearing a suit. Felt like he was choking half the time. That was the beauty of being a PE teacher – tracksuit and trainers were the order of the day.

'I need you there at six,' Mel told him.

'Okay.' At least there'd be time for a few pints after work before the big dinner for the designers.

It wasn't until he was in the car that Jay remembered he was meeting Jenny after school. She'd texted him last night to say she'd be on Bracken Hill at five. No way he was cancelling her for Gerald Maguire's Big Night Out. Mel would be upset with him if he turned up late, but he'd cross that bridge when he came to it.

* * *

Jay had left school later than planned due to an unexpected meeting with a parent. Parking his car at the base of Bracken

Hill, he jogged up to the summit in less than five minutes. It would take others double that time or more. He had the body of a god. Just one of the reasons why Jenny worshipped him. He crept forward through the scattered trees, wanting to surprise her. They usually climbed the hill from different sides to avoid being seen together.

And there she was. Standing in the clearing, looking down over the edge of the hill at fields of sheep and cows. Jay moved stealthily forward then grabbed Jenny up in his arms, swinging her round and round in the way that she loved. He fell back onto the grass, still holding her, flipping her over him so they were face to face, but her expression today stopped him dead. She'd been crying, her eyes red, cheeks blotched.

'What is it, Jen?' If that father of hers had laid a finger on her, he'd swing for him.

The tears started up again, dripping warm onto his face. He moved them both up into a sitting position, found her a hankie, gave her a drink from his water bottle. Hugged her close, begging her to tell him what was wrong. The women's magazines would have been proud of him.

'Jay ...' she whispered. 'I don't know what to do ...'

Her blue china-doll eyes, brimming with tears, stared at him with a pleading expression. Jay's mouth went dry. Some sixth sense told him that whatever it was, he'd not like it.

'I'm pregnant, Jay,' she blurted out.

His brain stopped working. He couldn't think beyond those words. Didn't want to consider the implications. Wanted to be off this hillside and safe at Mel's dinner. What was he supposed to do now? 'Are you sure?'

She nodded and spoke through gulps and hiccups. 'I've missed ... two monthlies ... and I got dizzy a few times. I've started ... being sick in the mornings. I did one of those test things yesterday ...'

'But, Jen, we've always used condoms,' he said puzzled.

'Not the first time!' sobbed Jenny. 'Remember?'

She was right. At the beginning of September they'd done it in his car. He hadn't been able to resist. How ironic if conception happened then. Jenny had been a virgin, and they'd had a couple of false starts. She hadn't even enjoyed it, not wanting to do it again but for his pleading.

Jenny was clinging to him. 'Jay ... Jay ... you do love me, don't you?'

He did love her fragile beauty, and how she made him feel like a teenager again, but he didn't want to spend the rest of his life with her. He was already married and a father. He'd wanted something different with Jenny ...

'Jay ...'

The distress on her face was too much. He caved in and lied. Took the easy way out for now. 'Course I love you. And we'll work this out, I promise. First thing is to get you to a doctor. To check you really are pregnant. Those chemist kits aren't always reliable ...'

'I am pregnant! I know I am! See?'

She grabbed his hand and placed it on her breast. The new swelling there confirmed the nightmare. Made him feel sick. He pulled his hand away as if it had been burned.

'Like I said, Jen – I'll get you an appointment with a clinic in Galway. As soon as possible. Then we'll decide what to do. Don't tell anyone – not yet. Promise?'

Finally she nodded her head. Then she wanted them to cuddle for a bit, wrapped up in the blanket she'd brought. Jay lay there, staring at the sky, his mind in overdrive. This baby couldn't happen. It would mess up his whole life. Screw up Jenny's life, too. He had to make her see that abortion was the only answer. She'd have to go to the UK and he'd go with her. Couldn't let her go alone. God only knew how he was going to manage that, though.

* * *

'This is a swell place you've got here, Melissa,' said Lance from Venice Beach. Mel would have enjoyed the compliment more if the American's hand wasn't resting a little too low in the small of her back. He'd been sniffing around her since he'd arrived with the other guests at The Fat Pheasant half an hour ago.

'Won't you take a seat, Lance?' she suggested. 'Dinner is about to be served. We've put you over here.' Thankfully on the opposite side of the room from where she would be sitting.

Mel glanced around the restaurant, her radar finely tuned for any problems. The tables gleamed with silver candlesticks and cutlery. She'd made the waitresses polish the wine glasses three times. The ironed folds in the napkins were so sharp that they could cut someone. Aileen something-or-other, a damned expensive musician from Galway, was in the corner producing exquisite Bach from her cello. Twenty-four guests – half from California, half from various corners of Ireland – had come to mix business and pleasure in her restaurant. Pierre Lévêque, the food critic Henri had invited from *Le Bon Weekend* magazine, seemed mellow and relaxed with his aperitif. He would see the place at its very best.

Mel signalled to the waiting staff to begin taking orders, and then joined her father at his table. As the compliments flowed in her direction, Mel basked in the glow of a job well done. All the tension and stresses of the past week faded away.

'Here's to you, Mel.' Her father raised his champagne glass in her direction.

At that moment, all the lights went out.

* * *

As darkness engulfed the restaurant, the cellist's bow skittered across the strings and then Bach was no more. A moment later, the guests all began talking at once.

'Say – what's the idea?'

'Forgot to pay the electricity bill, Mel?'

There was still a faint glow in the restaurant from the street lights in the square outside, and as Rachel's night vision kicked in, her eyes searched for and found Mel, who was stumbling across the floor to the desk. 'Get candles!' she hissed at the servers.

Rachel had been promoted to waitress for the evening, and she fled into the depths of the kitchen with the others, hearing Mel behind her, trying to soothe the guests.

Henri was barking orders like a general in his finest hour. No one would have guessed he'd caused all this. Rachel had no idea how he'd managed it, but he'd told her earlier that his father was an electrician and had passed on detailed knowledge about fuses and circuits.

The ovens were all gas-fired, so in theory the chefs could continue cooking – but they needed light to do that, and Colette soon discovered there weren't enough candles for both the kitchen and the dining room.

'Why the hell not?' demanded Mel, who'd come behind the scenes to see what could be salvaged from the chaos. No one offered an answer, although Rachel knew why – she'd secretly halved the supply yesterday. The remaining candles were being lit, one by one, on the counters beside her, and the flickering flames showed the panic on Mel's face. She turned to the cashier. 'Karen, go and ask Daniel Quinn for all the candles he's got. Tell him I'll buy replacements. And have him say a prayer while he's at it. You servers – get out there and ply the diners with wine. Henri – what's happened to the generator? Why didn't it kick in?'

Henri shrugged. 'It is dead as the doorknob, Madame. Will is now pulling and pulling the cord but nothing.'

Rachel had to hand it to Henri. His acting skills were second to none. He sounded desolate.

'Mel, what's happening?' Gerald Maguire came into the gloomy kitchen, radiating anger. 'Should I take my guests elsewhere?'

'No, no, Daddy,' moaned Mel. 'The food can still be

cooked. We're getting more candles. Twenty minutes and we'll have the starters on the table, I promise.'

'Why don't I check the fuse box?' suggested Gerald, and Rachel caught her breath. 'A flick of the switch and everything could be fine.'

'*Non, non*, Monsieur Maguire,' said Henri gravely, holding his big fleshy hand up in protest. 'You are a guest. It is not permitted. No insurance cover. We cannot have you go up in the puff of smoke. Besides, the candlelight is more romantic, *n'est-ce pas*? Better atmosphere.'

'Let's go back through, Daddy. Everything's under control here.'

Gerald and Mel returned to the dining room, and the servers started to take the candles through to the guests.

Henri gave Rachel the briefest of winks. The show wasn't over yet.

* * *

'I can't see well enough to read the score,' Aileen the cellist was whining in her darkened corner.

'You must know some music by heart,' snapped Mel. 'Play anything. I'll double your fee.' That did the trick. She was scraping out a tune on her cello before Mel had even turned round.

The guests had settled down, now viewing the power cut as a bit of an adventure. The candles gave the room a warm glow, providing atmosphere as Henri had said. If the chef got Mel through this evening, she swore she'd be a lot nicer to him. She might not even replace him. There was nothing like a crisis to bond people together.

The starters began to flow out of the kitchen, and Mel returned to her father's table. He was deep in conversation with one of the Americans. She picked at her foie gras, not really tasting it. Where the hell was Jay? She discreetly checked her phone under the table – no messages. He knew this was a big night for her. Was it too much to ask for a bit of support?

'Mrs Cole, could you come through to the kitchen for a moment?'

Rachel had appeared at Mel's elbow. She looked worried. What now? She excused herself to the guests and followed Rachel. 'What is it?' she asked.

'It's Henri,' whispered Rachel. 'He's not well.'

Mel's heart sank. Was Big Bear Breton going to let her down at the last minute?

In the kitchen, Henri was seated on a chair. The other chefs were clustered around him, anxiety writ large on their faces. They'd unbuttoned the top of his chef's jacket. Will was making him sip some water and Colette was fanning him with a menu. He was breathing heavily, and sweat was pouring down his face. Mel tried not to be irritated by the fact that no one was cooking right now. 'Henri, what is it?' she asked.

'He went all dizzy,' Will told her. 'Said he had a pain there.'

He pointed to the chef's chest. Dear God, her head chef was having a heart attack. In the restaurant. With all the guests waiting for their main courses. 'Someone drive him to the hospital,' commanded Mel. The last thing she wanted was an ambulance siren alarming the guests.

'*Non, non,*' protested Henri, levering himself up from the stool. 'I am fine now. Everybody – start the cooking.'

The chefs drifted back to their stations, and Mel thought they'd weathered yet another crisis. Henri took a few steps forward, smiled at her, and then staggered, clutching the counter for support. As he fell, his hand swept all three platters of dressed salmon down with him onto the floor.

They were still picking lemon wedges out of Henri's hair as Calum got him into his car and drove off to the nearest hospital.

* * *

'I'm afraid the salmon's off,' Rachel told the guests. 'Might I recommend the steak?'

'How can the salmon be off?' grumbled an American woman, swathed in gold jewellery. 'You haven't served any main courses yet.'

'Chef wasn't happy with the quality,' said Rachel. Back in the kitchen, there'd been some debate as to whether the salmon could be salvaged, but closer inspection with a candle revealed their feet had pulped most of it. So the options for the diners were narrowed to steak or the crab linguine.

After her table had ordered, Rachel offered them another carafe of claret. Quite a few of the guests were slurring their words now. By the end of the evening, they might not even remember the food. Back in the kitchen, Will and Eddie were manning the meat station, peering at the cooking steaks, and Karen was lighting fresh candles from the bundle she'd got from Daniel.

Henri had faked the heart attack. It was his idea. Tomorrow he'd come and tell Mel the doctor had insisted he take a break from being a chef for a while. The next day, he'd be on his way back to Toulouse. Rachel had been shocked when he'd first told her the plan. The other chefs would think he was sick for real, and she felt bad about that, but Mel was going to fire Henri. Kick him out to the kerb when it suited her. This way he could leave with dignity, his reputation still intact. His chefs loved him and would surely not grudge him that.

'Where's the key to the wine cellar?'

Rachel started at the unexpected voice behind her. She turned round. Mel looked exhausted and must surely be wishing this evening was at an end.

'Henri always keeps the key,' Will told her, and then his face slowly registered the implications of what he'd just said. Henri was miles away.

'But we're running out of wine,' protested Mel. 'There's still dessert and coffee to come. What can we do?'

They found a couple of bottles of claret in the kitchen, and there was sweet Sauterne in the fridge. The brandy and port, though, was in the locked cellar.

'Eddie and Rachel – run over to the off-licence and buy five bottles each of brandy and whisky. The best they've got. Hurry.'

Mel gave her a handful of notes, and Rachel followed Eddie out into the cold night.

* * *

A few of the steaks had been overcooked. Mel could hear some of the guests bitching about it. Let them try to produce a perfect filet mignon by candlelight. This was probably the last time her father would ever ask her to host his guests at the restaurant. And who could blame him? The evening had been a disaster. A joke. She was now a joke. Those bloody servers were all local girls. They'd dine off stories about her failure for months to come.

The desserts were appearing. Wonderful concoctions of spun caramel, chocolate and strawberries. Henri said Colette was one of the best pastry chefs he'd ever met. At least things were going to end on a high note …

The front door crashed open and Jay staggered in. Drunk as a skunk. He was scanning the room for her. Mel wanted to hide under the table.

'Hey, buddy, why dontcha close the door?' she heard Lance say.

'Whassat?' mumbled Jay. 'Whezza lights? Mel?'

She stood up, ready to pull him through into the back. He saw her and stumbled forward. His arm caught a candle near the window. The candlestick seemed to topple in slow motion, landing on one of the tables. Then there was a whooshing sound and the tablecloth and runner were burning. Panic-stricken guests jumped back quickly, knocking the table to the ground, and flames started to lick at the legs of the next table.

'Fire!' shouted Gerald. 'Everybody out! Now!'

One of the servers pulled the fire alarm and the noise jarred people into motion. They scurried for the door, some of the women shrieking their way out into the night. Two men were shoving Jay out of the restaurant ahead of them.

Will and Sam suddenly appeared, brandishing fire extinguishers. Aileen was dragging her cello out of the corner. 'Leave it!' yelled Will.

Mel sprang forward and pulled Aileen with her to the door, as the chefs sprayed the fire. Outside, the two women slumped down on the pavement, panting and coughing. The shrieking of the fire engine's siren deafened them. People helped them up and out of the way, Gerald leading Mel over to a bench in the square. The firemen unrolled their hoses and went into the restaurant, ejecting Will and Sam.

Rachel was approaching, clutching bottles of brandy. The girl took off her white coat and draped it around Mel's shoulders. Only then did Mel realise how cold she had been in the night air in her sleeveless gown. Rachel knelt in front of her and unscrewed the cap from one of the brandy bottles, pouring some of the liquid into it. 'Drink – you'll feel better,' she said. Mel gulped it down and the brandy started to revive her a little.

Lance wandered over to the bench. 'Say – you Irish really know how to put on a show,' he said.

Mel stared at him, then started laughing hysterically. It was the only sane response in the circumstances.

* * *

Rachel flicked the lamp on. Her watch said twelve-thirty. She'd been tossing and turning for an hour. Molly was already in bed when Rachel got back from the restaurant, so there was no one to talk to about the evening's events. She'd thought about calling Finn, but he didn't know any of the people involved tonight, and she hadn't yet told him why she was here. He wouldn't really understand what she was feeling.

Rachel got out of bed, wrapping herself in the quilt, and paced up and down the bedroom. Images from the disastrous dinner kept flashing into her mind. She could never have predicted Jay would deliver the final blow, more effectively than anything Henri had thought up. The firemen put out the blaze fairly quickly, leaving a couple of damaged tables, charred curtains, and the stink of smoke. It could have been much worse. Thank God no one was hurt.

Tonight Rachel had been playing God. Like Gilbert Stokeley in his paintings. It was a feeling like no other. Exhilarating and terrifying at the same time. Like the world was a chessboard, there for your amusement, and the pieces waited for your command. There was one thing that bothered Rachel, though. The reason for her sleeplessness. She had imagined taking revenge would feel much better than it did. Why wasn't she more satisfied, more at peace? Wasn't this the start of closure? Yet she felt hollow inside, as if something had been chipped away and nothing had taken its place.

Rachel picked up the old school photograph and looked at the four circled heads. She'd made a promise to herself that they'd all pay, and she always kept her promises. She couldn't start breaking them now at the first sign of difficulty. So much of her life had been consumed by weakness and the desire to forget. She'd never really be her own person until this thing was done.

Rachel sat down at the desk and took out the diary. She'd brought it with her to Ireland to strengthen her resolve, and she needed that more than ever tonight. Huddled in the quilt, she opened the diary to a day of humiliation and shame.

1 April
I don't know when I ever felt so embarrassed. Mel organised it, I know, because I heard her whispering with Katie Shaw when we all came back to the changing room after games. I went for a shower and when I came

out everyone had gone – AND SO HAD ALL MY CLOTHES! All I had was the towel so I had to peep out from the changing room and call a teacher. Miss Murphy came with a coat and took me into the teachers' room in the PE block. I heard her say to another teacher that it was April Fools' Day so what could you expect? I don't know what happened to my clothes because the janitor looked everywhere in the school and couldn't find them. Then I had to search for something to fit me from the Spare Box, which is there for when kids have been sick on their own clothes, or have wet themselves. When I went back to the classroom, Jay Cole made a comment about 'Urinaldi'. Ha ha ... NOT!

And now I have no uniform to wear, and Mam has to buy me another. She was really mad, as though it was my fault, though she calmed down after. She asked me if everything was okay at school, and I didn't answer. Just went up to my room. I don't know how much longer I can stand this. I don't have any friends here. No one to confide in. I can't tell Mam because she's busy and stressed all the time. What could she do anyway? Mel, Jody, Jay – they've got important parents. And the teachers are too busy to do anything. I have FOUR MORE YEARS at this school with these people. It's like being in prison for a crime I didn't commit.

Chapter Fourteen

Jay froze as he heard Mel coming downstairs. He'd hoped to have left for work before she got up. All was not lost, though. There was still the breakfast tray.

Mel walked into the kitchen, saw Jay, and gave him the don't-mess-with-me-this-morning look as she sat down at the table. She was still in her dressing gown, her hair unbrushed. That was not good. His memories of yesterday evening were patchy, but he remembered knocking over a candlestick, and then there was chaos: flames and sirens and someone hauling him out into the street. He'd woken up an hour ago in the spare room, still in his clothes.

Grabbing the tray, Jay set it down in front of Mel, hoping she wouldn't decide to sweep it off the table. He'd made a bowl of fresh fruit salad, keeping the strawberry halves aside to create a love heart on a saucer. The orange juice was freshly squeezed, and he'd added a red rose plucked from the flower display in the dining room. She sat there silently taking in his apology breakfast.

Back at the counter, Jay poured them both a strong coffee. Mel's went into the 'You're My Supermodel' mug, and he placed it next to the tray with the slogan facing her. He sat down opposite and delivered his prepared speech: 'I'm so sorry about what happened, Mel. I'm a total idiot. I was drunk and I shouldn't have been. I'll help with the damage. Anything you need me to do, name it.'

He watched her anxiously, hoping there'd be some kind of response. Even anger was preferable to women and their long, loaded silences. A car swished by outside. The coffee machine hissed.

Finally, Mel picked up the orange juice and drained it to the dregs. Perhaps he'd have the glass thrown at his head. At least he wouldn't have to go to school then.

'It's my father you need to apologise to, Jay, not me.'

His heart sank. He'd rather drink poison, but if that's what she wanted. 'Okay. I'll call him today.'

She nodded, picked up the coffee, and left the kitchen. He was used to Angry Mel, Silent Mel, Tearful Mel, Jealous Mel. This Disappointed-in-Him Mel was new. Whatever else, she'd always supported him, always had his back. He needed to win her over again – and soon – in case he couldn't contain this nightmare with Jenny. He'd plan a romantic weekend away – Paris, perhaps, her favourite city. And he'd apologise to that old goat, Gerald Maguire, though the words would stick in his throat.

Eating the strawberries from the pathetic love heart, Jay's mind returned to the challenge and the threat of Jenny O'Neill.

* * *

The Fat Pheasant's front door and windows were wide open when Rachel arrived just after nine. The temperature had dropped below freezing in the night, and Molly had loaned her a red crocheted scarf, which wound twice around her neck and still reached the knees. Not very stylish, but warmth trumped fashion on a day as cold as this.

She walked into the restaurant to find the acrid smell of charred wood was still strong. The burnt cello lay in the corner, fit only for the scrap heap. Mel was standing at the top of a stepladder, unhooking the brass rings of the charred velvet curtains. She glanced over her shoulder at Rachel. 'Restaurant's closed today.' She sounded weary.

'I know,' said Rachel, moving over to the foot of the ladder and picking up the heavy weight of the curtains, making Mel's job easier. 'I thought you could use a hand.'

The look of suspicion on Mel's face was understandable. A virtual stranger was offering her unpaid help when none of the other regular staff had shown up. Who wouldn't think that odd? Though Mel might do some soul-searching and realise that the people who actually knew her didn't want to help. Maybe she could learn something from that.

Rachel wasn't even sure herself why she'd come. Not to gloat, she knew that much. The brief flare of victory she'd experienced last night had soon diminished, leaving her with the uncomfortable feeling that two wrongs didn't really make a right. She'd tried to convince herself it was Jay's actions that caused the fire, but it was ultimately down to her that they'd been using candles. Well, her and Henri – but it was Rachel who'd instigated everything. It wasn't a nice feeling.

Mel climbed down the stepladder, and they both surveyed the damage. A blackened wall and some ruined floorboards, the curtains beyond repair, and two tables that were now only fit for firewood. But it was the smell of smoke lingering in the restaurant that was the worst.

'Will you be able to fix it up in time for the reunion?' Rachel asked.

'Sod the reunion. They can hold it at the school. Without me. I'm done with organising things that nobody appreciates.'

Rachel's heart skipped a beat. If Mel decided not to go to the reunion, Jay might cancel, too. That would ruin her chance to publicly confront the bullies and those who'd just stood by, to shame them with the damage they'd done. It would be ironic if last night's revenge deprived Rachel of that opportunity. 'A school can't compare with a restaurant, though,' she said. 'And you've done so much work on the reunion already. It would be a shame not to see it through. We can fix up the restaurant in a few days.'

'I've got no chef,' Mel complained. 'Henri just phoned. He's okay and back from the hospital, but the doctor told him to take it easy, so he's going back to France.'

Rachel had already phoned Henri. The hospital had – unsurprisingly – diagnosed non-specific chest pain, and advised him to rest more, maybe take a holiday.

'Will's a great chef,' said Rachel. 'Henri says no one can

cook fish like him. I'm sure everyone will do their best for the reunion dinner.'

Mel gave her a curious look. 'Why do you care?'

Rachel had sounded too eager for a lowly kitchen assistant just passing through. 'People should stick together in a crisis, don't you think?' she said. That sounded lame, and she quickly changed the subject. 'Why don't I make us some coffee?'

'Electricity's still off,' said Mel, picking up the bundle of curtains. 'The electrician should have been here already.'

'I'll boil some water on the stove,' Rachel told her. 'Then what should I do?'

Mel moved through into the kitchen and Rachel followed. 'Box up Henri's things from the office.'

'Okay.' Rachel busied herself at the stove, filling a pan of water and measuring out the ground coffee.

Before she went back into the dining room, Mel called Rachel's name, and she glanced at her boss across the expanse of kitchen. 'Thanks.'

'You're welcome,' Rachel answered, and felt a stab of guilt.

* * *

'So that's confirmed for five-thirty on Thursday, sir.'

Jay grunted a goodbye and shut down his phone. It was done. He'd drive Jenny to the private clinic in Galway after school. Then they'd know for sure about the pregnancy. He'd have to pay cash. Mel always checked the credit card statements.

If Jenny was pregnant, the next step would be to get her to agree to an abortion. That could be tricky. The church's anti-abortion indoctrination had probably stuck. He'd plead with her, maybe even cry a bit. Remind her Catholics shouldn't divorce, so he couldn't leave Mel ... hope she wouldn't pick up on the hypocrisy of what he as a Catholic was choosing to do and not to do. And he'd tell her she shouldn't ruin her life this way. And that her family might throw her out.

Jay sat in his car in the school car park mulling over arguments for – there were no arguments against. Not as far as he was concerned. He'd learned his lesson now. This would be his first and last affair with a pupil. The risk was too high.

The bell signalling the end of break rang out across the playground. Jay left his car and strode back towards the school, keeping a wary eye out for Jenny on the way. He was avoiding her as much as possible.

* * *

'Rachel, I'm sorry but I'm closing up now.'

Daniel was standing at the entrance to the chapel. He'd agreed to let her stay on after the regular visiting hours were over, and it had been helpful to work on the murals without tourists blocking her view.

'Okay.' She packed the notebook into her bag.

They exited the chapel and walked up the side aisle.

'Will you be at the Lantern Parade this evening?' asked Daniel.

'Yes, I'm going with Finn.'

Daniel didn't say anything in response. Either he didn't approve of Finn or he was a little bit jealous of him. There was no way of knowing which it was because after they'd reached their understanding about his kiss at the party, Daniel had kept a discreet distance between them. He was courteous, but not much more.

They reached the exit, and he held the door open for her.

'Bye, Daniel,' Rachel said with a smile. As she stepped out of the church, she was startled to see Jay striding up the path towards her. What did he want? To her relief, he bypassed her without a word or a glance.

She heard him say, 'Let's go through to the office, Danny. This is important.' Then there was the clunk of the heavy oak door behind her, and the rattling of the lock and the thud of the bolts.

Rachel turned and swerved round the side of the church. She picked her way through the graveyard, pulling her camera out of her bag. If Daniel – or anyone else – saw her, she'd claim she was taking some shots of the building.

One of the windows was slightly open in the office. Rachel didn't dare peek inside in case she was seen. She took cover behind a large evergreen shrub banking the church wall. Jay had something important to tell Daniel. He was unlikely to have found out who she was, but Rachel needed to be sure.

There was silence in the office for a good five minutes or so, and then a door opened and the talking started. Rachel had to strain hard to hear but didn't dare shift position and risk giving herself away.

'What's so urgent, Jay? I've not got much time. It's the Lantern Parade tonight.'

Jay sighed. 'Another bloody boring Kilbrook tradition.'

'Tone down your language. This is a house of God.'

There was a muffled apology. 'Have you got anything to drink?'

'No, I haven't. And please don't suggest the communion wine. So, tell me, what's wrong.'

'I've got a girl into trouble, Danny.'

'Christ!' hissed Daniel. Seemed he'd forgotten he was in the house of God. 'Who is she?'

'Jenny O'Neill.'

'Sean O'Neill's daughter?'

Rachel missed the next part of the conversation because her mind was racing. Jenny O'Neill! The girl who was playing the role of Belle, Scrooge's youthful love. The one who'd got dizzy on stage last week and whose dress had had to be let out. Signs of her pregnancy. But she was just a schoolgirl …

'Sixteen,' Jay was saying. 'So she's legal.'

'Legal! She's a pupil, Jay, and you're her teacher! Do you know what you've done?'

'We were using protection. It was an accident.'

Daniel gave a harsh laugh. 'And that makes it all okay, does it? You just don't get it! Can't you see that what you've done is wrong – very wrong? What in hell possessed you? You've had affairs before, but never with a child.'

'She's not a child!' snapped Jay. 'She's a young woman. People can get married at sixteen. And she wanted it as much as I did.'

A chair scraped backwards and Daniel moved over to the window. Rachel heard him sigh, and she crouched lower behind the shrub. 'So ... what are you going to do?' Silence. 'You'll have to do the right thing. Tell her family. Support her through this. Take care of her and the child financially—'

'No.' Jay's refusal sounded final. 'I can't do that to Mel. Anyway, Jenny said she wants an abortion.'

'For the love of God ...' Daniel sounded close to despair. All of a sudden, he pulled the window closed and Rachel lost the transmission. She'd heard enough, though. Enough to make her sick to the stomach. Jay Cole was rotten through and through. He'd ensnared this poor young girl. Probably ruined her life.

She'd have to move now, so she could get back to her car before Jay left the church. Grabbing her bag, Rachel made a run for it through the churchyard, mentally apologising to the dead as her feet knocked some flowers flying.

* * *

Daniel didn't know how long he'd been praying, but his knees were aching. He'd told God everything about Jay and his predicament and begged for guidance. For a way to persuade Jay not to let Jenny O'Neill commit a mortal sin. *Thou shalt not kill.* The Catholic Church was crystal clear on abortion. It was murder. Morals might be changing in parts of Ireland, but not in Kilbrook. Jenny was from a devout Catholic family who'd be scandalised by her situation. Who might even throw her out onto the street. She was damned if she terminated the pregnancy, damned if she didn't. No young girl – no schoolgirl – should have been put in this position.

His heart heavy, Daniel stood up and left the pew, genuflecting before the altar. Perhaps God would show him the way later. He'd have to get a move on to make it to the Lantern Festival on time. As he left the church, the day was darkening, and he started his usual tour of the grounds to make sure everything was in order. Near the evergreen outside his office window, he spotted a notebook and picked it up. Rachel had a blue one just like it, and he recognised her looped handwriting as he flicked through the pages.

What was it doing here? He'd escorted Rachel out before Jay came in. She'd headed towards her car … or had she? Daniel's skin started to prickle at the thought that Rachel had … No! Why would she be listening outside his window? That made no sense. But she'd had the notebook with her in the chapel – he distinctly remembered her snapping it shut and putting it in her bag.

She must have forgotten something. Tried the front door and found it locked. Came round the back to the office, seen he had company, and left. That was it. She'd likely confirm as much when he gave her back the notebook.

Still – that office window had been open. Had she heard part of his conversation with Jay? That was a disturbing thought.

* * *

Daniel sang along with the five-year-olds as they made their way from the church towards the village square.

In the dark winter night
We shine a little light

Pupils from every primary school class were walking behind them, shepherded by teachers and helpers.

The Lantern Parade was one of Daniel's favourite events. The late Victorians had started the tradition, and in those days people had donated precious candles to the church all through the autumn months so that every child – rich or poor – would be able to carry a lantern at the parade. The lights were supposed to be a guide for the coming Christ Child. A sign of the villagers' faith. Nowadays, of course, the children carried lanterns with battery flameless candles for safety reasons, but the effect was the same. Leanne was clutching Daniel's hand and holding her lantern on a stick in the other.

'My arm hurts, Daniel,' she complained.

'Let's hold the stick together,' he suggested.

It was hard to look at Leanne and not be reminded of her father's predicament. The little one would soon have a half-brother or sister, please God. Jay was unpredictable, though, and when he wanted something, it was hard to stop him.

'Look! The Square!' squealed Leanne.

This was her first time as part of the parade and, like the others in her class, she was excited at the novelty of it all. The children would sing songs, then march with their lanterns to leave them in a special display area in the park.

The square was crowded around the edges with parents and onlookers. Leanne spotted Jay and ran to him, jumping into his arms.

'Take a picture, Daniel! Take a picture!' shouted Leanne, still clinging to her father. Jay gave Daniel a wary smile.

'Shouldn't Mel be in the picture as well?' Daniel said to Jay, looking around for her.

'Mammy's at home. She has a headache,' announced Leanne.

Daniel snapped a few shots with his camera phone. Leanne's eyes were glistening with the excited tiredness of a child up past her bedtime. Jay looked stressed. Mother absent. Not exactly a happy family shot. 'I'll send the photo to your dad,' Daniel promised Leanne.

'Children! All children over here, please!' The music teacher was clapping her hands.

'Let's get you to your classmates, Leanne,' said Daniel, and she jumped down and ran to him. 'Catch you later, Jay.'

His friend nodded, eyes still on Leanne. The reality of his lack of judgement over Jenny – and the consequences of his error – looked like they were hitting home. Good. A bit of suffering would help Jay's soul in the long term.

Once Leanne had joined her group, and the singing started, Daniel moved to the side and snapped a few shots of the children and their lanterns. Moving through the crowds to get a better angle, he spied Rachel and Finn MacKenzie sitting on the library steps watching the show. They were chatting and laughing, and looked so right together, it made Daniel's heart ache. He was a fool to have let his thoughts run away with him, but Rachel would be going back to London soon. He had only a couple more weeks of torment to endure.

They didn't see him as he approached from the side. He heard Finn do an impeccable impression of Cary Grant, and Rachel applauded. An odd choice for an impersonation. Not many in Daniel's generation watched movies with Cary Grant, or the other old Hollywood movie stars. He supposed actors were always remembered by other actors, but for some reason, it niggled.

'Hello, Rachel,' he said, and she turned round, smiling a greeting. 'What do you think of our Lantern Parade?'

'It's so beautiful. I love old traditions like this.' She turned to her companion. 'Finn, have you met Father Daniel Quinn? He's letting me study the Stokeley murals.'

'We've met,' said Daniel. 'I told him Helen did a great job with the play.'

'Finn acts too – in Australia,' said Rachel.

'Yes – I just heard your Cary Grant impersonation. Very good. Don't hear that too often these days.' He was giving Finn an ego boost, but he'd not be churlish in front of Rachel.

Surprisingly, Finn looked uncomfortable and said nothing. A sign, perhaps, that he wasn't quite the show-off Daniel had him down as. The next minute, he scrambled up. 'Just going over to the food stall. Can I get you something, Danny?'

Daniel shook his head, somewhat surprised by Finn's familiarity. 'Not for me, thanks.'

He made small talk with Rachel until he saw Finn on his way back, then he said a quick goodbye and moved off through the crowd, taking photos as he did so, but he couldn't resist turning back to look at Finn and Rachel together on the library steps. They were eating from the same stick of candyfloss, and laughing as it stuck on their faces, and Daniel was suddenly fourteen again, with memories he'd sooner forget. For a moment, he struggled to take control of jumbled thoughts. Feeling like a private detective, he took a photograph of the happy couple, and then it was like someone turned the light on in his brain. 'No,' he whispered to himself. 'It can't be.'

* * *

Finn was deep in conversation with the lighting technician from the theatre. Something about adjusting the followspots for Scrooge. Rachel's attention drifted away from their talk to the scene in front of her. A young boy from the group of schoolchildren was singing a solo about snowy winters. Would there be a white Christmas for Kilbrook? She involuntarily flinched when she caught sight of Jay Cole walking past the library steps, but he didn't turn in her direction.

As her eyes followed him, a flash of blonde hair blocked Rachel's view, and she became aware that Jenny O'Neill was following Jay at a distance, weaving her way through the spectators. Few people spared her – or Jay – a glance because their attention was focused on the choir who had begun a rousing singalong hymn. Jenny came up alongside Jay, who swerved suddenly to the right. Jenny followed him behind the library, where there was a lane for parking and not much else.

Leaning over to Finn, Rachel told him she was going to walk around and take some photos and that she'd be back in ten minutes or so. She had to raise her voice to be heard over all the singing. Finn nodded and kissed her gloved hand.

Rachel wandered along casually, snapping some shots, until she reached the spot where Jenny and Jay had vanished. Like them, she swerved to the right, thankful she wasn't wearing noisy heels. The steps to the library loomed up to her right and Rachel took them, clambering up awkwardly because she was keeping her head low. The columns running along the back of the building would make good cover, plus she'd have the advantage of height and a bird's-eye view.

Peering from behind the first column, Rachel spotted Jay and Jenny, sitting together in a car in the lane. Rachel slipped out her phone, turning down the volume, and set it up for video recording. Zooming in, she was just able to make out their faces, thanks to the streetlight nearby.

Jay was talking and Jenny was listening, head bowed. Useless. It could be a teacher giving his student advice, or a family friend having a chat. Nothing really incriminating, especially in this small village where many people knew each other and boundaries blurred. The talking went on for some time. Her battery wouldn't last much longer, and her arms were cramping. She should give it up, but then Rachel thought about Jenny. A schoolgirl, pregnant at sixteen by a teacher who'd broken the rules and who should have known better. Maybe Jenny wanted an abortion, maybe she didn't, but Jay would probably make all the decisions. Scare Jenny into doing exactly what he wanted. It wasn't fair. It wasn't right.

Just then, Jay put his arm round Jenny, pulling her in close. She turned her face up to his for a kiss, and he obliged. Not for long. They got out of the car, and Jay locked it before walking away. Jenny waited a few moments before going in the opposite direction.

Rachel was about to stop recording when Jenny suddenly

turned and started running after Jay, calling his name. He swivelled round, frowning. She reached him and threw her arms around his neck. They were much closer to her now, and Rachel could see tears on Jenny's face. Her heart went out to the girl.

Jay was kissing Jenny's face, smoothing away the tears, his manner reassuring, but his eyes were like a cat's, roaming the lane and the surrounding buildings. Rachel prayed he wouldn't spot her in the shadows, or catch the glint of her phone. She was totally exposed, and had no convincing excuse for skulking here when the action of the evening was happening behind in the main square.

Jay untangled Jenny's arms from around his neck, gave her a final kiss on the cheek, and hurried off, leaving the girl behind, tearful in the lamplight.

Rachel stopped the recording, feeling for the first time like a voyeur. This wasn't some film – it was real life. Jenny was crying like her heart would break. Rachel slipped away down the steps to give the girl some privacy.

Now she had to decide what she was going to do with the recording.

* * *

25 April
Today at the morning break, Jay asked for my maths homework in the corridor so he could copy it for the next class. Well, he didn't ask – he demanded it like he usually does. I told him I hadn't done the homework. I don't know why I did that. I must be mad. He tried to pull my bag from me but Miss Murphy was walking by and she told him to report to the headmistress at lunchtime. She made me walk with her for a bit, asking me questions about home. When class started, Mr Collins asked for the homework and I forgot what I'd told Jay earlier. I handed it in. And Jay was watching me!!! He got told off

for not doing his, and I could feel his eyes boring into the back of my head.

I sat in the library at lunchtime to avoid him. Right next to the librarian's desk, which is safest. You can't eat in the library but I don't mind going hungry because it's peaceful there. Then I pretended I had a bad headache just before mid-afternoon break, so the teacher let me go to the nurse. When the bell went, I hid in the toilets till I thought all the kids had gone.

I was taking the long way home when I heard them coming up behind me. They never go that way, so they must have been waiting for me. I ran as fast as I could but they caught me. Jay held me and Mel spat in my face. Jay looked at me like he really hated me, then punched me in the stomach. It hurt so bad I thought I would die. I fell over, and Jay pulled me up by the hair and got hold of my face and squeezed really hard. I cried all the way home. At least Jody and Danny weren't there to join in.

That's what I get for standing up to them. I thought I could ignore it all. It was possible when it was just words but now it's physical. I feel so scared. They could really hurt me. Tomorrow I won't go to school. I'll drink some salt water to make myself sick. Mam won't think I'm not ill for real because I've always liked school. Well, I used to. I'll miss the maths test but I just need a day when no one is pushing me around.

Rachel put away the diary and replayed the video recording on her phone once again. This was hard evidence of Jay and Jenny's relationship. Anyone who knew Jay could recognise him. And Jenny's distinctive hair colour was such a giveaway. She froze a shot of them kissing and sent it to her portable printer on the floor.

What should she do with the photo? She could post copies anonymously to the school, to Mel, to Jenny's parents. And then Jay Cole's world would turn upside down. She now had tremendous power over him. That would truly be revenge for everything he'd done. All the bruises he'd inflicted. But Jenny's world would turn upside down as well. Did she have the right to do that?

Rachel wished she could talk to Finn about it all. Get someone else's perspective. She didn't need to reveal Jenny's identity. Didn't even need to lie. Just say what she'd overheard from the church office. The temptation to do that was so strong. To confide in someone, but it wasn't fair to involve Finn. He was just passing through. And Helen would be living in this village for a while longer – if she got involved in bringing down Jay Cole, things could be very unpleasant for her in the future. No, this burden was Rachel's alone. She'd wait and see what happened next. Try to let Jenny know she was there for her if the girl needed someone to talk to.

Chapter Fifteen

Rachel sipped at her morning coffee in Gulliver's. Finn had just texted to say he'd be a bit late because he had to finalise some arrangements for his London trip. His agent was in England for a few days and wanted to talk over some details regarding the new TV show. Then Finn would be meeting up with some old friends. He'd be leaving this afternoon and staying in London for two nights. He'd told her all this yesterday, and looked apologetic as he said it couldn't be helped. Rachel didn't mind the agent part, but his seeing friends rankled. She had a limited amount of time to spend with Finn before he returned to Australia, and every moment was precious. Clearly he didn't see it that way. She'd almost suggested that she go with him – she lived in London after all, and she could see Sophia, which would be great. But there was too much to hide from him. It just wouldn't feel right.

The café door jangled, but it wasn't Finn. It was Daniel. Strange for him to be in here at this time. Hopefully he wouldn't stay to chat. Rachel wanted time alone with Finn.

Kelly moved up to the counter. 'Yes, Father, what can I get you?'

'Coffee and a bacon sandwich to go, please.'

When he looked over in Rachel's direction, she gave a smile and a little wave. 'Morning.'

'Good morning.'

He came over to the table. 'May I?' he asked, indicating the chair, and Rachel invited him to sit down. His sandwich would take five minutes or so to prepare and then hopefully he'd be on his way before Finn arrived.

'I don't usually see you here at breakfast time,' she said.

'Actually, I was looking for you. I phoned Molly and she told me where you were.'

'Is there something wrong?'

He pulled out her blue notebook from the plastic bag he'd laid on the chair next to her. 'I think this is yours.'

Rachel took the notebook, surprised. 'Yes, it is mine. Where did you find it?'

'Outside the church. Under the office window. I found it last night.'

Rachel almost cursed out loud. How could she have been so careless? Yesterday, outside the church, she'd taken out her camera and not closed the bag. It was open all the time she was hiding in the bushes, and the notebook must have fallen out. She'd need to improvise. 'Of course, that makes sense. I got in the car and called Finn. Then I realised I'd forgotten something. The church door was locked, so I came round the side to the office, but I heard voices. I didn't want to disturb you, so I left.' Surely she deserved an Oscar for that. She flicked through the pages of the notebook so she didn't have to look at Daniel. She didn't trust her eyes not to betray the lie. 'I'm so glad you found it. If I'd lost all these notes ...'

'What did you forget?'

'What?' She looked at him, puzzled.

'You said you were in the car and realised you'd forgotten something, so you came back. What was it?'

No easy answer came to mind. 'D'you know, I can't for the life of me remember. I must be having a senior moment. Can't have been very important, anyway.'

Daniel nodded, but his expression was closed. It was hard to know if he believed her or not. Of course he was on alert. He was worried she'd overheard his private conversation with Jay. And she hadn't anticipated that last question. The most obvious one. She'd have to be a lot more careful from now on.

Thankfully, Finn came in just then. She wouldn't have to endure any more questions from Daniel. However, Finn's smile froze in place when he saw Daniel at their table, and he gave the priest an almost surly greeting before he kissed Rachel on the cheek.

'Hi, Finn. Daniel's just waiting for his breakfast to take back to his office.'

'Oh, yeah.' Finn sat down and opened up his newspaper.

Rachel was shocked by his blatant rudeness. It was so out of character. Surely he couldn't be jealous of a parish priest?

'There's a review of *A Christmas Carol* in the local paper,' said Daniel. 'They're calling it a roaring success.'

'That's great!' said Rachel, but Finn stayed silent. What was going on?

Daniel didn't seem to register the rebuff. He kept on talking. 'Seems like we've got some real acting talent in our humble little village. Maybe some future Hollywood stars. The next Cary Grant? A new Clark Gable? Jodie Foster?'

Finn rattled the paper open to the next page. Feeling sorry for Daniel, even though he was behaving a little oddly, Rachel made small talk with him until Kelly called that his order was ready.

'Well, I must be going,' Daniel said. 'You know, Gulliver's always brings back memories for me.'

'Good ones?' asked Rachel.

'Not really. Makes me think of someone I knew. Left the village suddenly, years ago, when there was a problem.'

Rachel got the chills. Daniel's statement was very close to the bone. Gulliver's … a sudden disappearance. Had he guessed who she was? Recognised her? She couldn't help staring at him as he got up from the chair.

He turned to Finn. 'Tell Helen not to forget it's Advent this Sunday. You're very welcome to come along too, Finn. And you, Rachel. See the great unveiling. There'll be a Mass, of course. And I'm hearing confessions every day this week between two and three.'

And with that cryptic statement, he collected his coffee and sandwich and left the café. He'd used the word confession

– was he expecting Rachel to confess to him who she really was? She wouldn't do it. Not when the reunion was so close. He couldn't bully her into giving that up ... but maybe she was overreacting, looking for suspicion because she was hiding something. A bystander would find nothing odd about Daniel's conversation. If he suspected something, let him come right out and say it. She wouldn't be helping him along.

Finn was still absorbed in the newspaper. Rachel pulled it down so she could see his face. He was scowling. 'You were quite rude to him, you know.'

'I need the loo.' Finn scraped back his chair and walked off.

Whatever the problem was, it had spoiled the mood of their breakfast together. And now she wouldn't see Finn again until Friday when he was back from London. Rachel heaped two spoons of sugar into her coffee. She hadn't done that in years. Sod the calories – she needed the sugar rush to get her through the rest of the day.

* * *

Daniel sat back in the armchair in the office, and closed his eyes. He had one of his headaches. Couldn't get Rachel and Finn MacKenzie out of his mind. Confession had just ended, and only his regular parishioners had shown up. He had dangled the bait but it hadn't been taken. With a sigh, Daniel got up and went over to the desk, ready to deal with the usual paperwork, but then there was a knock at the door.

'Come in,' he called, and Finn walked in, no longer looking like the confident Aussie, but standing there like a child who'd been caught scrumping apples.

'I guess I'm too late for confession.'

'It's never too late for confession,' said Daniel, standing up and walking round the desk. He held out his hand. 'It's been a long time, Spook.'

* * *

Finn shook Daniel's hand, and then allowed himself to be grabbed into a hug. Their friendship as troubled teens had been forged out of a fear of Jay Cole, but it had actually been genuine, and Finn had missed Daniel after the incident in the church drove them apart. He missed Mrs Quinn too, because she'd looked out for him, and tried to compensate in some small way for the fact that no one else was. On visits to the happy Quinn household, he'd felt like part of the family and was able to display a very different personality to the one he had a reputation for – a personality that was hidden beneath a total lack of self-esteem and confidence.

'What gave me away?' he asked.

Daniel picked up an old photograph from his desk, and held it out. 'Group of friends on the library steps enjoying the Lantern Parade, fifteen years ago. You made yourself sick with candyfloss.'

'The candyfloss? You're in the wrong job, mate. You should have been a detective.'

Daniel laughed. 'Candyfloss, mannerisms, your eyes – when I finally saw them without the glasses. It was the Cary Grant impersonation that made me think, though. You used to do it to wind your brother up. And calling me Danny last night seemed a bit familiar – especially as you were really offhand with me when we did meet! I presume you were on edge in case I recognised you? Anyway, it all just resonated. So, what's with the mystery, Jody? Have a seat. Tea? Coffee?'

Finn shook his head, then sat down in the armchair, resting one long leg on his knee. 'I'm not Jody James anymore. I left him behind years ago when I went to Australia. I don't want him resurrected. Please.'

Daniel sat down behind the desk and nodded. 'It's like being in a parallel universe. You're so different. I don't know if I'd have recognised you without the other clues.'

'I was a mess back then. Overweight, insecure, foul-tempered. I reckon I'd have been a prime target for bullying if I hadn't been the son of a guard. Harry wouldn't have stood for anyone bullying his kids. That was *his* job.'

'What the hell did you do to yourself?' asked Daniel. 'Fairy godmother?'

Finn smiled. 'In a manner of speaking, yes. I went to Australia to visit Helen, and she was willing to take me on. Living with someone who actually cared about me made a big difference to my attitude. And I got proper meals instead of having to microwave my own. Kids in Australia can be tough on a newcomer, though. I was bullied a bit. How do you like that one? Karma. But I had people onside who encouraged me to get in shape.'

'And the name change?'

'Took up acting and decided to be someone else permanently. Took Helen's name and said goodbye to Jody James. And I *am* someone else. I don't have a history with anyone here – I'm a stranger. Helen MacKenzie's nephew. Do you know what I'm saying?'

'Yes, I do. And don't worry, I won't tell anyone who you are. Keeping secrets is part of my job. But someone else might put two and two together. How much longer do you plan to stay here?'

'Another few weeks. There's a court case coming up. My darling mother is contesting Harry's will, and she's not going to get the house if Gabe and I can do anything to stop it. She deserves nothing.'

Finn couldn't hide the deep resentment he felt towards the mother who had abandoned him. Desire for revenge wasn't healthy, but perhaps he'd be able to move on after the court had made its decision.

'What happened to you, Jod … Finn? You just disappeared after the Halloween fiasco.'

It still hurt Finn to talk about it. There were times, even now, when he would think about that night. His father's rage and the madness in his eyes as he assaulted his youngest son. Finn had been terrified and thought he was going to die.

'I ran away. Harry – I don't ever think of him as my dad anymore – beat me black and blue with a buckled belt. All over my body, except my face. He was very careful not to leave visible signs. Wouldn't have looked good on his CV. And he ripped my arm out of its socket for good measure.'

Daniel frowned. 'I'm sorry he put you through that. Although I can't say I'm surprised. He always had it in him.'

'Love and understanding was never his strongest point,' agreed Finn. 'That's why I never invited anyone back to mine. As it happened, though, it was probably the best thing he ever did for me. He thought I'd just take it, but when he was asleep, I helped myself to fifty euro and did a runner. Caught the ferry to England. Gabe took me in, like he did Cary after Harry beat him.'

'You were a right pain in the proverbial after Cary left,' Daniel told him.

'I missed him, and I never forgave Harry,' said Finn. 'Cary was all I had. Harry drove us all away. Gabe didn't want to be a guard, but Harry kept trying to push him into it. We all made the right choices though. Gabe loves Brighton, Cary travels the world as an engineer – he's in Dubai at the moment – and I'm in Oz and loving it. None of us left in Ireland. We all wanted to get as far away from our parents as we could, though my mam doesn't live so far from Gabe now – she's in London. Still waiting for Hollywood to call, probably.'

'Sounds like you've all done okay. None of you gone off the rails – a lot of kids would have in your circumstances.'

'Well, I was already off the rails,' Finn said. 'I needed to get back on them, and I did, thanks to my brothers, and Helen. Do you ever think about it, Danny, what we did? Being bullied myself brought it home. I still think about Ella. I never thought I'd come back here, but Helen needed help and when I found out about the reunion, it seemed a chance to try and make amends. Just in case Ella turns up.'

'Would *you?*' asked Daniel. 'Come back here if you were her?'

'It's a long shot, I know, but I have to try. I hope maybe she's made something of herself and will come back to show us all.'

Daniel was silent for a moment, as though absorbing what Finn had said. 'Yes, I do,' he said finally. 'Think about it. Often. It's one of the reasons I became a priest. To give something back to society. I helped make that girl's life a misery, and all because I was scared it could be me.'

Finn nodded. Daniel's eyes were saddened by the same guilt that dogged himself. 'Helen read me an article once about the human brain. It said the frontal lobe develops really late in teenagers, and that's why they can make such bad decisions.'

'I think that would be cold comfort for Ella.'

'I know. She probably still hates us.'

'Or she doesn't think about us at all. That would be the best thing.'

'It would serve us all right if she did come to the reunion,' said Finn thoughtfully. Some things needed to be atoned for.

* * *

Helen was driving Finn to Shannon Airport for his flight to London. He'd offered to take the bus, but she'd insisted on taking him herself. He was stretched out on the back seat, not because he was tired but because a car journey was easier for him if he didn't have to look at the road ahead. Finn had just finished telling Helen about his meeting with Daniel.

'Well, Daniel's discreet,' said Helen. 'As a priest, he has to be. If he says he'll keep quiet about who you are, you can rely on him. Besides, any time someone in Kilbrook asks about Jody James, I always tell them I haven't seen or heard from him in years. I think the rumour going round is that Jody landed up in prison. That actually works in your favour. Puts people off the scent.'

Jody the jailbird. Quite fitting in a way. It would seem to people that he'd finally been punished for his bad behaviour. It did pain him, though, that people had such a bad opinion of him. Maybe one day he'd be able to put the record straight. He hoped Helen was right, and that Daniel would keep his mouth shut. The only way he'd been able to bear being back in Kilbrook was because he could move around incognito. If everyone knew who he really was, he didn't think he could stand the shame. 'Daniel doesn't think Ella will come back for the reunion.'

'It's a long shot, for sure,' agreed Helen. 'If she doesn't show, we could always hire someone to find her.'

'Perhaps.' She'd suggested that before, and Finn had always resisted because he couldn't imagine telling a stranger about his embarrassing past. Discussing it all with Daniel today, though, had been difficult but also cathartic. Maybe he did need to find Ella and try to lay these ghosts to rest.

'Will you tell Rachel about Ella? About your identity?' asked Helen.

Finn gave that some thought. 'Yes – but only when we're away from Kilbrook. Away from Ireland.'

'Well, that sounds promising.' Helen was smiling.

'What does?'

'You're obviously planning to keep in touch with Rachel after you leave here.'

'Why not? I like her a lot.' A lot more than he was letting on to Helen. Perhaps he'd not tell Rachel about Ella at all. He wanted to be honest, not to have secrets, but he didn't want to lose Rachel. 'She probably thinks I'm a git after the way I behaved in the café this morning. Daniel caught me so off-guard, though. It was obvious he'd guessed who I was, and I didn't want him to bring it all up in front of Rachel. I want to be able to tell her about it in my own way. Plus I was stressing out about this trip. I'll make it up to her when I get back.'

'Do you think this trip is a good idea, Finn?' Helen asked. 'Marilyn's hurt you so much. You're vulnerable around her. Maybe it's better to keep a lid on the past.'

It wasn't the first time Helen had tried to put him off the meeting, but it was something he needed to do, whatever the risk to his sanity.

* * *

Rachel sat on the bed, staring at her open suitcase on the floor. To leave Kilbrook or stay – that was the question. Daniel's cryptic comments that morning had worried her so much that she'd come back to the house and stayed put. It was her day off work, there was no performance of *A Christmas Carol* that evening, and Finn had left for London, so Molly hadn't seemed to find it odd that Rachel was hanging around more than usual. She'd made herself useful, clearing out some junk in the attic for Molly, and all the time she'd been waiting for the phone or the doorbell to ring. The fact that it hadn't happened didn't mean she was safe. Daniel might just be biding his time. Playing cat and mouse.

How could he have found out, though? As far as she knew, she hadn't given herself away with any careless remark. Someone might have recognised her, maybe at the Lantern Parade, but then surely they would have confronted her on the spot. No reason for them to go to Daniel.

Maybe his comment about confession had been aimed at *both* Rachel and Finn. If he thought they were sleeping together, he'd want to avert them from what he saw as a sin. Rachel's references on her CV included Father Bennett from her Catholic boarding school, and Helen said she'd been to Mass a few times at St Kilian's. Daniel would therefore assume Finn and Rachel were both Catholics and needed his guidance.

That seemed like a convoluted explanation for the priest's behaviour, but it was enough to persuade Rachel that she shouldn't leave Kilbrook just yet. And she should stop skulking around the house, which could arouse suspicion. She'd go to the church tomorrow as usual, giving Daniel the chance to confront her if he wanted. She had one ace up her sleeve – he'd kissed her at his party – but she really didn't want to play that card unless it was absolutely necessary.

Rachel closed the suitcase and shoved it under the bed. She'd fight on another day. The reunion was less than a week away. Time to read another diary entry.

15 May

Today was strange. Miss Murphy asked me to get some paper from the store cupboard, and Spook was in there! He was obviously hiding, and he wasn't like he normally is. Not so cocky or aggressive. I asked him if he was okay, and he said he was, but he sounded weird, like he'd been crying, and he looked like he had, too.

I just got the paper for Miss Murphy, and as I was leaving Spook said his brother Cary had run away from home. That means he's on his own with his dad now – his mam went off ages ago, according to Father Milligan. Mr James is a guard, but everyone says he's not a nice man. Maybe that's why Spook is like he is. I sat down next to him but didn't really know what to say, so I asked why he's called Spook. Apparently, he was born on Halloween – and he hates his real name, Jody.

I thought I'd better not stay any longer in case someone came looking for me. Before I left I said I wouldn't tell anyone. He mumbled a thanks and kind of smiled at me, though he still looked sad. I don't like him, but I do feel sorry for him. He doesn't have much going for him. When he smiled, he looked different, though, like I suppose most people would. He does have nice eyes. Maybe things will be better now – even if only because he won't want me telling people he was crying in the store cupboard.

Chapter Sixteen

Rachel sat in the chapel, gazing critically at the mural of the Expulsion of Adam and Eve from Eden. Lough Corrib was part of the setting. In the painting, Stokeley had filled the lake with his own face – reflected as God's face from an unseen place above. And it was the saddest expression she'd ever seen. A parent watching his children mess up.

The archangel Michael with his sword in his hand had no mercy in his eyes, though, as he expelled the sinners. Adam was dragging Eve behind him. She was grabbing a handful of flowers to take with her as a memento from Eden. It was hard not to think of Jay and Jenny as Adam and Eve, although Jay had been responsible for Jenny's fall from grace, which made him more like the serpent.

'Tragic picture, really, isn't it?'

Rachel jumped at the sound of Daniel's voice behind her, and her notebook fell to the floor.

'Sorry, did I startle you? Here, let me.'

Daniel stooped and picked up the book, handing it to her. Rachel quickly scanned his face. He was smiling, and there seemed nothing but benevolence in his expression.

'Do you have a minute?' he said. 'I want to ask you about something.'

Rachel's mouth went dry, and her heart was thudding. This was it then. He'd found her out and was going to confront her with his evidence.

'Rachel?'

'Sorry, I was … still thinking about the mural. How can I help?'

'Come with me, and I'll show you.'

Rachel picked up her bag and followed him out of the chapel and into the back rooms of the church. He didn't lead her into the office as expected but into the room next door. It was a storeroom, packed full with stacked chairs, boxes, and church ornaments. Daniel pulled at a white sheet and uncovered a wooden statue of a kneeling Virgin Mary. Another white sheet came off and revealed the baby Jesus in a manger. Rachel stood there, dumbfounded. What did it mean?

'As you can see, the paint is very faded,' said Daniel. 'Especially on the shawl here and the swaddling. I wondered if you'd be willing to give them a touch-up. We've just had a donation of paint.'

'Me?' It was all Rachel could manage to say. Her brain was still trying to assimilate what was happening.

'Well, I heard you did a great job with the sets for *A Christmas Carol*. Who better to do it than an artist? We can pay you with a donated gift token.'

So Daniel hadn't found out who she was. She'd overreacted yesterday – big time. The relief almost brought Rachel to her knees.

'I don't want you to feel I'm taking advantage. If you're too busy …'

'I'm not too busy. I'd be happy to help, Daniel. For free. Why don't you show me the paint. And let's see what kind of brushes you have.'

She'd have painted the whole church if he'd asked. Anything to keep him on side, and her secret safe.

* * *

Jay was waiting impatiently in the clinic's car park. Why was it taking so long? He'd told Jen he couldn't go in with her in case someone they knew spotted them together. He didn't tell her he'd been to this clinic once before, a couple of years ago. That time it had been a false alarm. Perhaps his luck would hold.

Half an hour later, one glance at Jenny's strained face as she left the clinic told him his luck had just run out.

She climbed into the car. 'I'm definitely pregnant, Jay,' she blurted out, and burst into tears.

He held her close and murmured the soothing noises he used when Leanne was fretful. He no longer thought of Jen as his pouting little sexpot. She was now a noose around his neck. A mistake with a capital M. He found himself wondering if she'd miscarry. She was so young – perhaps that was a possibility. 'Jen ... Jen ...' She looked up at him with her tear-stained face. 'We need to talk about ... about options.'

'Options?'

He swallowed hard. Better get this over with. He couldn't look at her. Just stared out the windscreen at the brick wall in front of the car. That's what it felt like he was up against – a brick wall. 'Well, obviously you could have the baby, although your family would be none too happy about that. Or you could give the baby up for adoption. Or ...'

His voice tailed off and she shrugged out of his embrace, twisting round in the seat to look at him. 'Or what?'

He sighed. 'Jen, we have to talk about all the possibilities. I'm married, you're still at school. You've got a bright future ahead of you.'

'Are you talking about our baby here or my leaving certificate?' Her tone was sharper than he'd ever heard it.

'I'm saying this might not be the best time for you to have a baby.'

'You want me to go somewhere to have an abortion, don't you?' Her voice was ragged, her breathing panicky. 'You want me to kill our baby!'

She wrenched open the car door and a rush of cold air hit him hard. 'Where are you going, Jen? We have to get back.'

'I'm taking the bus.'

'No you're not.' He grabbed her arm, but she wriggled free and was out of the car before he could stop her. She slammed the car door shut with more force than he thought she had in her. By the time he'd got the car in gear and reversed out of the car park, she was nowhere in sight. He cruised up and down the streets for a while, scanning all the bus stops, but she'd just vanished. Sick to his stomach with worry, Jay headed home.

* * *

'Rachel!'

The normally unflappable Helen had worry etched across her face. The curtain was going up in less than an hour, and Rachel was organising the props table at the side of the stage. Chatter and laughter filtered through from the dressing rooms. 'What's wrong?'

'It's Jenny,' whispered Helen. 'She's drunk.'

'What!' Rachel had a brief vision of Jenny, stumbling around, telling the world she was going to have Jay's baby. 'Where is she?'

'I put her in my office, but she can't stay there. If the kids see her, there'll be gossip, and it'll get back to the parents.'

'Should I take her home?' As soon as she said it, Rachel realised that was the worst idea.

Helen was thinking along the same lines. 'Best not. Her father's got quite a temper. Jenny's mother is not coming to the show tonight because one of the younger ones is sick. I promised to take her home after the performance, so take her back to my house, Rachel.' Helen handed over her house keys. 'Get as much black coffee down her as you can manage. See if you can find out why she's drunk. And where she got the booze.'

'Bring her out the back door,' said Rachel. 'I'll have the car ready and waiting.'

Helen squeezed her arm. 'Bless you. I just knew you'd be good in a crisis.'

* * *

Finn shifted uncomfortably in his seat, aware that the blonde at the bar was, as Helen would say, giving him the eye. He looked at his watch. Gabe was never on time, not even if it was to see his brother for the first time in two years. Maybe Finn would wait outside. He gulped down the rest of his lager, but the blonde got to the table as though some sixth sense told her he was about to do a runner.

'Have you been stood up?' she asked. 'I find that hard to believe.'

Finn looked at her, feeling sick. She was hitting on him! Platinum blonde waves of hair curled around her face, her lips red and glossy, and set in what was probably intended to be a seductive pout. She looked like a cross between a fifty-something Marilyn Monroe and Barbie's grandmother. Any moment now he expected her white halter-neck dress to billow up and expose her legs. God forbid.

'No,' he mumbled, his head down. 'I'm just early.'

She moved closer to him. 'Is that an Aussie accent?' she purred. 'Lifeguard on Bondi Beach?'

Despite himself, Finn raised his head, and looked directly at the woman. She smiled at him. Did she think her luck was in? He was embarrassed, and part of him wanted to scream at her that he felt nothing but revulsion. A bigger part of him wanted to cry.

It was a huge relief when Gabe appeared, arms outstretched before engulfing Finn in a bear hug. A glimpse at the blonde told Finn she was more than a bit confused.

'Gable?' she asked. Finn couldn't remember the last time he'd heard his brother called by his full name. To all those close to him, he was just Gabe. He'd hated Gable maybe even more than Finn had hated being called Jody.

'Well done!' Gabe replied. 'That's a good guess after seventeen years.'

'You haven't changed that much,' she said, but her eyes were locked on Finn. 'Oh my God, *Jody*?' she eventually said with a gasp.

162

'Finn,' he mumbled, still feeling uncomfortable. 'I ditched the girl's name.'

* * *

'Can I buy you both a drink?' Marilyn asked.

Finn didn't attempt to prevent a sardonic snort. Marilyn looked at him, irritation obvious on her heavily made-up features. 'It's a bit late to try and be civilised, don't you think?' he asked her.

'You called *me* and asked for this meeting, remember?' Her tone was sharp, and triggered unpleasant memories from childhood for Finn.

'I'll have a Guinness,' Gabe told Marilyn. 'Finn?'

'Same,' he muttered, and stared at her as she went over to the bar. 'She's unbelievable.'

'I know how you feel, but we don't want to antagonise her,' warned Gabe.

'It won't make any difference. The woman has no conscience. If she had, we wouldn't be here.'

'We have to try. For Helen.'

Gabe was right of course. Now wasn't the time – not when they wanted Marilyn's co-operation. Maybe afterwards Finn would get the chance to tell his mother what he thought of her. *His mother*. That was a laugh. She was the woman who'd given birth to him, that was all. The woman who'd left when he was eleven years old because he was a disappointment to her. Because he wasn't a girl. That's what she'd said, and what Harry had taunted him with on the numerous occasions he'd blamed Finn for her leaving. She'd wanted a girl so badly she'd named him Jody after Jodie Foster. She'd always been obsessed with Hollywood, but at least his brothers were named after men. At least she'd given him the more masculine spelling.

Marilyn returned to the table with a tray of drinks, one of which she placed in front of Gabe. 'Guinness,' she said. 'A *man's* drink.'

Removing her own glass, she pushed the tray towards Finn, her eyes studying him for a reaction to the half-pint glass of lemonade. He'd obviously touched a nerve with his earlier comment, and she was either telling him he was childish or that he was just a kid – she might as well have bought him a bottle with a straw in it. The woman was pathetic and he wouldn't give her the satisfaction of thinking he was bothered. He held up the drink. 'Cheers.'

'So, what are you up to these days, Gable?' Marilyn asked her eldest son.

Finn shook his head. Did she have no shame, no sensitivity? Wasn't she embarrassed that she had no idea what her sons were doing with their lives?

'I'm in computers,' Gabe answered, but volunteered no further information. He'd had a mother throughout his childhood, but a lack of any bond was obvious. 'What about you?'

They knew that Marilyn was living in London now. Harry's solicitor had been obliged by law to track her down and inform her about Harry's will, and then she'd wasted no time in making a claim on the estate, but they knew nothing else about her life now.

'I get by,' she said evasively.

She hadn't been interested enough to ask what Finn was doing, but then Gabe told her, 'Finn's an actor.'

The shock in her eyes was evident, as was the envy. 'What kind of acting?' she asked.

She probably expected him to say local theatre or rep. He was going to enjoy this. 'Stage,' he told her. 'But I'm branching out. Lead role in a new TV series back in Australia.'

Now she was rattled. Marilyn was no proud mother who would shout from the rooftops her son's achievements. She'd never loved him. Now she probably hated him. Despite himself, Finn could still feel that pain of rejection eating at his gut.

'Who'd have thought it?' Marilyn mused. 'You were such an unattractive child. Now you have my looks.'

'And you'd like them back?' Finn was quick to respond, but if Marilyn heard the barb, she ignored it.

'Poor Harry was never blessed in that department,' she said.

'Nor the wife department.'

Gabe glared, and Finn didn't blame him. He may have inherited his looks from his mother, but it seemed he'd inherited a fair bit of the temper both his parents had.

'What do you know about anything?' Marilyn snapped. 'Trapped in a backwater village, when I could have been someone!'

'Well you weren't – and aren't,' Finn responded. There was no point in trying to be nice now. The damage was done. 'Stop blaming us for the fact that you messed up your own life. You didn't have to marry and have kids.'

'Believe me, if I could change the past, I would.'

Nice. She was wishing none of them had been born.

'So, if you didn't want Harry, or his kids, why do you think you're entitled to his house?' asked Gabe.

'I cooked, cleaned, slaved for that man for nearly twenty years, putting up with his moods – and his demands.' She pulled a face and shuddered. It was obvious what demands she meant. How inspiring it was to know the James brothers had been conceived from such love, and yet Marilyn's harsh words somehow brought comfort to Finn. She hadn't left because of him. She didn't care about any of them.

'My solicitor says I have a very strong claim because I'm the official next of kin. A wife takes precedence over a sister.'

'You and Harry were separated for seventeen years,' said Gabe. 'I hardly call that a strong claim.'

'Better than Helen MacKenzie's. She swanned off to Australia as soon as that theatre director snapped his fingers. She visited Harry a handful of times. Hardly the devoted sister.'

Finn couldn't help himself. 'Are you jealous because she had a career in acting and you didn't?'

Marilyn sighed and rolled her eyes. 'Don't try to psychoanalyse me.'

'I won't,' snapped Finn. 'Although perhaps someone should.'

Marilyn swivelled in her chair, turning her back on Finn and directing her attention on Gabe.

'Look, if you get Helen to agree to let me have the house, I'll make sure she doesn't go empty-handed.'

Surely she wasn't serious? Finn would sooner trust a death adder. Or maybe a black widow was more apt. Before he could say that, Gabe spoke. 'No deal. We're going to fight you. Harry wanted the house to go to Helen. It was his dying wish.'

'And then when she dies, to you, no doubt,' Marilyn scoffed. 'I doubt your motives are completely altruistic.'

'Thankfully, we haven't inherited all your traits,' snapped Finn. 'Morally, you have no right. Can't you for once in your life do the decent thing?'

Marilyn shot him a look of pure steel over her shoulder. 'Seems like you've inherited your father's traits. He was very bad-tempered.'

'And what about your temper?' snapped Finn. 'Don't get me started on that.' He could feel his anger approaching bursting point as the past flared up in front of him.

As if sensing this, Gabe took over the conversation. 'I never blamed you for leaving Harry, but why couldn't you have taken Cary and Finn with you? Cary left home because Harry battered him – and then he did the same to Finn.'

Marilyn coolly sipped her drink. 'I needed to be by myself. I'm not the maternal type. They'd have been no better off with me.'

'That's true,' muttered Finn.

'After Harry battered him,' Gabe continued, 'Finn spent

166

nearly a day travelling to me in the UK, covered in bruises, and with a dislocated shoulder. Harry ripped his arm out of its socket – a neat little trick he'd learned to disarm criminals. Don't you feel guilty about that?'

Marilyn shrugged. 'You both seem to have done okay. People have all kinds of hard luck stories, but there's no point in harping on about the past.'

'That's it?' snarled Gabe. 'That's the best you can come up with after seventeen years? Well, you're right about one thing – you're not the maternal type.'

Marilyn stood up. 'I must go. It's been ... interesting. I'll see you both again in court. Oh, and Gable – don't worry too much about Harry's wishes. He wasn't even your father.'

* * *

Jenny was crying as if it was the end of the world, and perhaps for her it felt like that. The effects of the alcohol were wearing off, and life was probably crashing back over her like a tidal wave. Rachel was out of her depth. Not a counsellor, not a parent, not a doctor. Not qualified for anything but to analyse paintings. Helen's faith in her seemed sorely misplaced.

'I don't know ... what to do,' Jenny blurted out, between hiccups. She was curled up in an armchair in Helen's living room, clasping a third cup of black coffee. Her hands, with bitten fingernails, trembled slightly. Tears had washed away her make-up, and she looked young, scared and vulnerable.

'What's wrong, Jenny? Maybe I can help.'

With the truth, though, would come responsibility. Did Rachel want that on her shoulders? Don't ask, don't tell. The coward's way, but it would make things easier.

'I'm ... pregnant,' whispered Jenny. Her eyes widened slightly, as if in surprise that she'd finally found the courage to say the words.

Rachel gave a long exhale. A line had now been crossed, and she'd just been pulled into a world of trouble. Jenny was crying again, chewing her nails. Some of the coffee slopped onto her jeans. Rachel stood up and moved across the living room. She took the coffee cup and placed it on the side table. Kneeling down next to Jenny in the armchair, Rachel asked 'Do you want this baby, Jenny?' Perhaps the abortion had already been decided. Or maybe it wasn't the pregnancy that was the issue, but whether Jay would leave Mel.

'Yes,' Jenny finally whispered. Then she covered her face with her hands and Rachel had to strain to hear her next words. 'But he doesn't ... he wants me to have an ... abortion!'

The raw emotion, the desperation in Jenny's voice, sparked anger in Rachel. Jay had used this girl. Abused his position as a teacher. Betrayed his wife. And if the past was anything to go by, he'd charm his way out of the whole thing. Everyone else would be left to pick up the pieces.

'That's why ... why ... I was drinking.' Jenny's voice was muffled in a tissue as she dried her eyes. 'To forget he doesn't want me anymore ...'

'You shouldn't have to deal with this on your own. Can't you tell your mum?'

A vehement shake of the head. 'They won't understand! Having a baby when you're not married is the worst sin ever! My da will kill me!'

Rachel tried to comfort her during another bout of weeping and wished she didn't feel so helpless. It was getting late. The play would be finishing soon and it would be time to drive Jenny home. Her face was blotched from crying – the O'Neills couldn't help but notice something was wrong. Questions would be asked. Perhaps Helen would be blamed for hiding the fact that Jenny had been drinking. Sex and alcohol – big no-no's.

'Jenny ...' Rachel had just thought of a temporary solution of sorts. 'Do you think you could talk to Father Quinn? He's a priest. If you tell it to him in confession, he has to keep it secret. But he might be able to give you advice.'

'Maybe,' whispered Jenny.

That would place a wedge between Daniel and Jay. It might even ruin their friendship. Rachel couldn't help but like Daniel in spite of what he'd done all those years ago. He'd changed, become a kinder and more caring person, but Jenny had to be the first consideration. If helping this girl put a dilemma in Daniel's way ... well, Rachel would just have to write that off as a kind of watered-down revenge.

* * *

Rachel was driving in almost total darkness, bar the beams of the car's headlights that picked out the road a few yards ahead. It was as if God had switched off all the lights. Maybe the farming community went to bed at sunset.

'It's good you're directing me, Jenny,' said Rachel, 'or I'd have surely been in a ditch by now.'

Jenny didn't respond. She sat slumped in the front seat, her flaxen hair shimmering in the gloom. Her crying bout was over, but her mind was clearly on her precarious situation – a gymslip mother with a married lover.

At last they started up the track towards the O'Neill's farm. A couple of collies ran alongside the car, barking, and Rachel prayed she wouldn't run them over. The lights were on in the farmhouse, and a door swung open. A woman hovered in the doorway and called the dogs to heel.

'You won't say anything, will you?' asked Jenny, clutching at Rachel's arm.

'Of course not, Jenny, but remember I'm here if you need me. Any time. You've got my mobile number now.'

Rachel switched off the engine, and they got out of the car. The woman moved forward from the doorway towards them. It had to be Jenny's mother, although there was little similarity. Brown hair scraped back in a bun, dowdy shapeless clothes.

'Mam, this is Rachel. She's helping out with the play.'

Rachel shook hands with Mrs O'Neill. 'Nice to meet you. You've got a very talented daughter.'

The woman smiled. 'Well, thank you. She's my treasure. Thank you for giving her a lift home.' Her treasure was slouching beside her, hands in jean pockets, looking as if she wished the ground would open up beneath her.

'Won't you come in for some tea, Rachel?' Mrs O'Neill asked.

Jenny's eyes widened and she gave a warning shake of the head at Rachel. 'Maybe some other time, Mrs O'Neill. I should be getting back ... I'll see you soon, Jenny.'

'Yup. Bye.' A brief smile and then the girl was heading inside. Rachel gave the mother a goodbye wave as she got back into the car. Moving down the driveway, the scary darkness swallowed her up again. Rachel wondered what to do. Those parents should know about Jenny's pregnancy, but the girl was no longer legally a minor and would surely resent Rachel butting into her business. There was no easy answer.

* * *

Finn had been looking forward to catching up with Gabe, having a meal and a pint or two, and generally making up for lost time. It was proving hard, though, for the brothers to talk about anything other than Marilyn. Although Finn had believed he was past being affected by his sorry excuses for parents, seeing his mother had been unsettling. Helen had been a wonderful substitute in his teenage years, but he'd never known the comfort and security of maternal love. There'd been no bedtime stories and goodnight kisses; no supportive mother encouraging him from the sidelines on Sports Day; no loving protector to shield him from his father's rages. And now, in a sense, it was like she was trying to take his brother away from him.

'Do you think she was lying about Harry not being your dad?'

'It wouldn't surprise me,' Gabe said, setting down his knife and fork. 'But if it's true, it doesn't really bother me. It's not like I was close to Harry. None of us were.'

'But aren't you curious?'

'A bit,' Gabe admitted. 'But I'm not crawling to Marilyn to find out more.'

'No,' agreed Finn. 'Don't give her that satisfaction. Helen might know, though.'

'I think she'd have mentioned it by now, don't you?'

'Well, I'll ask anyway – if that's okay with you?'

Gabe nodded. 'I hope us talking about Harry's violence won't go in our darling mother's favour. She might tell her solicitor about it. I should have kept my mouth shut. I don't want you to have a tough time in court.'

Giving evidence in court would be hard, but Finn had volunteered to do it in order to help Helen's case, and he wasn't about to back out now. 'No, I'm glad Marilyn knows what happened. What she left us to cope with. In court, I'll tell them Harry was never as bad before she left.'

They both fell silent, picking at their food.

'Let's change the subject,' said Gabe. 'You're looking good, kiddo. Proud of you. I bet you've got the girls queuing up.'

Finn thought about Rachel and smiled. 'I've met this one amazing girl. Rachel.'

'In Australia?'

'No, in Kilbrook. She's an art student. Not local – from London. I really like her. I'm Finn MacKenzie to her, though. She doesn't know I'm incognito. I just need to find the right moment to tell her about who I was and why I left.'

'If she's that amazing, she'll understand.'

'Maybe. But I don't know how she'll react when she knows what kind of kid I was. Rachel likes Finn MacKenzie, but I'm not so sure she'd like Jody James.'

'Then tell her all of it. Tell her what made you behave like that. Tell her how Marilyn neglected you before abandoning you. How Harry blamed you for her going. How you were more or less bringing yourself up and existing on junk food because Harry worked all the hours he could rather than be at home – and how when he *was* at home, he was either ignoring you or ranting. Tell her everything.'

Finn shook his head. 'I went along with bullying Ella Rinaldi, though. I don't want to make excuses.'

'They're not excuses – they're *reasons*,' said Gabe, taking a swig of his beer. 'It's no wonder you were screwed up. I've felt guilty ever since I met you off the ferry. I should have done more – should have taken you away from there before it ever got that bad.'

Gabe was a good man, and Finn had always admired his determination and strength of character, so it pained him to see the sadness on his brother's face.

'Don't blame yourself, Gabe,' he said. 'Maybe I wouldn't be who I am today if things had been different – and I like me now, which I never did before.'

'Most of the girls in this bar seem to like you now, too, you lucky sod,' Gabe said, with a smile. 'Proves my earlier point.'

Finn glanced around and saw a number of women giving him the eye. A couple of weeks ago, he might have chosen one and taken her to his hotel room. Now, he only wanted Rachel. It was a surprisingly good feeling. 'Forget the girls. It's just us – and beer – tonight, bro.'

Chapter Seventeen

Finn gulped down the black coffee like his life depended on it. He'd slept all the way on the plane from London to Shannon, and he'd had to be shaken awake by a flight attendant. Helen, bless her, had come to the airport to pick him up. She'd taken one look at him and then parked him in the nearest café, plying him with coffee.

'Sorry, Helen,' he said with a croak in his voice. 'We overdid the grog. Didn't get to bed till four.'

'Boys will be boys.' She rummaged in her handbag and brought out a packet of painkillers. 'Take two of these.'

Finn gulped the tablets down, praying they'd quickly banish that small man with a big hammer from his head.

'C'mon,' said Helen, picking up her keys and phone. 'You can crash out in the back seat.'

'I love you, Helen,' he mumbled, gratefully.

'Yes, yes, Finn. Now, ups-a-daisy. No – leave that mug. It belongs to the café.'

He trailed blindly in Helen's wake like a toddler in unfamiliar territory.

* * *

Why didn't that seagull shut up? He'd have to get up in a minute and throw something at it. The screeching continued. But ... seagulls ... in Kilbrook? God, the weather out at sea must be rough if they'd come this far inland.

As Finn opened his eyes, his first thought was that his legs had been amputated. There was no sensation there at all. Dear God, why was he sprawled in the back seat of a car? He struggled up and cricked his neck as he did so. 'Ow!'

'Oh, look who it is. Welcome back to the world.' Helen

was looking round at him from the driver's seat. A crossword puzzle was propped against the steering wheel.

'How long have I been asleep?' Finn asked, trying to massage some life back into his legs. 'And where are we – Bondi? I heard seagulls.'

He became aware of the birds flying overhead now, squawking loud enough to wake the dead. Finn looked out the window and was shocked to find they were parked near the sea. Great grey rollers were throwing up spray onto a beach. 'Did you get lost, Hel? We were aiming for Kilbrook, a small landlocked village in the west of Ireland.'

'We're in Kilrush,' she told him.

'O-kay,' he said puzzled. 'And we're here because …?'

'Marilyn's mum lives here.'

Finn felt his brain cranking slowly, slowly, slowly into gear. He vaguely remembered Gabe telling him at the hotel that morning how he'd phoned Helen and told her about their mother's throwaway remark last night. 'Marilyn told Gabe he had a different dad.'

Helen nodded. 'And that's what we're here to find out – if we can. Your gran – Marilyn's mum – might be able to tell us more about that.'

His gran. Lilian. Finn couldn't get a clear picture of her in his mind. 'I haven't seen her in years. She might be none too happy about me just turning up on her doorstep.'

'I phoned ahead,' said Helen. 'She's agreed to see us at twelve.'

'What time is it now?'

'Eleven. We can get a quick coffee from that stand over there.'

They got out and Finn almost ducked straight back into the car. It was freezing. He'd need thermal gloves if the weather continued its Arctic trend. The woollen ones he'd bought in Kilbrook market were as much use as an ashtray on a motorbike.

'How did you know where Lilian lived?' he asked.

'There was an old address in Harry's phone book. I looked there before coming to meet you. She'd moved, but a neighbour told me where to find her. And here we are.'

His grandparents hadn't been a big part of his life. There'd been trips to Kilrush to visit them when he was a kid, but Marilyn had always ended up arguing with her mother. He had a memory of a birthday party when he was eight or nine and they'd given him a new bike, but they stopped visiting after that and no one would tell him why. Later, after Marilyn left home, Harry said Marilyn's parents wanted nothing more to do with the James family.

It would be strange to see his grandmother again after all this time. Perhaps she wouldn't be that happy to see him. Nothing new there in his dysfunctional family. Still, this had to be done.

Finn glanced at his watch. 'I'd better phone Rachel. I was supposed to be meeting her for a quick coffee before her shift.' Unfortunately, Rachel's phone was switched off so he sent a text instead, hoping she'd be understanding of the sudden change of plans. He'd make it up to her later.

* * *

Rachel stared out at the frosty village square from the warmth of Gulliver's café. A group of burly young men were setting up trestle tables and booths in preparation for the opening of the outdoor Christmas Craft Fayre that afternoon.

The men were in high spirits, fooling around and laughing, their breath like plumes of smoke in the chilly air. They made Rachel feel a little less glum. She'd been worrying about Jenny, of course, but the real reason she was out of sorts was the text she'd just received from Finn, telling her he was with Helen. He hoped to be back around four when they could meet up and give the Christmas Fayre a whirl. He'd signed off with 'Miss you,' which was some compensation. She'd sent a cursory confirmation, and then felt childish for such pettiness. She certainly had it bad.

Two customers bundled into their coats and scarves and went to the till to pay. As Rachel watched them leave, a flyer on the noticeboard announcing Mel's reunion dinner caught her eye, reminding her that she was still one bully short. It was too risky to raise the topic – and perhaps the alarm – with Mel or Daniel. Perhaps Kelly would know something?

Rachel called the waitress over and ordered another cappuccino. Then she went straight for it. 'Kelly, have you ever heard of someone called Jody James?'

'Jody James? God, that's a blast from the past.' Kelly frowned. 'He's not back here, is he?'

Rachel shrugged. 'I just heard Mel mention the name to someone. I don't even know who he is.'

Kelly pulled up a chair and sat down. 'He was in Mel's year at school. My older brother was in his class. Jody was a real bully, big for his age – his nickname was Spook, and with good reason. Scary kid. Used to hang around with Jay Cole. Everyone hated them. Not a nice pair at all.'

Hated them, yet did nothing to stop them. Rachel felt as much resentment for the bystanders as she did for the bullies, but she kept an expression of mild interest glued to her face. 'You said he doesn't live here any more. What happened to him?'

Kelly scooted her chair closer. 'He got into some kind of trouble, but no one's really sure what happened. He just disappeared. His dad said he'd gone to live in England with his two brothers.' Kelly lowered her voice. 'Rumour has it he's in prison now. Which is ironic, really, because Mr James used to be the local Garda.'

'So I guess he won't be showing up for the reunion dinner,' commented Rachel.

'Hope not. We don't need his sort around here.'

The phone rang and Kelly got up to answer it. 'Helen

MacKenzie would know about Jody,' she offered as a parting shot.

'Helen? Why?' asked Rachel.

'She's his aunt. Although she says she hasn't heard from Jody in years. Garda James was her brother. That house she's living in now is the one he bought when he came back to Kilbrook a few years ago – apparently he hoped to tempt his wife back with it.'

The café seemed to start spinning as Rachel absorbed that piece of information. If Helen was Jody's aunt, Finn was his cousin. She didn't know whether to laugh or cry, but it served her right. Some stones were better left unturned.

* * *

'So how long has Lilian been in this place?' Finn asked.

The Forest Vale Nursing Home was a bit dingy, but the front windows looked out onto the sea, which had to be a plus.

'About a year,' Helen told him. 'She went downhill after she lost your grandad, and there was no one who really bothered with her. Seems Marilyn was as bad a daughter as she was a mother.'

'No inheritance for her to get her hands on, then?' Finn could hear the bitterness in his voice.

'Obviously not.'

'Ouch!' Finn jumped aside as a Zimmer frame caught him in the ankles.

The owner was a plump, white-haired woman, who looked at him with a twinkle in her eyes as she asked, 'Are you looking for me, son?'

'All my life.' Finn smiled and winked, and the old lady chuckled as she made her way over to an equally spry looking elderly man and took his arm.

'Bet she was a goer in her day,' Finn said to Helen.

Helen laughed. 'Still is, I think.'

They asked at the information desk where they could find Lilian, and a carer took them to the lounge. Card tables had been set up, and some of the residents were playing with fierce concentration. They were led over to a woman in a wheelchair sitting alone, staring out of the window at the beach.

'Hello, Lilian.' The carer touched the old lady gently on the arm. 'Your visitors are here.' Turning to Finn and Helen, she said quietly, 'I don't know if you'll get much response. Depends what mood she's in, but I'll leave you to it.'

Lilian had remained impassive, looking down at her hands and twiddling her thumbs. Finn squatted in front of his grandmother, tentatively taking hold of her hands. 'Lilian ... Gran – do you remember me? It's ... Jody. Marilyn's son.'

For a moment Lilian was unresponsive, then she lifted her head and studied Finn, who didn't feel uncomfortable under such scrutiny. He felt only compassion for this old woman, who'd been rejected the same as he had been, but at least he had his brothers and Helen – and Rachel. Lilian had nobody.

Lilian spoke. 'Jody. Her youngest. The sulky one. You've changed. You look like my Bob, when he was young.'

Lilian obviously still had all her faculties. That was a relief. Hopefully she could shed some light on the truth or not of Marilyn's bombshell about Gabe's father.

For nearly an hour, Finn and Helen listened patiently while Lilian talked about her beloved Bob. Most of the time it was as though she was talking to herself, but gradually she reacted more to Finn's and Helen's presence.

'Do I know you?' she suddenly asked Helen.

Helen shook her head. 'No, Lilian. We never met. I'm Helen, Harry's sister. I moved to Australia.'

Lilian's face clouded. 'Harry James? I knew from the start they wouldn't last, but Bob thought he would tame her a bit. She was so headstrong. All those dreams of being an actress. That's why she changed her name to Marilyn. Insisted we call her that. Got hysterical if we forgot. But there was nothing wrong with Marion – that was the name we gave her. Anyway, even when it didn't work out in London, she couldn't get them dreams of Hollywood out of her head. Harry was besotted with her, but she never loved him.'

'What happened to her in London?' asked Finn. He knew something about Marilyn's days, pre-marriage, but she always spoke of it as if she could have been The Next Big Thing if she'd stuck with it.

Lilian shook her head, disapprovingly. 'She got married over there, to an actor. We never knew anything about it until she came back home, penniless. Bob didn't want her to get a divorce – it's not right – but she said this husband beat her up and she couldn't stay with him. I didn't know whether to believe that or not. Marilyn was always a one for tall tales.'

'Do you remember the actor's name?' asked Helen. 'Her first husband.'

Lilian sat there lost in thought for a few minutes. 'It was an odd name ... Waterbury was his last name, I think ... John Waterbury ... no, that's not right ... Jonathan – or it might have been Johnson ...'

Finn barely registered that Helen was making notes. He was reeling from the news that his mother had been married before. 'Gran, Mam told Gabe that Harry wasn't his dad. Is that true?'

Lilian looked pensive. Finn guessed it was hard for her to talk about her only child in this way. Marilyn had obviously been a real disappointment to her parents.

'After she left that first husband, Marilyn went and got herself pregnant by an agent who had promised her a starring role in a film. He was lying, of course. She came back home and met Harry who talked her into marrying him to give her child a name. She was very depressed, and I suppose he seemed like a lifeline. They moved to Kilbrook after he finished his training. A fresh start for them. For a while she was grateful and tried to make the best of it. Stayed with him because she had nothing else and had lost her confidence. He wanted his own child, though, so eventually she had Cary. Then she got it in her head that she should have a girl – one she could get into stage school and all that – she could have lived the life she felt she should have had through her daughter. Became an obsession really, but she lost a couple of babies – and both were girls.'

'No wonder she was disappointed in me then,' said Finn, but he didn't feel any compassion for his mother. You shouldn't blame a child for not being the gender you wanted.

'Harry stopped me seeing you, you know. You must have been about nine, or maybe ten.' Lilian was talking again, looking at Finn now with tears in her eyes. 'Because I told him he shouldn't be so hard on you boys all the time he wouldn't let me come to visit anymore. Or phone. I sent birthday cards, but you probably never got them. Then I got a letter from him a couple of years later, telling me your mammy had left. He said it was best if we stayed out of your lives because it made you think about her, and then you'd get upset. I didn't know what to do for the best, then Bob became ill, and I couldn't put him through the stress. I wrote you all a letter, you know – ten years or so ago – telling you we loved you and that we'd always be there for you, but I never got any reply.'

'Harry had moved away from Kilbrook by then,' Helen said. 'After Finn left home, he sold up and moved to Galway. More recently, he moved back to Kilbrook, but to a different house.'

It occurred to Finn that neither he nor Helen had told Lilian that Harry had passed on. Perhaps now wasn't the right time for that. Finn took Lilian's hand and stroked it. 'When did you last see Mam?'

'A few months after I wrote you boys the letter. I thought she might be able to intervene with Harry. Reconcile with him even. She'd gone to London again. I kept pushing Bob to track her down. I wish I hadn't.' Lilian shook her head and lowered her voice. 'We found out she was one of them … escorts. It's just a fancy name for a … prostitute, you know. Bob and I were so shocked. We asked about you boys, but she said she'd cut all ties. And that was that. Bob said we weren't to be in touch with her again. That we had each other, and that would have to be enough.' She was crying now. 'Still – I did miss my grandsons.'

So his grandparents hadn't just abandoned Finn and his brothers. That was something of a revelation, and Finn held his grandmother in his arms, trying to soothe her.

* * *

'Well, that was … disturbing,' said Helen.

They were driving back to Kilbrook, and Finn wasn't sure whether he was more shocked about the fact his mother had been married before to a man who had long since disappeared from the scene, or that afterwards she'd worked as an escort. Maybe she was still doing that in London. Most of all, though, he was angry that he'd been deprived of his grandparents. His feelings about Harry and Marilyn James were now truly at rock bottom.

'I wonder if we could track down this Waterbury guy.'

'Why would we do that?' Helen asked.

'He might have some information that could help our case, sway a judge against her. And maybe he'll know the name of that agent – Gabe's real father.'

Helen sounded doubtful. 'I don't know, love. Perhaps it's better not to dig too much into the past.'

'But her barrister will attack us, Hel.'

'Then don't take the stand, Finn. I never really wanted you to do it, anyway. It's not fair on you.'

'No, I'm giving evidence. I'm not afraid of Marilyn. We have to fight her. I'll phone Gabe and update him. See what he thinks we should do.'

'Sounds like a good idea.' Helen glanced across at Finn.

'Anyway, Lilian was happy to see you. Will you stay in touch?'

'I'll make sure I go there again before I leave. Then I'll write and phone,' Finn agreed. 'And get Gabe and Cary to come and visit. She'd love to see them – and her great grandkids, I'm sure.'

'Good lad.'

For much of the way back to Kilbrook, Finn thought about the meeting with Lilian. No matter how much he tried to be stoical, it hurt that he'd never had the security parents should provide, that his father had never played football with him, that there had never been family days out, that he'd missed out on being the pampered youngest child, that he'd never been loved by the two people who brought him into the world. He was fine if he didn't think about any of these things – he'd learned to be grateful for what he had – but when he was confronted by the reality of his childhood, it cut deep. Now, though, there was an element of contentment he wasn't used to. He'd found his grandmother, and she cared.

* * *

It was after three when Jenny O'Neill knocked at the door of the church office. Daniel had begun wrestling with his weekly sermon and would normally have welcomed any interruption. However, one look at Jenny's haunted expression awakened intense feelings of guilt. He'd known of her affair with Jay – and the pregnancy – and done nothing constructive about it, except to metaphorically slap Jay's wrists. A desire not to rock the boat too much had won out over action.

'Do you have a minute, Father?'

He forced his voice to sound normal as he said, 'How can I help, Jenny?'

'I need you to hear my confession.' Her cheeks were flushed, and her fists were clenching and unclenching.

It had always been a possibility that Jenny would confess

her condition – he could see that now – yet for some reason Daniel hadn't prepared himself for it. There was no way he could deny her request, though. 'Okay, Jenny. Go into the confessional and wait. I'll be there in a few minutes.'

When she left the office, Daniel closed his eyes and tried to clear his mind. Once in the confessional, he became God's representative. A priest through and through. No longer Daniel Quinn, son, brother, reluctant friend of Jay Cole. His sole purpose was to help a penitent reconcile with God. It sounded so simple, but in reality it was the most complicated and emotionally exhausting part of his job. The whole course of someone's life could change because of the words he would say.

The irony of it all was that it should be Jay begging for forgiveness, not Jenny. But Jay hadn't confessed his sins since schooldays, and even then he'd boasted that he'd lied through his teeth. Jay's conscience had been asleep for a long time.

Slowly, with a heavy heart, Daniel left the office.

* * *

'Bless me, Father, for I have sinned. It's been a while since ...' Jenny's voice tailed off, and Daniel heard the telltale sniff of tears.

The familiar wave of claustrophobia washed over him, something he'd never been able to shake. The confessional reminded him of a coffin. The Freudians would have a field day with that, no doubt. He shifted slightly on his stool and waited. After a minute, he spoke into the gloom. 'What is it, my child?' He never used names in confession to preserve the impression of anonymity, although he knew the voices of many of his flock. 'Share with God what's troubling you. He is always merciful to those who repent.'

The silence continued. This clearly wasn't going to work. He'd have to take Jenny back into the office, give her some tea ...

There was a shuffling on the prie-dieu kneeler in the other booth. Out of the corner of his eye, Daniel saw the outline of Jenny's head coming closer to the grille that separated them. She whispered, but he heard the words clearly enough. 'I'm ... going to have ... a baby.'

How many other priests had been in this situation? Probably hundreds of thousands over the centuries of church history. Condemning the sin, chastising the unwed mothers, hearing their act of contrition, counselling them about their next steps. It was the first time in conservative Kilbrook that Daniel had had to do this, but it likely wouldn't be the last. He struggled to remember his pastoral training. 'Do you know for sure? Have you seen a doctor?'

'Yes,' whispered Jenny.

'Have you told your parents?'

'No!' The word came out like a small moan of pain. 'They'd kill me.'

From what he knew of Sean O'Neill, Jenny wasn't far wrong. The man was a relic from the dark ages. Still, her mother was a kindly soul, and Jenny would need her support to get through this. 'I can come with you, if you like, to help you tell your parents.'

'I can't tell them,' insisted Jenny, her voice fearful.

'You're very young. You can't go through this on your own.'

The silence returned, and he hoped Jenny was seriously considering his advice.

'What if I have an abortion?'

Daniel sighed and passed his hand over his eyes. When he spoke, his tone was firm. 'Every human life is sacred in God's eyes, and that includes the life of your unborn child. If you have an abortion, you commit a mortal sin. A mortal sin is like turning your face away from God. If you die unrepentant of that sin, you'll be shut out forever from God's grace. And that's a terrible thing.' Although it did have its shock value, he couldn't bring himself to use the word hell.

'The baby's father wants me to have an abortion,' said Jenny, choking on the final word.

There was no way to avoid the next question, although she might not answer it. 'Who is the father?'

'Jay Cole.' The name seemed to echo around the two booths, and Daniel's claustrophobia suddenly got much worse. At least he was bound by the confidentiality of the confessional. He didn't have to share what Jenny had revealed to him with anyone. He didn't have to be the one to blow the whistle.

'I know you're friends,' Jenny continued. 'I wondered ... Father, could you talk to him for me? See if you can change his mind. He loves me, you know, not his wife. He's always said so.'

That was an impossible hope. Cruel of Jay to let her believe he would leave Mel and Leanne. Jenny was poor, Mel was rich – end of story.

'Father?'

'I will talk to him – as your priest, not as his friend. But you really need to think about telling your parents. Remember, I can be there with you when you do.'

'Okay.'

Her voice was so trusting it made Daniel's heart ache. How sordid this whole thing was. Anger flared again at Jay's irresponsible actions. 'I can also give you the name and phone number of a counselling service. Everything you say to them will be confidential.'

After Jenny had prayed the act of contrition and received her penance, Daniel said the words of absolution, and back in the office he gave her the details of the counselling service.

'Take care of yourself, Jenny. You can come and talk to me any time.'

'Thank you, Father.'

She left, and he heard the heels of this child-woman clicking along the wooden floor of the side aisle, then the heavy entrance door clunked shut behind her. Daniel put his head in his hands. Perhaps he needed to rethink his vocation.

* * *

'Hello, you.'

Strong arms enfolded Rachel from behind, and she smelled Finn's now-familiar musky aftershave. Instinctively, she smiled to herself and grabbed hold of the hands around her waist, as Finn nuzzled her neck.

People milled past them, more focused on the Christmas Fayre stalls than the lovers in their midst. Daylight was fading, and the old-fashioned lamp posts cast patches of gold onto the village square. Carol singers in Victorian dress started a rendition of 'God Rest Ye, Merry Gentlemen'.

'It looks like a Christmas card,' Finn commented, close to her ear.

It really did. And it would all have been so perfect but for Kelly's bombshell about Jody James. Rachel had thought about little else all day.

She turned round to face Finn, still encircled by his arms. He pulled her in closer and gave her the sweetest, most sensual kiss, which there was no way she could resist. When they came up for air, he said, 'Missed you.'

He meant it, she could see that, and all the half-baked notions she'd had about digging for information on his cousin Jody suddenly seemed pointless. She was in love with Finn, way past the point of return. And he wasn't his cousin's keeper. Finn was Australian. Probably didn't know Jody that well, if at all. He wasn't a blood relative, and she shouldn't taint him by association. Rachel realised with a start that Jody James was about to get a free pass, to catch a lucky break from a victim's revenge. All because she couldn't risk losing Finn. And yet that wasn't really fair ...

'Hey – what's wrong?' Finn tilted her chin up and she felt a tear roll down her cheek. Rachel buried her face in his jumper, afraid of what her eyes might reveal, despite the gathering darkness. He stroked her hair, gently, and waited.

When she was sure the tearfulness had passed, Rachel raised her head and attempted a smile. 'I missed you so much.'

'Maybe I should go away more often,' he quipped. 'That way you'll turn a blind eye to my many faults.'

'I don't want you to go away – ever.' Her voice held an urgency that surprised her. And it must have surprised Finn because he became serious again, stroking her cheek. 'Sorry,' she murmured. 'Christmas is a bad time for me. I always get over-emotional.'

'Well, we can't have that,' he said decisively. 'Christmas should be fun. Silly songs and tinsel and sausage rolls. Now – Helen's out tonight. You're coming home with me. I'll cook. A great big steak is what's needed here to banish the winter blues. What d'you say?'

She smiled her agreement, and the spectre of Jody James was banished temporarily to the darkness.

'Why don't you go to that cake stall over there, and buy us some treats,' Finn suggested. 'I'll meet you back here in ten minutes. I just want to pick up a Christmas present for Helen.'

He kissed the tip of her nose and then disappeared into the throng of shoppers. Rachel's imagination raced forward through time to all the Christmases she and Finn would share – as newly-weds, proud parents, doting grandparents. She'd never wanted anything so badly in her whole life, and never been less certain that she would get it.

* * *

Finn tasted the Béarnaise sauce and added more pepper. A sauce could make or break a steak, so it needed careful watching and stirring. He wanted to impress Rachel with his cooking skills. Make her realise what a good value package he was. Although perhaps there was no need to impress. That look in her eyes in the village square had been quite a shock. There was desire there, but love, too, and he guessed she was feeling vulnerable because of that. They'd only known each other for a short while and they lived in different countries. On paper, it wouldn't look like an obvious match.

'Did Helen teach you how to cook?' Rachel was seated at the kitchen counter, watching him. The bottle of burgundy they were sharing had seemed to relax her.

'Helen? No way. I love her to bits, but she's a disaster in the kitchen. Can't even boil an egg. I learned from cooking shows.'

And ex-girlfriends. Best not to mention them, though, when Rachel was feeling so fragile. He checked on the roast potatoes and started to baste the steaks.

'How was your relative? The one you saw this morning,' asked Rachel.

'Seventy-six and in a wheelchair, bless her. She doesn't get many visitors.'

The radio started blaring out a breezy Christmas tune, and Rachel leaned over and turned it down. Her expression was grim. This girl had a serious hang-up about Christmas.

'I didn't visit my mum much, either,' she said quietly. 'A few times a year at best.'

Finn moved the steaks aside and sat down opposite Rachel. 'Why not?'

She stared down at the counter, pushed her glass of wine away. 'She was an alcoholic.'

Finn waited, not wanting to push her with intrusive questions.

'My dad died when I was ten. A workplace accident. His fault, they said, so we never got any compensation. Money was tight, but Mum did her best. Then my sister died – she was really unwell. I think that's what finally tipped Mum over the edge.'

He wanted to reach out and hold her hand but realised his

own hands were wet with spices and meat juice. 'I'm so sorry, Rachel. How bad did her drinking get?'

Her voice when she spoke was hollow, flat, as if she were reciting someone else's story. 'I'd find vodka bottles stashed around the flat. In the airing cupboard, under the sink, in her boots. I'd pour them down the sink when I found them, but she wised up to that. She started decanting the stuff into water bottles which she carried around with her.'

'But you said she was hard up. How did she get the money for booze?'

'My uncle was helping us out financially. She hid the problem really well for a while. Was always sober when we went to visit him ...' Her eyes met Finn's, but they were unseeing. She was back in the past, reliving a nightmare. 'Once, just before Christmas, I came home and found her passed out in the kitchen. I couldn't wake her. Had to call an ambulance. She almost died from alcohol poisoning. When my uncle found out, he sent me off to boarding school with my cousin, and got Mum into rehab.'

'You poor thing ...'

'No!' Rachel shook her head, vehemently. 'Don't feel sorry for me, Finn. I had four great years at boarding school, and my uncle paid for my university education. I was lucky, but my mum spent the rest of her life in misery, just waiting for the moments she could get her hands on some alcohol to make her forget. No one could help her because no one could bring my sister back. Do you see that?'

He nodded. 'I do. But it's still very sad.'

'She died a year ago. Cirrhosis of the liver. She was fifty-eight. I was with her in the hospital when she passed. The last word she said was my sister's name ...'

Finn wished they'd known each other then. He'd have gone with Rachel to the hospital, been a shoulder for her to cry on.

'Everyone assumed I'd feel guilty after she died because I didn't visit much. But guilt is such a useless emotion. She didn't want me, she wanted my sister. I was just a reminder of what she'd lost. And she felt ashamed when I visited and knew she'd been drinking. She just wanted to be left alone with her memories.'

The torrent of words stopped. Rachel looked over at Finn, and this time her eyes were clear. 'Finn, I'm so sorry. Dumping all this on you. I've ruined our evening.'

He shook his head. 'You haven't ruined anything. I'm glad you trust me enough to share such sad memories. I want to know everything about you.'

Her cheeks reddened, and she glanced down at the counter. 'Maybe some things are best left unshared ...'

Maybe. Finn *would* tell Rachel about his past, though. Once they were free of Kilbrook – when she was in Australia with him, or he was in London with her. Someone was going to have to change location in the future – and he'd do it if he had to – because this was a relationship too good to lose.

'I'll just go and freshen up,' said Rachel, slipping off the stool and leaving the kitchen.

Finn drank deeply from his wine glass, already planning how to tell Rachel about the bully he'd been, the pain he'd inflicted on a young girl, and the regret that had haunted him for years.

* * *

Daniel had been waiting in the rectory living room for the last half-hour. He'd left a message on Jay's mobile, telling him to come round this evening or else Daniel would show up at his house. It was unlikely Jay would risk that. Mel would be curious because Jay and Daniel usually met here at the rectory, or in the pub.

The doorbell finally rang – a long, angry buzz that jangled Daniel's nerves. Gulping down the remainder of his brandy, he went into the hallway and opened the door. Jay stood there, scowling. This wasn't going to be easy. 'Come on in.'

The cold night air accompanied Jay into the hall. The temperature outside had barely risen above freezing all day, and snow was forecast. 'Take your coat?' offered Daniel, but Jay shook his head. He could sulk for Ireland when he wanted to.

They went through into the living room. Jay slumped into an armchair, and folded his arms, a visible barrier against Daniel and whatever he might be going to suggest.

'Do you want a drink?'

Jay glared at him. 'Let's cut the small talk, shall we? I don't appreciate being threatened. Stop hassling me about Jenny O'Neill. She's my problem, not yours.'

'She's not a problem – she's a sixteen-year-old schoolgirl who's pregnant.'

'I know that!' snapped Jay. 'Stop stating the obvious. I'll deal with it.'

'How? By forcing her to have an abortion?' Daniel's anger was bubbling to the surface.

Jay stood up. 'I'm not going to have this argument again.'

'Okay, okay.' Daniel made a placatory gesture. 'Sit back down … Please.' The word almost choked him, but at least Jay took his seat again. Daniel stood with his back to the fire. 'Sooner or later, Jay, Jenny is going to come to me for confession. And she might ask me to help tell her parents about the baby.' He widened his eyes and nodded, willing Jay to understand he wasn't talking in hypotheticals. He couldn't break the confidentiality of the confessional, but his friend needed to understand how close he was to disaster.

Jay stared back at him, his hostile look gradually changing to a thoughtful expression. 'Well, if Jenny won't have an abortion … perhaps I could set her up in a flat far away from here. Give her some money to take care of the kid …'

That was an improvement, for sure, but still fraught with complications. 'That could be quite an outlay. Do you have savings?' Daniel asked.

Jay shook his head, then said, 'I don't suppose you could loan me some money?'

'I don't have any savings, either. I'm just a poor parish priest. Could you get a bank loan?'

'Maybe ...'

Neither of them suggested asking Mel for money. She'd likely want to know what it was for, and then just as likely refuse to give it. And who could blame her. There were few women who would support their husband's illegitimate child. The more Daniel thought about it, the more the whole scheme seemed crazy. Sean O'Neill would complicate things, for a start. 'Jay—'

'I've got to go. Don't worry about this anymore, okay? I'll sort it out.'

Jay gave the ghost of a smile, then turned on his heel and left the room. He was out of the house before Daniel even made it into the hallway. Had he helped, or just made things worse? Hard to know. The thought of being part of a cover-up didn't sit well with him, though. His teenage years had been blighted by the secrets and lies surrounding Ella Rinaldi. He was experiencing the same feelings of guilt now.

He sat down on the stairs and said a quick prayer.

* * *

Rachel lay wrapped in Finn's arms, her head close to his chest. His heart rate was slowing, and he gave a deep sigh that she knew was contentment.

They'd started kissing on the sofa after they'd finished their meal, but when Finn had tried to ease her jumper off, Rachel told him she didn't want Helen to walk in on them, so Finn had led her upstairs to his room.

There'd been a new urgency to his lovemaking, an intensity that reassured Rachel he hadn't been put off by her revelations in the kitchen. Intimacy was always such a risk. Not the intimacy of being naked in front of each other, but the greater exposure of sharing your weaknesses and failings.

'Well,' murmured Finn, 'I never thought heaven would be found in a cramped bedroom with shabby green curtains. Life is full of surprises.'

His words seemed to fill the room with a tender, glowing warmth. Rachel leaned up and kissed his neck and chin, reaching out for his hand, laying it across his chest so their fingers could entwine.

Finn suddenly pulled his hand free and sat up, swinging his legs over the side of the bed.

'What's wrong?' she whispered.

'Nothing.' His voice was muffled because he was bending over, rummaging around in his bag. He lay back on the bed, facing her, his expression gentle, still happy. He handed her a box. 'I was saving this till Christmas, but I want you to have it now.'

She opened the box. Inside was a Claddagh pendant, hanging from a delicate silver chain. 'Oh, Finn, it's beautiful!'

'I bought it today in the market. When I sent you off for cakes.'

'Well, aren't you the devious one?' She reached over and kissed him. 'Thank you so much.'

'Try it on. Sit up and I'll fasten the clasp for you.'

He moved her hair gently over one shoulder, then draped the necklace. The cold metal made her skin tingle, contrasting with the warmth of his fingers, brushing her neck as he secured the clasp. 'Turn around,' he murmured.

She did so, and he looked at the necklace appreciatively. Then his glance swept down her body. 'Perfect ... and the necklace looks pretty good, too.'

She smiled, and they moved together into an embrace. Later, as she leaned over Finn, the necklace caressed his cheek, a visible token of love on his beautiful face.

Chapter Eighteen

'You need to move them higher,' Mel said from the base of the ladder.

Jay resisted the urge to wrap the party lights around Mel's neck. He was giving up an hour of his free time on a Saturday to help decorate the restaurant for the reunion on Tuesday, and all she could do was point out what he was doing wrong. Some people were never satisfied.

Mel set down a tray on one of the restaurant tables, and started filling the two cups. 'I've made some tea.'

'Thanks.' Jay abandoned the lights for now and descended the ladder. He wiped his hands on a cloth, and sat next to her, not directly opposite. He didn't want Mel to have a clear view of his eyes.

'I want this place to look amazing on Tuesday,' said Mel, sipping her tea. 'It'll be a reunion to remember.'

Jay wasn't looking forward to it. Didn't see the point. They'd kept up with the people who mattered. Everyone else from their class was irrelevant. Making boring small talk for a whole evening wasn't his idea of fun. Still, Mel would serve some good wine. He could get quietly pissed in a corner, then take off after a couple of hours. And Spook might surprise them all and show up. It would be good to catch up with him ... good to see someone who had always been on Jay's side. Even if it was because he was too scared to be anything else.

'What about a new chef?' he asked Mel. 'Found one yet?'

'The agency in Galway has shortlisted some candidates. I'm interviewing next week.'

The conversation petered out. Did all marriages reach this mundane stage? Nothing left to talk about but work and day-to-day trivia. Still, at least they were companionable today. He was helping her out with the lights. Perhaps she'd feel grateful enough to help him out. 'Mel, I need to ask a favour.'

Out of the corner of his eye, he saw her turn to look at him. 'Is it money?' she asked.

'Yes, it is. I need a loan. For Dad. He's got himself in over his head with a few investments. He's been worried sick. I had to force it out of him. He's too ashamed to ask you for help himself.' She'd believe the lie because he'd already shared with her his father's chronic mishandling of money.

'I see.'

Jay cast a nervous sidelong glance at Mel's face. She was frowning, staring down at the table. 'I hate to ask, Mel, but when it's family ...'

'How much does he need?'

How much could he safely ask for? 'About twenty thousand.' He'd never asked for that much before, but it was surely a drop in the ocean for the Maguires. Jay had never really known Mel's true financial worth. It had never been an issue. If he wanted something, most of the time she got it for him. Hopefully, his luck would hold. It seemed like an eternity before Mel finally gave an answer.

'I'll check with the bank. See what the contingency fund's like.'

'Thank you so much.' He leaned over and kissed her cheek. 'And I'd appreciate it if you didn't mention it to him ... to Dad.'

She gave a brief smile, then stood up. 'I'd better get back to the office.'

Jay fixed the lights in record time. It was almost ten. He'd call Jenny and arrange to meet her. He'd push for the abortion one last time, then if necessary switch to Plan B.

* * *

Jay waited impatiently on Bracken Hill. Mel thought he was meeting a fellow teacher. She'd be taking Leanne to the ice rink, so the coast was clear. With any luck, all this skulking around would be over soon. He'd take a break from extra-marital affairs for a while. Play the happy family man. Protect and shore up the comfortable life he had.

Ten minutes later, Jenny appeared on the summit of the hill. Her cheeks were flushed and her breathing laboured. She was pregnant, and all that climbing probably wasn't good for her, though maybe … he couldn't help thinking how much easier it would be if Jenny lost the baby naturally. He spread out the blanket on the ground and urged her to sit down, but she shook her head.

'I can't stay long.'

Her expression was wary, and she kept her distance. They hadn't spoken since that day outside the clinic, when he'd suggested the abortion. 'How've you been, Jenny?'

She shrugged, hands stuffed deep in her pockets. 'I'm not going to have an abortion, if that's what you've come to ask.'

There was a firmness in her voice that told him her mind was made up. Plan B it was then.

'I know that's not what you want.' Jay made his tone calm, reasonable, soothing – the exact opposite of what he was feeling. He deserved an Oscar. 'So I'm going to take care of you and the baby.'

Jenny's expression softened, and she moved closer. 'I knew you meant it when you said you loved me.'

She reached out her hands, encased in childlike mittens, and he pulled her close. 'I'll sort something out. Rent you a flat. A childminder can take care of the baby while you take some acting classes.'

It would work out, he knew it. She'd meet some arty type, or some well-off director later; she'd get married, and he'd be off the hook. Might not even have to send her any child support.

'When are you going to tell Mel?'

Jay froze, alarm bells ringing at the question. 'We don't need to tell Mel. We can sort this out ourselves.'

'I think she'll notice, Jay, when you move out.'

She'd got it all wrong. Assumed he'd be living with her. 'I can't leave Mel, Jen,' he said carefully. 'There's Leanne to think about ...'

'What about *our* baby?' Jenny wrenched her hands free, and he was left holding one pink mitten. He stared at her bare hand, clenched into a fist.

'I'll visit you. You'll want for nothing. I promise you.'

She stared at him, tears glinting in her eyes. 'But I won't have you.'

'Jenny ...' He moved towards her, but she turned on her heel and ran through the trees. He heard her feet crunching through the undergrowth, and then the sound faded away, leaving him alone on the hill.

Jay stared down at the mitten in his hand, stroked it gently for a second, then stuffed it in his coat pocket. When she'd had time to reflect, Jenny might rethink his offer. After all, it was a chance to get away from her father and the farm, to train as an actress. Hopefully Mel would come through with the money. If not, things could get very ugly – he would lie and deny everything, but of course now they had those wretched DNA tests.

God, he needed a drink. And this was the last time he'd ever come to this bloody hill, the scene of his potential downfall. He headed back the way he'd come, noticing for the first time the leaden sky. They'd been forecasting snow, a rare occurrence in Kilbrook. He'd make snow angels with Leanne, reassure Mel he was a good father, a good husband.

* * *

Mel drove further along the road which curved round Bracken Hill and parked in a side lane under the cover of some trees, not wanting Jay to catch sight of her car. She'd followed him here to Bracken Hill and watched him climb the slope to the top. It was something he liked to do for exercise, so perhaps she was here on a wild goose chase. Perhaps she was being foolish, skulking around the back lanes, spying on her husband, but Jay had never asked for that much money before. There was something in his voice and the way he avoided looking directly at her that had activated her intuition. Something was wrong here.

Movement at the top of the hill caught her attention, but the figure running down the hill, arms out to the side for balance, was definitely not Jay. Mel saw the glint of light blonde hair and knew at once it was Jenny O'Neill. The farmer's daughter. She was in the school play – Scrooge's long-ago love. Mel had heard people in the audience commenting how beautiful the girl was, with that distinctive hair colour.

She *was* beautiful. She was also just a schoolgirl. Dear God, was Jay cradle-robbing now? She couldn't see Jay. For a brief moment, she told herself it was just in her imagination. But her gut told her it wasn't. It was woman's intuition, not paranoia. Jay was messing around with a pupil. He could get fired for that. And Jenny O'Neill's father was a violent man. He'd once shot a poacher with pellets and served two weeks in jail. If he found out about Jay and Jenny, he might come round to the house or the restaurant, waving his gun.

The biggest fear of all, though, was that this young beauty was exactly the kind of girl married men might leave their wives for.

Mel sank her head down onto the steering wheel and let the tears come.

* * *

They were decorating the fir tree that grew in the village square. A man in a bucket truck was carefully wrapping a garland of lights around a tall pine tree while a group of children waited at the base, clutching red ribbons and plastic snowflakes. Those were Rachel's favourite Christmas colours – snow-white and heart-red and green-pine.

She touched the Claddagh pendant around her neck. She hadn't taken it off once – not when she went to bed, not even when she showered. It was a hope that Finn would stay true to her, even when he found out what she planned to do. He'd been bullied himself in Australia, so there was a chance he would sympathise. She didn't need him to condone her revenge – just to understand why she was doing it and to forgive her.

Rachel glanced at her watch. Almost eleven. Finn would be here soon for a quick coffee before her shift. It had become a habit between them. She'd already spent an hour on her research in the church, and after work they were meeting Helen for a late lunch in Donegan's before going to the theatre to prepare for the evening's show. The last performance of *A Christmas Carol* would be on Wednesday, the day after the reunion dinner. A big wrap party had been planned, but Rachel might not be welcome after she'd revealed her identity. Unless Kilbrook had grown a heart since she'd last lived here.

The café door jangled open and Rachel glanced over, expecting to see Finn, but it was Jenny. Face flushed, long hair tangled, looking like the sky had just fallen. She ordered a tea at the counter, and turned with her drink to find a seat. Rachel caught her eye and smiled, indicating the empty chair next to her. Perhaps that was a mistake – Jenny might prefer to be alone with her problems – but the girl came and sat down at Rachel's table. Hunched into her jacket, she stared out at the crowds in the square.

'How are you, Jenny? I've been worried about you.'

'I'm fine,' Jenny replied, with a sigh. A sigh of misery not frustration. 'Will you tell Helen I can't do the play tonight?'

'Okay … are you not feeling up to it?'

'I'm telling my parents today,' whispered Jenny, and took a quick sip of tea. 'About the … you know …'

'Oh. When?'

Jenny glanced at her watch. 'Soon … Father Quinn's coming with me.'

So Jenny *had* spoken to Daniel, and he'd agreed to help. That must have hurt him – the choice between a parishioner and Jay, his friend. Rachel regained some respect for Daniel, but when Jenny said she wasn't going to reveal the identity of the baby's father, Rachel couldn't help asking if that had been Daniel's advice.

Jenny shook her head. 'It's just ...'

The café door opened, and suddenly Finn was there, leaning down to kiss Rachel's cheek, saying hello to Jenny, asking if they wanted another drink. As soon as Finn went to the counter to order, Jenny scuttled out. Rachel watched her cross the square and stop for a moment to stare up at the Christmas tree, which had just been crowned with its star of Bethlehem. Her face briefly showed the wonder of a child, but was quickly replaced by the worried frown of a young girl about to grow up too fast.

'Something I said?' Finn set down his mug and glanced at the now empty chair.

Rachel smiled and shook her head. 'She's not feeling well. She won't be at the performance tonight.'

It was ironic that Jenny's real life contained even more drama than what took place in the theatre.

* * *

The frenzied barking of the farm dogs heralded Daniel's arrival so effectively that Susan O'Neill had already opened the front door of the farmhouse before he had switched off the car's engine. No chance to back out now. Unless Jenny changed her mind at the last minute, which was a possibility. She would know, though, that she couldn't postpone the revelation indefinitely. The truth would have to come out eventually.

Susan's expression was that familiar combination of anxiety and exhaustion. Daniel didn't think he'd ever seen her smile. Of course, marriage to Sean O'Neill could hardly be a bed of roses – she'd hinted as much in the confessional but always stopped short of outright disloyalty.

'This is a surprise, Father. Is everything okay?'

He closed the car door and approached the house, wearing a smile that he was sure looked part grimace. The dogs had been called to heel but still sniffed at Daniel's shoes suspiciously. 'Can I have a word with you and … Mr O'Neill?' Few people called him Sean to his face. They wouldn't dare.

'Who is it?' Sean's voice bellowed from within, right on cue.

'It's Father Quinn,' Susan replied, ushering Daniel into the farmhouse, then closing the door firmly on the dogs.

The hallway was a clutter of boots and umbrellas and crates, but Susan's kitchen was neat and brightly decorated in lemon yellow. The O'Neill family were seated around the big oak table, halfway through their lunch. The two younger daughters stared at Daniel in curiosity. Jenny sat as if turned to stone, staring at her mostly uneaten plate of stew.

Sean was already getting out of his chair. 'Welcome, Father. We don't see you here often.' He gave Daniel a bone-cracking handshake. However coarse and aggressive Sean could be, he was a devout Catholic who rarely missed Mass. That could be helpful because whatever Daniel advised, Sean might feel bound to follow the advice of a church representative.

'Get a chair, woman. Set Father Quinn a place.' Sean spoke roughly to his wife, and she scurried to obey.

'No food, thank you, Mrs O'Neill. I've already eaten.' A lie, but Daniel's insides were so churned up with nerves he'd be unable to swallow anything.

One of the daughters hauled over a rickety wooden chair for him. As he took his place at the table, the seat creaked alarmingly, the only thing to break the awkward silence that had now descended on the family group. They were all, bar Jenny, staring at him expectantly. He resisted the urge to run out of the farmhouse as fast as he could. 'I'm sorry to interrupt your meal,' ventured Daniel, 'but I wanted to catch you together.' He glanced at Sean and Susan. 'Do you think we could talk privately?'

'Girls, take your plates through to the living room,' instructed Susan, and the younger daughters scrambled to obey, grabbing bread rolls and their cutlery. They exited the kitchen, chattering about some TV programme they could now watch. 'You too, Jenny.'

'No, she needs to stay.' The urgency in Daniel's tone caught the parents' attention. Susan's face started to lose some of its colour. Did she suspect about her daughter's condition? 'Jenny has something she needs to tell you.'

He prayed she would do the actual telling, not leave it up to him. Jenny had also said she wouldn't mention Jay but, just in case, Daniel had left his friend a phone message advising he make himself scarce that day.

'Well, girl, what is it?' demanded Sean. 'I hope you're not planning on leaving school. Your mother might fill your head with acting dreams, but you'll be going to college. Learn about accounts so you can help me out with the farm.'

Jenny had slunk down in her chair, and the look of absolute misery on her face sparked a similar feeling in Daniel. A young pregnant girl needed supportive parents, but Jenny had only a bully and a timid mouse to rely on. How could any of this end well?

'Cat got your tongue? Come on – spit it out. We haven't got all day.'

Susan reached out and took Jenny's hand. 'Tell us what it is, love.'

Jenny glanced up at her mother's kind face. 'I'm pregnant, Mammy,' she whispered.

Susan's expression became a mixture of concern and deep sorrow. Not a trace of anger. Just one woman's compassion for another. Daniel had seen such a look on the face of a carved Madonna in a church he'd visited on a tour of the Rhine. It had convinced him that most mothers were nearer and dearer to God than anybody else could be. Jenny had an ally in Susan, for sure.

Sean's hand suddenly swept the dishes nearest to him off the table, and the crash of breaking pottery shocked Daniel so much that he jumped up in alarm, the chair skittering away behind him. The younger girls ran into the kitchen to find out what was going on, but they fled again when Sean bellowed 'Get out!'

Daniel could hear the dogs barking in a frenzy outside. It was all so much worse than he could have imagined. This man was a volcano.

Sean got up from his seat and towered over Jenny, menacingly. 'Who was it? Who did it? I want a name!'

If Jenny told him, Jay was surely dead. The man had a shotgun, and a vision of Jay being wheeled into emergency wounded – or worse – danced before Daniel's eyes.

'It's none of your business!' cried Jenny, clamping her hands over her ears.

Sean yanked his daughter out of the chair by her hair and slapped her so hard that she crashed back into the kitchen counter, slipping slowly downwards to lie like a crumpled rag doll on the floor.

Before he could move in again, Susan was there, placing herself in front of Jenny, her eyes flashing a warning. 'If you lay another finger on her, Sean, I'll have the law on you!'

'Get out of the way, woman!'

Susan didn't budge. 'I mean it! Aren't you ashamed of yourself? Behaving like that in front of Father Quinn.'

Sean had clearly forgotten Daniel was there. He glanced across at him now and hesitated. Daniel could see him struggling to keep his rage in check. What would he do if Sean started the violence again? Daniel was a natural born coward. Useless in a fight. Even Susan O'Neill had more guts than him.

Thankfully, his mettle wasn't going to be tested today. Sean kicked the chairs out of his way and stomped into the hall. 'I want a name!' he yelled again, before slamming the front door after him so loudly that it sounded like a gunshot. There was the sound of an engine, a screech of tyres, and then silence, except for Jenny's muffled sobbing.

Daniel's heart was beating so fast it felt like a heart attack. He'd have welcomed some brandy and a lie down.

'You'd best go after him, Father,' Susan said. 'When that mood's on him, he could do anything. He'll likely go to the pub, make a ruckus. Get the guards, if you have to. Perhaps a few hours in a cell will calm him down.'

Daniel stared at her. Here he was, thankful to be all in one piece, and now this woman wanted him to go after her husband and risk his towering wrath again. She must be mad.

'Go, Father. Hurry.' Something in her expression told Daniel he'd have to do it. Susan had shown a different side today. The lioness defending her cub. And she clearly expected help from the Church.

He watched as she knelt down on the kitchen floor and took the crying Jenny in her arms, rocking her daughter and soothing her with gentle words, as if she were a precious newborn again.

Daniel turned and crunched his way through broken plates to the door. Susan's neat kitchen looked like a war zone now, and this whole situation would likely get much worse. Sean O'Neill was a man who wanted answers – specifically the name of the guilty party. Pray God, Jenny didn't give it to him.

* * *

'How do you celebrate Christmas in Australia?' Rachel asked her companions. She was enjoying lunch, seated between Helen and Finn in Donegan's.

Finn smiled. 'Drunk – and with much merriment.'

'We usually celebrate it on the beach,' Helen told her. 'Along with thousands of others. You stake out your spot early, set up the deckchairs, and there are communal grills you can use to barbecue burgers and shrimp.'

'Then we barbecue ourselves in the sun,' added Finn.

'Sounds like heaven.' The only fun Christmases Rachel could remember were those when her father was alive. Later ones were all spent watching to see her mother didn't down too much vodka. That tended to kill the festive spirit fairly quickly.

'You know, you're very welcome to spend Christmas with us, Rachel,' Helen said, with a smile. 'Although, I suppose you'll have plans already. Kilbrook can't compete with London.'

'Well, no, I don't have any definite plans—'

Rachel's words were cut short by the pub door crashing open. The brash Christmas music played on, but the chatter in the pub noticeably dropped. A thickset man in overalls scowled in the doorway. He cast his eye over the people in the pub before stomping over to the bar and ordering a drink.

'Who's that?' she whispered to Helen.

'That, my dear, is Sean O'Neill. Jenny's father. As mean as they come.'

Jenny must have told her parents about the baby. Her father was here to drown his sorrows, or perhaps he'd found out about Jay and was looking for him. Surely Daniel would have protected his friend's identity, though?

Rachel had picked up her glass, ready to drink, when she noticed Sean O'Neill staring across at their group. He reminded her of a bull about to charge. Perhaps Jenny had told him Rachel advised her to speak to Daniel. The bull in overalls stalked over and glared down at Helen. 'My Jenny won't be in your play any more.'

'Why not?' Helen's voice was calm.

'Because that theatre's a den of vice. God knows what goes on backstage. It shouldn't be allowed.'

Helen stood up. She barely reached Sean's shoulder, but

when she spoke, she showed no fear. 'There's nothing but acting goes on in that theatre, Sean, so I'll thank you not to make accusations.'

Rachel was aware of Finn getting to his feet, so she felt she had no choice but to stand up as well. Everyone in the pub seemed to be looking at them now.

'We're having a quiet lunch here. Please leave us alone.' Finn's voice was calm enough, but there was an undertone of menace there.

Sean stared at him. 'Was it you with my Jenny?'

'What!'

Rachel was as shocked as Finn sounded. No – she was more shocked, because she knew what the man was implying. This was insane.

'I remember you,' Sean continued. 'You were with her ...' he nodded his head in Helen's direction '... that time she drove Jenny back from the theatre. And when I came to pick Jenny up a few weeks ago, you were having a very cosy conversation with her.'

'I was talking her through her lines!' Finn protested. 'She was upset because she kept forgetting them – now we know why.'

'This is my nephew,' said Helen. 'And he hasn't done anything to you – or to Jenny – so back off.'

'Don't play the innocent with me. He probably had my Jenny with your approval.' He glared again at Finn. 'Filthy bastard ...'

Before she really knew what she was doing, Rachel had thrown her wine in Sean O'Neill's face. The unjust insult to Finn – and Helen – had been too much to bear.

Sean rubbed the alcohol from his eyes and lunged towards her. Rachel gasped as Finn's fist connected with Sean's jaw. The man staggered backward into the landlord, who twisted Sean's arm up behind his back. 'Now then, Sean, we don't want trouble. Folks are enjoying their lunch. Why don't you just go home?'

'Get off me!' yelled Sean, kicking back with his foot and wrenching himself free as the landlord roared in pain. Sean headed towards their table again but the bartender, who'd come round to help, stuck out a foot and tripped him up. Sean crashed into another table, and there were shrieks and the tinkle of breaking glass.

Some people were scrambling to their feet and making for the exit. Suddenly Daniel was there with a guard in tow, and they dragged the dazed Sean to his feet, carting him away outside while he shouted curses and protests.

'Oh my God.' Helen looked badly shaken. 'What was all that about?'

'I don't know,' said Finn, nursing his right hand. 'But let's go home now – while we still can.' They headed through the wreckage to the door.

'I've forgotten something,' said Rachel, and darted back to their table. As she collected her scarf from the back of her chair, she heard a woman's voice from the next booth.

'No smoke without fire. Something funny must have been going on in that theatre.'

Rachel wanted to defend her friends, but Finn was waiting for her at the door. She didn't want him to be exposed to any of that hurtful gossip, and surely there'd been enough fighting for one day. She'd let the insult pass – for now.

* * *

'That's the sixth mother to call and say her child is sick and won't be in the play this evening,' Helen announced, as she came into the living room. 'A virus certainly travels fast in Kilbrook.'

'So does gossip.' Finn was worried. This was a serious blow. Helen had put her heart and soul into the play, and Sean O'Neill had jeopardised all that with one unjust accusation.

'I suppose it really could be a bout of sickness,' said Helen, as she sat down with a sigh in the armchair.

'No.' Rachel shook her head, frowning. 'I heard someone in the pub say there was no smoke without fire.'

Finn walked over to the window and peered out. He'd been nervous about coming back here but was sure his changed identity would protect him. Now the village was turning against him for reasons unknown. 'What is it Sean O'Neill thinks I've done?'

'Had a fling with Jenny, I'm guessing.'

'I didn't.' Finn turned round, came back over to the seated women. 'I swear I didn't.'

'Of *course* you didn't, Finn! We don't think that for a minute.' Rachel looked very upset. He was grateful to her for automatically taking his side.

Helen grabbed his hand. 'You're a stranger here, love, so it's easier for them to point the finger at you. And Sean is very traditional, very protective of his girls. If someone winks at them the wrong way, he takes it as a personal affront.'

'Well, I know I've never so much as winked at her, but Jenny herself must have said something,' persisted Finn. 'Else why would Sean be making accusations?'

'He said "*was* it you?" not "it *was* you",' Rachel pointed out. 'He didn't know anything for sure.'

'I think we'll have to have a conversation with the O'Neills,' decided Helen. 'Not tonight, though. Sean will still be raging. Maybe tomorrow I can get a private meeting with Susan or Jenny. Find out what's going on.'

'We should go *now*.' Finn wanted the whole thing cleared up as soon as possible. It was his name in the mud. How could he go anywhere with Rachel with this hanging over his head? He'd not want to expose her to any name-calling.

'Leave it till tomorrow, love,' Helen advised. 'Then we'll get to the bottom of it, I promise. Right now I need to go and let the theatre staff know the show is cancelled for tonight. I'll get them to put up a sign. Finn – can you call the parents whose children are still coming and let them know? The list is in the hall. I've ticked the names of the ones who've already cancelled. Will you be okay to do that?'

Finn nodded but clenched his jaw in frustration. Cancelling the show felt like giving in, admitting guilt where there was none.

To his dismay, Rachel got up from the sofa, saying, 'I'm sorry but I have to go. Molly asked me to do something for her.'

'I'll drop you,' offered Helen.

'That's kind, but I'd rather walk. Get some fresh air.' Rachel turned to Finn and gave him a hug and a kiss. 'I'll be back in a couple of hours. Just hang in there, okay?'

Finn nodded, but once Helen and Rachel had left the house, that place at the back of the mind where all dark things were stored threw up the tiniest of doubts. Did Rachel wonder if Finn was guilty as charged by Sean O'Neill?

* * *

The church was still open, though all the lights were on to banish the late afternoon gloom. A few tourists were wandering round, gazing at the murals or flicking through their guidebooks. Rachel made her way up the side aisle and through into the back rooms of the church. She prayed Daniel would be able to help her. It was impossible to shake the memory of Finn's troubled face.

She knocked at the church office door and was startled when it opened quickly.

Daniel was standing there, papers in hand, looking surprised. 'Rachel … um … I was expecting someone else.'

Jay, perhaps? She didn't want to run into him, so this would have to be quick. 'Can I talk to you?'

'It's not really a good time …'

Rachel could tell he wasn't rejecting her as such – any visitor would have been unwelcome at that moment. He looked stressed and tired. 'Please, it won't take long.'

Daniel swung open the door. 'Come in. Have a seat.'

He sat down, clasping his hands on the desk in front of him. There was the tiniest hint of impatience as he tapped his thumbs together. She'd get right to the point. 'We've had to cancel this evening's performance of *A Christmas Carol*.'

'Why? What's happened?'

'Sean O'Neill's what's happened.' She had Daniel's attention now. 'In the pub this afternoon, just before you came in, Sean seemed to accuse Finn of having an improper relationship with Jenny. After that, six mothers phoned Helen claiming their children were too sick to perform. What those mothers are really saying, though, is that they believe Finn is guilty. And he's not. I know he's not.'

Daniel was looking more than a little uncomfortable now. 'You know, it could be just coincidence. Maybe the kids are sick ...'

'I'm pretty sure they're not. This is a small village. Rumours spread quickly.'

She saw Daniel glance discreetly at his watch. Who was he expecting? 'Look, Sean O'Neill is a man with a bit of a temper. He's not always rational. Everyone knows that.'

He was giving her the brush-off, and Rachel was having none of that. 'Finn's got a right to be upset. Jenny's pregnant, but he's not her baby's father.'

Daniel's jaw dropped open. 'How did ...' he started to say, then quickly changed tack. 'As a priest, I can't discuss something like that.'

And he was right, of course. He shouldn't break the confidentiality of the confessional. But if he thought Jenny had already told Rachel everything, perhaps Daniel would be more willing to discuss it. 'I understand you need to be discreet. But Jenny's already talked to me about it. I know that Jay Cole is the father of her baby.' Two unconnected sentences, but both true. Rachel hadn't lied, except by implication.

Daniel took a sharp intake of breath. He clearly hadn't

expected that, thinking Jay's secret was safe with him. Rachel could see him mentally working through various responses. He was in a bind, and she sympathised, but Finn came first.

'I'll need to think about all this ...'

Rachel tried to hide her frustration. There was no time for delay. He'd need more proof. She took the photo out of her pocket and passed it across to Daniel.

As soon as he'd peered at the image of Jay and Jenny locked in an embrace, Daniel dropped the picture as if it had burned him. 'Where did you get this?' he whispered.

'I was taking photos of the Lantern Day Festival.'

'I wish you hadn't shown it to me.'

'I'm sorry,' said Rachel, and she was. Over the past few weeks, she'd become increasingly unsure about taking revenge on Daniel. He'd changed, and she liked him. Now she had the chance to make him suffer, but it didn't feel right.

'Has anyone else seen it?' Daniel asked.

'No. I wouldn't betray Jenny.' And that was the truth – it was the one thing that had stopped her posting the pictures to Mel.

'Then please don't show it to anyone,' Daniel appealed.

If only it could be that simple. 'Daniel, I'm not going to let Finn take the fall for Jay Cole.'

He gave her a long, searching look, but Rachel didn't break eye contact, hoping he would understand just how determined she was.

'I'm just trying to protect the man I love, Daniel – an innocent man – and I don't know how to do that. You know this village and the people who live here. I was hoping you could find a solution that clears Finn's name and protects Jenny's confidence in you.'

Daniel sighed and dropped his chin into his hands. 'Oh, what would I give right now for the wisdom of Solomon.'

'I know,' she murmured. It seemed impossible to resolve

this mess without someone getting hurt. She hoped Daniel could come up with something.

'Give me twenty-four hours,' he said. 'I'll do my best.'

'Thank you – so much.'

He was no longer meeting her eye. Did he feel guilty about Jay, or did he resent her for putting him in this situation? Probably a bit of both.

She stood up and reached over for the photo, but Daniel picked it up. 'May I keep this? Just in case I need it.'

'Of course.' Most likely he'd show the photo to Jay. 'I'd appreciate it if you didn't tell anyone it was me who took it.' The last thing she needed was Jay Cole raging on Molly's doorstep.

Daniel nodded agreement. He put the photo in his desk drawer. He looked drained. She was sorry she'd had to put this burden on his shoulders, but the look on Finn's face still haunted her.

'Bye, Daniel.'

'Goodbye.' He went back to looking at his papers.

She hurried out of the office, praying she wouldn't meet Jay on the way out.

* * *

This time the knock on the door heralded Daniel's expected visitor: Susan O'Neill. He ushered her in, thankful she was late. If she'd arrived on time, she'd have met Rachel, who might have blurted out what she knew about Jay. God seemed to be on his side – for now, at least.

'Time for a cup of tea?'

'I shouldn't really, Father. Garda Farrell's waiting.'

Daniel was going to accompany Susan to the police station. The landlord of Donegan's wasn't pressing charges, but the police wanted Daniel to have a sobering chat with Sean, to make sure he didn't repeat his behaviour. He'd been put in an interview room for a few hours to cool off.

'Ten minutes won't make a difference, surely,' Daniel said, and poured them each a cup of the strong brew. He needed it as much as Susan probably did. Rachel's revelation had been quite a shock. She was a woman in love, and that would make her very determined. Protective. If Daniel didn't act soon, who knew what she might do.

'How's Jenny?' he asked, thinking back to the awful scene he'd witnessed in the O'Neills' kitchen earlier that day.

'She's sleeping now. And I've told her to stay in her room when her father gets back. Best to keep them apart for a while.'

Daniel murmured agreement.

'Father Quinn?' Susan hesitated, looking down at her cup.

'What is it?'

'Jenny told you who the father of her baby is, yes?'

He should have declined to discuss that at all, but Susan was on Jenny's side. A mother truly concerned about her daughter. 'She did, but she told me in the confessional. You know I can't share that information.'

Susan nodded, and sipped thoughtfully at her tea. 'I know. She said you're the only one she's told. My question is, does … does the father know she's pregnant?'

'Yes,' murmured Daniel, realising too late that he'd probably crossed a line there, but he was busy absorbing what Susan had just said. Maybe Jenny really had told no one else about the baby, and Rachel had lied to him to try to get him to reveal that Jay was the father. Perhaps she had overheard Jay talking about it that time when she was outside the church office window. Now he was starting to feel manipulated, and a small seed of mistrust was springing up in his mind. Had Jenny lied to her mother, though? It was all getting very complicated.

'Father? What do you think?'

'I'm sorry – could you repeat that?' He tried to refocus.

'In your opinion, will the father do the right thing by Jenny?'

It was such an old-fashioned phrase, but it summed up the

situation well. Jay was the least likely person to do the right thing if it didn't benefit him. Such a shame that Jenny hadn't understood that before she got involved with him.

'In my opinion – no, he won't.'

'Will you talk to him?'

'Jenny asked me to, so I'll try, but I wouldn't bank on him.'

He saw the hope in Susan's eyes extinguished. Better she know the truth of the situation, though. That way she could start making alternative plans. He got up and went over to the filing cabinet, rummaging through until he found what he needed. 'This is some information about the counselling service in Galway. I've already given their details to Jenny. They're very experienced in dealing with ... situations like this. And everything is confidential.'

Susan accepted the pamphlet and tucked it into her handbag. She stood up. 'Shall we go then?'

As he was putting on his coat, Daniel thought again about Rachel. And Finn – his childhood friend who was now under suspicion, mostly because he was believed to be a stranger here, and it was easier for the villagers to reject an outsider than one of their own. 'You know, Sean created a bit of a problem in the pub this afternoon ...'

Susan sighed. 'I know, I know. We'll pay for any damage.'

'No, I don't mean that. He accused the wrong person of being responsible.'

Susan's face registered dismay. 'Who?'

'Finn MacKenzie. Helen's nephew. Probably because Jenny's in the play and he's helping out with it. Trouble is, some of the mothers wouldn't let their children show up for the performance this evening, so it had to be cancelled.'

'Oh, no. It just keeps getting worse, doesn't it?' Susan seemed close to tears. 'And Finn is such a nice lad.'

'This is a lot to ask at a time like this, I know, but I wondered if you could make some kind of a show of support for Helen and Finn. Stop the gossips in their tracks.'

'How?'

'Well, it's the Advent unveiling tomorrow. A lot of people will be there. Although perhaps you won't want to go ...'

Susan straightened up and there was some of that steel in her again that he'd seen earlier in the day. 'I'm not going to hide away. Let he who is without sin cast the first stone. Sean's messed up, but I'll set it right. Leave it with me, Father ... Now, let's go and see the jailbird.'

She headed out of the office, and Daniel followed, impressed for the second time that day by this woman he'd wrongly judged to be a doormat.

Now the only thing that remained for him to do was talk to Jay, but he wasn't answering his phone. Typical. The cause of all the trouble had gone to ground, likely planning a way to wriggle out of it all, but there was hard proof this time – Rachel's photo. Sleepy Kilbrook was in for a shock if that was ever revealed.

* * *

'It's getting heavier!'

Rachel's face was glowing like a five-year-old's. She was almost dancing with excitement on the doorstep at the sight of the snow, which had been falling for an hour or more. Finn smiled, reaching out to brush the flakes from her hair.

'Come on!' she cried. 'Let's go for a walk.'

'Well ...' Finn thought about the whispers and pointing fingers the villagers might subject him to. He'd rather stay inside.

'Go on, Finn.' Helen had come through into the hallway. 'When did you last see snow? You'll enjoy it.'

'He's just scared I'll beat him in a snowball fight,' joked Rachel.

Her delight at the snow was infectious. Finn had been indoors all afternoon, brooding over Sean O'Neill and the cancelled performance, and he was going stir crazy. Likely getting on Helen's nerves. She probably needed a break. He grabbed his coat and scarf, then pulled on a beanie, tossing Rachel one of Helen's spares. 'Let's go, Frosty.'

The air was fresh, but there was no hint of a wind, so the snowflakes dropped gently from the black night sky, dusting the streets below. As Finn and Rachel walked along, arm in arm, they could hear shrieks of delight from various gardens as children played in the winter weather bonus.

Finn's spirits lifted, and he hugged Rachel close. 'Where do you want to go?'

'Let's go to the park. To the ice rink – our first date, remember?'

'I'm not much in the mood for skating,' Finn protested.

'We'll not skate – we'll just watch it all through the trees.' She gave his arm a squeeze. 'I'll be so cold by then, I'm sure I'll need you to warm me up.'

The thought of that put a spring in his step, and they crunched their way through the fresh snow, turning back every now and then to see their footsteps in the thin layer. Rachel began to hum a Christmas tune, and Finn was glad she seemed, for a while at least, to have put aside her gloom at the festive season.

When they reached the park, Rachel hit Finn with a handful of snow scooped from the gate rungs. She ran away, laughing, and he chased her through the trees, eventually catching up with her in a clearing and dousing her head with a light snowball. Breathless, they came together in a snowy kiss. He could taste it on her lips, could feel the coldness of her nose. He pulled her in close against him, and they both spun slowly round in the starlight.

'I'm dizzy,' she told him after a while, and he guided her over to a log, where they sat with arms round each other. The lights from the ice rink were visible through the trees, and music drifted over the park to the clearing. The snow continued to fall, blanketing their boots. If it kept up like this, it would be really thick by morning, just right for the children to make snowmen. Not just the children ...

'Finn, can I ask you something?'

'Sure.' The lighthearted note seemed to have disappeared from Rachel's voice. He hoped she wasn't going to mention Sean O'Neill.

'You don't know very much about me. And ... well, there are things I've done that you might not ... agree with ... or like.'

He turned her head towards him, saw the worry in her eyes. 'Hey, that's the same for everybody, you know. I'm no angel, either.'

Smiling weakly, she said, 'But once you know more about me, what if you don't love me the same?'

'Rachel, let's agree to accept each other, faults and all.'

This was important. Whatever it was she was worried about, he had his own concerns – he was hiding his identity because of a shameful past.

'Deal,' she said, kissing his nose.

They walked home in a more thoughtful mood. As they passed the church, Rachel slowed then moved them over to the bench by the lychgate. 'I need to tell you something. It's about today.'

Finn's heart sank. She *was* going to mention Sean O'Neill. Just when the spectre of the man had been banished from his mind. He opened his mouth to speak, but Rachel beat him to it.

'It's about Jenny. And this is strictly confidential, Finn. You mustn't breathe a word of it to anyone. Well, you can tell Helen. You've been blamed for something you haven't done, and that's not fair. You have a right to know what's going on.'

Her solemn face was enough to make him promise to keep the secret.

'Jenny's pregnant. That's why Sean O'Neill's so mad. And I know who the father is.'

Finn panicked. 'Well, it's not me, if that's what she's been saying.'

'Of course it's not you, you idiot!' chided Rachel.

'Who is it then?' Curiosity was now burning inside him.

'Jay Cole. Mel's husband.'

The news hit Finn like a ton of bricks. Jay, his old partner in crime. The irony of the two of them being linked together with a problem in the village was not lost on Finn. It seemed like the gods had chosen to swat them both with one fell blow. And if Finn was to clear his name, it could only be by implicating Jay. What a mess.

'Jenny doesn't want to tell anyone who the father is,' Rachel was saying. 'And I have to respect that. Don't worry though, I think I've found a way to make sure people know you're not involved.'

'How?'

'I spoke to Daniel – Father Quinn. He said he'd try to help.'

Dear God. Daniel – Jay – Mel. All embroiled in this situation, and Finn had been dragged into it, too. What a sick joke. If he'd thought so before, he knew it for sure now – it had been a big mistake to come back. Why hadn't he listened to his instincts? Never go back, they said …

'Are you okay, Finn?'

He glanced down at Rachel's worried face. If he hadn't come back, he'd never have met her. She was worth putting up with a little complication. They'd both be gone soon anyway, leaving Jay Cole to clean up the mess he'd made.

'I'm fine,' he told Rachel. 'Let's forget about all of them. We've got each other, and that's all that counts.'

They sat there, kissing on the bench, until the church clock chiming the late hour sent them indoors to the warmth.

* * *

Daniel took another sip of his brandy. The drink wasn't having its usual relaxing effect – not surprising really, given the day he'd had. Snatches of conversation kept replaying in his memory, and it always came back to one thing. Had Rachel lied to him? And if she'd done so today, she could have lied to him before. About not being outside the window, for example, when Jay had confided in Daniel about Jenny's pregnancy. Perhaps she was even lying about being a student.

He went through into the study and found the file containing her documents. He glanced at the introductory letter from her university professor. It seemed genuine enough and could be easily checked. The application form for study permission listed Rachel's home address as London. Emergency contact was given as Sophia Ricci, a cousin, who lived at the same address. There was nothing out of the ordinary.

Rachel's CV listed her Catholic boarding school – St Anne's Convent in Manchester – and her postsecondary qualifications, including the postgraduate thesis on the Pre-Raphaelites and their circle. Gabriel Stokeley fitted in perfectly with that. She spoke fluent French and Italian, and had spent study time in both those countries. That's why she'd been so close to Henri, of course, because of her French. Interests were listed as theatre, cinema, and travel. Her three references were her current tutor, her former headmistress, and the priest at St Anne's. There was no mystery there. Everything above board.

So why did he feel like he was missing something? 'You're not,' he told himself, sternly. Daniel had never been a great believer in sixth sense – it was just the brain working overtime, trying to find connections where there were none. He was attracted to Rachel, so his mind was obsessing over her. Picking up on every little detail. She'd overheard his conversation with Jay outside the church office window, but she'd not told anyone about it. If she'd lied to him today, it was because she'd wanted him to talk about Jay but knew he couldn't if Jenny hadn't revealed it to her first. It was as simple as that.

He was as bad as Sean O'Neill, jumping to conclusions, and maybe wrong ones. He left the file about Rachel on the desk, picked up his drink and went back into the living room. He'd watch some mindless soap opera and force himself to relax. With luck, Susan would find a way to help him out, and he'd be off the hook.

* * *

Rachel sat at the desk, staring unseeing at the diary in front of her. Her fingers stroked the pendant round her neck, her mind full of Finn. She'd taken a big risk tonight, telling Daniel that she knew about Jay and Jenny. Lines and boundaries were getting blurred, and it was hard to keep track of her plan because she was having to improvise so much. Still, the reunion was coming up. She wouldn't have to keep up the deception for much longer. Then she could let out all the pain and anger.

31 May
I'm still shaking as I write this, waiting for Mr and Mrs Maguire to phone Father Milligan and complain about what I did. I attacked Mel in the cloakroom. It happened because I was late for school this morning. Rosie had a bad attack in the night and had to go to hospital. I slept in and Father Milligan wrote a note for Miss Murphy. Mel was writing on the board and I saw her look over the teacher's shoulder and read the note. At the end of the day, I was getting my blazer from the cloakroom and Mel was there. She turned to one of her friends and said in a loud voice that Rosie Rinaldi wasn't really sick – she was just retarded. All the Rinaldis were retarded. I flew at Mel and pushed her back against the wall and held her throat. I think I was shouting 'Bitch!' She actually looked scared. I've never seen that before. Then I let her go and ran home. Only Father Milligan was there, sleeping in

the armchair. Mam had left a phone message that she was staying overnight at the hospital. I made sandwiches and I've been hiding up here in my room. I'm going to be sick tomorrow. And the next day. We've got exams, but I don't care. It's given Mel something to think about, but I really think Jay might kill me for what I did.

Sitting alone in her room at Molly's, Rachel wiped away a few tears. That diary entry had shown a bit of spirit, a bit of fight. Even some optimism that the bullies could be beaten. But how misplaced that hope had been. Ignorance about the future had definitely been bliss.

Chapter Nineteen

The snow had stopped next morning, but it lay deep enough on the ground for boots to give a satisfying crunch on contact. Kilbrook's children were in seventh heaven – skimming the snow off walls and fences to make snowballs to catch the unwary.

Rachel, Helen and Finn were on their way to the church to watch the unveiling of the Christmas nativity scene, a long-standing tradition at the start of every Advent. It would take place just after morning Mass.

Finn hadn't wanted to come, feeling his presence would only add fuel to the fire of village gossip. Helen had been adamant, though. 'We're not going to hide away, Finn. Then they'll only think they're right. We've done nothing to be ashamed of.'

Last night, Finn and Rachel had agreed he could tell Helen in strictest confidence about Jenny's pregnancy, and about Jay. Over their breakfast earlier, Helen had told Rachel she was sympathetic to the girl's plight. 'That father of hers is such a bully. And a strict Catholic. He'll likely pack Jenny off to a relative until she's due, and then the baby will be put up for adoption. He'll make her life hell for that.'

Rachel wondered again if she'd done the right thing by going to Daniel. Jenny hadn't revealed Jay was the father, so what right did Rachel have to force the issue? It might make things much worse. Sean O'Neill was so volatile. He could really hurt Jay, and physical violence was never something Rachel had seriously contemplated in her quest for revenge. Perhaps she'd try to have a word with Daniel after the unveiling.

'Here goes,' said Helen.

They were approaching the church. She linked arms with Finn and Rachel on either side of her. A united front.

* * *

As he came out of the church after his parishioners, Daniel shivered in his thin priest's robes. The snow certainly looked pretty, but it brought freezing temperatures.

There was quite a good turnout. For some of the children, excitedly chattering in groups, it would be the first Advent unveiling they'd seen – or rather, the first unveiling they'd remember seeing, since they'd likely been brought along before as babes in arms or toddlers. Chairs had been set out for seniors and the disabled. Molly had bagged the best seat, front row centre, and she gave Daniel a smile and a little wave. As he scanned the crowd, he saw Mel with Leanne. No sign of Jay, which was probably a good thing. Then he saw Rachel, standing off to the side with Helen and Jody – no, Finn. It was hard to remember his alias. He wondered if Rachel knew his true identity yet, but he guessed not. Best get on with the ceremony before they all got chilblains. More snow had been forecast. At least it would make the nativity scene look truly seasonal. He signalled the choir and they launched into song, a sign to the villagers to gather together and get ready.

As the villagers assembled around the draped nativity scene, Daniel heard a surprised murmur from the crowd. Like them, he watched with bated breath as Susan O'Neill, followed by her younger daughters, crossed the snow-covered grass, in full view of everybody, and stood right next to Finn. She whispered something in his ear, and he smiled. Helen craned her head round to mouth a hello to Susan. She also received a smile. The gossips would be dumbfounded. Susan had kept her word.

It was with a lighter heart that Daniel proceeded with the rest of the ceremony. There were the usual gasps as the simple but elegant newly-painted wooden figures of the nativity scene were revealed. Most people had seen them before many times, but perhaps the memory of this touching family scene dimmed throughout the year. Some of the statues also had single words carved on them – 'Love' for the Virgin Mary,

'Hope' for Joseph, 'Joy' for the angel, and 'Peace' for the baby Jesus. Such simple messages, yet a simplicity that reached the heart. Advent symbolised that all those things were coming for everyone, through the birth of a miracle baby.

The choir started to sing a hymn about an end to strife and quarrels, and Daniel vowed he'd work for peace in Kilbrook. He'd help Jenny and the O'Neills in whatever way he could. Jay was smart enough to take care of himself. Time would pass and things would work out in the end.

He looked over at Rachel. Surely she'd be happy now? She'd landed a difficult burden on his shoulders, but she'd done so because of her love for Finn. However misguided, love came from a pure place. He tried to catch her eye, but she was staring intently at the nativity scene. She looked almost tearful, and he remembered she'd told him about being orphaned at a young age. Times like Christmas could be especially hard for those without family.

When the hymn was over, Daniel started to speak. Rachel turned to look at him, and he was so shocked by her expression that he almost forgot the familiar words of the blessing. Her eyes seemed full of anger and resentment, and a kind of judgement. She diverted her gaze quickly, but that was worse because he saw she was now focused on Mel. Some sixth sense of danger prickled the back of his neck.

* * *

Leanne pulled Mel over to the nativity scene so she could inspect the crowns of the three kings more closely. Mel had only come to the unveiling today because Leanne insisted – many of her classmates were going, and she didn't want to be left out. It was supposed to be a family event, and it looked like everyone else had their partners with them. Jay, however, hadn't come home last night, or this morning. He'd texted Mel to say he was staying with his friend Garrett in Galway, but when she'd called Garrett's number, there'd been no answer.

It wasn't the first time Jay had pulled an all-nighter, drinking and clubbing with friends from his university days. Usually he came home in a very good mood, with gifts for her. Guilt gifts, perhaps, but it was still a nice feeling that she was important enough for him to want to keep her sweet. Now that she suspected he was having an affair with Jenny, though, things were different. A sixteen-year-old schoolgirl on his home turf. That was stupid and dangerous. Suddenly she heard Jenny's name mentioned by a group of women off to her right. Mel inched Leanne over in their direction, making some throwaway comments about the statues to her daughter as she did so.

'I bet Jenny's pregnant,' one of the women said, and Mel almost gasped aloud with shock. 'Sean O'Neill was in Donegan's yesterday accusing Helen MacKenzie's nephew of messing around with his daughter.'

'That can't be right,' a second woman said. 'Will you look at Susan O'Neill now – she's talking away to Helen and the boy as if they're all best friends.'

'Well, Sean will get to the truth soon enough. And then there'll be fireworks …'

'Mammy! Stop pulling me!' Leanne wailed, but Mel ushered her past the statues. She needed to get away from this crowd of gossiping women who'd made her sick with worry.

'When's Daddy coming home?' asked Leanne as they reached the car.

'That's the million dollar question, isn't it?' she replied absently.

'What does *that* mean?'

'Never mind. Let's get you to Shauna's house.'

Mel fastened both their seat belts. Lucky Leanne was having lunch with her best friend. Mel would have to spend Sunday lunch in the company of her parents, who would want to know where her husband was. And she had no answer to give them. Damn Jay!

* * *

'The rumour I heard at the Advent unveiling this morning is that Jenny O'Neill's pregnant.' Mel delivered this information matter-of-factly, as if she were announcing the price of fish.

Jay's fork clattered onto his plate, and he mumbled an apology. He'd been expecting some kind of gossip because Daniel had phoned him yesterday to warn that he was helping Jenny tell her family about the baby. He hadn't expected the gossip to come from Mel, though. He wished he hadn't made it to lunch now, but he'd tried to do the right thing for a change.

'Oh, my! Who's the father?' asked Tessa.

Jay concentrated intently on his beef.

'I think the girl's keeping it secret.'

'Sean O'Neill's probably roaming the streets now with a shotgun,' joked Gerald.

Jay gave a nervous glance out of the dining room window. He prayed Jenny would continue to keep his identity secret. She knew her father's rages. Surely she wouldn't expose Jay to that.

'My bet is he's a married man,' declared Mel. 'Jay?'

He started guiltily as she said his name, but she was only offering him the bowl of sprouts.

Or was she? There was something in her eyes that wasn't right. Resentment? Accusation? He couldn't be sure. Her hand trembled slightly as he accepted the dish of vegetables.

'That would be quite a scandal, wouldn't it?'

Jay wished Tessa would shut up and eat. Pity Leanne wasn't here – they'd never have raised such a topic in her presence.

'And quite a risk for a married man,' continued Mel, slicing sharply into her meat. 'To give up house, children, and maybe career, for a bit of skirt.'

'Goodness, Mel, that's perhaps a bit too blunt for the lunch table,' said Tessa, and for once Jay agreed with his mother-in-law. He couldn't quite shake the feeling that Mel was really talking about him, yet maybe that was just a guilty conscience. His appetite had almost completely vanished, and he wished the meal was over.

'How are the numbers shaping up for the reunion dinner, Mel?' asked Gerald.

Thankfully, the conversation had changed tack, but now Jay was worried what might be in store for him once his in-laws had left.

* * *

Mel carved the cheesecake into portions, not caring that they were uneven. Once the slices were in the bowls, she dolloped ice cream carelessly on top. She could have done without the ritual of Sunday lunch today, but she hadn't been able to think of a good enough reason to cancel, and her father would have asked for one.

When Jay had swanned into the dining room as if he hadn't a care in the world, Mel wanted to slap his face, and that had shocked her. Part of her was starting to question all those years of pandering to him. Had he ever really loved her, or was that just a word he tossed around to get his own way?

'Hey.'

And suddenly Jay was there, in the kitchen, coming up behind her, planting a kiss on her cheek. Even now, after all these years, the physical closeness of her husband was enough to spark Mel's desire. Not today, though – she couldn't let that happen today. She needed the truth.

'Sorry I didn't get back last night,' he was saying. 'Garrett's having some problems with Amy, and he wanted advice.'

Mel moved sideways away from him and transferred the dessert bowls onto a serving tray.

'Is everything okay?' he asked.

She swivelled round, pinning him with her gaze. 'I don't know, Jay. Is it?'

227

There was a flicker of something – panic? uncertainty? – in his eyes before it was quickly masked. 'Well, the lunch is great. Excellent roast beef—'

'I'm not talking about the fucking food!' The curse shocked them both into silence.

'Can I help, darling?' Tessa wandered through into the kitchen, exuding her usual vagueness. She often blundered blindly into tense situations without the faintest idea that anything was wrong.

'We'll be right there,' said Mel, not taking her eyes from Jay's. 'Why don't you put some music on for us?'

'Will do,' Tessa said, and drifted off again.

'What's wrong, Mel?' Jay asked, crossing his arms.

And suddenly she couldn't keep it to herself any longer. 'Jenny O'Neill – that's what's wrong.'

Strains of Rachmaninoff swirled through from the dining room into the kitchen.

Jay frowned. 'What's she been saying?'

'Nothing – yet. I'm waiting for the silent phone calls to start.'

Jay rolled his eyes. 'What am I being accused of now?'

'You were with Jenny O'Neill yesterday on Bracken Hill. And if you dare say it was a chance meeting, I'll dump the rest of this ice cream on your lying head!'

The accusation hung in the air between them. Despite her anger, she willed him to deny it – to convince her it was all in her mind. He seemed lost for words – a first for Jay. Mel waited, not helping him out.

'What's the hold up?' Now Gerald sauntered into the kitchen. His slightly irritated expression enraged Mel. Could he not give them five minutes of privacy? She picked up the tray and handed it to her father. 'You can take this and make a start. We'll be through in a few minutes.'

'O-kay.' Gerald drew out the syllables, clearly judging her lacking as a hostess, yet he did as he was told.

Jay closed the door behind his father-in-law. 'Mel, we can't discuss this now,' he pleaded.

'Why not?' she demanded. 'The whole village was discussing it this morning. All kinds of speculation as to who the father is. I wouldn't be surprised if they were taking bets.' He was silent. 'Well, what do you have to say?'

His face clouded, and there was anger there now. Not what she'd expected. 'I am *not* the father of Jenny O'Neill's baby, Mel.'

Her knees suddenly felt weak, and Mel realised she wanted to believe that, so badly. It would take away the nightmare that had haunted her since yesterday.

'But I did have an affair with Jenny ... months ago ... and I'm sorry about that.'

'Months ago ...' she echoed. How far along in her pregnancy was Jenny? Not far, surely, if her father had only found out now.

'I was always careful about protection,' he said in a low voice. 'When we split up, she started seeing a local boy her own age. *He* got her pregnant, but now she's trying to palm it all off on me.'

Protection ... split up ... pregnant ... affair ... Each of the words cut Mel like a knife. Although it wasn't the first betrayal, and she should have been used to it by now, this was the first time they'd talked openly about his infidelity. It was too much, and to her horror she started crying.

Jay was at her side in an instant, hugging her, and she hadn't the strength to push him away.

'Sorry ... sorry ...' he whispered, kissing the side of her head. 'It won't happen again, I promise. I'm an idiot. I don't know what gets into me. It's like a sickness. Will you help me, Mel? Help me never to be so stupid again?'

His words surrounded her, engulfed her in the possibility of change and a fresh start. The desire to believe in him, to trust him, almost – almost – drove the doubts away.

'Now, why don't you go upstairs and lie down. I'll tell your parents you have a blinding headache. As soon as they go, we'll curl up on the sofa and watch any film you want. I'll even go and get some wine and chocolate.'

He held her face in his hands, encouraging her with his smile.

It took everything she had to push him away. Grabbing some kitchen roll, she wiped her eyes dry. 'I do have a headache. You gave it to me, but it's going to take more than a few glasses of Beaujolais to get rid of it. Let's get back to the dining room.' Mel brushed past him, turning as she reached the door. 'You'd better not be lying to me, Jay, or I swear I don't know what I'll do.'

He didn't come back into the dining room. She heard his footsteps on the stairs and told her parents he had a headache and had gone to lie down.

* * *

Finn swerved the steering wheel and they crashed into another car. Rachel screamed, but the sound was swallowed up in the blare of music surrounding them. He turned the wheel and they were off again, blazing a trail through the other over-excited couples in dodgem cars. He was like a child, and his laughter was a real tonic.

Finn had been so stressed at the unveiling of the Christmas nativity scene. He'd put a brave face on it all, but Sean's accusation yesterday – and people's easy willingness to believe it – had clearly troubled him. It was Helen's suggestion that they both get out of Kilbrook for a while.

'Go out for the day,' she'd advised, once the unveiling was over. 'They have a funfair in Loughrea. Spend some time being kids again.'

And so they had. The funfair was a riot of colour and music and excitement. They'd ridden side by side on the carousel, gorged on candyfloss and shot at the firing range. Rachel had won him a little teddy bear. The chance to forget about the bullies and the reunion and poor Jenny was very welcome, even if it was only for a short while.

She'd suggested the dodgems as a safe way to get him behind the wheel of a car again. He'd been reluctant at first, but now he couldn't seem to get enough.

'Let's go one more time,' he said, his eyes shining.

She paid the fairground worker, and smiled at Finn. 'Go for it.'

* * *

The Ferris wheel glided smoothly round against the backdrop of the winter sky. The stars were out, twinkling brightly down on the funfair below, a splash of bright colour against the white snow.

Rachel was snuggled against Finn. 'It's all so beautiful, isn't it?'

'*You're* beautiful,' he murmured, tilting her face up for a kiss. He couldn't get enough of this woman. When they came up for air, he murmured 'I love you.' The words just came out naturally, no thought required.

The breath caught in Rachel's throat, but the next moment she responded with 'I love you, too.'

They stared at each other, wide-eyed, both feeling the gravity of the moment. It felt to Finn like they'd both unlocked a door and could now walk through it together into a magical place, but …

'I'm scared, Finn,' Rachel whispered.

'It's okay, it'll be over soon.'

'No, it's not the ride I'm scared of.'

'What then?'

Her face was pale and anxious. 'I'm scared I'll lose you.'

He gently kissed her forehead. 'You won't lose me.'

'Promise?'

'Yes.' She still looked troubled, and he tried to think of a way to reassure her. 'Let's make a promise on a star.'

'Which one?'

He scanned the sky, then pointed. 'There. That one. See. It's really bright.'

'Yes,' she breathed.

He slipped his hand under the neck of her jumper and pulled out the pendant he'd given her, then he took her hand in his, so they were both holding the Claddagh. 'Not just on the star, but on this. The Claddagh means love, fidelity and eternity. An Irish promise. And I promise, Rachel Ford, that you won't ever lose me.'

'No matter what happens,' she said sounding anxious.

'No matter what happens.'

Then it was her turn, and her expression was deadly serious as she made the same vow. It was obvious she really meant this. It touched Finn's heart and they sealed their promise with the longest, sweetest kiss.

* * *

The snow had started again in earnest when Daniel arrived to take Molly to the carol concert at the church. He'd have to get the church volunteers out in force tomorrow to clear garden paths for the elderly and the disabled. As if to confirm the need for that, Daniel slipped and fell forward onto his knees in the cold wet snow just before he reached Molly's front door.

'Damn!' he said, then glanced quickly round to confirm he was alone. People here wanted their priests perfect – no cursing, no drinking in public and always pleasant. It was a lot to live up to.

Scrambling up from the treacherous path, Daniel checked out the damage. Snow had soaked through the lower part of his trousers, and his right knee was stinging – perhaps a cut. He'd be a sorry sight at this evening's performance, for there wasn't time to go home and change. Sighing, he pressed the doorbell, and Molly appeared a few moments later. She was bundled up in fur coat and fur hat, like someone out of a Tolstoy novel.

'Come on in. I'll just get my handbag.'

As he stepped into the hallway, he said, 'I'd best stay here – I fell out there, and I'm soaking wet.'

He indicated his trousers, and she became all motherly concern. 'You can't sit in a draughty church like that, you'll catch your death. Go on upstairs to the bathroom and do what you can with some clean towels from the press.'

His protests were useless, and time was running short, so he took the stairs two at a time. He flicked the light on in the first room he came to. It was a bedroom not a bathroom. About to leave, he noticed a blue notebook lying on the small white dressing table. This was Rachel's room. His conscience prickled, but he managed to ignore it. The temptation was too great.

At the dressing table, he flicked through the notebook, scanning Rachel's writings on Stokeley and the murals. Daniel gently opened one of the drawers. Inside he saw a purple book and pulled it out. It was a diary from years ago. What had the young Rachel been like? His curiosity got the better of him. He turned to the first page – New Year's Day – and the shock at what he read there almost floored him. He dropped the book on the dressing table as if it had burned him. Ella Rinaldi's diary! How could that be?

His mind tore through possibilities – Rachel was a journalist, looking for a story, or she'd somehow found the diary in Molly's house – which was unlikely – or Rachel had known Ella Rinaldi.

Or, dear God, could she actually be Ella Rinaldi?

Daniel stood there, staring at the diary, lost in the nightmare his mind had conjured up, and then he noticed the edges of a paper sticking out of the back of the book. Pulling it out he discovered an old school photograph, with rows of pupils in their best clothes, smiling or frowning at the camera.

It was his class! The second year at Kilbrook Community School. Four heads had been circled in red ink, and Daniel's heart skipped a beat when he realised his own head was one of them. The others belonged to Mel, Jay and Jody. Four friends, four bullies. Fear gripped Daniel like an icy hand. What did it mean? The four red circles looked like nooses around the necks of himself and the others. His partners in crime ...

'Are you almost ready?' Molly's voice floated up to him. Thankfully, there was a turn in the staircase, so she couldn't see where he was.

He replaced the photo and quickly shoved the diary back into the drawer. He switched out the light and made a beeline for the stairs. His wet knees forgotten, Daniel's only thought was to get out of the house as fast as he could.

* * *

Rachel and Finn slipped into the church, and some people squeezed up to make room for them in the back pew. The concert had already started, and the singers' voices soared up to the vaulted roof. Finn took Rachel's cold hand and stroked some warmth back into it. She snuggled up close and rested her head on his shoulder.

The church looked beautiful. Candelabras at the front brightened the gloom and threw flickering light onto the faces of the choir and small orchestra. It all had a timeless feel, as if the centuries had melted away and the spectators were the faithful from medieval times, crowding together in a place of warmth and light.

The combination of music and dimmed lighting lulled Rachel into a waking doze. She'd come to Kilbrook with anger and revenge in her heart, but she'd found love instead. God certainly worked in mysterious ways. Perhaps He'd granted her this blessing because of all her past suffering. The future would be a kinder place ...

Rachel spotted Daniel, sitting on a chair by himself near the pulpit. His face was pale, strained, and he looked preoccupied, not even seeming to hear the music. Maybe he was thinking about Jay and Jenny – two members of his flock who had gone seriously astray.

Cocooned in the glow of happiness Finn wove around her, Rachel could feel pity for Daniel. He'd been a lost sheep himself in his teenage years, but he'd reformed as an adult. When she'd needed help for Finn, he hadn't hesitated. She hadn't the heart to pursue revenge against him anymore. It didn't feel right. It was enough that he was embroiled in Jay's secret. That surely wouldn't sit easily on his conscience. She wouldn't post the photos of Jay, either – she'd not put Jenny in a difficult situation. If Jody James showed up at the reunion, she'd give him a piece of her mind and be content with that. And then she'd reveal all to Finn and hope he'd forgive her.

'Love you,' Finn whispered, kissing her head, and that was enough to convince Rachel she'd made the right decision.

* * *

It was past nine when Daniel got back to the rectory. The concert had been its usual success, although he'd hardly heard a note. His mind had been relentlessly active, helping him piece together fragments and suspicions into a worrying theory.

Without even taking his coat off, Daniel went into the study in search of Rachel's CV. He picked up the phone and dialled the number of her third referee – Father Bennett of St Anne's Convent. Of course, no one answered at this late hour on a Sunday, but there was a recorded message. The man's voice sounded old, a bit breathless, but not unpleasant. After the beep, Daniel spoke.

'Father Bennett, this is Daniel Quinn, priest of St Kilian's in Kilbrook, County Galway. I need your help. I have some urgent questions about a former student of yours – Rachel Ford. Or she might have been called Ella Rinaldi. If you could give me a call back first thing tomorrow, I'd be most grateful.'

He left his number then went to bed, where he had nightmares about a darkened church and a screaming girl.

* * *

It was an effort for Rachel to think about reading a diary entry. The carol music had been so beautiful, and then she'd gone with Finn to Donegan's, where they'd shared a nightcap and a lot of kisses in a private booth. When she'd first arrived in Kilbrook, she couldn't wait for the reunion to come but now she couldn't wait for it to be over. She wanted to get back to her life in London, to invite Finn to her flat there, have him meet Sophia and the rest of the family. Usually Rachel hated New Year's, but this time it could be very different. 'Almost there,' she told herself, and opened the diary.

30 June
School is over, THANK GOD!!! Two months of peace and quiet. I'll stay at home, just reading in the garden or maybe it'll be okay to go to the library sometimes. Mel's going to France for a month with her family, and apparently Jay goes camping with his cousins. Daniel's going to Ballycotton, so that leaves only Spook, and I swear he hasn't been so bad since that time in the stationery cupboard.

Today, the last day of school, was horrible as usual. We had to have our class photo taken. On the way to school, Jay pushed me into a muddy bank so my uniform was filthy. I hid in the back row, so I hope the photo doesn't look so bad. Mam always likes to frame school photos. If I had my way, though, I'd burn it.

Still, Rosie's feeling better and Father Milligan said he'd take us on a few drives this summer. Anywhere that isn't Kilbrook is HEAVEN!

Chapter Twenty

It was six o'clock and Kilbrook was slowly waking up. The roads had been cleared but the pavements were gathering the falling snow into solid layers that took effort to walk through. The news reports said snow was now blanketing most of the country, a rare phenomenon.

Rachel wondered how Jenny was doing. She'd slept fitfully last night, imagining Jenny trapped on the farm with her belligerent father. She wanted to go and visit but after that scene in the pub, how could she? Sean O'Neill would likely run her off the property. Although she'd tried texting Jenny, there'd been no response. It seemed there was nothing more she could do.

Finn was also an early-riser so there was a chance he'd be awake and they could have breakfast together. As she headed for Helen's, Rachel quickened her pace in anticipation of that pleasure. Nearing the house, she heard signs of activity. A scraping shovel and the soft thud of snow. The hedge hid Rachel's approach and the snow muffled her footsteps. She scooped some of it up and moulded it with her gloved hands. Peering round the hedge, she saw Finn standing on the path, his back to her. Leaning on the shovel, he seemed to be catching his breath.

'Hey!' she called, and he spun round.

The look of joy when he saw her made Rachel's heart skip a beat. She'd lock that away in her heart. It seemed a shame to wipe that expression from his face. Still …

She tossed the snowball and it found its target, exploding on Finn's cheek.

'You little …' he spluttered, shaking his head vigorously and lurching for the gate.

Rachel darted behind Helen's car, gathering more snow for

ammunition. Finn chased her round the vehicle a few times before she allowed herself to be caught and pulled into a hug.

* * *

'A parent has lodged a complaint about you, Jay, with the Chair of the Board of Management.'

Jean Donovan, Principal of Kilbrook Community School, delivered her bombshell in a muted voice, staring at the papers on her desk rather than at the teacher seated across from her.

Jay forced himself to remain calm. This might be about nothing more than a pupil he'd called lazy or some shirker whose pathetic excuse note he'd chosen to ignore.

'It's a serious complaint,' the principal continued, dashing Jay's hopes. 'Sean O'Neill claims you're having an … improper relationship with his daughter, Jenny.'

'That's ridiculous!' retorted Jay, with as much indignation as he could summon up. 'The girl's lying!'

Mrs Donovan's expression was not unsympathetic, so there was still hope. 'Actually, the girl herself hasn't accused you. Mr O'Neill is basing his allegation on … another source.'

'Who?' Jay's mind sorted through the possibilities. Mel – unlikely. Daniel – possibly. Or perhaps someone else had spotted him with Jenny even though they'd been so careful.

The principal sighed. 'I'm afraid I can't go into that right now. Mr O'Neill is submitting his written complaint and evidence this afternoon. I'll make sure you get a copy of that. You should supply your own written statement about the case in the next day or so.'

'And then?'

'There'll be a meeting with the Board of Management on Thursday, and you'll be able to make a presentation of your case. You're allowed to have a friend present to support you.'

Hopefully it would be Jay's word against O'Neill's. The principal hadn't even mentioned a pregnancy, so perhaps the family were trying to keep that under wraps. Jenny obviously wasn't co-operating, so what did they really have? Gossip and rumour. Unless Daniel had spoken out against him. A priest's word would carry considerable weight.

'Thank you,' Jay stood up. 'If that's all, I'll get back to my class.'

'I'm afraid you can't do that,' said Mrs Donovan. 'You'll have to take a leave of absence until the hearing. I've arranged a sub to take over.'

'What! I haven't done anything! Not letting me teach makes me look guilty.'

'It's standard procedure, Jay. You'll still be paid, of course, but you can't be on the school premises or have any contact with the O'Neill family.'

Jay choked back his anger. It wouldn't do to alienate the principal. He needed all the support he could get. And he needed to find out what evidence Sean O'Neill had. If Daniel had betrayed him, Jay was lost. And their friendship was over.

As he walked out of the principal's office, Jay saw the school secretary duck her gaze and focus intently on her computer screen. How long would it be before the whole school – and the whole village – knew about the accusation? And what would Mel say?

* * *

Father Bennett from St Anne's Convent had phoned earlier. He wasn't prepared to discuss details about Rachel over the phone, but he did agree to talk in person. One of Daniel's cousins, a travel agent, had been able to book him on a cheap flight at one o'clock that afternoon from Shannon to Manchester. It was almost nine now. He'd be cutting it fine to get there in time, but the radio reports said the snowploughs were working around the clock to clear the main roads. More snow was forecast, but if the weather took a turn for the worse, he could always stay overnight in Manchester and return next morning because the ticket was open-ended.

Daniel slipped Rachel's CV into his holdall, then shrugged into his coat. He'd left the church keys with the deacon, telling him only that he had to leave on urgent business. It was all a bit irregular, but Daniel had been there for seven o'clock Mass as usual so his main duty for the day had been taken care of.

It *was* urgent business anyway – if Rachel was Ella Rinaldi, here in disguise, she'd hardly confide it to his face, because he'd been one of the bullies. He needed proof before he confronted her, and he had to get it today. The reunion was tomorrow – surely the reason she'd come back. He recalled the circled heads in the photo. Mel's special dinner had been a fiasco and perhaps the reunion would be hijacked in some way too. Rachel also knew about Jay and Jenny. And she was in a relationship with Jody – did she know who he was, and was setting him up for the biggest fall of his life? She was definitely keeping her enemies close. He felt a sharp stab of regret to think that she must hate him, too. He just hoped after he'd stopped whatever it was she had planned that he'd have a chance to apologise to her, and say how much he regretted what he'd done.

The doorbell rang – once, twice, a third time – and was followed by someone hammering aggressively on the wood. Please God, don't let it be Sean O'Neill. Daniel toyed with the idea of taking off out the back door, but his car was parked at the front. He'd have to deal with whoever it was quickly and then be on his way.

Daniel hadn't even finished opening the front door when Jay barged his way through and into the hall. Dressed in his school tracksuit, he stood there, almost quivering with rage. At least it wasn't Sean O'Neill, though Jay in a temper could be just as bad.

'Why aren't you in school?' Daniel asked.

'Did you tell him?' demanded Jay. 'Did you tell Jenny's father it was me?'

'Keep your voice down,' warned Daniel, closing the front door. 'No, of course I didn't say anything. Why?'

'He's made a complaint to the principal that I'm having an improper relationship with Jenny. I've been suspended, pending a meeting with the Board of Management this Thursday.'

'Oh God, so Jenny told him?'

'No, the principal says someone else told Sean O'Neill, and I want to know who it was.'

Rachel. Daniel's heart sank. She'd promised to keep it to herself, but of course why should she? This was a perfect opportunity to take revenge on Jay. And on Daniel. Both Rachel and Jay himself had told him that Jay was the guilty party, so Daniel was in a way free of the confines of the confessional, but he'd used that as an excuse. Done nothing. Jenny wasn't a minor, yet she was a schoolgirl being sexually taken advantage of by her teacher. It had been Daniel's duty at least to mention that to the school principal. If everything came out, Daniel could get caught in the crossfire, and he deserved it. There'd been no real punishment all those years ago for their appalling treatment of Ella, so payback was long overdue.

'Daniel?'

He refocused to find Jay glaring at him. 'Did you talk about this to anyone else?'

'Of course I bloody didn't!' he snapped.

'Then who was it?'

He wasn't about to drop Rachel in it. In a rage, Jay was capable of anything, and Daniel wouldn't have that on his conscience as well. And after all, Jay was the one at fault. He'd made the error of judgement that could cost him his job. 'I don't know who told him, but if Jenny doesn't admit to it, then surely they've got nothing.'

'Will you speak for me to the Board of Management – as a character witness?'

Daniel stared at Jay, saying nothing as his mind processed

the request. Could he in good conscience do that – perjure himself?

'You know, I kept it secret that you were kissing Rachel Ford at your party.'

Daniel glared at Jay. 'That sounds like blackmail. I don't like that.'

'Thanks for nothing, friend!' Jay snapped and bolted back out the front door, slamming it shut with more force than the rectory had likely seen in centuries. Daniel sighed. Right now, he had to get moving before the snow got worse.

* * *

'Where's Mrs Cole?'

One of the local farmers dumped a large crate of carrots and potatoes, dusted with snow, on the floor. He stood there, hands on hips, glaring around at the kitchen staff. Rachel wondered if Mel was behind on payment of her bills.

'She's in the office,' said Will, pointing to the closed door.

The farmer strode over and opened the door without knocking. The staff could hear Mel's angry protests at the interruption.

'That's the last delivery of vegetables I'll be making here,' said the farmer. 'I'll expect you to settle your account by the end of the month.'

'Well, that's completely unprofessional. Just where am I supposed to get another supplier at short notice? And I have the reunion dinner tomorrow evening.'

The fury in Mel's voice stopped all work in the kitchen. Rachel's chopping knife hovered over a carrot as she tried to figure out what the problem could be. The last thing she wanted was the cancellation of the reunion dinner. The snow was already worrying her on that count.

'Sure, and that's your problem,' said the farmer, curtly. 'I don't think you'll find anyone else round here who'll supply you.'

242

'And why not?' snapped Mel.

'Ask your husband.'

The farmer stamped out of the office and out of the kitchen, slamming the back door after him. The staff started whispering frantic questions to each other. Only one of them was local. They wouldn't know yet about the scene in the pub on Saturday, or the gossip about Jenny. Silent in the corner, Rachel was putting two and two together. Sean O'Neill had somehow discovered Jay was the father of Jenny's baby, and his farmer friends were sticking by him. The shunning of Mel and Jay had begun.

But who had revealed the secret? Perhaps Jenny had caved in under pressure. That wouldn't be surprising. Or maybe Daniel had finally done what he should in the name of duty to a young girl in trouble – perhaps one of the bullies had found his conscience at last.

* * *

Finn's cold fingers fumbled the key into the lock, and he shouldered the door open, ushering Rachel inside. They were both drenched and shivering. Chasing each other and generally behaving like children had ended with them falling down a snow-laden bank in the park. Finn shed his jacket and helped Rachel off with her wet coat, then brought some towels from the airing cupboard. His hair was dried quickly, but Rachel's curled damply around her face. The effect was enticingly erotic until she sneezed – twice.

'Take your clothes off,' he ordered, and pulled his own jumper and T-shirt over his head.

Her expression of surprise was priceless. 'Finn ... I don't think ... I mean, what if Helen comes in?'

'Then we'll have to be quick,' he teased.

Her jaw dropped open, and he laughed. 'Helen's in Galway. She won't be back till late. Rachel, we're both soaking. We'll catch our deaths if we stand around here much longer. Give me your clothes and I'll put them in the dryer while you go upstairs and run us a bath.'

She stared him boldly in the eye with a you-asked-for-it look, then slowly took off every stitch of clothing till she stood there in front of him, naked. It was Finn's turn to stand there, open-mouthed.

'See if you can find us some wine,' she whispered, stroking his cheek.

He swallowed hard and watched in admiration as she sashayed up the staircase. Grabbing her clothes, he stuffed them with his into the dryer, then blessed the gods as he found a leftover bottle of champagne in the fridge.

* * *

Rachel relaxed back against Finn's chest, and he slowly trailed the sponge over the contours of her body. She'd poured bubble bath into the water, and the hibiscus fragrance helped her imagine she was in some faraway tropical place rather than a cramped bathroom in snowy Ireland.

Before long, Finn abandoned the sponge, and his hands took over, gently caressing her curves and her most intimate places.

'Feeling warmer now?' he whispered, nuzzling her neck, and her body responded to the erotic charge of his voice.

She could only murmur agreement, beyond speech now. Finn's hands were everywhere, his touch relentless, until her body finally tipped over the edge, and she called out his name into the steamy, fragrant air.

* * *

Finn handed Rachel a glass of champagne. 'It's warm now. Sorry. I got a bit distracted.'

'I'll say,' murmured Rachel, with a smile, as she accepted the glass.

The sheets were in total disarray around them, and the

bedside lamp was broken on the floor, a casualty of their passion that had taken over once more as they'd sensually towelled each other dry.

Finn hoped he hadn't been selfish. It had been hard to hold back when Rachel's legs wrapped round him and her nails scratched down his back. She looked contented enough now, though, propped up against the pillows, sipping her bubbly. Pity they ever had to leave this bed. Everything he wanted was right here.

He wanted to say that to Rachel but was worried about moving too fast and possibly scaring her off with his intensity. That was the problem when you'd had a string of casual relationships. You lost your sense of timing for the serious stuff. Maybe it was time to test the water.

'Rachel, I'd really like us to spend Christmas together.'

She set her glass down on the bedside table, and then she was leaning over him, holding his face gently in her hands.

'If you ask me that again after tomorrow,' she whispered, 'I'll say yes.'

Before he could question her further, she'd set aside his glass and was kissing him as if her life depended on it.

This girl was certainly an enigma, but no one had ever stirred his passion like she did.

* * *

The austere grey stone of St Anne's Convent was softened by the snowflakes swirling steadily down from a leaden sky. England was getting almost as much snow as Ireland. The taxi driver had driven at a cripplingly slow pace, and Daniel had checked his watch every minute in frustration. It was after three. At this rate, he'd have no choice but to stay overnight in Manchester. It would depend how long his conversation with Father Bennett took.

As Daniel approached the entrance, the doors swung outward and a stream of schoolgirls poured out, shrieking as the cold snow pattered their cheeks. A young nun emerged behind them, telling the girls to calm down and *walk, not run* to the art building. With a deferential smile at the sight of his dog collar, she gave Daniel directions to Father Bennett's office, then followed her pupils.

The interior of St Anne's was all polished wooden floors and light blue walls. The classrooms were named after female saints, and Daniel caught a glimpse through doorways of rows of girls, neat in blue uniform, hair tied back, heads bowed over textbooks.

The door to Father Bennett's office was open, but Daniel paused in the doorway as the elderly priest was with a pupil – a young girl of about ten, her face dwarfed by glasses that made her look like an owl. She was helping herself to a chocolate from a box that Father Bennett was holding out to her.

'Take two,' the priest suggested with a kindly smile. 'That'll sweeten your temper. Now, back to class with you, and apologise to Sister Catherine. And say three Hail Mary's at prayers tonight – Our Blessed Mother will give you guidance.'

As the girl skipped out of the office, her mouth crammed with chocolate, Daniel walked into the room and introduced himself. As they shook hands, the old priest's face cracked into a smile, one that reached his eyes, and Daniel wondered if he himself would be so kindly and joyful at the end of his many years of priesthood. Perhaps such a state of grace was the reward for years of devotion to the church. It was something to hope for anyway.

Father Bennett rang for tea, and they settled in comfortable chairs on either side of the fireplace.

'My old bones need the heat these days,' the priest said, holding out his gnarled hands in the direction of the blazing fire. 'I spent time in Africa in my youth, you know. The sun was heavenly.'

Daniel let the old priest rake over his memories for a while. As he listened to the soothing voice and the snowflakes fluttering against the windows, the reason for his visit, the urgency he'd felt that morning, seemed to recede. He even caught himself dozing once or twice.

All that changed, though, after a nun delivered and poured tea for them. At Father Bennett's instruction, she closed the door behind her and was to put up the 'Do Not Disturb' sign. Taking a sip of his tea, he said, 'So, you've come about Rachel. Does she know you're here?'

The old man's eyes were eagle-sharp now, and Daniel knew he wouldn't get away with any half-truths. He shook his head. 'I don't even know if I'm on the right track, Father, but if she is who I think she is, then I'm worried about what she might do. I think she's after revenge for what happened to her at school in Kilbrook.'

'Indeed.' The priest's expression was guarded and Daniel knew they were both skirting a fine line of confidentiality. 'And who exactly do you think she is – and what is it you think happened to her?'

Daniel looked at his cup, couldn't meet the old man's eyes, didn't want to see the inevitable judgement he deserved there. 'It's not what I think, Father, it's what I know. You see, I ... I was one of the bullies who made her life a misery.'

Shame burned his cheeks, but when he glanced up, there was only compassion in his fellow priest's eyes. That was somehow worse. Daniel wanted to be berated, to be told what a hypocrite he was, and that there was no forgiveness from God for him. That's what the background voices in his head had been saying ever since that fateful night long ago in St Kilian's church.

'Have you confessed to this?' Father Bennett asked.

'Many times,' whispered Daniel, appalled to hear his voice crack with grief. 'But it didn't help.'

'So you will have done penance for the sin, and God has forgiven you. That would be true for any member of your flock, yes?'

Daniel nodded, but the misery and guilt inside him didn't shift. 'It was a terrible thing we did. And none of us were ever really punished.'

'Oh, I think you were,' said Father Bennett. 'You punished yourself. You've probably lived under the weight of guilt for years. Perhaps it was even one reason you joined the priesthood?'

The old man seemed to have a window into Daniel's soul. It was disturbing yet reassuring at the same time. 'I thought ... if I could do some good as a priest ... help people ... it might make up for ...'

The memory of that night in the church blazed back into Daniel's mind, in full, horrifying technicolour, and he felt despair loom close. He'd never be free of it.

'Perhaps you should have changed your name to Thomas.'

Daniel stared at the old priest. What was he talking about? Was his mind wandering?

'*Be not faithless but believing,*' Father Bennett quoted. 'Thomas doubted Jesus; you doubt God's forgiveness, his love. The sins of those who truly repent are absolved. It's the central tenet of our faith, what gives us hope and courage to go on. God has forgiven you—'

'But Ella Rinaldi hasn't!' Daniel blurted out. Catholic dogma was of no consolation to him, trapped in the middle of some nightmare revenge tragedy. 'She's back in Kilbrook, plotting against us, I'm sure. Who knows what she'll do?'

The cup shook in Father Bennett's trembling hand, and Daniel wondered if he'd gone too far. Shouting at a fellow priest. He was surely losing it.

Father Bennett set down his cup and levered himself out of the chair. Daniel expected to be dismissed, but the priest walked slowly over to his desk. Rifling through a manila folder, he pulled something out and brought it back over to the fireplace. 'Let's start over, shall we, and share what we know.' He held out a photograph for Daniel to see. 'Can you tell me if this is the same Rachel you know?'

Daniel stared intently at the picture. 'It's her.'

Father Bennett nodded and settled himself back down in his chair. 'Please understand, Father Quinn, what I'm about to tell you is said in confidence. It should go no further than this room. Is that clear?'

Daniel nodded.

The old priest stared down at the photo, still in his hands. 'Rachel came to us here at St Anne's after suffering a deep trauma. She was very fragile. Her soul was troubled ...'

As the priest shared what he knew, the burden of guilt on Daniel slowly intensified, and started to manifest itself as a ferocious headache. He only suffered from migraines occasionally – probably brought on by stress, the doctor had suggested. By the end of the revelation, the pain behind Daniel's temples was so bad that he welcomed Father Bennett's suggestion that he lie down and rest in one of the school's guest rooms.

* * *

Arriving home, Mel saw Jay's car parked at a slant in the driveway, blocking access to the garage. The au pair had had to park behind him, so there was no room for Mel. Furious, she left her car on the street and trudged through the uncleared snow up to the house. Jay's car had a good five inches of snow layered on it, which meant he'd been home longer than the couple of hours since classes had finished. Perhaps the school had declared a snow day. Lucky for some.

Closing the front door behind her, Mel allowed herself to experience the exhaustion that had dogged her all day. She hadn't slept well last night after Jay's confession about Jenny, and now the farmers had taken against her.

There were sounds of splashing water and shrieks from upstairs – bath-time for Leanne. At least that part of her life was normal. Ilsa knew she had a cushy number here, and she wouldn't react to village gossip – likely didn't even understand half of it with her broken English.

Mel picked up the mail and went in search of Jay. He hadn't answered any of her calls, and as she walked into the living room, she could see the reason for that. He was passed out on the sofa, an empty bottle of whisky on the coffee table beside him. Hopefully Leanne hadn't seen him like that. A fine example of a parent he was.

She shook him roughly, snapping out his name, but Jay just mumbled something incoherent and rolled over with his back to her. A piece of paper was sticking out of his tracksuit pocket, and Mel took it and unfolded it.

As she read the copy of the complaint which had been lodged against Jay, her heart sank and despair loomed close. This must be why the suppliers had turned against her. They were closing ranks. Sean O'Neill had found out what had been going on. The girl must have talked, trying to blame Jay for her condition. Things were about to get very messy, and instead of dealing with it, Jay had disappeared into the bottom of a bottle. He was absolutely useless in a crisis. Mel was on her own.

Suddenly Jay's mobile thrummed and Mel fished it out of his pocket. She almost fainted when she saw who the text was from: Jenny O'Neill, begging Jay to call her right away. The stupid little cow! It wasn't enough that she'd screwed another woman's husband, now she'd endangered his job, and probably wanted to break up his family. All this mess had happened because the girl hadn't had the wit to use proper protection with her equally dim teenage boyfriend, and now she wanted to come out of it all smelling of roses.

The anger took such a tight hold of Mel that she could hardly breathe. She should phone the O'Neill girl back and chew her out. Set her straight. She'd not drag herself down to that level, though. She still had her pride.

Then another thought drifted into Mel's mind. She had Jay's mobile – she could put an end to this nightmare once and for all.

She was alone in the room with Jay, but still Mel glanced behind her as if afraid of lurking witnesses. Clicking 'reply', she hesitated, battling her conscience. Glancing down at Jay, curled up helplessly on the sofa, she knew she'd have to protect him. From himself, if necessary.

She started typing the text, all fingers and thumbs so she had to keep deleting her errors. Once the message was finished, she read it through:

It's over, Jenny. Why can't you accept that? Have you no shame? You've ruined my life. I never want to see you again. Jay.

Mel pressed send, her heart thudding, and the text clicked through. She waited a few moments, but there was no reply. She flicked to *Sent Messages* and deleted the incriminating text. There was no trace of what she'd done. Then she deleted Jenny's message. Hopefully Jay wouldn't be subject to further emotional blackmail from little Miss O'Neill. Mel would persuade Jay to deny all accusations to the Board of Management. They'd weather this together.

A gust of wind spattered snow against the window. She strode over and rattled the curtains closed. Bring it on, Kilbrook. Melissa Cole was ready for battle.

* * *

'How does it look?' Rachel was perched on top of a chair, trying to make sure the star at the top of Helen's silvery Christmas tree was straight. It was only the first day of December, but Helen always put her tree and decorations up early.

Finn was holding Rachel's waist in case she fell, and all he could see in front of him were the glorious curves emphasised by her short, tight skirt. 'The view from here is fabulous,' he murmured.

Rachel gave a playful backward kick. 'I meant the star.'

He peered round her body and up at the tree. 'Pull it a little to the left … a bit more … perfect.'

Finn helped Rachel down from the chair, and then pulled

her in close for a kiss but was distracted when her mobile beeped. Disentangling herself, Rachel pulled the phone from her pocket. 'Sorry, Finn ... I need to see if this is important.'

Rachel read her text, then made a call, frowning as she held the phone up to her ear. She clicked the off button and stared at the screen again. 'Finn – read this.'

Surprised, he took her mobile and saw a message from Jenny O'Neill:

Rachel, thanks for everything, for being my friend. No one else understands. They all hate me for what I've done, even Jay. It hurts so much and I'm tired of it all. Tell Father Quinn I'm sorry. Bye. Jenny.

'God, poor kid,' said Finn, handing the phone back. 'All this is really getting to her.'

Rachel grabbed his arm, and there was real alarm in her voice. 'Finn, I think this is more than teenage angst. She's saying goodbye.'

'Why? Where's she going?'

Rachel read part of the message out loud: 'Tell Father Quinn I'm sorry.'

She was looking at him as if he should understand something he was clearly missing. Then a light went on. 'Is she going to have an abortion?'

Rachel shook her head impatiently. 'No, I think she's going to try to kill herself.'

'What!' Finn felt like he'd been slapped in the face. Surely Rachel was misinterpreting the message.

'Do you have the O'Neills' home number?' she asked.

'In the address book on the hall table, but—'

She was out of the living room before Finn could finish his sentence. He hurried after her into the hallway, where she scanned a page in the address book before picking up the phone. Her fingers seemed to be trembling as she dialled. Reaching across for the handset, he clicked 'speaker' so they could both hear who answered. After a few minutes of ringing, a small voice answered, 'Hello?'

Rachel spoke. 'Hello? Is that the O'Neills' farm?' There was only a faint crackling sound. 'Hello? Who's that?'

The small voice spoke again. 'Sally O'Neill.' Finn mouthed 'sister' to Rachel.

'Sally – this is Rachel. I work with Mrs MacKenzie on the school play. Can I speak to your mam?'

'She's out.'

'Is your dad in then?'

The phone line crackled again, and Rachel had to ask Sally to repeat what she said. The girl's parents had gone to Willow Farm, to help their nearest neighbours whose sheep had escaped when the snow made part of the barn roof and wall collapse.

'Can I speak to Jenny?' asked Rachel.

'Okay.'

It was a long wait until the girl came back on the line, and she sounded anxious now. 'She's locked the bedroom door, and she won't answer.'

Rachel set the phone down on the hall table, putting on her coat and scarf as she continued talking. 'Sally, don't worry. I'm coming over now to try to talk to her, okay?'

'Okay.'

'See you soon, Sally. Bye now.'

Finn had put on his coat, too, and was shrugging into his boots.

Rachel pulled out her car keys. 'I don't know how long it will take us in the snow. Once we're in the car, I think you should phone an ambulance. And see if you can get hold of Jenny's parents at Willow Farm.'

'Okay.'

Perhaps Jenny was just passed out drunk, and he and Rachel would end up looking like fools. Better that, though, than the alternative.

* * *

253

Rachel had never driven in such conditions before, along slippery roads and tracks packed with snow, and by the time they arrived at the O'Neills' farm, her hands were cramping from gripping the steering wheel so tightly. Finn had managed to get through to the emergency services for an ambulance but had no service after that and was unable to reach the O'Neills at Willow Farm.

One light burned inside the farmhouse. They got out of the car and plodded through the deep snow to the front door. Rachel knocked loudly, but nothing happened so Finn started hammering at the weathered wood.

'I think the wind's too loud for anyone to hear us.' Rachel had to raise her voice against the gale that was brewing around them. She tried the handle, and the door swung open, jerking her arm and crashing against the hall wall.

Two little girls stumbled into the hallway, looking scared. Jenny's sisters. 'Hello. I'm Rachel.' She looked at the older girl. 'Are you Sally?' A nod. 'We spoke on the phone a little while ago – remember?'

The girls were staring nervously at Finn as he shut the door behind him. 'It's okay. This is Finn – he also works with Jenny in the play. Where is Jenny, Sally? Can you take us to her?'

The farmhouse was all on one level, so they were led down the hallway to a room at the back. Finn knocked at the door and called out Jenny's name. There was no response. He turned the handle but the door was locked. He glanced at the girls and whispered to Rachel, 'Keep them back. Over there.'

Rachel put her arms round the girls' shoulders and moved them with her to a spot where they couldn't see into the bedroom.

Finn kicked out at the door, just under the handle, and there was an almighty crack that made the youngest girl shriek. The door was open now.

Finn glanced quickly into the room and then stepped back, crouching down to talk to Sally. 'Sally, where's the phone?'

'Kitchen.'

'Can you find the number for Willow Farm and call them? Say your mam and dad should come back right away. Can you do that?'

Sally gulped, her eyes wide and scared. 'What's wrong?'

Finn kept his voice very calm. 'Jenny's a bit sick. We're going to help her. Now, you go and phone Willow Farm. Then get some milk and biscuits for you and your sister. Wait there for us in the kitchen. Okay?'

Sally nodded and moved backwards slowly down the corridor, holding tight to her sister. When they were out of sight, Finn bolted back into the bedroom and Rachel followed.

Jenny was curled up in the foetal position on the bed. An empty packet of pills lay on the bedspread next to her. Rachel froze at the sight, felt her knees trembling. Memories crowded her mind – her mother sprawled unconscious on the kitchen floor ... the stark open grave at the funeral ...

She watched as Finn looked at the pill packet, grabbed Jenny's wrist to check her pulse, shouted her name. There was the faintest flicker of the girl's eyelids and a small moan. He scooped her off the bed, held her upright against him, tried to walk her up and down the bedroom, but she was swooning against him.

'They said it could take two hours for an ambulance to get here,' said Finn. 'They're backed up with emergencies.'

'We'll have to take her ourselves,' decided Rachel. The thought of getting back in the car and fighting her way through the blinding snow filled Rachel with horror, but Jenny could be dying. There was no choice. 'I'll get the car started. Can you dress her warmly?'

Finn pointed to a pink phone on the bedside table. 'Take Jenny's mobile in case the batteries run out on ours.'

* * *

After Rachel had left the room, Finn laid Jenny down on the

bed. Rummaging in her wardrobe, he found boots and fitted them onto her feet. He wrapped the duvet around the girl and picked her up easily in his arms – she weighed next to nothing.

In the hallway, he glimpsed Jenny's sisters at the kitchen table, all biscuit crumbs and milk moustaches. Someone at Willow Farm had promised to get a message to the O'Neills who were out in the fields somewhere rounding up stray sheep. 'Sally, tell your mum we've taken Jenny to the hospital in Galway. Okay?'

She nodded. Finn was worried about leaving them alone but there was no choice. Taking them in the car on a journey in such hazardous conditions would be totally irresponsible. They were safer at home. Outside, the wind tore at Finn's hair and the snow temporarily blinded him. Rachel honked the car horn and he stumbled in the direction of the sound. He saw the car lights, and then Rachel was there beside him, opening a rear door.

'You stay in the back with her, Finn. Keep talking to her. Try to keep her awake.'

The journey to the hospital was tortuously slow, and Jenny moaned at every bump and slide in the road. She threw up into a bag, and then she started saying a few words in response to Finn's questions to try to keep her awake. They'd just passed the sign for Galway when Jenny cried out in pain. As Finn reached for her pulse, she whispered, 'I think I'm bleeding.'

Chapter Twenty-One

Rachel slumped into a chair in the reception area of the Emergency Department. They'd made the journey in just under an hour. Now they'd have to wait and see if Jenny would be okay. The adrenaline surge that had helped Rachel cope with the discovery at the farmhouse and the dangerous drive to the hospital was subsiding, leaving an exhausted melancholy in its wake.

The image of Jenny lying curled up on the bed, dying slowly and alone, wouldn't leave Rachel's mind. Why hadn't she gone with the girl to tell her parents the minute she found out about the pregnancy? Why hadn't she told the O'Neills that Jay was the father? Instead she'd played some stupid waiting game and baited Daniel to see what he would do. There must be something twisted and sick inside her.

But it was the bullies who'd made her that way, with their total lack of compassion and decency. They'd ripped all feelings of hope and safety from her. Anyone who said bullying was just a phase clearly hadn't met the adult Mel and Jay. Even Daniel was still the coward he'd always been, only interested in helping himself. Jenny should weigh as much on their conscience as on Rachel's, yet that was unlikely.

Well, they'd hear her out this evening at the reunion dinner. Then she was through with Kilbrook. She'd put the past behind her and try to rebuild her life. Finn might be appalled by Rachel's deception and want nothing more to do with her. That would be heartbreaking, but she had no control over that. Nothing and no one was going to stop her revelation tonight.

* * *

A kindly nurse had taken pity on Finn and took him to the

Intensive Care Unit for a glimpse of Jenny. He peered through the glass and saw her lying still and silent in the hospital bed. Blood from a transfusion bag was dripping slowly into her veins, and a machine monitored her vitals.

Susan O'Neill sat by the bed, smoothing back Jenny's hair. Her face was as white as her daughter's. Sean O'Neill, listening to the doctor, looked smaller than usual, shrunken somehow, all the usual fight gone out of him. The nurse told Finn that Jenny was out of danger, and he turned away from the window and slowly walked away down the corridor. A door opened behind him and he heard Sean O'Neill call his name. Oh God, he couldn't cope right now with a confrontation.

He continued walking until he felt himself pulled around and, to his astonishment, Sean O'Neill gave him a big man-hug, then he was shaking his hand in a bone-crushing grip.

'Thank you ... thank you,' Sean said, his voice breaking with emotion. 'She'll be okay, but she's lost the ...' He stopped short of saying there'd been a miscarriage, but it wasn't a surprise to Finn. When the nurses had unwrapped Jenny from the duvet after their arrival, there'd been a frightening amount of blood.

'If you hadn't ... if she'd ... I don't know what I'd have done. You're a hero.'

Finn suddenly thought about Ethan and the grief hit him afresh. He'd not been able to save his friend. He was no hero. It was all down to luck – who lived and who died. The despair of knowing that made him unable to respond to Sean, apart from a reassuring hand on the shoulder and a feigned smile.

As he walked back down the corridor, Finn had to resist the urge to run. He needed to get out of this place as quickly as possible, and he needed to come clean about who he really was.

* * *

Mel glared out at the snow through the kitchen window. Was there no end to the stuff? The worst winter weather in a hundred years and it had to happen around the time of her class reunion. Everybody else seemed to be delighted with it, though. Switching on the TV, she actually saw the weatherman rubbing his hands with glee. She'd have fired him on the spot for that.

The boiler had packed up in the school, so there were no classes today. Ilsa was playing with Leanne in the back garden. Their shrieks and laughter irritated Mel, but at least they were out from under her feet and she'd been able to call her solicitor in peace and quiet.

Pouring a mug of strong coffee, Mel went through to the living room where Jay was still sprawled on the sofa. Last night, she'd propped a pillow under his head and thrown a blanket over him. She'd also locked up the drinks cabinet. He needed to be sober today. She rattled the curtains open, letting in the unnatural white light from the snow. Jay eventually responded to her shaking, and he cursed and groaned as he levered himself upright.

'What time is it?' he asked, his voice hoarse.

'Just gone nine.' Mel perched on the ottoman. What she most wanted to do was slap his face, but strategy not hysteria was what was needed.

'Gotta get to school,' mumbled Jay, looking around him in a daze.

Mel scooped up the letter from the table and waved it under his nose. 'They've suspended you – remember?'

His expression clouded, and his shoulders slumped.

'Here, drink this coffee.'

Jay did so with the obedience of a child. Hopefully he'd do everything else Mel asked of him today as easily.

'Simon's coming to see you at two o'clock. Make sure you're here – and sober.'

'Simon? Our solicitor?'

Jay looked startled, and it occurred to Mel he might think she was filing for divorce. Which was what he really deserved. 'He's going to help you prepare the written statement to the Board in response to the complaint,' she told him.

'The union rep—'

'Some fifth-rate nobody isn't likely to get you out of this, Jay. We need the best. You'll be denying any relationship with this girl, of course.'

'Well ...'

'Denying it all,' said Mel, firmly. 'The girl had a crush on you. You tried to talk her out of it. End of story.'

He couldn't meet her gaze. She had him on the ropes now. With a bit of luck, he might have been so burned, he'd never stray again. Just one more thing ...

'By the way, you're not coming to the reunion dinner this evening.'

A flare of resentment flickered in his eyes. 'Yes, I am.'

'The whole village will likely know about Sean O'Neill's accusation by now. Best lie low till Thursday. Why give them the chance to whisper and finger point?'

At least half of the reunion class no longer lived in Kilbrook, and most of the set that still lived here would be on Mel's side. At least, they wouldn't dare gossip in her hearing. If she could just get through this evening successfully, she'd be able to focus properly on all the other problems.

Jay was searching in his pockets. 'Where's my phone?'

'I've just set it to recharge in the kitchen,' Mel said, neglecting to mention that she'd left it on all night with the ringer turned down so the battery would go flat. And that she hadn't properly plugged it in this morning. No chance of Jay phoning Jenny for a while, and he'd not risk using the landline with its itemised bills. Anyway, Jenny O'Neill now thought Jay didn't want anything more to do with her, so with luck she'd steer clear of him.

As she got ready for work, Mel felt quite proud of herself.

She'd fixed things pretty well. She was truly one of the movers and shakers of this world. Of Kilbrook anyway.

* * *

'Tell Mel you're sick today,' suggested Finn, as Rachel pulled up outside Helen's house. He watched her as she sat with her hands resting on the steering wheel, gazing at the white world outside. She looked as exhausted as he felt. They both needed sleep. 'Why not give the reunion dinner a miss? They'll cope without you.'

'No!'

There was an edge to Rachel's voice as she shook her head. The stress of everything was obviously getting to her. All the more reason he should persuade her to give work a miss today.

'Some of the staff might not make it through because of the snow,' she explained. 'Mel will probably be short-handed. I can't let her down on the big night.'

Finn didn't see why not. 'Considering the trouble her husband's caused, I don't think she should be high on your list of priorities.'

Rachel sighed. 'She's not responsible for what Jay did. Let's just say I'm one woman supporting another. Does that sound crazy?'

'Yes,' Finn replied, and she gave him an anxious sideways glance. 'I understand, though,' he added.

'Anyway, she's promoted me to waitress for the evening. I don't want to miss out on my star turn. I'll catch some sleep now. I don't have to be at the restaurant until three because lunch service has been cancelled. Then I'll come round to see you when it's all over.'

'Okay.' Finn was desperate to know if Ella would turn up tonight, but there was no satisfactory way he could attend the reunion without revealing his identity. He planned to tell Rachel who he really was tomorrow – and he wanted to do that when they were alone. Daniel had agreed to get a phone number from Ella if she showed up, and then Finn would contact her later to apologise.

Rachel leaned over and kissed him, stroking his face. 'You were amazing last night,' she whispered. 'The way you just seemed to know the right things to do. You're quite something, Finn MacKenzie.'

The glow her words of appreciation gave him was cut short by her use of his name, and the guilt that provoked. He'd had no trouble forgetting Jody James when in Australia, but here, back in Ireland, he was in danger of forgetting Finn MacKenzie.

* * *

'You're welcome to stay another day,' said Father Bennett, peering outside. 'Apparently, there are quite a few flight delays.'

'I'll manage,' Daniel said.

He'd slept right through the night, knocked out by the medication the school nurse had given him for his migraine. Now, apart from a dull ache in his left temple, he felt surprisingly refreshed. Physically at least. He'd just had a solid breakfast of bacon and eggs in the school dining hall, and the shy smiles and whispers of the adolescent girls all around him had done his ego no end of good. He was ready to go back to Kilbrook and face his past. His flight left Manchester at midday. The reunion dinner started at six. If the roads were clear, he could make it.

As he said goodbye to Father Bennett, the elderly priest put his hand on Daniel's shoulder. 'Go easy with Rachel. Remember – revenge is a confession of pain.'

And this was a woman who had every reason to want revenge. She'd suffered so much pain, and was a danger to herself and others because of it. The reunion had to be her target. It couldn't be a coincidence that she was here in Kilbrook at the same time as that. He had no idea what she'd planned, but it surely couldn't be good.

The wind whipped and scourged Daniel as he slid and stumbled towards his parked car. He prayed he'd get back in time.

* * *

Simon Moore was wearing a suit that must have set him back at least two grand. The legal business clearly had its advantages, but Jay knew he would never have had the patience for all the paperwork. As if on cue, Simon pulled out a folder from his briefcase and flicked through it. How the hell had the solicitor found time to put together a dossier? Mel had only phoned him that morning. Perhaps it was all for show. Make the client feel they were getting their money's worth.

'I've got a copy of Sean O'Neill's statement – his allegations against you.' Simon's voice was like polished steel. Sent a chill right through you. And his beady eyes missed nothing. 'Why don't you read through it now, and then we can discuss it … Take your time.'

Jay read the statement twice. It wasn't looking good for him. Sean had got hold of Jenny's mobile, which was registered to him, and asked the phone company to give him a printout of the numbers called in the past three months. Jay's number was on that list, and it was clear to see that Jenny had called him numerous times. More than she'd called anyone else. He cursed Jenny's carelessness with her phone. And he cursed himself for always using his name when he answered a call. He'd received a couple lately where the caller had just hung up. He realised now that it was probably Sean O'Neill trying to identify the owner of the number. Still, just because Jenny called him didn't mean anything untoward had taken place. He could brazen this out. 'Jenny phoned me for advice. End of story.'

Simon raised his eyebrows, clearly not buying that. 'Well, before we get into that, I must tell you that there's been a development. Jenny's mother, Susan, has been in touch with the school. The family are willing to drop the allegations against you.'

'What!' Jay felt light-headed for a moment. Was there really a way out of this nightmare?

'There is a condition, though.'

Simon's expression told Jay he wasn't going to like it. 'What condition?'

'You are to leave Kilbrook Community School. The school will likely have to conduct their own investigation regardless, but without the family pressing the allegation, they don't really have a case against you.'

'Leave! That makes me look as good as guilty!' Jay sprang up from the chair and prowled the room. 'Why are they even willing to drop the allegations? Isn't that suspicious? Doesn't that tell you it's all lies?'

Simon leaned back in his chair, looking a bit smug. 'Well, that's where things start to look more … promising for us. Last night, Jenny took an overdose. Her parents were out, but some couple …' Simon glanced at his notes '… Finn MacKenzie and Rachel Ford … managed to get her to hospital. Clear evidence that the girl is unstable.'

Jay sat down before he fell down. 'Oh my God, poor Jenny. Is she okay?'

'Seems to be. Your concern is touching but this girl is out to destroy you. She might just have handed us a win—'

'Get out!'

'I beg your pardon?'

'I can't do this now. You'll have to go.'

'There's not a lot of time, Jay. The meeting is on Thursday.'

'I know. I'll come round and see you tomorrow.'

'Why are you so upset?'

Jay glared at Simon. 'A girl just tried to kill herself. I think most people would be shocked by that. Most people who aren't solicitors, clearly.'

264

Simon sighed and put the file back in his briefcase. 'Mel wanted this sorted out today. I tried.'

'I'll deal with Mel.'

'Okay. We'll talk tomorrow.' At the door, Simon turned back. 'One more thing, Jay. Don't even think about going to see Jenny O'Neill. Or phoning her parents. They are all off limits to you. I'll see myself out.'

The minute the front door closed, Jay went to pour himself a whisky, but the drinks cabinet was locked, so he had nothing to blur the mental image he had of Jenny lying in a hospital bed. He was relieved because her action meant there was a way out of his mess, but he was concerned too. He had cared about her. Still did. In fact, if she'd been a bit older ... Still, what was done was done. There'd be gossip for a while but it would fade away eventually. The O'Neills would surely pack Jenny off somewhere to have the baby ...

The baby! Had Jenny's suicide attempt harmed the baby? That would be better all round, so why was he feeling so upset about it? He'd have to toughen up, put her out of his mind. He couldn't live a life without money or comfort, and he couldn't enjoy those here in Kilbrook if he was mired in a scandal. He'd have to make a decision ... and soon.

The front door crashed open and Leanne called his name. 'In here, sweetheart,' he responded.

She ran into the living room, straight at Jay, and he picked her up, whirled her round, and held her close, feeling her cold cheek against his flushed one.

'Shauna has a new doll's house, Daddy. There's a living room with a white rug and real plants in a little box ...'

As she chattered on, Jay knew he was going to buy Leanne a doll's house for Christmas. The best he could find. And her smile might make him feel okay again. He was a bastard. Had even prided himself on it. A cold, hard realist who knew people had to make their own luck and opportunities, and no one was going to get in his way. So he'd been as shocked as everyone else by the rush of love he'd felt after holding baby Leanne for the first time. He couldn't properly explain it, but the trust in her wide blue eyes and the way she grasped so tightly to his finger had touched a softer part of him he'd never known was there. Children were innocents in the battleground of life. Jenny's baby – his baby – was an innocent.

'Time for your lunch, monkey,' Jay said, carrying Leanne through into the kitchen, where Ilsa was opening a tin of alphabet spaghetti. 'I've got to go out for a bit.'

'Take me with you! Take me with you!' Leanne pulled his hair, playfully.

'I can't – there's too much snow. You'll disappear up to your chin.'

'You can give me a piggyback. Please, Daddy, pleeeeeease.'

It was hard to resist her. And perhaps it would be hard for others to resist her. Maybe she could help him get the answers he needed.

'All right. Let's go. Back in half an hour, Ilsa.'

* * *

The snow had slowed to a few drifting flakes. Kilbrook's do-gooders were out on the streets with shovels and virtuous smiles on their faces. Probably wittering to each other about community spirit and all that. One or two gave Jay a long stare as he walked past. Perhaps if Leanne hadn't been hoisted high on his shoulders, they'd have said something. Throw stones and think after – that was the usual motto in Kilbrook. No matter, he was at his destination now.

As she answered his knock at the door, the shock on Helen MacKenzie's face was quickly replaced by a frown and a look that told him she'd really like it if Jay dropped dead there and then. He'd only spoken to her once in the three years she'd been here, to ask if she knew where Jody was, and after a sharp denial, she'd turned her back on him and walked away. He'd got the message and never again attempted contact.

266

'Hello,' chirped Leanne from behind and above his head. 'Did you make that snowman in your garden?'

Helen's expression softened, as he'd thought it might.

'No. My nephew made it.'

'Can I play with him?'

'He's sleeping now, sweetheart.' Her eyes flicked back to Jay. 'What do you want?'

'I need a wee-wee,' Leanne declared.

Jay hastily swung her down from his shoulders. 'Could she use your bathroom?' he begged. God bless Leanne – she'd wangled him a way in.

Helen opened the door wide, and they both crossed over the threshold. Jay looked around. This had been Harry James's house, but not the one where Jody had grown up. His father sold the old one after all his family left him. Took off not long after Jody had, and returned without him years later.

'There's a little bathroom just here,' said Helen, opening a door down the corridor. 'Do you need some help?'

'Course not.' Leanne's voice was scornful. 'I am five, you know. I go to school and everything.'

Helen's mouth twitched. 'Right you are.'

As soon as the door closed on Leanne, Helen swung round to face Jay, her eyes flashing anger. 'What do you want?' she asked again. Not once had she used his name.

'Can I speak to Finn?'

'No, you can't!' she snapped. 'As I said, he's sleeping. Whatever it is, you can ask me.'

Jay took a deep breath. He only had a few minutes before Leanne would reappear. No time to lead up to this. 'I've just heard Jenny O'Neill's in hospital ... that Finn found her ... I wondered if she's okay.'

Her look would have sent the strongest of men running for cover. 'Isn't it a bit late now to be concerned?'

So she'd heard the rumours and had already judged him and found him guilty. Although of course he was. Guilty as charged. Sometimes he forgot that. 'Please ... I need to know ...'

Helen looked him up and down, the distaste evident on her face, and said, 'She's okay, but she lost the baby.'

Jay felt his shoulders sag. Relief and grief weighed him down in equal measure.

'You don't really care about anyone but yourself, do you?' Helen said, folding her arms. 'Jenny was just a bit of fun. And you fucked up Jody's life all those years ago. Not to mention Ella Rinaldi's.'

The curse coming from this grey-haired pensioner shocked Jay, and her words stung. 'That incident in the church wasn't my idea, you know. It was Mel's. And Jody didn't need asking twice.'

She sighed. 'You know, you and Mel deserve each other.'

The bathroom door clicked open and Leanne came out. Jay didn't want her to hear any other insults Helen might be tempted to throw at him, so he swung his daughter up again and onto his shoulders, then marched down the hallway.

'Thank you!' Leanne sang out to Helen, as he opened the door and headed down the path. She chattered about everything and nothing all the way home. He let her down as they reached their driveway, and he suddenly felt her fingers brush his cheeks.

'Are you crying, Daddy? Your face is wet.'

'No – it's just the cold, little monkey,' he lied.

* * *

Rachel stood in The Fat Pheasant's lounge area, staring in shock at the huge photo of the high school graduating class that greeted her when she arrived for work. Prominently displayed, it was a canvas that must have cost a fortune, though her idea of a fortune probably differed a lot to Mel's. Mel was easily recognisable in the centre of the front row, ever the Queen bee. And there in the back row, arrogance personified, was Jay Cole, his intimidating manner apparent, even on canvas. There was no Ella Rinaldi in the picture of course, and Daniel's parents had taken him to England not long after the incident. No Jody James in the picture either. Maybe he'd already disappeared by then. As she studied the eighteen year olds in their final year before moving on to colleges, apprenticeships, or whatever, Rachel realised that getting to know the adults the bullies had grown into had done nothing to lessen her resentment, even for Daniel. She'd initially had a grudging respect for him, but he'd let Jenny down badly because he'd decided to protect Jay. History had repeated itself, and the bullies were all sticking together while someone else suffered. Tonight, though, it would be different.

* * *

Daniel was on the last part of the journey from the airport because by luck he'd fallen in behind a snowplough. However, that meant moving at a slower pace than he would have liked. It was after five and dark now, and the roads to Kilbrook would be much trickier to navigate. The reunion was starting in an hour – perhaps he'd get there too late.

Parked in a service station, he tried Finn's mobile for the umpteenth time. Still nothing. The freak weather was obviously interfering with the signal. Daniel ducked inside the building in search of a landline but gave up when he saw a queue of at least ten people waiting impatiently to use the phone. Best if he just kept going.

Daniel revved up his car and followed in the wake of a farm truck with a snow blade. More slow-going, but every mile brought him closer to home.

* * *

'Right, don't forget – tonight is to be perfect. Especially after the recent fiasco. If there's a repeat of that, you can all kiss your jobs goodbye.'

Mel was her usual charming self. It was just as well she had no idea what Rachel had planned for the evening. Had she heard yet about Jenny's suicide attempt and miscarriage? Probably not. There'd been no gossip about it in the kitchen – they'd all been working flat out with no time to chat. The food would be glorious: a choice for main course of lamb medallions with parsnip purée or seared halibut with roasted baby carrots or a truffle risotto. And Colette had outdone herself on the dessert – a huge red velvet cake with white icing. It was a feast fit for a king for the guests to enjoy before Rachel hopefully ruined their appetites.

She'd been tempted to tell Finn of her plans. It didn't seem right to keep it from him – he was her best friend now, her lover, and she surely had an obligation to be honest with him. In the end though, she hadn't been able to. He might have tried to talk her out of it, and she'd come too far now to back out at the last minute, with the bullies in her sights.

'Right, Rachel, I want you to stand in front of the drinks table and give everyone a glass of champagne as they come in. Make sure you keep the tray full. And smile.'

So she did. Rachel plastered a smile on her face as the reunion class began to arrive, despite the fact that inside she felt sick. How was she going to feel at the end of the evening, and would Finn understand her deceit, or would her actions destroy their relationship?

* * *

'Where exactly are we going?' Finn hurried along behind Daniel, getting increasingly frustrated by the man's monosyllabic answers. The priest had knocked at Helen's door ten minutes ago, insisting Finn had to come with him, that it was important and he needed his help.

At first Finn had thought it might be something to do with Jenny, but Daniel had been away since yesterday and hadn't known anything about the suicide attempt. When Finn briefly recounted what had happened, he'd looked shocked and said he'd go to the hospital tomorrow morning to see how she was. Then he'd clammed up again. Just kept kicking his way through the snow until they reached the main square, where finally he stopped and pointed at the restaurant. 'We're going to the reunion.'

'What!' Finn wondered for a moment if the wind had distorted Daniel's words.

'I need you to come with me to the reunion.'

'No way!' Finn started to back away, but Daniel caught hold of his arm.

'Please! It's important! No one will recognise you. You can be there as Finn MacKenzie. I'll tell Mel you came to get me when my car broke down. That you're my guest for the evening.'

'Are you mad? I'm not going in there!' The thought of mingling with the likes of Mel and Jay and drinking toasts to their golden schooldays made Finn feel sick to the stomach. Daniel had clearly lost it. 'You're on your own, mate.'

'I think we'll find out what happened to Ella.'

Finn's heart skipped a beat, and he stood there rooted to the spot, unable to move. 'How ... how do you know that?' he asked, hoarsely.

'Something I heard yesterday ... I can't go into it now ... I can't break a confidence ... but, by the end of the night, I'm pretty sure we'll know a lot more.'

And suddenly she was there, in Finn's mind. That awkward Italian girl with the perpetual hangdog expression. Now he imagined he could hear her screams as they locked the church door on her. How could he ever face her?

Daniel moved close, a burning intensity in his eyes. 'We were cowards then – let's not be cowards now. This is a chance for closure.'

Finn followed Daniel across the square and into the light and chatter of the restaurant. Still in a daze, he found himself seated next to the priest at the end of a long table. As if by magic, wine and plates of food appeared in front of them. If he wasn't so nervous, he might have laughed aloud as he wondered what people would make of him, a total stranger as far as they knew, being Daniel Quinn's guest. Tongues were probably wagging already. Finn took a long gulp of alcohol. Only then did he dare to look around him, scanning the faces for the one he was dreading to see.

* * *

Rachel nearly dropped the tray of food she was holding when she saw Finn and Daniel enter the restaurant. What the hell was going on? Daniel spoke to Mel and then guided Finn to a table in the corner. Finn looked uncomfortable and a bit dazed. He spotted her and gave a smile and a wave. He flicked his eyes over to Daniel and shrugged his shoulders, his expression telling her he had no idea why he'd been brought along.

Perhaps she should just drop the whole thing. Endure this reunion and tell Finn later – much later – about what she'd almost done. But she'd waited so long for this moment, for the chance to confront the bullies and bystanders. To have it taken from her at the last moment was so unfair …

'Rachel – are you waiting for a bus?' Mel hissed in her ear. 'Serve those plates at once!'

Rachel lurched forward on autopilot, her brain still trying to come up with a plan.

* * *

Rachel looked at the clock. The evening had been underway for nearly two hours. So far, everything had gone according to plan. To Mel's plan, at least. She was in her element, microphone in hand, thanking everyone for coming, surrounded by fawning guests, people who had probably been just the same in their schooldays, impressed by wealth and position, or anxious to stay on the right side of Gerald Maguire's spoilt little princess.

A man took the mic from Mel and voiced his thanks to her for organising the reunion, saying how wonderful it all was. How wonderful she was. Rachel wanted to throw up. Her plan was in tatters. Ever since Finn had come into the restaurant, her courage had slowly drained away. How could she stand up in front of him and confess her deception? Disappointment or anger on his face would crush her.

Suddenly Finn was there in front of her, taking a glass of champagne from her tray. 'Bet you didn't expect me to be here. I didn't expect to be here either. Daniel asked me.' He took her silence for tiredness. 'I still wish you hadn't come to work today. You must be exhausted. Still, it'll all be over soon.'

Yes, it would. And she would have failed. Except she had Finn now – that had been an unexpected miracle. Love found in a dark place. 'I love you, Finn,' she whispered.

His smile lit up the room. 'I wish I could kiss you right here and now.'

'Mel would probably sack me on the spot.'

'Might be worth it.'

His hand was on her waist when a huge bear of a man suddenly appeared next to them. He took a glass from Rachel's tray and then placed an arm round Finn's shoulders, hugging him.

'Well, young Jody, you've been avoiding me all night. You're looking well, lad – not the lazy lump you used to be, eh? I wouldn't have recognised you if Gable hadn't put photos on Facebook. He's very proud of you.'

'Mr Moran ...'

Finn's words were lost by the sound of a silver tray falling to the floor, and the shattering of glass.

* * *

Finn inwardly cursed his old form teacher for blowing his cover before he was ready.

'Please tell me you're not Jody James,' Rachel said. Her

273

face was the colour of chalk, and she was looking at Finn as though he was the devil incarnate. 'You're his cousin … aren't you?'

What was going on? What was the big deal – had Rachel heard the rumours about Jody being in prison, or worse, the lies that Daniel told him Mel and Jay had spread about Jody being the main instigator of the bullying of Ella Rinaldi?

'I'm Finn MacKenzie,' he told her. 'But I was Jody James … a long time ago.'

Rachel just shook her head, her expression a mix of disbelief and anger. Finn was about to reach out to her when Mel walked between them.

'What the hell is going on?' she hissed.

'Sorry, Mel,' said Mr Moran. 'I was just catching up with Jody here, and your waitress seems to have had a bit of a shock.'

Mel's mouth literally dropped open as she stared at Finn. 'You're *Jody*?'

He shrugged and nodded, feeling some satisfaction that he was so transformed. As a child, Mel had teased Jody about the way he looked, pretending she was joking, but she wasn't. He'd just put up with it, laughed it off. Didn't want to alienate her or Jay and end up bullied like Ella Rinaldi.

Mel smiled. 'Well, you've certainly changed.' She took his arm. 'We've got a lot to catch up on.'

There was a crunch of glass underfoot as Rachel started backing away.

Mel glared at her. 'Rachel – get this mess cleared up – now.'

The look on Rachel's face was one of pure venom. 'Clean it up yourself.'

'How dare you!' snapped Mel. 'I won't be spoken to like that. You're fired!'

'Oh, you've heard nothing yet,' Rachel said, and she snatched the microphone from the hand of a startled guest.

She marched over to the small stage that had been set up for the evening and called for attention. All eyes and ears were on her as she started to speak.

'I've been watching everyone tonight. Adults trying to be teenagers again – remembering how great it all was at Kilbrook Community School, glossing over the reality.'

'Rachel, what the hell are you doing?' asked Finn, totally confused by the turn of the events.

'I'm being honest!' she replied. 'Probably the only honest one here. Everyone is either in denial, or they've just forgotten what utter bastards the kids of this school were.'

'Hey – hang on …' came an anonymous voice from the crowd of ex-pupils.

'Rachel, I don't know if you're drunk or just insane,' said Mel, moving forward, 'but you'd better get off that stage right now or I'm calling the police.' She grabbed for the microphone, but Rachel held it out of reach.

'No! Let her speak!'

Daniel was suddenly in front of the stage, blocking Rachel from Mel.

'Daniel … get out of the way!' Mel said, anger crackling in her voice.

'Let – her – speak!'

His voice was firm, his presence commanding. There was silence for a moment. It seemed no one was willing to take on a priest. Finn was beginning to feel decidedly uncomfortable. There was no way Rachel would be talking like this if she was a stranger here. Something was wrong, and Daniel apparently knew what it was. He'd said they'd find out what happened to Ella …

Rachel started speaking again. 'Once a bully, always a bully, eh, Mel? Or are you so convinced of your own superiority, you don't even realise you're doing it? Do you ever think about what you did back then … the pain you caused?'

Finn was in pain right then. A sudden debilitating fear had

descended, as though someone had reached in and gripped his heart, squeezing it until it felt like it would burst.

'Actually, to be fair,' continued Rachel, 'I haven't always been honest myself. Until now, I've not been entirely truthful. This isn't my first visit to Kilbrook, and my name isn't Ford ...'

And then Finn knew. As sure as night followed day, something was coming that he wasn't going to like one bit. Was Rachel actually Ella Rinaldi? If so, no wonder she was so upset. She'd been sleeping with Jody James. Her childhood tormentor. Finn had no idea how, or if, he could ever make things right between them.

'How many of you remember Ella Rinaldi?' Rachel asked. 'Those of you who do either bullied her or stood by and let others do it. Those of you who don't remember – well, you're just as guilty of making someone's life a misery. Being ignored, overlooked, made to feel worthless – that's not much better than getting the kind of attention she got from some of you ...'

Someone at the front said, 'Ella?'

Rachel shook her head sadly. 'No, I'm not Ella. My name really is Rachel although my nickname was Rosie because of a birthmark. I'm Ella's little sister. At least there's an excuse for most of you not remembering me – I was sick with rheumatic fever for most of the time I lived here.'

'You're still sick,' said Mel. 'Coming here just to gripe about something that happened years ago, and making such a drama out of it? Did she put you up to it? She never did have much backbone.'

Any minute now, and Mel might lose her teeth. Finn wouldn't put it past Rachel to use the microphone as an offensive weapon, but she seemed strangely composed as she looked Mel square in the eyes.

'You've got a daughter. Do you think it will be okay if she's ever treated the way you treated my sister?'

'I hope she'll have a sense of humour and not take everything so personally,' Mel retorted, but she looked uncomfortable.

'Being locked alone in a church on Halloween, after a group of morons convince her they've raised demons, is funny?' spat Rachel. 'Not to mention all the emotional and physical abuse that came before. And you call me sick?'

'Yes, well, you've had your say. Now get out – not just of my restaurant but out of Kilbrook. Tell your sister you've had your fun and ruined my reunion night. You can have a good laugh about it.'

Rachel was looking at the floor, and when she lifted her head, Finn was shocked to see huge tears on her cheeks. It was as though the fight had gone out of her, and he wanted to take her in his arms, protect her and grovel his apologies. Anything that might stop her talking because he didn't want to hear anymore.

'I wish we *could* have a laugh about it.' Rachel's voice was little more than a whisper, until she raised the microphone. 'Two months after we left here, Ella hung herself. My sister is dead. Should we blame it on her having no sense of humour – or on the Kilbrook bullies?'

* * *

Daniel felt the tears in his eyes as Rachel revealed what he'd learned yesterday from Father Bennett. There was total silence in the restaurant as people absorbed what they'd just been told. Finn looked like he might collapse.

Rachel handed the microphone to Daniel and started to walk through the crowd to the door. People quickly created a space for her as if afraid she was going to suddenly start wielding a machete. She took a glass of red wine from one of the tables and turned to face them all, raising the drink in a mock toast. 'Happy reunion,' she said, then turned and hurled the glass at the huge portrait of the Kilbrook Community School pupils. There was a shocking splintering of glass. Her aim had been true: the red wine spattered all over the young Mel's face.

'You little bitch!' Mel ran forward and grabbed hold of Rachel's hair, pulling her backwards.

'Leave her alone!' yelled Finn, and within seconds he had moved forward and grabbed Mel's arms, jerking her away from Rachel.

Mel started screaming and scrabbling at Finn's face as he backed her into a corner. Two of the waiters sprang forward and wrestled him to the ground although he was putting up a hell of a fight. There was noise and confusion everywhere. Things were getting out of hand.

'Stop this!' yelled Daniel, and had to repeat himself several times before the babbling subsided. 'Let him go!' As he approached Finn, the waiters hesitated then obeyed. Daniel reached out a hand and Finn took it, hauling himself up, wiping at a small cut on his cheek.

'We've all had a shock tonight, but that doesn't mean we should be acting like this.' Daniel glanced at the faces around him. 'What happened to Ella Rinaldi was unforgivable. We'll have to live with that.'

'How do we even know it's the truth?' Mel was clearly trying to re-establish her control. 'That woman – that Rachel – she came out of nowhere a few weeks ago. She could have been put up to it all by Ella ...'

Daniel gave her a scornful look. 'It is the truth. I went to Rachel's boarding school yesterday. The priest there confirmed everything. Rachel was the one who found her sister's body. Can't you, Mel – or any of you – find some compassion inside yourselves? We shouldn't be trying to tear her apart. We should all be apologising and telling her how wrong we were. Let's do that now, all of us. Rachel ... Rachel?'

He looked over the heads of the crowd, but she didn't come forward.

'She's gone,' said someone at the back.

Finn cursed and pushed his way through the crowd to the door and out into the night. Daniel took off after him.

Chapter Twenty-Two

As the restaurant door banged shut behind him, the cold night air hit Finn like another body blow. Ice on the ground made it hard to stay on his feet, and the effort was painful. The waiters had slammed him down so hard on the floor it felt like a few ribs were bruised, but that wasn't what was important. What mattered was Rachel and the look of horror on her face when she'd realised who Finn really was. He had to find her, to explain just how much he regretted his actions fourteen years ago.

The door opened behind him, and noise from the restaurant flared out briefly into the night. Turning, Finn saw Daniel, and despite the pain in his ribs, he grabbed his friend by the lapels and slammed him against the door frame. 'You knew? Why the hell didn't you tell me?'

'I only found out yesterday. From the priest at Rachel's boarding school. He asked me to swear I wouldn't tell anyone. Besides – it wasn't my secret to share.' Daniel squinted up at Finn, blinking as the snow coated his eyelashes. 'Surely you can understand that? I didn't know if she had some revenge planned, but I thought if she did, she'd likely not go through with it if she saw you.'

'So you *used* me!'

'In a way, yes. Then I planned to get you two together privately so you could come clean about your identities. I didn't bank on Mr Moran. I'm sorry, Jody.'

'Don't call me that!' Finn snapped, and Daniel flinched. 'Don't *ever* call me that again!'

Although what did it matter now? He'd tried to leave Jody behind, to pretend he'd never existed, but the teenage bully was a part of himself and couldn't be expunged with a mere change of name. How many actors got conned by that one and came to believe their facade was real?

'Where are you going, Jo … Finn?'

He hadn't even realised he was moving. His body seemed to have a will of its own. It trudged him through the mounting snow on the pavement, and he welcomed the sting of snowflakes on his face. It felt good to walk. He'd gladly walk forever. Pity the world wasn't flat because then he could finally reach the edge and tip off into oblivion.

'Come to the rectory with me.' Daniel was slushing along beside him, desperation in his voice.

Finn turned left into a street leading off the square, and he suddenly knew where his body was taking him. 'I've got to see Rachel.'

'Don't you think she might need a bit of space?'

'Yes, but first I need to get down on my knees and apologise to her.'

'Isn't that a bit dramatic?'

Finn stopped dead and glared at Daniel. 'Doesn't it bother you what we did? We tormented Ella so much that she killed herself. I'll never forgive myself! Never!'

'I know,' whispered Daniel.

A wave of despair washed over Finn. 'I love Rachel, Danny, but I've lost her. And it serves me right. Your God really does punish, after all.'

Daniel was starting to shake in his thin priest's coat. The temperature was dropping. They could both freeze out here discussing the shameful past they shared but which nothing could change. 'Come on then,' he said. 'Let's go and do what we should have done years ago. If Rachel will see us.'

Ella Rinaldi's sister had come back to Kilbrook for revenge, and Finn couldn't blame her. He'd probably have done the same thing himself. All he could do now was let her know how devastated, how broken, he was. Perhaps Ella's ghost might be appeased by that.

* * *

'She's gone to Shannon to try to get a flight back to London.'

Finn stared at Molly. 'What?'

'Some kind of family crisis. Her cousin, I think she said. She looked awful cut up about it.'

Finn wanted to crash his fist into Molly's front door. He'd wasted precious time in the restaurant.

'When did she leave?' asked Daniel.

'About ten minutes ago.'

Finn guessed she must have already had her suitcase packed, not knowing how things were going to work out at the reunion.

'I did tell her to wait till morning,' Molly continued, 'but she said she had to get away as soon as possible.'

The subtext in that statement was not lost on Finn, and the weight of guilt on his shoulders doubled.

'Perhaps I shouldn't have let her go.' Molly was sounding fretful. 'I did give her a blanket, though, and some bottles of water. Just in case she got stuck in the snow.'

'It wasn't your fault, Molly,' said Daniel, putting a reassuring hand on her shoulder. 'You couldn't have stopped her. Anyway, they'll be out clearing the motorways all night, and she has a mobile – if she needs help, she'll call. Now, you get back into the warm.'

However, once Molly's door had closed and they were walking down the garden path, Daniel sang a different tune. 'Finn, it took me ages to get back here. The roads are a mess. The radio reports are advising everyone to stay home. And there's worse weather coming tonight.'

Finn stopped with his hand on the gate and looked back at Daniel's worried expression. 'She'd turn back if the roads were really bad – wouldn't she?'

Daniel shook his head. 'She just told a roomful of people about her sister's suicide. She found out who you really were. I doubt she'll be thinking clearly … Finn! Finn!'

Daniel's shouts drifted out of earshot. Finn was running as

best he could, the crunching of his boots in the snow finally pounding away the self-pity he'd been wallowing in. No one should be out on the roads this night, and it was his fault that Rachel was driving into danger.

* * *

'I'll come with you, Finn,' said Helen, as she quickly packed a bag of food and drink.

'No. I might have to stay over somewhere.' Finn deliberately hadn't used the word 'stranded' or she would panic. 'It's the finale of the play tomorrow. One of us has to be here for that. The show must go on, remember?'

Her expression told him she wasn't convinced.

'Daniel can go with you,' she declared.

'No,' said Finn. 'He's got a church to run. And anyway, I need to do this by myself.'

Helen sank down onto the kitchen stool and rubbed her forehead. 'Don't go, Finn, please don't. You haven't driven for so long and it's not a good idea to start now, with the roads so bad.'

She was thinking about Ethan and the car crash. It was there in Finn's mind, too, but he was keeping it at bay – just. He went over and hugged her. 'I'll be okay. I'm not going to take any risks. And your car's built like a tank.' He tipped her head up to look at him. 'I have to get over this not-driving thing some time, Hel. And Rachel needs me.'

'I know,' she whispered.

As soon as he'd arrived, he'd given her a quick outline of what had happened at the reunion, and she'd grasped it all quickly. The best thing about Helen was that she didn't ask a million unnecessary questions. She'd taken charge – started getting together the things Finn would need, sending Daniel out to put some tools and other supplies in the car. Even now that anxiety was taking hold, she'd not stop him doing what he needed to do.

'Right – everything's ready,' declared Daniel, coming into the kitchen. Snow was clinging to him everywhere. 'You've got almost a full tank of petrol, and there's a spare can in the boot. Hopefully it won't freeze. Have you got your mobile?'

Finn pulled it out of his pocket and checked it was charged. 'Both of you keep your mobiles on. I'll call as soon as I find her.' He gave Helen a quick kiss. 'Now, don't you worry about me.'

Helen and Daniel stood huddled in the doorway as Finn got into the car. It took him a few seconds to recall where everything was, but driving a car was like riding a bike – you didn't forget. As the engine roared to life and the windscreen wipers cleared a view for him, Finn tooted the horn and set off. He tried to clear his mind of everything except controlling the car and watching the road. He could do this thing as long as he didn't for one second let the memories in.

* * *

The car hit the patch of black ice under the bridge too late for Rachel to do anything about it. She felt the back end sliding right, and she instinctively steered in the opposite direction. Then the car was spinning out of control, round and round, and the wheels couldn't get any traction. As the skid slowed, Rachel tried the accelerator. Instead of moving forward on the road, however, the car lurched towards a snow bank on the hard shoulder. Hitting the brakes didn't help much. Momentum carried the car into the drift and an eerie whiteness blanketed the windscreen and front side-windows.

Rachel sat in the silence and stillness for a few moments, watching her hands trembling on the steering wheel. Stupid. She was so stupid. Only a fool would drive in weather like this. That skid could have been fatal. Once she was back on the road, she'd turn off at the next town and book into a hotel for the night. Wait for the roads to be cleared.

Rachel put the car into reverse and slowly revved the engine.

The front wheels spun and the car backed out a little way then stopped. Nothing would budge it after that. The tyres obviously needed some traction. Rachel leaned over the back seat and unzipped her suitcase, pulling out a couple of towels. Buttoning up her coat, she pushed open the door, thankfully free of the snowdrift now.

The wind cut through her like a knife and whipped her hair crazily around her face. Huge snowflakes whirled through the air, and Rachel could barely see the road. She considered trying to flag down a passing car if one came along but quickly dismissed that idea – if she was finding it hard to see, it would be the same for other drivers. They might accidentally mow her down. Instead, she moved to the front of the car and tried to scoop away as much snow from behind each tyre as she could before wedging the towels in place. She tried to rock the car a little, but it was useless without help. She'd have to hope the towels would do the trick.

Back in the car, Rachel eased off her gloves and rubbed her hands together to get the circulation going. This whole evening was turning into one mishap after another. She wanted to cry.

'Oh, get a grip,' she told herself, and then laughed out loud at the unintentional pun. Her breath formed a cloud in front of her. It was getting cold in the car. She turned on the ignition, flicked on the heater and the defroster to clear the windows, and tried to move the car again. Lots of noise, flailing snow, a small lurch, and then nothing. Still stuck.

Rachel grabbed the mobile from her bag and found there was a weak, fluttering signal. Opening the glove compartment, she fished out the documents for the breakdown service provider she'd signed up with at Shannon Airport. The call to their 24-hour helpline was predictably put on hold, and a recorded message told her to stay on the line or to leave details of her location. Patrols were currently taking two hours to reach stranded motorists. Drivers were advised to stay in their cars and keep warm. Rachel snorted. As if she was going to attempt anything else in this weather. She left a message, thankful she'd passed a road sign a few minutes before going off the road.

Rachel took the torch and set it on the back window to shine out. There were two spare batteries – hopefully that would be enough. Nothing else to do now but wait and try to keep warm. She'd run the engine and the heater no more than fifteen minutes every hour. For the rest of the time, she'd raid her suitcase for extra clothing and huddle into Molly's blanket.

Her mobile phone hummed, announcing a text message. Rachel flicked the light on to read it. Daniel. Asking where she was and if she was okay. Molly must have called him – been worried perhaps when she heard the weather reports. It was odd that Daniel still cared after what Rachel had done. He was a priest, though – not really supposed to judge people.

Rachel had finished with Kilbrook, but it wasn't fair to leave people worrying, especially Molly, who'd been nothing but kind to her. She briefly texted her situation and location to Daniel and told him the patrols would find her soon. A reply text bleeped a minute later: 'Stay in the car. Conserve your phone battery. Help is coming.' Unexpectedly, those last words brought a lump to her throat. She had no right to expect help from Daniel, yet he still cared. She was grateful for that, she'd not deny it. The wind was howling outside, and she felt terribly alone and vulnerable. Her mind suddenly summoned up an image of Finn, and she knew she was going to cry. Why hadn't he told her who he was, long before now? Before her heart had decided he was The One.

* * *

At one o'clock in the morning, Jay set out in search of Mel. Her mobile was switched off and no one was answering the restaurant phone. The reunion was scheduled to finish at eleven, so she should have been back by now. After he'd arrived home with Leanne, he'd gone to bed, pulling the covers over him, desperate for sleep, which had eventually come. He'd originally been angry when Mel had banned him from the reunion. Now he was glad – he wouldn't have been able to stand around and make useless small talk with a bunch of people he couldn't care less about. Not when his mind was still so full of Jenny.

He parked in front of the restaurant. It was empty now, but the lights were still on. Jay pushed open the door and the aroma of spices and cooked meat reminded him how hungry he was. The tables had been cleared, but the remains of the reunion cake stood on the counter near the till. He lifted the glass dome and cut himself a slice, stuffing it into his mouth. Not bad. His attention was caught by the enlarged reunion photo Mel had told him she'd ordered. A red stain was smeared across her face. What the hell did that mean?

Jay felt a lurch of fear and shouted out for his wife. 'Mel! Mel!'

His heart calmed when he heard her answering him from the back of the restaurant. Entering the dim kitchen, he saw her seated at the desk in her office, and he joined her there.

'So how did it all go?' he asked.

She looked up and there was anger in her expression. He noted the glass and half empty bottle of wine next to her elbow. Something was wrong. Maybe no one had turned up because they'd heard about the accusations against him. If so, he'd be in for it now.

'Oh, you should have been here, Jay,' she said, her words slurring slightly. 'It was quite the event.'

'What happened to the picture?' He sat down on the edge of the desk, bracing himself. 'Looks like someone threw wine at it.'

'That's exactly what happened.'

'Someone threw wine? Who?'

'Rachel.'

'Rachel?'

The same Rachel he'd made a pass at during Daniel's party? The one who'd rescued Jenny? Hopefully it wasn't the same person.

'Rachel Ford came to work here a few weeks ago. Claimed she was researching Stokeley's paintings. Daniel asked Henri to give her a job.'

'So?'

'Rachel Ford turns out to be Rachel Rinaldi.'

Jay frowned. 'Rinaldi? As in …'

'Ella Rinaldi's sister.' Mel poured herself more wine and gulped it down. 'I'd forgotten about her. She was ill most of the time. She's recovered now, of course – well enough to come back here and play a dirty trick on us all. Like a spider, spinning her web, biding her time.'

Jay tried but failed to summon up an image of Rachel as a girl. She was younger, though, and would have been at the primary school.

'So what did she do?'

Mel sighed. 'Got up on stage and shouted at everyone for not treating her sister like a princess. We're all guilty apparently because Ella killed herself.'

Jay felt his blood freeze. 'Ella did what?'

'Are you deaf?' snapped Mel. 'She hung herself. All because of a few practical jokes. Clearly she was unstable. I'm not taking the blame for that, no matter what Daniel says.'

'Daniel? Did he bring Rachel back here? Was he helping her?' Jay had no option but to ask question after question to try to piece everything together.

'I never thought about that,' mused Mel. 'It's a possibility. That bleeding heart of his always was a problem.'

'Where's Rachel now?'

Mel shrugged. 'Don't know. Don't care. Hope she gets the hell out of Kilbrook, though. And Jody, too.'

'Jody? Jody's here?' Jay wondered how he looked now. Still

the porker, or had he cut down on the TV dinners? He'd have to track him down, talk about old times.

'And that's the other big secret.' Mel poured the last of the wine, watching as the last few drops hit her glass. 'Jody James clearly had a fairy godmother who transformed him into none other than Finn MacKenzie, director of *A Christmas Carol* and current heart-throb of all the young girls in Kilbrook. He's been here in disguise, too.'

Jay was rapidly losing the plot. Rachel Rinaldi, Jody James ... 'I've seen them together.'

'Who?'

'Finn ... Jody and Rachel. They looked like a couple. Do you think they planned this together? Mel?'

Mel had started laughing, her head thrown back, shoulders shaking.

'What's the joke?' Jay asked, frowning. He hated when she was like this. She was a mean drunk.

Finally, she stopped laughing and after a few giggles, she wiped her eyes. 'That's the only good bit about this evening. She didn't know. Rachel didn't know he was Jody James until tonight. She must be feeling sick as a dog right now. I hope she screwed him – oh, I hope she screwed him. Serves her right, the little bitch.'

'Okay, let's go home. You need some sleep.' He needed to stop Mel running off at the mouth. It was getting ugly. And now was definitely not the time to tell her about Jenny and the O'Neills' ultimatum. That could wait until tomorrow.

* * *

Helen's Range Rover was proving itself king of the snowy roads. A lesser car and Finn would have been in a ditch by now, not only because of the poor weather conditions, but also because his nerves were shot to pieces. He kept pushing away memories of the crash that had claimed Ethan – the horror of the car rolling over and over, the smash of breaking glass, and being trapped with him for more than an hour, in pain, unable to move, just staring at the lifeless body of his best friend. The only thing that kept Finn going now was the determination not to see Rachel end up the same way.

Daniel had called ten minutes ago, saying she'd gone off the road but was okay. For now. A bad snowstorm was heading their way, building up strength as it swept down from the Arctic.

'All drivers are advised to stay at home,' said the radio announcer now, sounding more Dalek than human. The signal was patchy, blaring out intermittent snatches of music and weather reports. It was company at least on the long stretches of white monotony.

He passed a road sign that told him he was close now to Rachel's position. After a few minutes, he saw the bridge she'd reported to Daniel and felt the black ice that had sent her off the road. A scary moment of skidding and then the snow tyres did their job, connecting with the road again.

He couldn't see a car. Where was she? Panicking, Finn pulled over onto the hard shoulder, the Range Rover collapsing a high snowdrift. It was good to stop driving at last, and it was only now he fully realised how traumatic the journey had been. His hands were trembling, and the pounding headache, which had started once he joined the motorway, continued to rage just behind his eyes. He felt sick at the thought of the journey back to Kilbrook, but he'd have to do it.

Now to find Rachel. He put on his gloves and pulled his beanie down tight over his ears, then opened the car door. The snow whirled inside, coating his eyelashes and lips within seconds. He sounded the horn three times and listened carefully. Nothing. He did it again, and again, and again. Finally, there was an answering car horn. Three blasts. The wind made it hard to judge direction, but the sound seemed to be coming from behind him.

He grabbed the ice scraper and shovel and got out of the

car. The world was now a confusing blur of white, and the freezing night air made his body shake. He pushed his way through snow that in places reached his thighs. He veered over to the road, where it was clearer, and nearly had a heart attack as a car swished by dangerously close, blaring its horn angrily.

Rachel – at least, he hoped it was Rachel – was sounding her own horn again. Three blasts each time. Clever girl. The noise guided him to a large mound in the snow. Almost buried but he could see wheels sticking out at the rear. 'Rachel!' he yelled, then had to spit out a mouthful of snowflakes.

He started shovelling snow away from where he judged the driver's door would be. Then his hands scrabbled on a flat surface, and he used the ice scraper like a madman, flinging snow into the drift. Now he could see glass, and he polished it with his sleeve, peering inside.

Rachel's face peered back at him, her gloved hand splayed on the glass. Finn put his own snow-caked glove on the window over her hand and smiled. Her eyes showed relief, but then she pulled her hand away and reached for her suitcase in the back seat. She hadn't smiled, and it seemed she couldn't bear to touch him, even through glass. He had a sinking feeling as he realised he was probably the last person on earth she'd wanted to see. He started to clear more snow from around the car door, ignoring the grief that froze his heart much more than the winter cold.

* * *

It was good to be moving again, even if it was only at the speed of a cyclist. The hour or so that Rachel had been stuck in the snowdrift hadn't been pleasant. She'd got out once to clear the snow gathering on the roof and windshield, and her body temperature had plummeted. Back inside, she hadn't been able to stop shaking, and eventually she'd turned the heater on again, using up precious fuel reserves. As soon as she switched it off, the bone-chilling cold had settled around her. She'd almost cried when she heard the three blasts of the rescue car horn. Then she'd almost cried again when she saw her rescuer was Finn.

They hadn't spoken much – too preoccupied in transferring Rachel and her luggage into the Range Rover. Finn had wanted to head back to Kilbrook, but Rachel had protested. Told him he could drop her at the nearest town, and she'd make her way to the airport tomorrow by train. He hadn't argued, just said, 'We'll keep going, then.' Soon after, he'd switched the radio on, and the car filled with traffic updates and weather warnings, covering up the awkward silence between them.

Rachel had never expected to see Finn again so hadn't a clue what to say to him. She certainly didn't want to talk about Ella or the reunion dinner. If Finn was to judge her harshly for what she'd done, he'd get a slap in the face. And if he said he was sorry, and hoped one apology would change everything, he'd be mistaken. As for love – well, that had to be over now because she'd been sleeping with the enemy. The very worst thing she could have done. A betrayal of her sister. Love, though, wasn't a switch you could turn off. It would take her years to get over this, if she ever did. The return to Kilbrook was supposed to bring closure, but now she was experiencing as much pain and loss as when she'd first found Ella's diary. She should have kept love and revenge separate …

'We're being diverted.'

Finn's voice made Rachel jump. She peered into the gloom ahead and saw a tailback of cars, their crimson brake lights contrasting sharply with the white snow. There had been signs for Shannon some miles back, but they clearly weren't going to make it there. As they neared the turnoff, Finn rolled down the window slightly to talk to the guard waving cars off to the right.

'Pile-up just outside Ennis,' he informed them, his shoulders and hat covered with snow. 'Side roads won't all have been cleared. Best stop at the first bed and breakfast you see and wait till morning.'

Rachel's heart sank. She didn't even want to be delayed in a car with Finn, let alone a B&B. Why were the elements trying to stop her escape? She pulled the map out of the glove compartment and spread it across her knees. 'Maybe we can bypass Ennis …' She glanced across at Finn and for the first time noticed how tense he was, his fingers locked tight around the steering wheel. His face was white, his jaw clenched. She remembered then that he hadn't driven since Ethan's death, yet he'd braved the elements to come after her. He'd rescued her. But why? Was it out of guilt? Or love? Whichever it was, she couldn't in good conscience allow him to go on driving. It would be cruel. And maybe dangerous. These weren't conditions for a nervous driver. She'd have to concede defeat, admit the weather had won.

'Let's obey the voice of the law,' she said quietly. 'Stop at the first hotel we see and wait for morning.'

She heard a sigh, probably of relief, from Finn. Her own quiet sigh was one of exhaustion and despair.

* * *

Daniel pushed open the main door of the church and then locked it behind him. He didn't hit the lights. It was almost three in the morning, and he didn't want anyone reporting a suspected burglary. Anyway, the sky was strangely luminous with all that snow, so some light shone through into the church, lifting the gloom a little. The various stands of votive candles glimmered under their safety guards, throwing shadows on the walls.

Genuflecting and crossing himself, Daniel walked up the side aisle and through into the chapel with the Stokeley murals, Rachel's favourite haunt. Finn had found her, rescued her, and they were safe for now in some wayside inn. Later today, they'd be heading on to Shannon. Daniel might never see her again, and he regretted not having a chance to apologise to her in person. Really, though, what could he say that would be any good? His actions all those years ago had had terrible consequences. His punishment was to find a way to live with that knowledge. And to atone.

He looked at Stokeley's last mural, faintly visible in the chapel with its tall narrow windows. He'd painted a factory, built during the Industrial Revolution, which used to be situated a few miles outside of Kilbrook. Stokeley had painted the factory buildings, ugly and black in the lower half of the fresco. But it was dawn in that make-believe world and the most glorious sunrise was in motion, golden sunlight bathing the rooftops and making them shimmer. A group of factory hands representing the apostles had stopped to point at Jesus transfigured into the Son of God. It was a simple picture of hope, and the transformation that faith could bring. In the darkest hour, it was important not to despair. It was a good lesson.

Daniel left the chapel and stood in front of the altar. He crossed himself before the figure of the crucified Christ on the wall, knelt down on the cold, hard floor. Then he lay down flat, face to the ground. Copying the position of his saviour in his last torment, Daniel began his penance.

* * *

Finn's room in the Shanmore Bed and Breakfast was so cramped that the gap between the dressing table's edge and the bed was about the width of half a kneecap. He was wedged in that gap, trying to close the curtains. When he yanked hard at the tasselled velour material, the heavy wooden pole above gave up the ghost and clattered down onto the dressing table. Someone in the next room banged the wall and roared at him to effing keep it down.

He collapsed onto the bed and was alarmed by the groans of protest from the springs. Everything seemed to be on its last legs. The bulky TV set was a collector's item that had probably broadcast the 1966 World Cup. The old wardrobe, missing a door, leaned into the room at a menacing angle, and the 1970s blue and green flowery wallpaper was giving Finn a headache. This place wouldn't pass any inspection – unless perhaps the owner had just opened up some old rooms to help stranded travellers.

Still, they'd been lucky to find somewhere to stay. They'd tried three other B&Bs and all the rooms had been taken by other orphans of the storm. The Shanmore had one twin bed and two singles left. Finn didn't even try to suggest they share – he booked Rachel into the twin room and claimed one of the singles. He'd offered to carry her suitcase to her room, but she'd declined, tramping wearily up the stairs and taking a right while he took a left. That about summed up their relationship now. Opposite directions. Poles apart.

Finn's stomach rumbled. Hardly surprising, given it was now three o'clock in the morning and he hadn't eaten for hours. The owner had sold them crisps and bottled water from the bar. Some chocolate would have been heaven, but there was none to be had. He pulled a packet of crisps from his coat pocket, opened it, and started munching.

A toilet flushed next door and the pipes started a maniacal rattling and wheezing. Finn was tempted to tell his neighbour to effing well keep it down. With his luck, though, the man would be a big bruiser of a trucker who'd beat down the door and kick Finn around the room. They were far off the beaten track here. Probably wasn't even a garda station for miles. Best keep a low profile and get some sleep. They had a difficult drive ahead of them in the morning – if the roads had been cleared. Perhaps they'd have to take the train …

His mobile shrilled into life and he grabbed it from the bedside table at his elbow, taking the call quickly, not checking who it was in case Thumper on the other side of the wall started up again.

'Finn?'

'Rachel? What is it?' He sat upright in the bed, setting the squeaking springs into action again.

'Someone just tried my door handle.' She sounded scared. 'I don't want to be here alone ...'

'What's your room number?'

'Four.'

'I'm on my way.'

The only 'weapon' he could find was a small tin bin with a picture of a goose on it. Better than nothing. He locked his room door and padded along the dimly lit corridor, trying not to think of *The Shining*. He slowed as he turned the corner, but no one was there. Room six, five ... He gently tapped on the door of number four. 'Rachel – it's me.'

The lock clicked, the door opened, and Rachel peered nervously down the corridor. 'Did you see anyone?'

'Nope. But I came prepared to defend you.' He held up the bin. Her lips twitched.

'Do you mind staying with me a bit – just in case?'

'Have you got a mini bar?'

'I wish. I'm making tea. Come in.'

The room was more spacious than his, but the décor was worse. Blood-red flocked wallpaper, bedside lamps with fringed red shades, and red velour headboards on the twin beds. 'Well, if they ever do a remake of *The Masque of the Red Death*, this would be perfect.'

'Who do you think was at the door?'

'Vincent Price?' he suggested, but Rachel didn't laugh. 'I'd say it was some drunken guest who got the wrong room.'

She seemed to accept that and invited him to sit down, busying herself with the kettle and teabags. There were no chairs. Finn sat on the unused bed and leaned back, propping himself against the wall.

Rachel handed him a mismatched cup and saucer and settled down cross-legged on the other divan with her own drink. He sipped at the tea and swallowed with difficulty. 'Interesting taste. Like a mouldy Mars bar.'

'So, you eat mouldy Mars bars?' she quipped.

'Touché.'

The wind spattered snow against the window, and the two bedside lamps flickered alarmingly. Finn held his breath until they stabilised. Being stuck in this dump during a power cut would be dismal.

'Thanks for coming to find me,' said Rachel, staring fixedly at her teacup.

'I was worried sick about you.'

'I guess they'd have got me out eventually.'

'I wasn't just worried about the snowstorm,' Finn said tentatively. He had no idea how to navigate through this conversation. Here he was, the expert at improvisation, terrified that he might say the wrong thing.

'I don't even know what to call you now,' whispered Rachel. She drooped her head, and her beautiful chestnut hair shaded the side of her face from his view.

'Finn,' he said decisively. 'I never want to be called Jody again as long as I live. I'm too ashamed.'

She sat, unmoving, as the minutes ticked by. Finn waited for her to speak when she was ready. He had no right to push her. None of this was about him anymore.

Another spray of snow hit the window and it shook Rachel out of her thoughts. She twisted her body round and set the teacup on the bedside table. She gave Finn a long look, as if she could see into his very soul. He wanted to curl up and hide. He'd never felt so vulnerable.

'If you have questions, Jody, ask them now,' she said, 'because this is the last time I ever want to talk about this … situation.'

Her use of his real name was deliberate, and it hurt as much as a body blow. More. Finn MacKenzie was being consigned to the garbage. Now wasn't the time to fight his corner though, and he did have questions. So many, it was hard to know where to start.

'Why did you decide to come back to Kilbrook now? I mean, after all this time?'

She settled back on the pillow, not looking at him as she spoke. 'Like I said in the restaurant, I was sick most of the time I was in Kilbrook. In and out of hospital with rheumatic fever. It's all a blur, really, but it was a very bad dose. My heart was affected.'

'Are you okay now?' asked Finn.

'I seem to be. I have regular check-ups. Anyway, because of my illness, I didn't learn about all the bullying and the incident in the church until last year when my mum died. That's when I found … Ella's diary.' Her voiced had dropped to little more than a whisper. 'Ella hardly spoke at all after we left, and I didn't know why she killed herself. Mum refused to talk about it. The diary … well, it was all in there.'

'I'm so sorry.' Finn knew that was hopelessly inadequate, but he meant it. 'I wish I could go back in time and change everything. I'll never forgive myself.'

'I found Ella, you know.' Rachel closed her eyes, obviously lost in the memory. 'She'd hung herself in our bedroom. Mum and I had been out at the shops … Ella's face was all puffed and purple … I started screaming. Mum came into the room and did the same. I ran out of the house to get my uncle … We had to have a closed casket at the funeral … I could never sleep in that room again …'

The terrible story was tumbling out of Rachel randomly, and Finn bolted from the bedroom into the bathroom to be sick. Then he sank down onto the cracked linoleum floor, with his head in his hands, and let the tears come.

When it was over, Finn came back into the bedroom. Rachel had curled up under her blanket and switched off her lamp. She was turned away from him, so he didn't know if she was sleeping or not. A few days ago, he'd held her close. Now they hadn't even said goodnight. It was heartbreaking.

She'd left something on his bed. A purple book. Finn picked it up as if it might scald his fingers. Some long-ago pop stars graced the cover. A typical teenager's diary. Except this teenager never made it to adulthood because of him. He flicked the pages, scared at first to look too closely at the neat handwriting. Then he started to see names he knew: Mel, Jay, Daniel, Jody ... Spook.

He was reading the dates now – July, August, September ... He stopped when he found an entry dated the beginning of October. Taking a deep breath, he lay down on the bed and started to read.

29 October
On the 31st there's a Halloween party in the Community Centre, and Father Milligan wants to make it a kind of birthday party for Spook as well. Probably hoping to make it less of a Halloween party as he doesn't think Catholics should be indulging. He's planning to bring out a birthday cake but make it as though it's just a little gesture they'd do for anyone. He said he doesn't want Jody to be embarrassed because his own family (what's left of it) haven't bothered. Mam has been asked to buy a cake from the supermarket. How bloody sick is that – my mother getting a cake for someone who has made my life hell. Father Milligan feels sorry for Spook because his mother went off and his father's never around much. So that's a mother and two brothers gone, and a dad who apparently doesn't bother with him. Time to look in the mirror, I'd say, Spook.

30 October
Mel Maguire asked if I wanted to hang out with them at the Halloween party tomorrow! No idea why the sudden

change. Mel seemed pleasant enough and I know exactly what kind of party it is, so it's not like she's trying any tricks. I won't be dressing up even if it is Halloween. Been there, done that. I wasn't going to go but if I don't, I'll wonder if it could have been the start of a new page. I won't expect anything, though, then I won't be disappointed, but maybe they have changed. Maybe it's something to do with me not saying anything to anyone that time I found Spook crying in the stationery cupboard. I'll give them the benefit of the doubt. Again. What do I have to lose?

31 October

I've just finished helping to decorate the community hall for the party. It looks pretty impressive. We've hung black drapes with luminous painted ghosts over the window. I so want this to be a good evening. I shouldn't be pinning all my hopes on it, I know. Rosie was really looking forward to going and begged Mam to let her. I promised to look after her, but she's had another one of her funny turns. She must be feeling really bad as she's not even complaining about missing out. Just lying there with no colour in her cheeks. She said I was to have a good time, bless her.

At this point, Finn stopped reading, and closed his eyes, as the memory of that night materialised in his mind, as fresh as though it had happened yesterday ...

'Hurry up, Spook. Get it on!'

Jody looked at the hooded cloak, which Jay had lifted from the school's Drama department wardrobe. 'Why me?'

'How many more times? It's your birthday – Halloween – you're the one with the gift. The power.'

'We shouldn't be breaking into the church. My dad'll kill me.'

Jay rolled his eyes. 'We're hardly breaking in, seeing as Ella's gone to get the key. Just hurry up.'

Jody slipped the cloak on, still unsure about what they'd planned. Jay and Mel said it was just for a great Halloween joke, but was Ella going to find it funny? Somehow he doubted it, and he was feeling a bit guilty. After all, she'd not said a word about finding him upset after Cary had left home, and she could have done. Especially after the way they'd treated her.

'I feel stupid in this,' he complained.

'You look stupid, too – but you should wear it more often,' chipped in Mel. 'Covers a multitude of sins.'

That hurt. Jody was sensitive about his weight, but the others didn't usually tease him about it since he became one of them, and the rest of the class wouldn't dare. Jay would sometimes call him lardy or lard-arse but didn't seem to mean anything by it. He'd stood up for Jody a few times, but Mel was a right bitch. Always trying to impress Jay. Of course, he was athletic and good-looking, the lucky sod. Jody wondered what it must be like to have the girls fancying you, like they did Jay. He'd probably never know.

'Ella's coming,' said Danny Quinn. He looked scared. His mum and dad were very religious and wouldn't approve of anything supernatural. He'd had to convince them to let him go to the Halloween party – they'd only agreed because he said it was more a birthday party for Jody. It had been good of Father Milligan to do that, but it was still embarrassing. Everyone knew Jody's dad hadn't bothered to arrange anything. At least he'd got him a present and a card. Even signed it, 'Love, Da'. Probably in case anyone saw it, but at least it was more than he'd had from his mother. Not that he expected anything. It was nearly three years since they'd heard from her. The bitch.

'I got it,' said Ella, as she joined them. She looked pleased with herself. Jody felt a stab of guilt again but brushed it aside. It was just a bit of fun, Jay had said.

Once inside St Kilian's, Jay locked the door and pocketed the key. He looked at his watch. 'Nearly midnight – let's get started.'

They made their way to the apse, and Jody took his place at the altar, while Jay instructed everyone to stand in front of it. Ella was at one end of the line. Jay was next to her, then it was Mel and Daniel.

'Can he really do this?' he heard Ella whisper.

'That's why he's called Spook,' said Mel. 'Born on Halloween after his mother had sex in the churchyard nine months before. They say his real father was a demon, you know, and his mum was possessed. That's probably why she ran off.'

Jody wanted to punch Mel. Instead, he prepared himself for his big moment. He liked acting – it was the only thing he was any good at. He'd just forget about the others. Throw himself into the part. He started chanting a mixture of gibberish and the smattering of Latin he knew, calling on the demons of hell to show themselves and to prepare the way for their master. He threw in some names that sounded good, like Lucifer and Azriel, then he began the prayer: 'Lord Satan, by your grace grant me, I pray thee, the power to conceive in my mind and to execute that which I desire to do ...'

It had taken him ages to learn it, and he pushed away a sudden nagging fear that maybe it would work. What if the Devil really did appear? He hoped that when Jay and Mel had read up on it, they'd left out some of the essential stuff.

He'd closed his eyes for the incantation but opened

301

them to see what was happening. Ella had her head down as Jay had instructed. Danny was nowhere to be seen. Part of the plan.

'Where's Danny?' Mel was trying to sound panicky. She was a crap actress, though. Jody wouldn't have been fooled. The three of them looked round.

'Probably needs the loo,' said Jay. 'Get on with it, Jody – don't lose the spell. Girls, we have to close our eyes at this bit.'

Jody watched as Ella obediently shut her eyes. Mel quietly slipped away from the apse and made her way to the doors. Despite the fact he enjoyed giving the performance, Jody was starting to feel more than a bit uncomfortable with what they were doing.

'Oh my God!' said Jay. 'Mel's gone now.'

Ella opened her eyes, her expression fearful.

'Let's go and find Danny and Mel,' she said. 'They might be in trouble.'

At that, Jody's conscience really started to prick. Ella looked scared, but she was worrying about Mel and Danny, and wanted to help them. What they were doing just wasn't right.

'No, we can't!' Jay insisted. 'We'll anger the demons if we leave midway. It'll make it worse! We have to continue. We have to kneel now, with our hands on the floor.'

Jay got on his knees, and after a moment, Ella copied him. She was actually beginning to shake, but Jody continued, waffling nonsense, but sounding pretty good. Even if he said so himself.

Just then, a piercing scream rang through the church. Mel, on cue.

'Stay here, Ella,' said Jay. 'Don't move, whatever you do … and don't look round. Spook, come with me. We've got to help Mel and Danny. Ella, you'll be safer here, away from Spook.'

Ella looked frozen to the spot. Jody wanted to tell her it was okay, but Jay would never forgive him. He was being cowardly, but he couldn't help it. Couldn't face it if Jay and Mel turned against him, so he ran after Jay.

At the door to the church, they turned round. Ella was still on her knees, her back to them and looking at the floor. Jay quietly opened the door and ushered Jody outside, then he gave an anguished cry and turned the lights out. He left the church, leaving Ella with only the handful of flickering votive candles for light, as he locked her inside. At the side of the church, level with where the apse was, Mel and Danny had set up a ghetto blaster, and began playing a tape they'd recorded of evil-sounding cackling and howling wind. Mel was laughing so much the tears were streaming down her face, and she had her hand shoved in her mouth so she couldn't be heard. A crowd of people went by, but they were just other Halloween revellers, who ignored the schoolchildren.

As the four of them made their way out of the churchyard, Jody heard Ella calling their names. She sounded terrified. And he didn't sleep that night.

Finn closed the diary, sickened by what he'd read and the memories it had conjured up. He'd helped to kill Ella Rinaldi as sure as if he'd handed her a loaded gun. He turned to the last page in the diary. He didn't want to read it, but he had to. He had to face the truth about his part in a girl's suicide.

Chapter Twenty-Three

Rachel sipped her bitter black coffee in the bed and breakfast's dining room. It was just past seven and she was the only one in there. She had tiptoed out of the bedroom, not wanting to wake Finn, needing a break from that guilty look in his eyes, a constant reminder of the nightmare of Jody James being her lover.

Outside, the snow had stopped, leaving behind an eerie white moonscape, glittering in the faint dawn glimmer from the sky. Hopefully that pile-up outside Ennis had been cleared, opening up the road to Shannon Airport. Maybe Finn should leave Helen's car in the long-term parking at the airport and take the bus back up to Galway. And what would she say to him before they parted? Nothing, preferably, but wouldn't that make her a coward?

It was still early, but she'd try to phone Sophia. Get another perspective. Rummaging in her coat's deep pocket, Rachel's fingers closed around the cool metal of the phone and she pulled it out.

Only it wasn't hers. It was Jenny's. One glance at the baby pink colour reminded her of the night of Jenny's suicide attempt, when Finn had told Rachel to take the girl's phone in case the batteries on their own mobiles died. She should have remembered and given it back, but it had slipped her mind after the stress of the frantic drive to the hospital and then the reunion. She'd give it to Finn to take back to Jenny.

Turning the phone over and over in her hands, a thought occurred to Rachel. About Jay, and what he'd done. About what he might do. Deny everything, or emotionally blackmail Jenny into keeping quiet about their affair and the baby. Another cover-up. It would be so typical of him. And he might continue teaching at the school, watching and waiting for another young girl to take his fancy. Another life to ruin. Unless ...

Rachel switched on the phone, surprised that there was no PIN code lock. She'd assumed all teenagers were paranoid about nosy parents. Maybe she always deleted any personal stuff. Or perhaps subconsciously Jenny wanted someone to read her texts to Jay – a kind of cry for help. There was no signal, but she flicked to *Messages* and the last text received came up on the screen. She read Jay's words: It's over, Jenny. Why can't you accept that? Have you no shame? You've ruined my life. I never want to see you again. Jay.

If Rachel hadn't been sitting down, she'd have fallen down. Jay had sent this text just a few hours before Jenny overdosed. The connection was clear. The bastard. The absolute bastard.

Rachel felt hot and dizzy. She'd wanted nothing more than to escape from Kilbrook, but this was unfinished business. Jay Cole had to be stopped, made to realise the suffering he'd caused. She'd have to put aside her own anguish and take him down.

She was still clutching Jenny's phone ten minutes later when Finn barged into the dining room, scanning the room before his gaze settled on her. He seemed to breathe a sigh of relief and gave a small smile as he sat down at her table. The smile curled sly fingers around her heart, but Rachel ruthlessly shoved aside all memories of their romantic connection as she slipped Jenny's phone back into her pocket.

'I've just checked,' said Finn. 'The road to Shannon is clear.'

Rachel made up her mind there and then. 'We're going back to Kilbrook.'

The hope in his blue eyes almost chipped a hole in her defences. She was tempted for a moment to tell him about Jenny's phone and what she planned to do, but Finn had once been Jay's friend – his partner in crime – so he couldn't be trusted.

'There's something there I forgot to do,' she told Finn. 'And you shouldn't be driving alone. If at all.'

Finn reached out a hand towards her. Rachel slammed up out of the chair. 'You get some breakfast. I'm going to have a quick shower.'

She strode out of the dining room, praying he wouldn't follow her. This was all so hard. Her heart was still yearning after Finn MacKenzie, refusing to accept that he'd never really existed.

* * *

The radio news channel was awash with reports of the chaos that last night's snowstorm had brought with it. The road to Galway was hard-going, but the snowploughs were making headway. Finn hadn't been so lucky. His text to Daniel yesterday evening had been brief: he'd holed up with Rachel in some godforsaken B&B. Daniel didn't envy Finn that. What could you possibly say to the woman whose sister you'd tormented and driven to suicide? 'Sorry' didn't even come close. He'd done his own private penance last night in the church, but it was arguably much easier to face God's wrath than Rachel's.

'I hope Jay Cole doesn't have the nerve to show up at the hospital,' said Helen from the seat beside him. He'd agreed to give her a lift to the hospital to visit Jenny since Finn had commandeered her car. 'I wonder what Mel sees in him.'

'She's been in love with Jay since primary school,' he told her. 'It's just one of those things.'

And not a good thing, either. At school there was nothing Mel wouldn't have done to impress Jay. If he acted up with a teacher, she would do the same – but try to take it one step further. If he bullied, she bullied – but more viciously.

'Maybe she'll see him differently now.'

'Maybe ...'

Daniel didn't really believe that. With Mel, Jay was an

obsession. What must it be like to know your partner would eventually forgive everything you did? That wasn't healthy. Jay needed someone to rein him in. His parents had only ever half-heartedly told him off. He was surrounded by enablers, and Daniel had been one of them. Not any more. He'd definitely not be acting as a character witness for Jay. No more lies and cover-ups. He owed that much to Jenny. And to Ella.

* * *

Jenny lay small and fragile and very still in the hospital bed, the drip in her arm casting a long shadow over the white blankets. Susan O'Neill sat beside her daughter, knitting a long green scarf. Her hands were busy, but she seemed lost in thought, staring out of the window.

At the sound of their footsteps, she looked up and gave a small smile. Setting aside the scarf, she stood up. 'Father Quinn ... Helen ... so good of you to come by.' She shook Daniel's hand, kissed Helen's cheek. 'Jenny, look who's here to see you.'

The girl's eyes settled on the visitors, but she displayed not even the smallest spark of any emotion.

'I'll just go and get her some orange juice,' said Susan. 'Why don't you both sit down – have a nice chat.'

'Daniel, you stay. I just need a quick word with Susan.'

To Daniel's surprise – and dismay – Helen linked arms with Susan, and the two women walked away together, leaving him alone with Jenny. What to say to the poor girl? Counselling was part of his job, yet he felt so out of his depth. And he also knew he'd failed her as a priest. That guilt had shadowed him relentlessly since he'd learned of her suicide attempt.

He perched on the edge of the chair by the girl's bed. 'How are you feeling, Jenny?' he asked, and instantly regretted such a stupid, useless, pat question. One look at her face told him all he needed to know. She was suffering, both physically and emotionally.

She mumbled something about the baby, her voice faint and hoarse. Daniel leaned forward. 'I'm sorry, I didn't catch that.'

'I killed my baby,' she whispered into his ear. 'I'm going to hell, aren't I?'

'Oh, Jenny.' He gently smoothed her hair back from her forehead. 'You were in an impossible situation. You were in despair. God understands about that, believe me.'

Daniel held Jenny's hand and said a short prayer aloud. Outwardly, he must look like the perfect man of God, but rage was building within him. A white-hot anger against Jay and the damage he'd done. Not just to Jenny's body and her feelings, but to her soul as well.

The anger was so strong, Daniel had to excuse himself when Helen and Susan returned. He couldn't trust himself not to betray what he was really feeling. Muttering that he'd be in the cafeteria downstairs, he fled the ward as if the hounds of hell themselves were after him.

* * *

Daniel hadn't even touched his coffee when Helen joined him a half-hour later. He'd chosen to sit in a quiet corner near a window, needing to sort out the turmoil of his thoughts, but now he regretted that decision because he'd likely have to make conversation with Helen, who could read people like a book and also believed in speaking her mind. All Daniel wanted to do right now was sleep for a week.

Helen sighed. 'It breaks my heart to see Jenny like that. She had such a sparkle in those early days of play rehearsals. So much talent.'

Daniel nodded. 'It'll take time, but hopefully she'll get through.' How clichéd that sounded. Cavalier, almost. As if she were a name on a list, not a real person going through one of the worst moments in her life – in any life.

'I'm not leaving that to chance.' Helen's tone and expression were equally determined. 'I spoke to Susan about options for Jenny.'

'Options?'

'The story that's being put out is that Jenny had appendicitis, but the gossips might figure out what really happened, so she'll not be going back to school. She'll study for her leaving certificate via distance learning. Then, if she wants to try for drama school, I'll help her prepare for the audition. If Sean won't support her, she can try for scholarships and grants. Susan has a friend in Galway who can give her a cheap place to stay.'

'That's amazing,' said Daniel, and meant it. Helen had thought of real, practical steps to help – to show Jenny that all was not lost. 'Getting away from Kilbrook could be the best thing for her. A fresh start.'

'Getting away from Jay would certainly be a good thing.'

True, but Daniel wanted to avoid that topic, for too much guilt already lay on his own doorstep. 'Finn told me how much you helped him after he ran away from home.'

Helen nodded. 'He needed a helping hand – everyone does at times. You know, the one thing I remember is that Finn never complained about what had happened with his father. He didn't give in to self-pity. And he always took responsibility for his part in Ella's bullying. That puts him streets ahead of Jay Cole in my book.'

Daniel gulped at his cold coffee. This new topic was even worse than the one he'd tried to avoid.

Now Helen was looking at him with a strong curiosity, and then she asked the question he least wanted to answer. 'What happened to you, Daniel, after Ella left?'

Memories flooded into his mind. His mother weeping for days; his younger brothers and sisters uncertain, keeping their distance; and his father closeted away in the living room with Father Milligan. The shame of it all. Mel had been packed off to a boarding school abroad, ostensibly to '*get the French right*'. Within days, Finn had disappeared. Harry James told everyone he was staying with his brothers in England for a while. Jay skulked around, picking fights with anyone who looked at him the wrong way. And Daniel ...

'We stayed on in Kilbrook for about six months,' he told Helen, 'but it didn't work out. I was appalled by what I'd done. Couldn't sleep, wasn't eating, my schoolwork went downhill. I refused to go to church – couldn't bear to be in the place where Ella—'

He broke off, gulped more coffee. The headache was starting up again, but he'd have to finish this conversation or he'd look like the worst kind of coward. 'My parents decided to move. We went to England – to Liverpool. It was better in some ways, but the guilt and regret were always with me. I'm not complaining, believe me, Helen.' He scanned her expression anxiously for signs of disapproval. 'I got what I deserved, and I got off more lightly than poor Ella did.'

'And so you became a priest. To atone – or because it's the one job where you get to be forgiven?'

That stung. Helen was right, of course. His encounter with sin – his overload of guilt – made him seem more weathered than the other students at the seminary. The church almost bent over backwards to welcome him into the fold. As if they thought he would have some special connection with the sinners in his flock, some stronger ability to help them back onto the straight and narrow.

'I've never forgiven myself,' he told Helen. 'And I don't think I ever will.'

Helen nodded, thoughtfully. 'Two bullies stayed on in Kilbrook, two left. And it's the ones that scattered who truly repented ... Perhaps it's Jay's turn now to leave. It might do him some good to have to deal with the consequences of the misery he caused.'

But then little Leanne, who loved her father, would suffer.

Every action seemed to cause a negative reaction somewhere else. Even the one good thing that had come out of this whole mess – Rachel and Finn's love for each other – had been tainted. Daniel hoped that the two of them could work their way through it, and keep their relationship going. They were different people now – surely there had to be a chance for them, however remote. He cared for them both, especially Rachel, but he was a priest and it was time to forget whimsical fantasies of what might have been. 'I wonder how Finn and Rachel are,' he pondered, thinking out loud.

'Cold, confused and upset, I should imagine,' Helen answered with a sigh. 'I hope the roads are clear enough for them to get back. It's the final performance of *A Christmas Carol* tonight. A pity if Finn missed it.'

'Do you need any help?' It was the least Daniel could do, since he was partly responsible for this mess. Keeping secrets, deciding to let the cards play out, not alerting Finn earlier to his suspicions about Rachel.

'Don't worry, I've got it covered.'

That about summed up Daniel's position now. Useless. No good to anybody as a priest, or as a friend. He was at rock bottom. The only way was up, but experience told him that upswing could be a long time coming.

* * *

Mel tried to eat a slice of toast but her hangover meant she had little appetite. She topped up her coffee instead. 'What did Simon have to say yesterday?' she asked Jay. They'd talked a bit about Rachel's revelation, but Mel didn't want to waste any more time on that conniving bitch.

'He told me the O'Neills will drop their allegations if I resign.'

'What!' Mel forced her blurry mind to focus. Was this good news or not? 'If you resign, everyone will think you're guilty. The O'Neills win either way.'

Jay was silent, crumbling the remains of the toast on his plate like a child. He looked ready to give up.

'It's not just your reputation at stake here, Jay. I've already been blacklisted by farmers because of this and I'm having to get fresh produce from Galway, which is costing me an arm and a leg. And what will Leanne have to put up with at school?'

'I know.'

Jay's head drooped, and Mel put a reassuring hand on his arm. 'We'll get through this together. Okay, so you made a mistake. A stupid mistake, but the O'Neill girl made one, too – trying to pin everything on you. We should call her bluff – insist on a DNA test when the baby's born ...'

Jay put up a hand to stay her words. 'There is no baby. She lost it yesterday. Apparently she took an overdose of pills. Tried to kill herself. She's in hospital right now.'

That was a shock, but Mel honestly couldn't feel much compassion. Those stupid enough to get involved with a married man made their own beds. She didn't like the look in Jay's eyes, though – a sadness, but more than just that. Regret? Or was it guilt? No, she wouldn't go there.

'Well, that's probably better all round.'

Jay glared at her, and she realised how callous that must sound. 'I mean because her problem's solved, and her parents will want it all brushed under the carpet. Does Simon know?'

Jay shook his head.

'Phone him this morning and tell him. Now we have a bargaining chip. Better for the parents to drop the allegations and not drag their daughter through endless interrogations when she's in an unstable emotional state.'

It took a while to convince him, but eventually Jay agreed to her plan to fight the accusations. It was the only way, or they'd never be able to hold their heads up high in Kilbrook again.

* * *

The minute Finn closed the front door, Helen shot out of the living room and gave him a big hug. He stood there in the hallway, clinging to his aunt for all he was worth. Here was one person who knew him completely, inside and out, and still loved him.

'You look done in, love. Come on through and I'll fix you a drink.'

Finn let Helen pull off his jacket then lead him into the living room. Once seated, she poured him a brandy and he downed it in one. The warmth in the pit of his stomach began to take the edge off his chilled bones, but the despair inside was unchanged.

'How's Rachel?' asked Helen, refilling his glass.

In the car, Rachel had told Finn she would go and stay with Molly. A hint in case he needed one that she'd not be spending any time with him. He'd texted Helen then and asked her to let Molly know.

'She spent the last part of the journey asleep on the back seat. I couldn't wake her when we got here, so I just carried her up to bed. Molly said it was likely delayed shock.'

Helen nodded agreement and sat down in the other armchair. Her face was pale and the dark shadows under her eyes spoke of a sleepless night. One more thing for Finn to feel guilty about.

'How did the driving go?' Helen asked. 'God, I was so worried last night.'

Finn thought about that, and realised it hadn't been so bad. 'I think I'm over it. The fear of driving thing. It was hell on the way to find Rachel last night, but okay on the way back. I guess there are worse things than fear …'

'Well, whatever the reason, it's good that you're over it. No worries for you now about the TV series.'

Right now, Finn's career and Australia were thousands of miles away. How was he ever going to fit back into that life? Without Rachel. 'She hates me, you know.'

Helen shook her head. 'If Rachel hates anyone – which I doubt – she hates Jody.'

Finn gave a rueful laugh. 'That's hardly a consolation, Helen. We're one and the same, Jody and I. A name change doesn't let me off the hook.'

'You were a child when it all happened. Maybe that *does* excuse you more than if you'd been an adult.'

'No, Helen. I was fourteen. I knew right from wrong. Harry made sure of that. But it didn't stop me from doing it – from bullying Ella.'

'The law would still have treated you differently,' persisted Helen. 'As a minor, not yet able to make fully rational decisions. Can't you forgive yourself?'

Finn looked into Helen's kindly eyes. This woman had tried her best to put him back together again when she'd brought him to Australia, all those years ago. She'd almost succeeded. Almost.

As Finn had read the diary, Ella's face became more clearly defined. She'd stepped out of the shadows of his distant memory and stood there now as his accuser. 'It's only Ella's forgiveness that really matters. If she's looking down on us now, she wouldn't forgive – how could she? All those months when she'd have dreaded every day. Sometimes, in Australia, I used to convince myself she was happy somewhere, maybe with a family. I clung to that thought.'

'That shows you felt guilt, that you had a conscience. And some might say remorse is punishment enough.'

Finn gave a small laugh. 'That's what a priest said when I confessed, not long after I got to Gabe's. He gave me absolution because I was genuinely sorry. It didn't help one bit.'

Helen sighed. 'I don't want to see you broken by this, Finn. I think the sooner you get away from Kilbrook, the better. When the court case is over, you should make plans to go back home.'

Home. In disgrace. Without Rachel. The thought of that was unbelievably bleak.

Helen took his hand and squeezed it. 'I'm going over to the theatre soon. Are you coming with me?'

'Bloody hell! The finale! I totally forgot about it!' Finn glanced at his watch. 'It's after five. Why aren't you there already?'

'Relax. The whole show is like a well-oiled machine now. But I'd love you to be there tonight.'

'Well ...' The whole village likely knew Finn's real identity by now. He didn't think he could stand their pointing and staring and whispers.

'It's just a bunch of kids backstage, Finn. They don't care about something that happened years ago. You're one of the directors – that's all they know. It would be a shame for you to miss their last – and maybe best – performance.'

Helen was right. Finn was a performer through and through – the one thing he still believed in was that the show must go on. 'I'll not be up for the wrap party after,' he warned, 'but let's make sure tonight's finale is one to remember.'

Helen beamed. 'That's my boy. Let's get ready then.'

Off to the theatre to put on a show about ghosts from the past. The irony wasn't lost on Finn.

* * *

The church loomed up in front of Finn, the outdoor lights shining on the clock face telling him it was almost nine. The final performance of *A Christmas Carol* had been stellar, with three curtain calls. Helen had given a heartfelt speech to the audience, garnering a standing ovation. Finn had fled the theatre after that, in no mood for a celebration party. His time here was almost at an end.

He'd avoided the church as much as possible since his arrival. His memory never let him forget the sound of a girl screaming and begging to be let out. Even now, the wind whirling through the trees was uncannily like a human voice. Finn shivered and pulled his coat closer around him. He'd come here tonight as a kind of apology, but now he was here, he didn't know what to do. The church was all locked up, so lighting a candle for Ella wasn't an option.

Finn looked thoughtfully at an empty planter next to a bench and then set to work. He put a layer of fir cones in the planter base. What now? Walking a circuit of the church, he was able to gather some fallen pine twigs, ivy and winter honeysuckle, which he arranged in the planter. The nearby holly tree proved trickier because the branches were tough and hard to break off, but using the sharp edge of a stone, and ignoring the cuts to his hands, he finally cut some sprigs with their cluster of berries still attached. The result was a crude flower arrangement – not artful, yet it had a kind of rough and ready charm. Finn placed the planter by the church door and used his finger to scrape the name 'Ella' in the snow next to it.

'I'm sorry,' he whispered. 'I'm so sorry.'

The clock chimed the half hour, and Finn shivered. He'd been so intent on what he was doing, he hadn't registered the cold. There might be more snow on the way. Time to go home. He'd cook something for Helen in case she was hungry when she returned from the theatre.

As Finn rounded the church, heading for the street, he saw a car pull up outside the rectory. Perhaps he'd tell Daniel what he'd done. Update him on Rachel.

But it was Jay who got out of the car, not Daniel. He marched up to the rectory and pounded on the door, then moved over to peer through the dark front room window. Coming back to the door, he banged at it again, calling out Daniel's name. Then he turned abruptly from the door, and Finn found himself exposed at the church gate under the lamplight with no time to hide. Jay spotted him straight away, and walked up the rectory path and then over the road.

Finn had been in Kilbrook for two months, and had

316

managed to avoid Jay. The risk of recognition was too great. Plus he had nothing to say to his childhood collaborator.

'Hello, Jody. Look at you. Quite the ladies' man. I can't call you lard-arse anymore, can I?'

Finn flinched at the use of his real name more than the insult, and the sight of Jay close up set his heart pounding. The years seemed to fall away, and he felt like he was back in the playground, trying to keep on Jay's good side, to deflect his venom onto someone – anyone – else. With an effort, Finn pushed aside his hopeless teenage self.

'The name's Finn now,' he stated, keeping his voice deadly calm.

Jay smiled, but it was not a good smile. 'Oh, yeah, Mel told me about your little disguise. Not man enough to be yourself, eh *Jode*?'

Finn should have walked away then. Any conversation with Jay was likely to be a dead end. Something kept him rooted to the spot, though. 'I was hoping Ella might show up at the reunion. And then I could apologise to her.'

Jay's lip curled into a sneer. 'Apologise for what? We were kids, messing around. That's what kids do.'

The memory Rachel had planted of Ella's hanging lifeless body came clearly into Finn's mind. 'What – bully someone to suicide? You think that's what kids do? You're sick in the head, Jay.'

Finn turned away, but Jay caught hold of his arm. 'Don't rake up all that shit from the past. No one wants to be reminded of it. We've all moved on.'

Finn shrugged himself free of Jay's grip. 'No one should forget Ella Rinaldi, and if I have anything to do with it, they won't.'

'Yeah, that's easy for you, isn't it? You'll fuck off back to Oz and leave the rest of us to deal with the fallout.'

'Think of it as a farewell gift. You have a daughter ...'

Jay scowled. 'So what?'

'I'm guessing you'd not want to see her bullied. You'd protect her. Ella had no one to protect her.'

Jay slowly started to clap. Finn's words had had no effect. There was no getting through to the man. Best to leave now.

'Is this little charade all about getting back into Rachel Rinaldi's knickers? I wonder what your precious Ella would have to say about that.'

Finn stared at Jay as he processed the ugly words. But if Jay thought that, perhaps Rachel would, too. That was a depressing thought. Finn turned away, not up to any more conversation.

'I hear Rachel came back tonight. She's quite a looker. Maybe I'll go and see her – take a cue from you – play the apology card. She might spread them for me, too.'

Finn turned and launched a punch at Jay's jaw. All his years of fear and doubt and resentment went into it, and the man crumpled to the pavement.

'You little shit …' Jay groaned, caught unawares.

Finn hauled Jay to his feet and slammed him against the church gate, his hand at the man's throat. His voice when he spoke was surprisingly calm.

'I know violence is the only language you understand, Jay, so listen good. If you go near Rachel, I'll break both your legs. That's not a threat, it's a promise. Do you understand?'

Jay was staring at Finn in shock. Probably never thought Jody James had it in him. Finn tightened his grip on the man's throat. 'Do – you – understand?'

'Yes,' Jay gasped.

Finn forced him back down to the ground, and then he walked away, expecting to hear insults from behind him or approaching footsteps, but there was only silence. He glanced at the windows of the houses nearby, but there were no twitching curtains. Kilbrook was turning a blind eye to Jody James's payback.

* * *

Rachel gulped down the glass of water that had been placed on her bedside table. She'd woken up a while ago, startled to find herself back in her room at Molly's house, fully clothed and in bed. Had Finn brought her upstairs? She had no memory of any of it. Her watch said it was three o'clock. Obviously in the morning, as it was dark outside. She'd been asleep – unconscious almost – for hours, but she didn't feel any benefit from it. Her head was full of the events of the past few days. She'd done what she came here to do but because of her relationship with Finn, it felt like she'd betrayed Ella.

She got up and rummaged in her bag for the diary, then took it back to bed with her. Propping up the pillows, she forced herself to read her sister's last few entries. The handwriting was erratic, a sure sign of poor Ella's torment. They'd left Kilbrook, but Kilbrook had left an indelible mark on her.

10 November
I feel better now Mam's given me a pill but it won't last, it never does and then there are the long, long nights to get through, and the light has to be on and it hurts my eyes and I can't really read either because the words are always dancing on the page.

15 December
I know now there was nothing to be afraid of that Halloween, that it was just the bullies, but at the time it was so scary and I keep having nightmares about demons and devils. I should have worked it out that they were trying to trick me but for a while it had been such a good feeling – being accepted – and I guess I didn't want to lose that. I wanted to believe. But I have to face the fact that I have no friends because I'm obviously a freak. And now I'm another burden on Mam. She looks so tired these days because Rosie's been poorly again.

31 December

I>m supposed to start the new school soon. I can't face it, I can't go through all that again, everyone making fun of me.

The doctor says I have to stop the pills but I can't cope without them.

I wish Papa was here. I miss him. I want him to cuddle me, tell me everything will be okay.

I wish I could find some peace.

I wish I was dead.

Rachel closed the book, buried her face in the pillow, and wept.

Chapter Twenty-Four

Rachel woke up to the sun streaming through the bedroom curtains and a steady drip-drip-drip outside. The snow was starting to melt.

The doorbell chimed and Rachel stiffened. Please don't let it be Finn. She could only get through all this if she didn't have to see him. Her brain wasn't co-operating in her attempts to regard Finn and Jody as one and the same, and just being physically close to him was torture.

Molly's voice floated up the stairs, thanking someone. Then the door closed and there was blessed silence. Rachel would have to go down now, apologise to Molly for her deception. It was the least she could do. She dressed quickly but descended the stairs slowly, uncertain what reception she'd get. As she entered the living room, a blast of strong perfume almost overpowered her senses. There were vases of flowers everywhere – asters and chrysanthemums and lilies. All sorts. Was it Molly's birthday or something? She glanced at the card propped close to a vase at her elbow: *Rachel, we're so very sorry about Ella. The Dempsey family.*

Stunned, Rachel dropped the card. What was all this? She moved to other flowers, picking up the cards one by one. All the same – messages for her. There was a potted hyacinth from Daniel. His card read, *Dear Rachel, I'm more sorry than I can ever say. I hope one day you'll be able to forgive me.*

Still clutching the card, Rachel sank onto the sofa and started to cry. Great messy sobs that just wouldn't stop. She felt arms pulling her close and heard Molly's voice say, 'That's right, Rachel. Cry it out. Let it all out. You're not alone any more.'

* * *

'Hot chocolate.' Molly held out a Santa mug to Rachel, now seated at the kitchen table. 'Drink it all now. It'll pep you up.'

Rachel obeyed, sipping at the sweet liquid. She felt weak and drained after her bout of tears. And a bit embarrassed, although Molly seemed to be taking it all in her stride. The woman was amazing.

'Molly, I'm so sorry for not telling you who I was. That wasn't right.' Her cheeks burned at the shame of it.

'It's okay, darlin', I understand,' said Molly, setting down a plate of toast. 'If it were my sister, I might well have done the same thing. Everyone understands.'

'Do they?' Rachel thought of the class reunion at the restaurant. People who had stood by while one of their group was victimised.

'Read that.' Molly set down a leaflet on the table. 'Every seat at the theatre last night had one of these on it. And Helen announced it after the show was finished.'

Rachel picked up the paper. Her eye was drawn by her sister's name.

This evening's performance of A Christmas Carol *is dedicated to the late Ella Rinaldi, who was badly bullied when she lived here in Kilbrook. No child should be bullied, but the reality is that it does happen. In Ella's name we've set up a fund to establish a Bullying Helpline and website for Kilbrook and surrounding villages. Donations can be made at the bank. Please open your hearts and give generously.*

Helen MacKenzie

Rachel's hands were trembling by the time she finished reading. Whatever she had expected to happen on her return to Kilbrook, this wasn't it. It wouldn't bring Ella back, but it ensured her story would be known and her name not forgotten, and that other children in a similar situation would be helped.

'I must thank Helen,' she said.

'I expect Finn and Father Quinn had something to do with it too.'

The mention of Finn's name brought back painful memories of yesterday. His eyes when she'd told him about the way Ella had died. Was he involved in this to salve his conscience? No, she knew it wouldn't be for that reason. And at least he had a conscience.

'Eat up now. I want to see that toast finished.'

She had no appetite, but Rachel munched away to please Molly. She glanced at the clock. Almost nine. She remembered she had one last thing to do here. 'I need to see Daniel.'

'It can wait until you've finished your breakfast, surely,' said Molly, bringing more coffee. 'Anyway, I've heard on the grapevine that he'll be at the school today. There's a disciplinary meeting to do with Jay Cole. Sounds like he might be for the chop.'

'What!' Rachel shot up from her chair. Then she was in the hallway, stabbing her feet into boots, shrugging into her coat, and grabbing her bag, all at the same time.

'Sorry, Molly!' she called from the open doorway. 'I've got to catch Daniel!'

* * *

Rachel slid most of the way over to the rectory, cursing the slippery snow and her stupid city boots. Daniel wasn't answering his phone – not the landline or his mobile.

Stumbling up the rectory path, she rapped at the door, then had to double over to try to ease the pain from the stitch in her side. She was aware of the door swinging open but couldn't straighten up.

'What ... Who ... Rachel? What's wrong? That bloody holly tree didn't get you again, did it?'

Daniel said it so seriously that Rachel started to laugh, which didn't help with the stitch at all. She grabbed the door frame, and then he helped her inside and onto a hall chair.

'Should I get help?'

'No ... no ...' she gasped. 'Wait ...'

The stitch took its own sweet time to go, and all the while Daniel hovered over her, his face creased with worry lines.

Finally, she could speak. 'I think I just broke the four-minute mile. Pity no one had a stopwatch.'

'I could time you on the way back if you like.'

Rachel smiled. Despite everything that had happened, part of her couldn't help but like Daniel.

'I was on my way out,' he said, and for the first time she noticed his coat and scarf. She was just in time.

'I know – you're going to the meeting at the school – about Jay. Molly told me.'

Daniel sighed. 'No secrets in this village.'

'I'm hoping there won't be after today. I need your help. The thing is – I don't know if I can trust you, Daniel.'

His face fell, and then he knelt down before her. This was how it had been when they first met, when he'd bathed her hand. Funny how things had a way of coming full circle.

'You can trust me with anything, Rachel,' he said gently. 'And to prove it, I'll share with you something now that I shouldn't – something confidential. I'm going to tell them today that Jay had an inappropriate relationship with Jenny. I won't mention the pregnancy – that's not fair to Jenny. But I will tell them Jay came to me for advice, and that I didn't act on what he'd told me. I kept it a secret until Jenny came for confession.'

Rachel frowned. 'I don't think you need to go that far, Daniel.'

'Yes, I do. Because I can't talk to God again until I've told the truth. Of course, Jay will probably deny everything, and the O'Neills don't want Jenny to testify – understandably. Without proof ...'

'You've got proof,' said Rachel.

'The Lantern Festival photo? Yes, that would help. But it's your photo. I wasn't going to use it without your permission. They'd ask how I got it.'

'You have my permission to use it. And there's something else,' said Rachel, rummaging in her pocket. 'I've got Jenny's mobile. I took it from her bedside table as back-up when we rushed her to hospital, and I forgot to return it.' She pulled out the pink phone, switched it on, flicked to *Messages*, and then handed it to Daniel.

'Good God!' he said as he read it. 'How could he!'

Surely there was no escape for Jay now. Not with this proof, not with Daniel also speaking out against him. 'Can I take this phone with me?' asked Daniel, standing up.

Rachel nodded. 'Only if you take me with you as well.'

'It's a closed meeting, Rachel. They'll only let me in on Jay's say-so. He thinks I'm a character witness. I am – although he'll be sorely disappointed by what I have to say about his character.'

Rachel stood up. 'It's okay, I'll wait outside when we get there. Just promise me one thing.'

Daniel looked wary. 'What?'

'Make sure Jay knows it was me who gave you the phone and asked you to use it as evidence. Tell him it was me, Daniel. For Ella's sake.'

There were tears in his eyes as he gently brushed her cheek. 'For Ella's sake.'

* * *

'Come this way, Father.'

Daniel left Rachel in the waiting area and followed the school secretary down a long corridor. She stopped outside a door marked 'Conference Room', knocked, and went inside. 'Father Daniel Quinn,' she announced, and ushered him in.

The conference room was all gleaming dark wood and brilliant fluorescent lights. No twitch of the mouth or lowered eyes would go unscrutinised.

Jay was already there, dressed in a smart grey suit. Daniel was startled, though, to see an ugly bruise on his chin. Maybe Mel hadn't been too thrilled about his extra-marital affair.

The clock said he was five minutes late, and Daniel apologised.

'Take a seat, Father Quinn,' said Brendan Keeley, Chairman of the Board of Management. He was a strict man, but fair. At least Jay would get an impartial hearing. Jean Donovan, the school's principal, was also present, as well as a Mrs Gowdy from the Association of Community Schools.

The chairman read out the allegation against Jay. It all centred on gross misconduct. Jenny wasn't a minor, so there were no criminal charges to answer. Pity that – a stint in prison would have shaken Jay up a bit, although Daniel guessed he might have fitted right into the violence of prison culture.

The questioning started, a picture built up of when and how long Jay had been Jenny's teacher, what their interactions had been like, and when, if ever, he'd met her outside of school. Then it was crunch time. Jay was shown a copy of a record of all numbers Jenny had called on her mobile in the last three months.

'Note the highlighted numbers, Mr Cole. Can you confirm that is your phone number?'

'Yes, it is,' said Jay, glancing at the list.

'She called you twenty times in the past three months?'

'Yes, she did.'

There was silence in the room. Daniel wondered how Jay could sound so calm. Surely this was damning evidence.

'She was having problems. All kinds. With a boyfriend, with her family. She said she felt she could trust me. I suggested she talk things through with her mother or a close friend or a counsellor, but she said she couldn't. It wouldn't have been right to turn her away.'

'Why didn't you report this to your principal, to Mrs Donovan?'

'I should have. I see that now. But I think Jenny would have seen that as a betrayal of trust. It seemed like she had enough on her plate.'

The panel digested this information. Daniel could see Mrs Donovan at least seemed to be looking more favourably on Jay.

'Mr Cole, I'll ask you now – did you have a sexual relationship – or any kind of inappropriate personal relationship – with your pupil, Jenny O'Neill?'

Jay vehemently shook his head. 'Absolutely not. And these allegations have been extremely distressing to me, and to my wife. I feel sorry for Jenny O'Neill – I understand she's in hospital right now. Perhaps she's been under strain from difficulties with her boyfriend for some time. I also understand that Jenny herself has made no accusations against me, yet her parents are threatening my position as a teacher and as a member of this community. If you have proof against me –· other than some distressed parents' uncorroborated suspicions – then please bring it forward now, or find me innocent of these allegations.'

Daniel felt like he'd stumbled into an episode of *Law and Order*. Jay was running rings around the committee. Daniel remembered Jenny's pale face in the hospital bed, and anger stoked inside him.

'I have proof,' Daniel blurted out. They all stared at him, the chairman's laser vision making him break out into a sweat.

'I'm sorry, Father Quinn,' said Brendan Keeley, frowning, 'but I understood you to be a character witness *for* Mr Cole. Are you now saying you're not? That you have some evidence to substantiate the allegations?'

'Yes, I have evidence.'

'Then I'd like to hear it.'

'So would I,' said Jay. His voice held a challenge, a latent threat. The atmosphere in the room had suddenly become very charged.

'Jay came to see me about ten days ago at the church. As a friend – not for confession. He told me he'd been having an affair with Jenny O'Neill. He wanted advice.'

'Indeed.' The chairman peered over his glasses at Jay. 'And whom did you tell about this, Father Quinn?'

Keeley knew his stuff, knew that there were steps Daniel should have taken.

The shame flared up in Daniel's face. 'To my regret, I did nothing. I let my friendship with Jay blur my judgement. I advised him to break off the relationship, and I left it at that. I'll be confessing as much to the Bishop. I know my conduct was wrong.'

Daniel had taken a huge gamble by leaving out details of the pregnancy in his desire to shield Jenny. Jay couldn't really reveal that without exposing himself, but this was a dangerous game, and Jay was a master player.

'I know why you're doing this, Daniel,' said Jay, smoothly, turning in his seat to face him. His eyes were pure poison. 'I wouldn't have said anything, you know. You're my friend. It would have stayed between us.'

Daniel's mind was racing, trying to figure out what was coming up. 'I've no idea what you're talking about.'

Jay's face took on a pitying expression. 'Now you've left me with no option. I'll have to tell.' He turned back to the panel. 'Last week, Father Quinn made ... advances ... to my wife. Naturally, she rebuffed him. I was angry and had it out with him, but I assumed we'd put it behind us. I see I was wrong.'

Daniel's jaw dropped open. This was an attack of the lowest kind. 'That's a lie!' he protested. 'I'd never ... never ...'

The shock and confusion on the faces of the panel members

told Daniel he could be losing credibility. He stood up, quickly took out Jenny's phone and handed the mobile to the chairman. 'This is Jenny O'Neill's phone. Look at the text sent to her on Monday. As you can see, it's from Jay.'

Daniel glared at Jay over the chairman's head. This was war now, and he'd not stop till he'd brought his opponent down.

'How did you get this phone?' asked Keeley faintly.

'A friend – Rachel Ford – gave it to me. She and another friend, Finn MacKenzie, found Jenny sick at home on the night of the first snowstorm. They drove her to hospital. Rachel took Jenny's phone in case they needed back-up, and she forgot to return it. She found this text message yesterday and asked me to pass it on to you.'

'Rachel Rinaldi, you mean!' snapped Jay. 'She's just looking for revenge because of what happened to her sister years ago. She's out to get me! It's a trick! I never sent any text messages to Jenny.'

Jay was losing his cool. The calm, reasonable facade had slipped and now he was all anger.

'What does the text say?' asked Mrs Gowdy

Keeley read out the cruel words, his tone showing deep disapproval.

Jay sat there, looking stunned, saying nothing. Hopefully, he was experiencing shame now at his cavalier response to Jenny. Now Daniel would go in for the kill. He pulled out the photo and handed it to Mrs Donovan.

'Rachel was also recording the Lantern Parade. She inadvertently caught Jay and Jenny on camera. As you can see from this still shot, they're kissing.'

Mrs Donovan took a sharp intake of breath as she looked at the photo. The picture was passed along to the other committee members in turn, and then pushed across the table to Jay, who ignored it.

'In light of this new evidence, Mr Cole, we will need to retire to discuss—'

Jay stood up, his eyes fixed on Jenny's phone. It was as if he hadn't even heard the chairman's words. Jay at a loss was something Daniel had never seen before.

'I didn't send that text,' he declared. 'I wouldn't ... What time was it sent?'

'How is that relevant?' Keeley's tone was cool, critical.

'The time, man!' shouted Jay, and there were shocked murmurs from the committee. 'What's the time on that text message?'

Daniel glanced over the chairman's shoulder. 'Five-thirty. Why?'

Jay silently absorbed that information, then he turned and stalked out of the conference room.

* * *

Rachel heard a door click open down the corridor. An hour had passed. The meeting must be over. She stood up, waiting anxiously for Daniel.

But it was Jay who rounded the corner, his expression distracted. A man in a hurry. There was nowhere for Rachel to hide, and she hoped he'd just keep walking.

He stopped dead in front of her and raked her up and down with his glare. 'Quite the little detective, aren't you?' he said, and his voice sent a chill down her spine.

'You needed to be stopped.' Rachel wished her voice didn't sound so small, so insignificant.

'Well, you've certainly got more guts than your wimp of a sister.'

Rachel slapped Jay's face. Hard. Behind him, the secretary got up from her seat.

Jay raised his own hand and Rachel took a step back, but he only smoothed his hair back into line.

'Don't worry,' he sneered. 'I won't hurt you. Yesterday your boyfriend threatened to break both my legs if I went near you. Quite the little thug is Jody. You two deserve each other.'

And then, thankfully, he was gone. Rachel sank down into a chair, hoping that she'd done the right thing for Jenny.

* * *

'Was it bad?' Rachel asked Daniel, as she finished her late lunch of chicken salad. They'd driven to a pub in a neighbouring village, both feeling the need to escape Kilbrook.

Daniel had been picking at his fish and chips for the last half-hour, his mind clearly still back in the meeting, where there had been unanimous agreement to recommend to the Board the termination of Jay's appointment as teacher at Kilbrook Community School.

He glanced up. 'Without the text and the photo, he'd probably have gotten away with it.'

A small part of Rachel had wondered if Daniel would be able to go through with it – betraying a friend. Perhaps he was having second thoughts now. 'Do you regret using the evidence against him?'

'Absolutely not. It was the right thing to do. It's just …'

'What is it, Daniel?' she prompted.

'Me. As a priest. It's all wrong now.'

'I'm sorry, I don't understand.'

He gave up on his food, pushed the plate aside, and signalled for the bill. 'I should have done something about Jenny sooner. I kept quiet because it was Jay. That was wrong. And Jenny suffered because of it. The Church suffered because of it.'

He was right about that. Still, the original fault had been Jay's. 'Everyone makes mistakes, you know. I'm sure God understands that.'

Daniel smiled. 'You just stole my line.'

'It's a good line.'

'Yes, it is. But I'm not sure it applies to errant priests.'

His face was still troubled, and Rachel thought of what she could say to ease his mind.

'Daniel.' He looked at her, questioningly. 'I forgive you.'

Three little words, yet she could see how much they meant to him – and that he knew how much it had cost her to say them.

'Thank you.' His hand briefly touched hers in gratitude. 'I need you to do something for me, Rachel. It involves Finn.'

'What?' Surely he wasn't going to ask her to forgive him. That would be too much. It had been easier to forgive Daniel, but Finn was something else. How could she forgive him when she couldn't forgive herself? She'd betrayed Ella, and the guilt over that would take a long time to go.

She had to wait for his answer while the waitress scooped up their plates and left the bill. Daniel counted out some notes, insisting he pay. When he was ready, he made his request.

'Jay was angry when he left. You saw that. And he knows it was you who gave me the phone. He's probably getting plastered somewhere as we speak. And Jay drunk isn't good. He might get it into his head to pay you a visit …'

Jay looming over her *had* been intimidating, but he shouldn't be allowed to get away with that kind of behaviour. 'I don't care. If he shows up, I'll call the police.'

'Okay, but there's Molly to consider. She's old and frail. She shouldn't have to face Jay's wrath at her time of life.'

He was right. 'So what do you suggest?'

Daniel sipped at his water before answering. 'Molly should go and stay overnight with her friend, Mary Clarkson.'

'And me?'

He hesitated. 'You should stay at Helen's.'

'No way!' The diners at nearby tables glanced curiously at Rachel, and she lowered her voice. 'That's a very bad idea. Why can't I stay with you at the rectory?'

Daniel pointed to his dog collar. 'Because I'm a priest and you're a single woman. I can't deal with any hint of scandal right now, Rachel.'

'Then I'll take a train to Shannon. Find somewhere to

stay.' The cheapest flight she'd found back to London was on Saturday, so that was a day and two nights to get through in some soulless hotel or B&B with only her dark thoughts for company.

'You shouldn't be on your own. Helen will be there. And you can stay in the bedroom and avoid Finn if you want.'

It felt like Daniel had cornered her though his expression was all innocence. It was obvious what he was trying to do, but he could be right about Jay, so she'd do as he suggested. And Daniel was right. She shouldn't be on her own. She was feeling too weak and fragile for that. Even if it meant being near Finn. She'd plead exhaustion or a headache that evening and have an early night in the MacKenzies' spare room. She needn't be alone with Finn at all.

'Okay, Daniel, but I'm not happy about this. Anyway – Helen might not agree.'

'She already has.'

'What!'

'I phoned her while you were in the washroom.'

'Daniel Quinn! That's just devious!'

He held up his hands in submission. 'Guilty as charged. All in a good cause, though.'

'Everything all right here?' asked their waitress anxiously, as she picked up the bill and the payment.

'Everything's fine,' Daniel reassured her. 'She's just upset because I won't let her sleep with me. Keep the change.'

The waitress skittered away, shocked.

Rachel tutted, but couldn't resist a smile. 'I'm seeing a whole new side of you today, Daniel.'

'Hold on to your hat. There's more to come.'

And with that cryptic remark, he stood up and helped Rachel into her coat. Wrapped up against the winter chill, they left the pub. Pity they had to go back to Kilbrook at all. Rachel was feeling that longing for escape again.

* * *

Finn was at the theatre, listening to sappy love songs on the radio. He could have changed the station, but he was obviously a masochist. The scenery was getting the better of him, and it was his own fault. It really needed two people to dismantle it, but he'd refused help, wanting to spend time on his own. He unhooked the canvas from the sliding blocks, ready to roll it up for storage, but it crumpled to the stage floor and started curling up the wrong way. He moved his foot and heard a rip. 'Damn.'

'Need a hand?'

Finn glanced out at the auditorium and was shocked to see Rachel standing there. In her white wool coat, she looked like an angel, as eye-catching and lovely as when he'd first met her weeks ago. So much had happened since then. 'I'd love a hand, but it's dusty up here. Best take your coat off.'

Although he pretended to focus on the canvas, his attention wandered. And his imagination. Rachel was wearing a tight black jumper and skinny jeans, and he couldn't help but remember the curves underneath. As she walked up the treads onto the stage, Finn tried to read her expression. Calm, but reserved. As if the storm had passed and a decision had been reached.

'What do you need me to do?' she asked.

Forgive me. Love me. Spend the rest of your life with me. But he hadn't the courage to say any of those things. 'Can you help me roll up this scenery? Then we'll check off the props against the list – see what has to be returned. A quick tidy-up of the dressing rooms, and then we're done.'

They worked together methodically on the scenery. It went more quickly and more smoothly with her help. Then it was on to the props. They were scattered around the stage, waiting to be boxed for storage or labelled for return.

Rachel sat on a chair with the list, and Finn stood holding labels and ready for instructions. He was relaxing more now. The theatre was his element.

'One rubber turkey,' read Rachel from the list. 'There's a phrase I never thought I'd say. Belongs to Sarah Ryan.'

Finn grabbed the yellow thing with its flailing legs and labelled it. 'Helen said one year apparently they used a real turkey. By the second night, the front row were all barfing at the smell.'

Rachel giggled. 'Tableware. Ten plastic plates, saucers, cups, glasses. Three serving dishes. All belonging to the theatre.'

Finn piled all the dishes into a box. 'Next?'

'Ostrich feather fan.'

He picked it up and flicked it open, fluttering it in front of his face. 'To whom does this charming item belong?' he asked, in a high-pitched Southern belle accent.

'The theatre.' She giggled again, and Finn revelled in the sound.

They continued with the list. There was a sticky moment when it came to Scrooge's gravestone. Rachel's expression grew sad – she'd be thinking about Ella. Or perhaps her mother. Finn thought briefly about Ethan.

Scrooge's four-poster bed, still on stage, was on the list, and Rachel avoided looking at it. Finn hurriedly stuck a label on the headboard.

Next, there was an assortment of top hats and canes, kindly loaned by the Amateur Operatic Society in Galway. On a whim, Finn clapped a hat on his head and grabbed a cane. His boots gave a satisfying click as he tapped out to the centre of the stage and did a quick Chaplin impersonation.

Rachel clapped. 'Excellent. But can you do Fred Astaire?'

Finn switched immediately to a fluid tap routine, twirling the cane, tossing up his hat and catching it. All that dance training at drama school that he thought he'd never use was paying off now. Rachel was watching him, entranced.

Just then, and proving that God had a very warped sense of humour, Maria McKee's voice came out of the radio. 'Show

Me Heaven.' The song he and Rachel had danced to on Helen's landing.

Ditching the cane and hat, Finn held out his hand. 'Dance with me?'

'Finn, that's not a good idea.'

'Please. For old times ...'

'Well ...'

Rachel put her hand tentatively in his, and he pulled her gently up and close to him. Curving a hand round her waist, he waltzed her slowly round the stage. She was lightly holding his shoulder, her thumb on his bare neck. It was an innocent touch on her part, yet it electrified him. He wanted to go on dancing forever, but her movements told him she was getting ready to stop. He discreetly inhaled the floral scent of her hair, registered her soft hand in his. Finally, gazing into her deep blue eyes, he locked this beautiful moment away in his memory. He'd need it in the long days and months ahead. The memory of their first dance was killing him, reminding him that it had been the start of something special, but Rachel wasn't declaring her love. She was saying goodbye in the kindest way she could.

* * *

'What made you come here tonight?' Finn was sitting next to Rachel, his long legs dangling over the edge of the stage. They were sharing some leftover crisps and bottles of water they'd found in one of the dressing rooms.

'I wanted to thank you for driving us home yesterday. I was ... upset. I just couldn't think clearly anymore. Needed to sleep. I know it wasn't easy for you.'

'No problem. Probably did me a favour.'

The disappointment was plain in Finn's voice. He'd have been hoping to hear a different answer. Part of Rachel wanted desperately to hold him close, but the other part was warning her to keep her distance. How could she ever have a proper relationship with him now? Too much had happened, and she was sure she could feel Ella's ghost watching her. She didn't hate him. How could she? But what he'd done as a child would stand between them forever.

As a distraction, Rachel told Finn about finding Jenny's phone, and she relayed what Daniel had shared with her about the meeting at the school. Finn's response wasn't what she'd expected.

'You never told me about Jenny's phone, yet you trusted Daniel.'

Was that jealousy? Probably. 'I wasn't really sure what I was going to do about the phone until I woke up this morning. Then when I went over to the rectory to talk to Daniel, we had to get to the school very quickly.'

He said nothing, just swigged at his water.

'Molly told me about the Bullying Helpline.'

'Probably too little, too late.' He sounded so despondent.

'No, it's not, Finn. That helpline is important.'

He nodded but was silent, munching away at the crisps and staring out into the auditorium.

'Jay told me you warned him away from me.'

Finn's head flicked in her direction. 'Oh?'

'He had a bruise on his chin. Was that you?'

'I shouldn't have done that. It'll make you think of me as a bully again. But he said things about Ella … about you …'

Rachel reached out and touched his hand. 'Thank you for protecting me.'

He took her hand up to his mouth and kissed it. She didn't pull away. 'Rachel, I love you. I wish I could undo the past, but I can't. I'm different now, though …'

'I know,' she murmured. He was Finn MacKenzie. Jody James was dead and buried. But it didn't make any difference.

'Is there any way we can be together?' he begged. His eyes were full of a burning desire, and it was hard to look into

337

them, but she persisted. The next bit would be tough but necessary.

She pulled her hand away, and saw the expression of pain. 'I'm sorry, Finn. Ella's so much in my head right now. Being with you ... I don't see how it could work.'

He nodded and stared back out at the empty auditorium. 'If only this were a play, they'd have scripted a happy ending for us.'

'Look, Finn ... I can leave for Shannon today. See if I can get a hotel room. Sort out the car from there. You don't want me hanging around—'

'No.' He turned back to look at her and attempted a smile. 'Stay with us tonight. I won't hassle you, I promise. And I'd like you to meet my brother, Gabe. He's coming over from England for Helen's court case.'

She smiled, and things felt better between them. Not normal again, but at least they'd reached a plateau of calm, of understanding.

Finn stood up. 'You go and wait in the foyer,' he told her. 'I'll switch out the lights.'

Rachel jumped down from the stage, then walked away without speaking. There was nothing more she could say. As she reached the back of the auditorium, she turned to take one last look at the stage. Finn was now sitting on the edge of the bed, turning the top hat over and over in his hands. Rachel's eyes filled with tears of loss as she walked out the door.

* * *

Mel slammed the car door and rushed into the house. Jay had texted her a half-hour ago that he was back from the meeting and needed to speak to her at home. She'd immediately tried phoning him, yet he didn't pick up, so it had to be bad.

Mentally, she prepared herself for the worst: Jay's dismissal from the school. He'd have to get some other work in Galway or Limerick. Maybe even as far as Cork, or out of Ireland altogether. Her father would help with that. They'd move, of course, to get away from the gossips. Leanne would have to start a new school, which could be difficult, but they'd all have to make sacrifices.

'Jay?'

Inside the house, she went from the kitchen to the dining room to the living room, but he wasn't there. She'd expected to see him getting cosy with a bottle of Jamesons. Pounding up the stairs, she pushed open the door to their bedroom and stopped dead.

Two suitcases lay spread open on the floor, and Jay was dropping clothes into them. Mel felt the cold hand of fear on her neck.

'What are you doing, Jay?' she asked, amazed her voice could sound so normal.

He glared at her. 'I'm leaving.'

The idiot of a solicitor must have screwed up. No more retainer for him. 'Tell me what happened, Jay. It doesn't matter if it didn't go well – we'll sort something out.'

'It went swimmingly until Daniel gave them Jenny's mobile. He got it from Rachel Rinaldi.'

'Rachel?' That interfering bitch. She was trying to take them all down.

'There was a text message from me to Jenny on that phone. Sent on Monday. At five-thirty. When I was passed out drunk on the sofa. Is this ringing any bells, Mel?'

She swallowed hard, cursing her stupidity. Best to come clean. Jay already knew she'd done it. 'I just wanted her gone from our lives. I couldn't believe she'd have the nerve to contact you when she'd caused so much trouble.'

'She got that text and then she tried to kill herself!' Jay's voice was getting louder. 'Don't you feel *any* guilt about that?'

Something snapped inside Mel. 'Don't you dare lecture me about guilt! I'm not the one who screwed a teenager! A pupil!

You said yourself she was trying to pass the blame for the pregnancy onto you—'

'I lied. It was my baby.'

'What?' Mel couldn't – wouldn't – take in the words properly. 'But you said ...'

Jay dropped the shirt he was holding. 'Jenny was carrying my baby. I wanted her to have an abortion, but she wouldn't. And now it's dead, because of you, not because Jenny or I made that decision. I was going to set her up somewhere. She'd have the baby and I'd help her out with money.'

That was too much. Mel started to laugh. Couldn't help it. The shock had unbalanced her. 'You – take care of a baby! You hardly earn enough to pay the insurance for the house and the cars. What were you planning to do – rob a bank? Or lie to me and take money meant for Leanne and use it for your by-blow? Your *bastard*.'

Mel's hand went up to her mouth to stop the flow of venomous words. Jay had curled his hands into fists. Anything might happen now.

'Well, it's good to know what you really think of me, Mel.'

'I didn't mean ...'

'Yes, you did. You think I'm a no-good scrounger. That's what your father thinks, too. All these years of insults I've taken from the great Gerald Maguire. Probably the whole of Kilbrook has been laughing behind my back, too. Calling me Mr Mel Maguire.'

'Surely it hasn't been such a bad life,' whispered Mel.

'I suppose not. You made it all so easy.'

'It can still be easy ...'

He held up his hand. 'No, it can't. Because you've screwed things up. You sent that text message – you interfered in my life. I can't ever trust you again to have my back.'

'One mistake, Jay. I'm so sorry. I did it because I love you.' She was crying now. Couldn't hold back the tears, her grief.

'But I don't love you anymore, Mel.'

'No! No! No!'

And then she was clutching at Jay, trying to hold him close to her, but he was pushing her towards the door. She fell over one of the suitcases, grabbed hold of Jay's ankle. He dragged her, shoved her outside, locked the door. She pounded at the wood, ignoring the pain in her hands, calling his name over and over.

Finally, exhausted, she curled up on the carpet, weeping. The hallway grew slowly dim as daylight faded. When he unlocked the door later and came out with his suitcases, she knew it was too late. He stepped over her and went down the stairs.

'Jay,' she whispered.

He opened the front door, walked through, and slammed it shut behind him, never once looking back.

* * *

Rachel discreetly compared the two James brothers. Chalk and cheese really. Gabe was dark, Finn was fair. Gabe's features were sharp and angular, quite rugged. Finn's were smoother, more boyish. Both shared the same sense of humour, though. They'd cracked jokes throughout dinner, and Rachel knew Finn was trying his best to put her at ease.

'Lovely meal, Hel,' Gabe said. His voice was deeper than Finn's. 'Did you order in?'

'Cheeky bugger! How do you know I haven't had cordon bleu lessons since you were last here?'

Finn and Gabe both laughed like drains, and Helen rolled her eyes. 'All right, I confess. The food's from the supermarket. They do a lovely duck in red wine sauce.'

'You'll be back to shrimp on the barbie soon, Finn, eh?' said Gabe, topping up everyone's wine. 'And all that Australian sunshine. Lucky sod.'

Rachel felt a wrench of real grief at the thought of Finn leaving. Soon there would be thousands of miles between them. He didn't seem to be looking forward to it either because he only gave Gabe a quick smile.

'It's banoffee pie for dessert,' declared Helen. 'Any takers?'

Finn and Gabe clamoured for some, banging their spoons on the table to hurry her up while she served. Helen swatted at them both with a tea towel and told them to mind their manners, but she was laughing hard at their antics.

They were all close, Rachel could see that. And she had so nearly been a part of this family, of this irreverent fun, that the loss of what she'd never have made her feel sad. She'd be back in London soon, finishing her thesis, then applying for jobs. Alone again. Well, there was Sophia, who was great, but her cousin had hinted at forthcoming wedding bells for her and her boyfriend. The thought of dating again, of trying to find The One when Rachel had already found him, was a bleak thought.

'Don't you like it?' asked Helen.

'It's lovely,' said Rachel, and applied her spoon to her bowl. The last thing she wanted was to spoil the family's time together.

When they'd finished eating, Gabe told them he had a surprise. He brought his laptop over to the table and opened it up. He urged them to crowd round him. His wallpaper showed two giggling little girls at the dinner table, all pigtails and gap-toothed smiles.

'My girls, Tina and Becky,' Gabe told Rachel, proudly. 'Now, let's get this set up.'

Finn had told Rachel that Gabe worked with computers, and now his fingers flashed over the keyboard with breathtaking speed. He opened up Skype, tapped an icon, and after a few rings, someone answered. A man looking sleepy. A man with Finn's smile.

'Cary!' shrieked Helen. 'It's Cary!'

'Direct from Dubai,' said Gabe, pleased with his surprise.

Finn mouthed 'my brother' at Rachel, and then they were

all talking at once. Asking questions, sharing news, and Cary was wishing them luck for their day in court tomorrow. Finn was lit up to see his brother, and Rachel was glad to see him happy again after their difficult conversation in the theatre.

Rachel was an outsider here. By choice, but still it was hard to watch this show of family unity when her own family life had been so badly fractured. Taking some dirty dishes from the table, she slipped out of the room and into the quiet of the kitchen.

* * *

Rachel was elbow deep in suds at the sink when Helen bustled into the kitchen a little later, carrying dishes on a tray. 'Oh, there you are, Rachel. I thought maybe you'd gone to bed. You don't have to do that, love. Leave them till the morning.'

'It's okay, really,' said Rachel. 'I don't mind.'

She hoped Helen wasn't going to talk about Finn. It was too personal and her emotions still too raw to discuss their break-up with anyone.

Scraping the leftovers into the bin, Helen said, 'I was always asking Harry to get a dishwasher, but he said they were a waste of money. Personally, I think they're a godsend.'

'Me too.'

They smiled at each other, and the awkwardness eased slightly.

'I'll make coffee. The boys are discussing tomorrow's court case. Finn's going to be giving evidence.'

'I didn't know that.'

'I'd rather he didn't have to say anything, but he feels it's important. Has he told you much about the case?'

'Virtually nothing.' Finn's name had come up now, but the topic was neutral so Rachel felt able to answer. 'I got the feeling he didn't want to talk about it. He just said that your brother's wife was contesting the will that left the house to you.'

'That's right.' Helen sat down on a stool at the counter while the kettle boiled. 'If it was just me involved, I might not have fought Marilyn, but this house should be the boys' inheritance. Their father's last wishes should be respected. If I get it, I'll sell it and split the money four ways, but if Marilyn gets the house, she'll likely sell it and spend the money – there'd be nothing left for Gabe or Cary or Finn. And she'd do that to her own sons without a second thought.'

Rachel dropped the cup she was washing into the soapy water. 'So Harry's wife – the one who's contesting the will – is Finn's *mother*? I thought you were talking about a second wife.'

'Mother!' snorted Helen. 'Not much of a mother. Marilyn only ever thought about herself. Her real name was Marion, you know, but that wasn't good enough for her. She was obsessed with the idea of becoming a movie star. Modelled herself on Marilyn Monroe. Gave her three boys Hollywood names – Gable, Cary and Jody. She so badly wanted a daughter, she named Finn after Jodie Foster. Such a stupid woman.'

'So what kind of questions will they ask Finn in court?' Rachel scrubbed intently at a plate. She should change the topic now, but it was impossible to switch overnight to indifference about the man she still loved.

'Questions about his father. Whether he was abusive to Marilyn. If that could be a reason why she left.'

'Was it the reason?'

'I don't know. Harry wouldn't talk about it. He certainly had a temper,' admitted Helen. 'He could be a hard man to live with. But he adored Marilyn. Would do anything for her, more fool him. When she walked out, Finn said Harry took it very badly. Gabe had already left home by then, and Cary and Finn were left to their own devices. Cary was only seventeen, but he was more of a father to Finn than Harry was – and then he got himself into a bit of bother and ran away because Harry gave him a beating. He wasn't a bad boy, but Harry didn't know how to handle him. Didn't really know how to handle any of them because a few years later he did the same to Finn.'

The kettle clicked and Helen busied herself making coffee. Rachel finished the washing-up, emptied and rinsed the basin, wiped the countertop. All the time a question was forming in her mind. 'How old was Finn when Marilyn left him?'

'Eleven – nearly twelve, I think.'

'It's very young to lose your mother,' murmured Rachel. But the age was more significant than that. Jody had joined in the bullying of Ella at the time when he was living alone with his angry, rejected father. His mother had abandoned him and he'd lost both of his brothers. It wasn't an excuse. There could be no excuse. But it was a reason.

'So Finn came to live with you after … after Ella?' Rachel started drying the dishes, needing to keep busy.

'No, he went to Gabe and Cary in England first – Brighton. I persuaded him to come to me in Australia. I thought a fresh start would be best.'

'Lucky him – he got a second chance.' The words were out before Rachel could stop them.

Helen put a last cup on a tray and came to sit down again on the stool by the counter.

'Finn was bullied when he came to Australia,' she said. 'He had no friends, not for a long time. He was a prime target – a sullen, overweight Pom – but he got through it because he believed he was being punished, that he deserved it.'

'He wasn't punished. All the bullies got away with it.'

'It depends what you mean by getting away with it. There are more ways for someone to be punished than by justice being seen to be done.'

'So he felt guilty. That's not enough. My sister died because of what they did. And so did my mother.'

'I know.' Helen looked sad as if she knew Rachel was consigning Finn to yesterday. 'But believe me, Finn never went unpunished. He reached a point where … well, he didn't want to go on. He thought he was ugly, unlovable and, all in all, a bad person. After all, his own mother didn't want him. He became more and more depressed, and then he met Ethan, who took him under his wing. Made him feel worth something. When he died, I thought Finn would fall apart, but he's a fighter. He wanted to make something of himself for Ethan, and he has – but he hasn't been able to stop the nightmares. And when he drove after you the other night, it was the first time he'd driven since the crash. His nerves must have been shot to pieces. The news of Ella's death has hit him hard. He came back here to help me with the court case, but he was also hoping he'd be able to apologise to her at the reunion.'

'Too late.' Rachel's words were harsh, but she had enough of her own sadness to deal with. She couldn't take on feeling sadness for Finn's life too. Not when he was the cause of hers.

'It was a tragedy all round,' said Helen. 'It must have been very stressful for you to be back here. Has it helped at all? Did you get some closure?'

Closure. Rachel hated that word. As if emotions could be neatly packaged away in some sort of box. 'I don't know, Helen. I was so certain before I came about what needed to be done. But things turned out a little differently.'

'I still believe people can change, you know. Like Scrooge.'

'It's all so easy in a play, but this is real life.'

'Finn loves you, Rachel. He told me, although he didn't need to say anything. I could see it in his eyes. And you still love him. Otherwise, why are you here? Is it really because you're scared of Jay Cole – or is it because you can't let go?'

'Don't, Helen, please!' She felt like smashing every cup in the house.

'Sorry, I know I shouldn't be pleading Finn's case. It's wrong of me. Not fair on you, and he wouldn't thank me. Don't tell him I said anything. He's lost all hope you'll want to be with him. It's just that I'm a romantic old fool.'

Were there tears in Helen's eyes? Rachel sat down at the counter. 'I'm sorry about how things turned out, but it's good that I met you. You're an inspiration. And thank you so much for organising the Bullying Helpline.'

Helen's smile was warm and genuine. 'I'm glad you came back, Rachel. Even if only to give me the chance to say a proper goodbye. And, you know, if you're ever in Australia, you be sure to look me up. I'll give you the address.'

Rachel nodded, but she'd never go to Australia. That continent was out of bounds now because Finn would be there, and the temptation to see him would be too strong. It would be hard enough to forget him as it was.

'Let's get this coffee to the boys.'

'If you don't mind, I think I'll have an early night.'

'Okay, love. Sleep well.'

As Rachel climbed the stairs, she could hear Finn's voice in the living room, and it set off a wave of longing. He'd probably be in her dreams again, like he was last night. Dear God, how was she going to get over him?

Chapter Twenty-Five

'All rise,' boomed the court clerk, and Finn stood with everyone else as an elderly judge made his way to the tall leather-backed chair in the centre of the podium. 'His Honour Judge Raymond Kenneally presiding.'

The judge peered round his courtroom before sitting down, and then the clerk told everyone, 'Please be seated.'

Finn recognised what a great piece of theatre a courtroom was with its podium, witness boxes and the audience. If he could trick himself into thinking this was an audition or a performance, he might just get through it. Of course, Marilyn herself was quite the actress – or liked to think she was. She'd certainly gone for strong stage make-up today, and the neckline of her navy dress was just the wrong side of decent. Old Kenneally, though, might well be too short-sighted to see her clearly, or too aged to care.

Helen was sitting a few rows in front of Finn, next to her barrister. She'd dressed with care and an eye to today's testimony. Minimal make-up, hair twisted into a sweet little bun, her grandmother's pearls on a plain grey dress, and a walking stick beside her, which she only used once in a blue moon when her arthritis was playing up. She was Miss Marple against Marilyn's Blanche DuBois.

Finn wished his brother was with him, but he'd gone to the airport. The phone call from Gabe's witness early that morning saying he was flying over for the court hearing had been unexpected. The brothers had decided not to give Helen any details because then she'd have had to disclose them to her barrister, who'd have had to disclose them to Marilyn's barrister. Better that it all came as a complete surprise.

The clerk read out the details of the case, and then the questioning began. Marilyn was first up, answering questions from her barrister. She spoke of her twenty years of marriage to Harry, and her love for her three sons. It was only when Harry started drinking too much and becoming violent that she had reluctantly left. She had never divorced him, holding on to the hope that he might one day get his anger issues under control. His sister had not informed Marilyn of Harry's terminal illness, or she would have gone to see him. At the time of Harry's death, she was still legally his wife, and she believed the duration of the marriage and the contribution she had made in managing the home and raising the children of the marriage also entitled her to claim against Harry's estate.

Finn felt like breaking into applause but thought better of it in case the judge held him in contempt.

'Your witness, Counsel,' the judge said to Helen's barrister, who stood up.

'Mrs James, you abandoned your husband and children seventeen years ago, but that wasn't the first time you'd walked out, was it?'

Marilyn seemed prepared for the question and didn't try to hide anything. 'Yes. I'd left home eight years before that.'

'What age was your youngest son at that time?'

'Three.'

The judge stared over his glasses at Marilyn. His expression was not kind.

'Why did you leave?' asked the barrister.

'I had post-natal depression,' said Marilyn, affecting the slightest of tremors in her voice.

'Did you seek medical treatment?'

'No. I thought a change of scene would work better than pills.'

'And where did you go for this "change of scene"?' Helen's barrister asked, the scepticism evident in his voice.

'London. For three months.'

'And how did you spend your time there?'

Marilyn fixed a critical eye on the barrister. 'Recovering.'

The barrister picked up a piece of paper from his desk. 'You acted in a play at that time. This playbill lists you as Geraldine Barclay in the play *What the Butler Saw*. Is that correct?'

'Yes.'

There was an edge in Marilyn's voice as if she knew exactly where the barrister was headed.

'The role of Geraldine Barclay requires you to be naked on stage, does it not?'

The judge's head swivelled sharply in Marilyn's direction.

'For some of the time, yes, but it wasn't gratuitous. The play has a serious point to make.'

'Indeed.' The barrister wielded a disapproving tone. 'So this is how you spent your time "recovering" from your … condition?'

'Yes. I had rent to pay. I didn't want to ask Harry for financial help. He needed the money for the boys.'

Ouch. The judge seemed to approve of that response, slightly softening his laser gaze on Marilyn.

'Why did you leave London after three months?'

'I missed my family.'

'Mmm. According to newspapers at the time, the play you were in closed after three months of poor reviews and dwindling audiences.'

'Is that a question?' snapped Marilyn.

Old Kenneally was startled into a brief cough. Hopefully he didn't like women who talked back.

Helen's barrister delivered his final question. 'Was it a coincidence that you returned home at the same time as your career on the stage failed?'

'Yes, it was a coincidence. And my career didn't fail—'

'Thank you. No further questions.'

Marilyn stalked out of the witness box, glaring at Helen as she resumed her seat.

'The court will take a short recess,' announced the judge.

Everyone stood as Kenneally exited the courtroom, and

then Finn bolted for the doors. Out in the reception area, he dialled Gabe. No answer. Where was he?

* * *

'Daniel, is there nothing I can say to change your mind?'

The bishop was upset, and Daniel was sorry about that. The man had been a mentor to him, and the last thing he wanted was to appear ungrateful.

'I've given it a lot of thought – and I've prayed about it. God has guided me.'

And it felt like he had. Waking in the middle of the night, Daniel had known instinctively what he had to do and had wasted no time this morning in setting about it. He'd been lucky that the bishop had a cancelled appointment. Lucky – or was it God giving a helping hand?

'Then God give you strength in your new path, my son. Shall we say a short prayer together?'

Daniel bowed his head and closed his eyes, only half-listening to the bishop's words. He'd just taken an enormous leap of faith, but not the religious kind. He wondered what would be waiting for him on the flip side.

* * *

Helen was on the stand, talking about how she'd left her home in Australia three years ago to come back to Ireland to nurse her brother through his final illness. She detailed the two rounds of chemotherapy, which had debilitated Harry. He couldn't sleep properly, couldn't keep much food down and was in constant pain. His tumour shrank but finally returned aggressively. He'd died in her arms.

Finn felt for his aunt. She wasn't acting there on the stand. She was reliving the memories as she gave her testimony, and her sadness was evident for all to see. How was Marilyn taking all this? Would she feel pity for her one-time husband? Probably not.

'Mr James transferred the title deeds of his house in Kilbrook to you,' said Helen's barrister. 'Was that your suggestion?'

'No, it was not. I tried to talk him out of it, but he just got upset. He said he wanted me to have the house, that I was a widow and getting older and might be glad of the security.'

'And he didn't leave anything to his wife or three sons.' Finn saw Marilyn edge forward slightly in her seat. 'Did you agree with that?'

'He was estranged from his boys. Nothing went right for them as a family after Marilyn left.'

'Objection.' Marilyn's barrister sprang to his feet. 'Speculation.'

'Please restrict yourself to answering the questions, Mrs MacKenzie,' counselled the judge, though not unkindly. Helen's honest and touching evidence seemed to be having some effect.

'For the record, Judge, Mr James's three sons are aware of the contents of his will, and none has made an application for financial provision from the deceased's estate,' stated Helen's barrister.

'Objection. Irrelevant.'

'Counsel,' warned the judge.

The barrister murmured an apology and then asked Helen one last question. 'Did Mr James ever, in all the time you were nursing him, talk about his wife, Marilyn James, the plaintiff?'

'No,' said Helen firmly. 'He never once mentioned her.'

'Your witness, Counsel.'

Marilyn's barrister stood up, and Finn clenched his hands together. This wasn't going to be easy. Helen would know that, though, and be ready.

'Mrs MacKenzie, when did you emigrate to Australia?'

'In 1977.'

'And how often did you see your brother after that?'

'I came home four times, before coming home to nurse him.'

'Four times,' repeated the barrister, rolling the words around in his mouth. 'In thirty-four years.'

'Yes.' Helen was refusing to be drawn, keeping her expression calm.

'Would you say you were close to your brother?'

'We always kept in touch by phone.'

'How often did you speak to him by telephone?'

'Once a month.'

'Once a month.' Again, the barrister toyed with the words. 'Did your brother ever mention problems in his marriage?'

Helen didn't falter. 'Yes, he did. Marilyn wanted to pursue an acting career. Harry felt she should focus on the children.'

'A traditional man, yes?'

'You could say that.'

'A man who believed in supporting and providing for his family?'

'Objection!' Helen's barrister was on his feet. 'Leading the witness.'

'Sustained. Restrict yourself to questions, Counsel.'

'Yes, Judge.' He picked up a paper from his desk. 'Your husband died in 1999, Mrs MacKenzie, is that right?'

'Yes.'

'According to official records, he died bankrupt. Is that correct?'

'Yes. He was conned by his business partner. A man he'd worked with for years—'

The barrister cut her off. 'What did you live on after this bankruptcy?'

'I had a small inheritance from my father. Harry got the same.'

'Did you have to sell your house in Australia in order to pay your husband's debts?'

'Yes, I did.'

'Where did you live?'

'I rented somewhere from a friend at a reasonable rate.'

Finn thought back to the flat in Sydney that he and Helen had shared. Cramped, but she'd made a fine home of it. It had been a haven for him after the nightmare of living with Harry, who would fly into a rage if he left DVDs out of their covers, or if he opened cupboard doors from the corners instead of the handles – he lost count of how many times he'd get a cuff around the head, and would have to clean the paintwork.

'Did you work?' the barrister was asking Helen.

'Yes. I directed plays, and did some voice-overs and commercials.'

'Did that irregular work pay well?'

Helen gave a rueful smile. 'Not very. But I could support myself.'

'When did your youngest nephew, Jody James, come to live with you?'

'About three years after my husband's death.'

'Why did he move to Australia?'

'He'd had a fight with his father and left home. And he needed a mother figure. Every child does.'

'How old was he when he came to live with you?'

'Fourteen.'

'And you felt it was better he live with you rather than his own father?'

'At that time – yes.'

'Why?'

'He'd gotten into problems in Kilbrook – where he lived with Harry. I felt a fresh start would get him back on the right path.'

'So did he come to you immediately after he left home?'

'No, he first went to stay with his two brothers in England.'

'Whose idea was it – originally – that Jody move to Australia?'

'Mine.'

'I see. And did you receive payment from Jody's brothers for his upkeep?'

'Yes, I did.'

'That must have been very convenient for you.'

'Objection! Argumentative.'

'Sustained.'

Finn barely restrained himself from leaping over the seats and knocking the barrister for six. He was twisting everything, making Helen seem opportunistic.

'How did you learn your brother had cancer, Mrs MacKenzie?'

'He phoned to tell me.'

'Did he ask you to come over and nurse him?'

'No. I suggested it.'

'I see. Was your nephew Jody working by that time?'

Helen's face lit up. 'Yes, he'd started his acting career and was doing well.'

Her guard was temporarily down and Finn wanted to tell her to be careful.

'Had the maintenance payments from his brothers stopped?'

Helen faltered. 'Yes, but—'

'No more money from them, so you decided to prey on your brother next—'

Finn was on his feet in a second. 'How dare you say that! You don't know how much she helped me! Just leave her alone!'

Everyone had turned to stare and the judge ordered Finn to be quiet or he'd be removed. Helen was shaking her head at him. He'd screwed things up. Finn turned and fled from the courtroom.

* * *

Rachel waved as she saw Daniel enter the café. He'd given her a lift to Galway so she could make arrangements to have her rental car towed back to Shannon, but he'd not given her any details about the appointment he had there.

'Hey!' Daniel greeted her with a smile and slipped into the chair opposite, picking up a menu. 'Have you ordered yet?'

'Chicken soup and a sandwich. I ordered for you, too.'

'Okay. This is my treat.'

'What's the occasion?' she asked. 'My leaving tomorrow?'

'No, that's definitely not a cause for celebration. I'm really going to miss you, Rachel.'

Perhaps he was the only one who would, who might give her a thought from time to time. Finn wouldn't dare do that – he'd push her to the back of his mind. And she understood that.

'I'm leaving the priesthood,' declared Daniel.

Rachel felt sick. She'd come between a man and his God. Things were going from bad to worse.

'Say something,' he prompted.

'Is it what you want, Daniel? What you really, really want?'

'You do know you've just quoted the Spice Girls. Are you about to break into song?'

'Daniel!' snapped Rachel, exasperated. 'This is serious.'

'Sorry,' he said, but he had a grin on his face as he said it. 'No, correction, I'm not sorry. Because I've never felt more alive in my life. I've made absolutely the right decision.'

'This is all my fault,' moaned Rachel. 'If you think I wanted this – that it was part of my plan of revenge – you're so wrong. Now I wish I'd never come here.'

And that was true. Her playing God just showed what a warped mind she had. They ought to lock her away.

'Rachel, look at me,' Daniel said gently, and she did. 'I've thought hard about leaving the priesthood. Helen said perhaps I joined the Church because they'd give me the only forgiveness I was likely to get for what I did. And I think she was right.'

'Is that so terrible? You found peace as a priest, yes?' Perhaps she could change his mind about this drastic step. One less thing to weigh on her conscience.

'I did find peace for a while. But I know the Church isn't enough for me anymore.'

Something the nuns had said came to Rachel's mind. 'Perhaps this is God testing you.'

'I think he did that years ago. Now he wants me to make up my own mind.'

'I don't understand,' said Rachel, miserably.

The waitress came then with their order, and there was a lull in the conversation. Daniel didn't seem upset about his life-changing decision. In fact, quite the reverse. He seemed younger somehow, vibrant.

'I was looking at Stokeley's murals a few days ago,' he said, picking up his soup spoon. 'The last one in the sequence is The Transfiguration – Jesus appearing as the Son of God before the apostles. I always wondered why Stokeley didn't paint the Crucifixion, or the Day of Judgement. Or even the Ascension.'

The murals were the last thing Rachel wanted to think about at that moment, but she'd humour Daniel. 'Perhaps his patron chose that theme.'

'Perhaps. But I like that his last mural was about change. And hope for the future. Transformation. Something we're all capable of, although on a much smaller scale.'

'The Transfiguration is also about seeing things clearly for the first time – as they really are,' she told him.

He nodded. 'That, too.'

Had she changed? She was certainly different after her time in Kilbrook and seeing things more clearly. But she'd also found and lost Finn, which was heartbreaking.

They ate their lunch in silence for a while.

'When do you officially leave the Church?' Rachel eventually asked him.

'March. This will be my last Christmas in Kilbrook.'

'And then?'

Daniel shrugged his shoulders. How could he seem so

unconcerned about his future? 'Who knows? Maybe I'll go back to university to re-qualify.'

'Or you could become a private detective,' Rachel suggested, managing a smile. 'You've certainly proved your abilities in that area.'

He laughed. 'Oh, I'll miss you, Rachel. You're quite a woman.'

She smiled, but her thoughts shifted to Finn. 'I wonder how the court case is going. I hope the judge decides in Helen's favour.'

Daniel called for the bill, and then gave the waitress his credit card. They started putting their coats on.

'Why don't we go and find out?'

'Oh, no, I don't think Finn would like that.'

'Then we'll leave. But I think he might appreciate some support today. Especially from you.'

Although Daniel meant well, he didn't know the misery of her last meeting with Finn. She'd rejected him. Who would want to be reminded of that?

'Come on, Rachel. You took on Kilbrook. You took on Jay Cole, remember? Bravest girl I've ever known. Let's go see Finn and Helen.'

The waitress came back with his card and Daniel pocketed it. He stood up and held out his hand to Rachel. This new Daniel seemed invincible, like he'd found the courage of his namesake. They left the café, arms linked, and he made her laugh all the way to the courthouse.

* * *

Mel sat at a table in The Fat Pheasant, re-reading the article in the local paper. The headline blared, 'Local Teacher Dismissed for Sexual Misconduct'. No ambiguity there then. God knows how the paper had got hold of it so soon. Probably that Rinaldi bitch had given them the story. The paper had used a photo of Jay taken at the opening night of this very restaurant.

Mel had been so happy then, so sure things were going to work out well. Now she just felt like a fool.

The couple at the window table got up and left. She didn't know them. Probably tourists. They'd been the only ones in for lunch today. Normally the restaurant was fully booked, even on a weekday. Now the writing was on the wall: nobody would frequent the restaurant of the wife of a teacher who had screwed a pupil. And Jay had fled the scene of the crime, leaving her to deal with the fallout. Coward. But that niggling voice in Mel's head reminded her she wasn't blameless in this – she'd sent that text to the O'Neill girl. And Rachel Rinaldi had used it to take her revenge.

The restaurant bell announced a visitor. Mel looked up, hoping to see a surprise coachload of tourists, but it was her father, clutching his own copy of the local newspaper. His eyes swept the empty restaurant, and he frowned. Mel took a quick gulp of her gin and tonic. Talking to Gerald through an alcoholic haze would be much better than facing him sober.

He waved the waitress away, hung up his coat, then came and sat down at her table. 'How are you, Mel?' His hand touched hers.

'Jay's left me,' she managed to blurt out.

'Run away, you mean,' he growled, glancing at the open newspaper in front of her. 'Leaving you to cope with everything.'

'It's not all his fault, though. I ... I did something wrong. Used his phone to send a text message as if it was from him.' She remembered his words from last night. 'I betrayed him.'

Gerald shook his head. 'I'd say you were the one betrayed, Mel. And it's not the first time he's been with other women, is it?'

The humiliation of her father – and the whole village – knowing about Jay's affairs burned afresh in Mel's cheeks. But she only knew that she loved Jay, even now. It was like a sickness that she didn't want to be cured of.

'If I leave Kilbrook, Daddy, do you think there's a chance Jay will come back to me?'

Gerald buried his head in his hands for a moment. When he looked across at her again, his expression was one of thinly-veiled exasperation. 'He's not good for you. He's dragging you down with him. Have you no pride, Mel?'

'No, when it comes to Jay, I've got no pride. I love him. I always have. He's the only one for me. You know that.'

There was no fatherly rebuke, just pity in his eyes. 'Maybe you could both start afresh away from Kilbrook. Leanne's young enough so she'd adjust to a change of schools. We can sell the restaurant, or bring in new management.'

Mel nodded, trying to envision a future somewhere other than in Kilbrook, the only home she'd ever known. Running away from a problem wasn't her style, but her options were severely limited now.

'Do you know where Jay is?' asked Gerald.

'Probably staying with his friend Garrett in Galway.'

'I'll text him and ask to meet over a drink.'

Mel got up from her seat and went to hug her father. They weren't usually a demonstrative family, but he hugged her back and kissed her forehead.

'There's no guarantee, Mel, that I can get him back for you.'

'I know.'

But she couldn't give up on her marriage without a fight.

* * *

Outside the courthouse, Finn was staring at his phone, thinking hard. After a delay due to bad weather, Gabe said the plane had finally landed at Shannon. He reckoned it would be an hour or so till he got to the courthouse with their witness. Lunch was over, and they were due back in court soon. Gabe had advised Finn to stall, to say he was sick – anything to avoid taking the stand before his brother arrived with their star witness.

Stalling seemed like the coward's way. Especially since the brothers were the ones who'd pushed Helen to fight against their mother's claim. Marilyn's barrister had played dirty, painting Helen as some gold-digger, yet over lunch she'd surprised Finn by taking it all in her stride. Said it didn't matter. Their own barrister had told her Kenneally was a traditional judge who supported family values right down the line, and he'd seemed shocked by Marilyn leaving home to take to the stage. Would that be enough, though? Marilyn had been Harry's legal wife at the time of his death, and that counted for something under law.

He might have to lie. Under oath. Say that Harry hadn't been violent. Only Marilyn would know he wasn't telling the truth, and she didn't count. Helen hadn't been around back then and Gabe was still at the airport. He'd do it if he had to: lie to protect Helen's interests. What did it matter? He'd pushed a girl to suicide. He was banished forever from the moral high ground.

'Finn!'

He turned to see Helen standing at the entrance to the courthouse next to Daniel. And Rachel, who looked like an angel in her white coat. She gave him an uncertain smile, and he lost his clarity of thought. Walking over, he couldn't take his eyes from hers.

'Helen, let's meet them inside,' said Daniel, and the two of them quickly went through the revolving door.

'How's it going?' Rachel asked, her voice barely making it through the rushing sound in Finn's ears.

He told the truth. 'Marilyn's barrister rubbished Helen. Now he's going to try to do the same to me.'

'Oh God.' Rachel's hand went up to her mouth. Her expression told Finn how much she still cared about him and his family, and he loved her for that.

'Daniel thought we should come to show our support, but if you don't want me here, Finn, I'll go.'

'Of course I want you here.'

In twenty-four hours or less, she'd be gone from his life, so he'd take whatever he could get of her company. He'd have to tell the truth now, though. He couldn't lie in front of the woman he loved. Not anymore.

'Let's go in,' he said.

'Good luck, Finn. Be strong.'

Her lips brushed his cheek and then he lost sight of her through the revolving doors. A prelude to their final parting.

* * *

Rachel sat in the courtroom, her stomach in knots. Finn had just sworn his oath to tell the truth and was settling down in the witness box. His expression was tense, his mouth almost a grimace. It was okay, though. Helen's barrister was asking the questions first.

'Your birth name was Jody James, but you've since formally changed it to Finn MacKenzie. Do you prefer the latter name to be used in court?'

'Yes, I do.'

'Mr MacKenzie, in his will your father left nothing to you or your brothers. And before his death, he transferred his property to his sister – your aunt – Mrs Helen MacKenzie. Were you surprised by this?'

'No. My father was free to dispose of his property as he wished. If anyone deserves it, my aunt does. She must have gone through hell nursing him in his last months. She was there for him when he needed her.'

Finn was glaring at a woman sitting at the table directly in front of the witness box. It must be Marilyn. Rachel could only see the back of her head – soft blonde curls. She wondered if he looked like her.

'What kind of a person was your mother, Mr MacKenzie?'

Finn continued staring directly at the woman in front of him as he spoke. 'She was cold, distant, angry sometimes. As

362

I grew up, it became clear she resented many things. Being married, being a mother, living in a small village. Only a Hollywood career would have satisfied her.'

Rachel heard the slight sneer in his voice. He was clearly deeply angry at his mother.

'Did your mother work?'

'No.'

'Did she help you with your homework?'

'No.'

'Did she go to parent-teacher evenings?'

'No.'

'Was she ever abusive towards you?'

'Yes.'

Rachel leaned forward in her seat, clasping and unclasping her hands in her lap.

'When?'

'Whenever I disappointed her. Which was pretty near all the time.'

Oh, Finn. Rachel wondered if she'd be able to sit through this testimony.

'Can you be more specific?' asked the barrister. 'Give the court some examples.'

'She never wanted me. After two boys, she wanted a daughter. She never forgave me for being a boy. Never forgave my father for not giving her a girl. If she thought I'd misbehaved, she'd tell me I was bad. Useless. Then she decided I was overweight. I know now I wasn't, but she cut my food down. Said she didn't want me to embarrass her by being a fat, ugly child. I was always hungry. My brothers would give me chocolate, crisps, burgers, and eventually I did put weight on. Too much. It made her hate me more. Then she found a chocolate wrapper in my bed. She said no son of hers was going to be fat – she made me drink cooking oil until I was sick, and made me strip naked in front of a mirror so I could see how disgusting I was.'

'How old were you when this took place, Mr MacKenzie?'

'I was seven.'

Finn was silent for a few moments, thinking. Remembering. 'When I was five, I found …' He hesitated, then said 'Marilyn.'

'Your mother?' prompted the barrister.

'Yes.'

Dear God, he couldn't even bear to call her his mother. Rachel hated that he was having to go through this.

'I found Marilyn in the bedroom with a man I'd never seen before. I didn't understand what was going on at that time, but now I know they were having sex. I told my dad – innocently – and she denied it. Said I was lying to get back at her for disciplining me. She swore on *my* life she hadn't done anything, so Harry believed her. He always believed her – he was obsessed with her, but I think deep down he knew the truth.'

'Mr MacKenzie, do you know why your mother abandoned the family when you were eleven?'

'I only know what she told me. The day she left, I was making my breakfast before school, and she came into the kitchen and said she was leaving. I could see her suitcase in the hallway. I thought it was because she didn't love Harry anymore – I didn't realise at the time that she'd never loved him. I … I said I loved her, and would help her around the house more. I started to cry and said I didn't want her to go. She …' Finn paused, and closed his eyes.

'Mr MacKenzie, what did your mother say when you told her you didn't want her to go?'

Finn took a deep breath and looked directly at his mother. 'She said, "You should have been a girl then, instead of the useless waste of space you are," and she just turned and walked away. She never came back.'

'What was life like after your mother left?'

'Quieter. My father threw himself into his job. Worked all the hours he could.'

'Isn't it true that you took on a lot of what your mother should have been doing – cleaning the house, cooking for your father?'

'Yes. I was trying to make amends. I thought her leaving was my fault.'

'Thank you, Mr MacKenzie. Your witness, Counsel.'

Rachel wiped at the tears on her face. He'd never told her any of this, even after she knew who he was. He hadn't used it to defend or excuse his actions. And even though it couldn't excuse what he'd done to Ella, she understood the teenage Jody better now.

Marilyn's barrister stood up. 'Mr MacKenzie, why did you change your name?'

Finn shrugged. 'It's a stage name. I'm an actor.'

'Yes, indeed you are. And your performance here has been worthy of an Oscar. So the change was nothing to do with hating your father's name – and him along with it?'

Helen's barrister shot up. 'Objection. Argumentative.'

'Sustained. You know better than that, Counsel,' warned the judge.

'Yes, Judge. My apologies,' said Marilyn's barrister, and then returned to the attack. 'Why did you leave Kilbrook when you were fourteen, Mr MacKenzie?'

The hairs on the back of Rachel's neck prickled a warning.

'I needed to get away for a bit,' said Finn, evasively. 'Things weren't going well for me there.'

'Isn't it true that your father assaulted you just before you left?'

'He hit me, yes.'

'What are we talking about here, Mr MacKenzie? A slap on the wrist? A bit of pushing around? Or worse?'

'Objection! The witness has answered.'

'This question speaks to Mr James's potential for violence, Judge,' protested Marilyn's barrister.

'I'll allow it,' advised the judge. 'Please answer, Mr MacKenzie.'

'He beat me with a belt,' said Finn. 'And I deserved it. And to answer your previous question, I changed my name because I hated me, not because I hated my father.'

'Mr MacKenzie, isn't it true that your father beat you severely? That he dislocated your shoulder, and you needed to seek medical attention when you reached your brothers in England?'

'I was able to travel on a train and a ferry, so it was hardly a matter of life and death.'

'Did you seek medical attention?'

'Yes. Because my brother wanted me to. But like I said, I deserved it.'

'You may be unaware of this, but there are laws against assault and battery. Even within families. Especially with regard to minors.'

The judge leaned forward. 'Thank you for the lecture, Counsel. Perhaps you'd like to proceed with your questioning now.'

'Yes, Judge. After you left home, Mr MacKenzie, when did you see your father again?'

'I never saw him again.'

'Why not?'

'He didn't want to see me. I didn't live up to his image of what a guard's son should be. I was an embarrassment to him.'

'Did you go to his funeral?'

'No.'

'Why didn't you – or your brothers – make any claim on your father's estate?'

'I told you. His property was his to do with as he pleased.'

'Isn't it true, Mr MacKenzie, that your father was a violent man? Not just that one time after you were caught bullying, but on a regular basis?'

'My father hit us when we'd done wrong. End of story.'

'Did you ever see your father hit your mother?'

'No, I did not.'

'I would remind you, Mr MacKenzie, that you are under oath. Did you ever see your father hit your mother?'

'No, I did not.'

'Did you ever *hear* your father hit your mother?'

Finn fell silent. He seemed startled.

'Answer the question, Mr MacKenzie.'

Finn looked at Rachel as he answered. And she knew at that moment that he wouldn't lie because she was there, watching him. And that the case could be lost …

'I heard them shouting and screaming at each other a lot, and sometimes she had bruises—'

The door to the courtroom banged open, and everyone turned towards it. Gable was standing there with a man Rachel had never seen before. She glanced back at Finn, sitting drained in the witness box. But something was happening now. Marilyn was talking to her barrister, and then he approached the bench, going up to the judge, where they had a brief conversation.

'Court is adjourned,' declared the judge, a few minutes later. 'My chambers in five minutes, gentlemen,' he said to the two barristers.

'All rise.'

Rachel stumbled up from her seat. What had just happened?

* * *

Finn came back into the small waiting room to find Helen and Gabe deep in conversation with their barrister. Marilyn's first husband, Johnson Waterbury, was waiting just outside.

Finn had had to excuse himself earlier, and in the washroom he'd lost most of his lunch. His head was full of unwanted memories of his father and Marilyn – the aggression, the abuse, the childhood that was gone and would be the only one he'd ever remember. It was more than he could cope with.

'Hello, love,' said Helen.

'Marilyn's side have made an offer,' Gabe told him. 'She obviously saw Johnson in the courtroom and she knows what evidence he's got.' His eyes glinted a warning, and Finn understood. The barrister needed to think they'd tracked down Johnson early that morning. That way he didn't have to lie to the judge if he was asked if he'd known about this witness ahead of time yet failed to disclose it to the other side.

'Tell me about the offer.' Finn sat down with them all at the table.

'Marilyn will settle here and now for half the value of the house,' said the barrister.

'And if we keep on going?' asked Helen.

The barrister shrugged. 'The judge may let you keep all of the house, he may award you half of the house or some other division. Or you may walk away with nothing.'

'But what about Johnson's testimony?' asked Gabe.

'Marilyn's side will likely object to him because he's a late witness and they've had no time for discovery. The judge could accept that and refuse to let him take the stand. Or there could be an adjournment to a later date. I can talk to the judge and try to persuade him Johnson has critical evidence, but there's no guarantee I'll be successful.'

They all absorbed that information silently for a few moments.

'It's your decision, Helen,' said Gabe, taking her hand. 'We'll support you, whatever you decide. Finn, Cary, and I want this house for you. We have no other interest in it.'

'Finn and I went through hell in there,' said Helen. 'Marilyn didn't spare us anything. Why should we spare her now?'

'There's one other thing to consider,' said the barrister. 'Finn's testimony was interrupted. They may ask him to take the stand again.'

So the whole thing might not be over yet. Finn clasped his hands under the table to stop the trembling.

'What do you think, love? Are you up to it? And it's okay to say no.'

Finn looked at Helen, this woman he loved so much. Who had saved him when he'd been lost. She'd taken everything Marilyn's barrister had thrown at her. He could do the same. This thing needed to be played out.

'*I'll have my bond; speak not against my bond,*' Finn said to Helen.

'Shylock,' murmured Helen.

'And Marilyn.' Like Shylock, she'd shown them no mercy, so she herself should be shown none.

Gabe and the barrister looked puzzled, but the two actors in the room were communicating perfectly.

'We fight on,' declared Helen.

Chapter Twenty-Six

The hearing was about to restart. Judge Kenneally had been closeted away with the two barristers for almost an hour. Having heard what evidence Johnson had, he told the courtroom now that he judged it critical to the hearing so he would allow the testimony.

Finn smiled across Helen at his brother and gave a thumbs up. Gabe had found Johnson Waterbury through the wonder of Facebook. He'd posted notices on several 'Seeking Relatives' groups, and eventually, a friend of Johnson's had been alerted to them. Although Johnson was now plain William Johnson, his old stage name, ditched years ago, had still stood out.

Johnson himself was a giant. A head taller at least than Finn, and well-built. He seemed to dwarf everyone else in the courtroom. Even with his greying hair, it was easy to see how Marilyn had fallen for him. He exuded self-confidence and charm.

Helen's barrister established the preliminaries of name, age and occupation, and he requested Johnson to identify Marilyn in the courtroom. She was staring down at the desk.

'Mr Johnson, when did you marry Marilyn Buckley, as Mrs James was then?'

'In March 1975, when Marilyn turned eighteen. That way she didn't need her parents' permission.'

The barrister picked up a piece of paper. 'Mr Johnson, is this the certificate of marriage for you and Ms Buckley?'

A clerk showed Johnson the paper. He glanced at it and gave his confirmation.

'Why did you split up?'

'I found out she'd been sleeping around to try to get acting roles. She'd slept with quite a well-known director and his wife found out. Marilyn's name was dirt after that. She couldn't even get a job sweeping the stage.'

Johnson's testimony was matter-of-fact, but Judge Kenneally's eyes looked like they were about to pop out of his head.

'Did you start divorce proceedings?'

'Yes.'

'On what grounds?'

'Irretrievable breakdown. But I was told we needed to be officially separated for two years before we could be divorced.'

'When did you receive your decree absolute, Mr Johnson?'

'March 1978. I have it if you need to see it.'

The barrister picked up a piece of paper. 'Your honour, this is the wedding certificate of Harry James and Marilyn Johnson. The date of the marriage was November 1977. It was a civil ceremony that took place in the USA in Las Vegas. Marilyn was still legally married to Mr Johnson at that time. Therefore, she was guilty of bigamy, and her second marriage to Mr Harry James was invalid.'

Shocked murmurs ran round the courtroom. The judge called for silence.

'No further questions.'

Finn couldn't help a quiet, ironic laugh. So he really was a bastard.

* * *

Finn was pacing up and down the upper courthouse level. He couldn't keep still. Half-an-hour had passed. Johnson had been cross-examined, and they were now waiting for a verdict. Finn's nerves had been strained to the limit. He hoped it would all have been worth it.

A strong smell of perfume enveloped him, and he turned. Marilyn was walking past, accompanied by her barrister. She glanced scornfully at Finn and said, 'You've obviously inherited my acting abilities, Jody.'

'I wasn't acting!' he called after her, his temper flaring. She said something to her barrister, and their laughter floated back to him. Finn felt sick at the thought that he was connected to her in any way. He moved over to the railing and glanced down at the entrance and saw Daniel and Rachel coming through the revolving door. They'd gone to buy decent coffee for everyone. As she followed him through the metal detector, Daniel said something which made Rachel laugh. Finn remembered how she'd once laughed at his jokes. Now *he* was a joke. A walking cliché. A bully who'd been the victim of abuse and who'd taken it out on others.

He watched Rachel climbing the stairs, her cheeks flushed from the frost outside. She spotted him and said something to Daniel, who continued on to where Helen and the others were waiting outside the courtroom. Rachel walked up to Finn and handed him a coffee.

'Thanks.' He sipped at the drink, unsure how to begin a conversation. She helped him out.

'It must have been so hard for you, Finn, to talk about your past ... up there on the stand. I think you're very brave.'

'Or stupid.' The last thing he wanted from Rachel was pity. It was a poor second to her passion and love. 'I might have blown it all. That barrister knew exactly the questions to ask.'

'I don't think any of it put Marilyn in a good light. She's a bigamist.'

'Hopefully the judge agrees with you.'

'I'll be leaving tomorrow, Finn. Daniel said it's the finale of the Winter Festival tonight. Will you come with us? He wants to celebrate.'

'Celebrate?' What the hell did any of them have to celebrate? He wasn't interested in her answer. He could only focus on the fact she'd said 'us'. Her and Daniel.

'I hope he doesn't mind me telling you,' said Rachel, glancing quickly over to the group outside the courtroom. 'He's leaving the priesthood.'

'What!' The shock hit Finn like a body blow. And then he thought about Daniel and Rachel at the entrance of the court with their coffees. Laughing. And they'd arrived here together. Open-mouthed, he stared over at Daniel. No, it wasn't possible ... was it? Had he just been outmanoeuvred by a priest? A soon-to-be ex-priest?

The courtroom doors swung open, and an official stepped out. 'Parties in James versus MacKenzie – please take your seats. The judge is returning to the courtroom.'

'Finn?'

He glanced at Rachel, his mind all over the place.

'Let's go.'

Numbly, he followed, her white coat like a beacon in the darkness gathering around him. He would have followed her to her seat but then Gabe called him down to the front, where he sat down next to Helen.

'All rise.'

Finn stood up and then sat down again like some mechanical toy. He found it hard to follow the judge's words. Snatches and phrases penetrated his consciousness:

' ... an unhappy relationship ... abandoned the family home ... estranged from sons and husband ... no evidence of reconciliation ... a bigamous marriage ... an abusive mother ... clear wishes of the deceased ... Marilyn James ... unworthy to succeed ...'

Suddenly Helen was hugging Finn. 'What happened?' he murmured.

'We won, Finn! We did it!'

Gabe was thumping him on the back, and he managed to smile at them both. Then they had to thank the barrister. Finn tried to see Rachel and Daniel. He needed to talk to them.

'We'll drop Johnson off at the airport with Gabe,' Helen was saying now. 'Least we can do.'

They'd only brought one car! Damn! He'd have to go with them.

Finn pushed his way out of the courtroom. Another hearing had just ended, and the hallway was filling with people, all moving at a snail's pace.

When they finally all made it to the car park, Finn saw Daniel's car reversing out of his spot. Rachel was in the seat beside him. Daniel rolled down the window. 'Congratulations, Helen! See you back in Kilbrook. Make sure you come to the Fireworks Festival. Great way to celebrate.' Then the car revved and was gone, leaving Finn lonelier than he'd ever felt in his life.

* * *

It was just after six when Jay entered the bar in Galway. He'd spent most of the day crashed out in the bed in Garrett's spare room after their heavy drinking session the night before. It had been strange to wake up in a different place but great not to have anyone nagging at him for not behaving like a responsible adult.

Now Gerald Maguire was likely going to chew him out for leaving Mel, and for getting involved with Jenny. He'd almost not turned up for their meeting, but a chance to tell Mel's father what he really thought of him was not to be missed. It would be great closure.

Gerald was in a corner booth, and he didn't stand up when Jay came over. Didn't even offer him a drink.

'Been waiting long?' asked Jay, well aware that he was late.

'I've been waiting five years, Jay, for you to start taking your responsibilities seriously. Twenty minutes is nothing.'

So the insults had started already. 'And I've been waiting five years for you to back out of my marriage and show me some respect.'

'Respect!' exploded Gerald. 'Are you serious, man? My daughter is a laughing stock because you can't keep your hands off other women!'

'That's between Mel and me,' snapped Jay. 'Husband and wife. We understand each other. Or did, before you started trying to poison her against me.'

'I don't know what you mean.'

'Yes, you do. Running down my job every chance you get, criticising me for not earning enough money. If you didn't think I was good enough for Mel, why did you let me marry her in the first place?'

Jay's comments seemed to hit home. Gerald was silent for once in his life. Savouring his advantage, Jay stopped a passing waitress and ordered a beer.

'I didn't want Mel to marry you, that's true,' admitted Gerald. 'But she loved you. Loves you still. And she means everything to me. She's not happy with you, but she'll be miserable without you. That's just how it is.'

That was the truth. And it was a terrible truth because Jay didn't love Mel anymore. He probably never had. He certainly didn't want to be shackled to her for the next twenty, thirty, forty years. He wanted to be free. His beer arrived, and he gulped at it like a man lost in a desert.

'If you reconcile with Mel, I'll set you both up here, or in Cork or maybe Dublin – you name the place.'

Jay was stunned. Gerald Maguire was offering him a fresh start, not a kick in the teeth as expected. It was tempting. He could keep all the home comforts he'd grown used to, perhaps set up in business for himself. Give Mel another baby to keep her busy …

'But know one thing, Jay,' said Gerald, and his eyes were burning with dislike. 'If you cheat on Mel again, so help me, I'll run you out of her life – and out of this city.'

So that was the deal. He'd be a prisoner of sorts, in a gilded cage. Watched like a hawk, kept on a short leash. Only half a man.

'No deal.' The words came out almost automatically, and part of Jay felt uncertain about the enormity of what he'd done. But Garrett had told Jay that he'd likely get half of Mel's money if they divorced. He could set himself up in business, buy a flat, live modestly …

Gerald was buttoning up his coat, putting on his gloves.

He'd be wild that his famed negotiating skills had failed this time.

'Okay, Jay, I offered and you refused. But know this – the house doesn't belong to Mel. The deeds are in my name. I also own the restaurant. She has less than twenty thousand in her savings account. When you divorce, you'll be lucky to walk away with ten grand. Your car belongs to me, too – but I'll let you keep it. Something to sell when the maintenance payments for Leanne kick in.'

After Gerald left, Jay sat on at the table, drinking pint after pint, until the alcohol finally blurred his thoughts about the disaster his life had become.

* * *

The church choir was singing the traditional tedious medley of songs to mark the end of the Winter Festival. While everyone's attention was focused on the singers, Mel moved quickly up the side aisle and slipped into a space at the end of one of the pews near the front. Next to her was the deacon's aged crock of a mother, dozing off and drooling now. That was fine because the last thing Mel needed was dirty looks from one of the worst gossips in Kilbrook.

Her belief in God was shaky. Perhaps that would work against her now, but Mel was desperate. She'd try anything. Clasping her hands discreetly in her lap, she closed her eyes and tipped her head slightly forward to pray: *Dear God, I'm sorry for all the bad things I might have done. I'll be better in future, I promise. Just, please, bring Jay back to me. I love him, and I need him. Leanne needs her father. Bring him back.*

Mel opened her eyes, and then hurriedly whispered 'Amen' as an afterthought. There was nothing more she could do now but wait for Gerald – or Jay – to call. She pulled her phone out of her pocket and held it in her lap. It was on, but the ringer was turned down.

The choir kept going with their interminable 'hallelujahs'.

She noticed that Daniel didn't seem to be here, which was strange. He was usually wedded to his bloody church, buttering up the parishioners with his simpering smiles and good deeds. She'd never liked him, not even when they were young, but he'd ingratiated himself with Jay so she couldn't kick him out of the group. And now he'd tried to salve his conscience by stabbing Jay in the back.

Her thoughts turned to Jody James, and the way he'd turned out. Who'd have thought it? If he'd looked like that in school, she might have set her cap at him, instead of Jay. He was as bad as Daniel, though – all over Jay at school, when it suited them. Too cowardly to do anything else. Daniel, Jody, and Rachel Rinaldi – they were all bloody cowards and hypocrites. She and Jay were worth ten of them …

She felt a slight tremor from her mobile, and her stomach lurched. Glancing down, she clicked on the text message from her father: No use, darling. He wants a divorce. Chin up. I'll come and see you tomorrow. x

Tears dropped into Mel's lap, wetting the phone. It was all over now. She wanted to run out of the church, but everyone would see her and know she was upset. Nothing to do except sit there until the end of this wretched caterwauling.

Images of Jay flitted through Mel's mind: their first kiss, their wedding day, baby Leanne cradled in her father's arms. All over now. No more memories for them. As she sat there, a cold and fierce hate seeped into her bones and spread its tendrils outwards to include the church and Kilbrook and everyone in it. She loathed this village with its stupid traditions and backward people, so full of themselves because tourists flocked to see some dead painter's murals. Mel glanced over towards the Stokeley Chapel and an idea began to form in her mind. A way to take revenge on them all.

When the concert ended and there was the usual noise and bustle of departure, Mel slipped out of the pew and behind the large Christmas tree directly in front. She crouched down in the small nook between tree and pulpit, hidden from view. Nobody saw her, nobody found her. The noise of voices gradually faded away, and then she heard the deacon telling the choir master to leave the lights on because Father Quinn would be coming back after the fireworks.

The two men left and Mel heard them lock up. Like Mel and Jay and Jody and Daniel had done all those years ago to Ella Rinaldi. Only Mel wasn't afraid. She was exactly where she wanted to be. She'd do what she planned, then lever open the church office window. Make it all look like a break-in.

* * *

Finn waited in line to get some punch for Helen. All around him in the park people were celebrating the end of the Winter Festival. Their laughter and excitement left him untouched. He was happy that Helen would keep the house, but he was wretched at the thought that he'd lost Rachel.

He finally spotted her by the ice rink, sitting at a table with Molly. The two women were talking intently, heads close together. He wanted so much to speak to Rachel yet was afraid of what he might find out. It was one thing to have lost her, but quite another to have lost her to someone he knew. How could Rachel get involved with Daniel but not Finn? They'd both bullied Ella. It didn't make sense. Unless she'd just gone off him. Today in court, Rachel had heard all about his past. Perhaps that was too much emotional baggage for her to handle on top of her own.

Finn watched as Daniel approached Rachel and Molly and set down two cups of punch on the table. He pointed out to the ice. Rachel stood up, took Daniel's arm, and they headed up to the rink entrance, where they paid to rent some skates. They were laughing together.

Finn couldn't bear to watch any longer and walked away.

* * *

'Thank you for my reward,' said Daniel, unlacing his skates. Rachel had asked how she could thank him for helping her with Jay, and he'd chosen a spin around the rink, something he hadn't done in years.

'Happy to oblige,' said Rachel, handing back her skates. 'But my muscles won't thank me for that tomorrow.'

'A hot bath tonight will sort that. And right now, some more punch will take the edge off. Shall I get us some?'

Rachel hesitated. 'Daniel, there's something I'd like to do now.'

'What?'

'I want to go to the church and … say goodbye … to Ella.'

He nodded. 'Okay, I'll come with you.'

'I need to do this alone. Do you understand?'

'Of course I do.' He took the key to the church out of his pocket. 'I asked for the lights to be left on. I'll be going over there in half an hour to finish up some things. But you'll miss the fireworks if you go now – they're about to begin.'

She was already moving away. 'I think I've had enough fireworks for now. See you later.'

Daniel watched until she was just the tiniest speck of white moving through the park gates.

* * *

The fireworks were crackling up into the night sky as Rachel arrived at the entrance to the church. She looked back for a few moments at the silver rockets and red starbursts and green spirals lighting up the darkness. It was a beautiful way to end the festival.

Standing on the steps, Rachel realised this was where she had come in. On first arriving in Kilbrook, she'd stood in front of this church and sworn vengeance. She'd done her best. She'd burned and been burned. And now, full circle. Her entrance was now her exit. A final farewell to Ella, and then tomorrow she'd head back to her old life.

The fireworks fizzled and crackled noisily as she unlocked and pushed open the wooden door. It was all lit up inside, the Christmas tree glowing warmly at the front. This was not the dark nightmare place that Ella had known.

Dipping her fingers into the holy water stoup, Rachel genuflected and crossed herself, then slipped into a back pew. She said a silent prayer for the soul of her sister, and asked forgiveness for herself for playing God. She didn't know if anybody up there was listening, or even if there was anybody up there, but that wasn't really the point. She was trying to find peace inside herself. Make sense of the past, and prepare for the future.

There was a lull in the fireworks outside and the church was silent until she heard a noise to her left, from the direction of the chapel. Rachel was startled. She'd thought she was alone. She should be alone because she had the key. Perhaps it was just mice? Then there was another sound, of something being laid down on the ground. Oh God, had she come here in the middle of a break-in?

Cowering down in the pew, Rachel sent a text to Daniel: Intruders in church. Come now. But the circular signal told of a delay. There was more noise, and Rachel's heart thudded in her chest. Was someone stealing the church silver? The text still hadn't gone through. She'd better leave and find him herself. There was no way she was going to play the hero.

Then Rachel heard the most unexpected sound – someone was humming. And it was a woman's voice. Perhaps a choir member had stayed behind to practise. Daniel could come rushing in with the police, and Rachel would feel like a fool for overreacting.

'Fuck!' Rachel heard someone say. Obviously no chorister or devout Christian. And there was something familiar about the voice. She glanced at her mobile. The text was still on hold. She should get out of the church but curiosity was getting the better of her. She'd just take a quick look. Slipping out of the pew, Rachel looked around her and grabbed a candelabra stand. She crept slowly up the side aisle. Peering round the wall, she couldn't believe what she saw. Mel was standing there in the middle of the chapel, holding a wet paintbrush. Tins of opened white paint were at her feet. Glancing up at the wall, Rachel saw white streaks of paint covering the right side of Stokeley's Creation mural, and she screamed her anger.

Mel dropped the paintbrush in fright, whirling round to face Rachel. Then she started to laugh, a high-pitched ugly sound. 'I might have known it would be you. Rachel bloody Rinaldi. Determined to stick your nose in.'

Rachel moved slowly into the chapel, and Mel eyed the candelabra in her hand. 'What are you doing?' she asked. 'Stealing church property?'

'What are *you* doing, Mel?' Rachel wished her voice wasn't shaking so much. She heard the faintest of pings and knew her text to Daniel had finally gone through. All she needed to do was keep Mel talking until he arrived. Glancing around, she saw that Mel had only damaged one fresco with the paint, thank God.

'What does it look like? I'm redecorating.'

Rachel inched forward. 'Why?'

Mel darted down and picked up a paint can, backing away from Rachel. 'Because I don't like this church. The priest is a hypocrite. And I especially don't like this chapel.'

'Why not?' Rachel edged in closer. If she could back Mel into the corner near the votive candle stand, she had a better chance of keeping the frescos safe.

Mel pointed the paintbrush at Rachel. 'I don't like this chapel because *you* like it. And *you* have ruined my life.'

'Mel, please ...'

Mel put both hands around the tin of paint and swung it round, ready to throw it at the fresco. Rachel hit out with the candelabra and managed to dash the tin from Mel's hands. The liquid spattered some of the fresco on the opposite wall but mostly coated the floor beneath. Rachel launched herself physically at Mel, and they both crashed back into the votive candle stand. There was a shattering of glass and candles tumbled out around them. And then there was a *whoosh* as flame and paint met. Within seconds, the fire had spread to the wooden bench in the middle of the chapel. There was still an exit, though.

'Move, Mel, get out!' Rachel pushed at the woman sprawled across her. There was no response. Wriggling free, she turned Mel over. There was a small cut on her forehead and she was out cold.

Rachel started to cough from the smoke and wrapped her scarf round her nose and mouth. Then she grabbed Mel's feet and began to drag her slowly through the gap in the fire. Her muscles screamed in protest, but finally Mel was clear. Rachel dropped to her knees, breathing in great lungfuls of air, but then a huge flash seared across her eyes. God, the paint cans were going up now! Stokeley's murals! She dragged herself to her feet and stumbled along the aisle. Where was it? Where was it? Feeling along the wall, her fingers found the fire extinguisher. Heaving it free, she used it to smash the glass of the fire alarm and pulled the handle down. The ringing deafened her for a moment, and then she was off again, back to the chapel. She pulled out the locking pin and pointed the nozzle at the base of the fire. Foam flooded out and blanketed the flames in the centre of the chapel. The smoke was acrid and stung her eyes. Her arms felt like lead but she kept going, spraying all the area under the nativity fresco. She prayed there'd be enough in the extinguisher to finish the job.

There was a popping sound behind her and Rachel whirled round. The lid had come off an unopened paint can under the Creation fresco, and a flash of fire blinded her momentarily. She moved instinctively backwards and skidded on the foam. Her arms wheeled around frantically, and for a moment she was reminded of her ice skating sessions with Finn and Daniel.

And then she hit the ground, cracking her head. The scarf fell from her mouth and nose, and there was only smoke to breathe. Dimly, through her streaming eyes, she saw flames creeping closer, and then she lost consciousness.

* * *

Standing near the park gate, Finn saw Daniel running towards him, slowing as he reached the gate.

'It's Rachel,' he gasped to Finn. 'Something's wrong in the church.'

And then he was off again, racing across the road. His words penetrated Finn's brain, and he took off after the priest, soon overtaking him. Pounding the pavement, all kinds of thoughts ran through Finn's mind, but the worst was that Rachel had somehow tried to kill herself, like Ella ...

Finn vaulted the church gate and barrelled into the front door. As it slammed open, he found a scene from hell inside. The fire alarm was ringing and there was smoke everywhere, making it hard to see anything.

'Rachel!' he yelled, and coughed as his lungs protested at the lack of oxygen.

Pulling his coat jacket over his nose and mouth, Finn stumbled up the side aisle, and then tripped over something. It was Mel, sprawled out on the floor. She was coughing violently. He crawled back towards her, but she was pointing over to the chapel. Finn turned to look – and shouted out Rachel's name.

She was on the floor on her back. One side of the chapel was on fire, and the flames had licked their way to her white coat, which had started to burn.

'No!' He flung himself into the chapel and onto his knees. With his bare hands, he started to pat out the flames. The pain was beyond agony. He pulled off his jumper and swatted at the smouldering coat material, then he pulled Rachel over to the side of the chapel where the fire was out. Through eyes that were stinging from the smoke, Finn saw Daniel arrive with a fire extinguisher, directing it at the flames.

Finn's lungs were burning but, with what energy he had left, he pulled Rachel into his lap. Her face was grimed, her eyes closed. He couldn't tell if she was breathing or not.

'Rachel!' he whispered. 'Rachel!'

Her eyes flickered open, and she started gasping for air.

'Thank God, thank God, thank God!' moaned Finn, his voice cracking. He kissed Rachel's eyes, her cheeks, her lips, then hugged her close to him, blinded now by tears not smoke.

* * *

Rachel coughed herself awake. Her throat felt like it had been sandpapered and she could smell smoke. Smoke!

She bolted upright and found herself in a hospital bed. Vague memories of the horror in the chapel flooded back, and she started to cough again.

'Here, drink this.' A hand supported her head and brought a glass of water to her lips. She drank greedily and the pain in her throat eased a fraction. She leaned back against the pillows and looked up into Daniel's worried face.

'Hello you,' he said gently.

'You saved me,' she whispered. 'Thank you.'

Daniel shook his head. 'I didn't save you. Finn did.'

'Finn?'

'He came with me to the chapel. He got to you first. Your coat was burning. He put out the flames and pulled you to safety. You're lucky to be alive, Rachel.'

Now she remembered looking up into Finn's face, seeing the relief and love in his eyes. It was too much to cope with, and she drifted back to sleep.

* * *

Rachel stared through the ward window at Finn. He was

whiter than the hospital sheets, and a drip fed into one of his bandaged hands. Helen was in a chair at his bedside, reading something aloud from a newspaper.

Courage failed her for a moment, but then Rachel thought of him risking his life to pull her away from the fire. Daniel had said the second-degree burns to Finn's hands might need skin grafts. Months of pain, his career on hold – the least she could do was thank him. More than that she didn't think she could offer ...

Helen spotted her and came out into the hallway, smiling. 'How are you feeling today?'

'A bit better, thanks.' Clearly Helen didn't blame Rachel for what had happened, but that didn't help.

'Go in and see him. He's on morphine but not too much. He can carry on a conversation. I'll just get a refill of coffee.'

And then Helen was gone, leaving Rachel standing there with a heart that was breaking. She forced her feet to move, into the ward, and over to Finn's bed. He watched her intently with those blue-grey eyes as she sat down.

* * *

Finn struggled to keep his mind clear and focused. Rachel had told him that the Stokeley murals were being cleaned and would be okay, and now she was updating him on Mel, who'd had a concussion but had been taken home by her parents today. She'd got all this from Daniel, who obviously hadn't wasted a moment getting to see her. All Rachel told the police was that she'd found the chapel on fire and tried to put it out. She hadn't incriminated Mel because Jay had left her, so the woman had lost everything and now knew what loss felt like. It was revenge enough.

Her words burned themselves into Finn's mind. He remembered the pain of seeing Rachel and Daniel together at the ice rink. Was that also revenge? If so, it was game, set and match to Rachel. She'd destroyed him. But he had to be sure ...

'Rachel.' His voice was faint and raspy, but she stopped talking and leaned in closer.

'What is it, Finn?'

He wanted to beg her not to leave him. There was no shame in that because he had no pride left. That had been lost fourteen years ago. He didn't want to give her more pain, though, because she'd surely had enough for a lifetime.

'Is there any chance for us?' he whispered, scanning her face for a sign.

Her beautiful blue eyes brimmed with tears, and then she looked down at her hands. It was over, he knew. The love they'd shared, so brief and so intense, had burned down like a candle. The promise they'd made on a star couldn't hold because both of them had been hiding something. The gods didn't like deceivers.

'Finn, I wish that ...'

He held up his hand to stop her words. All he wanted now was to dial up the painkiller from his drip and sink into nothingness, but he'd not leave her wounded.

'I understand, Rachel. I do. I guess there's too much against us to make it work, but I'll never forget you or stop loving you ...'

He started to cough, and she had to put a glass of water to his lips. As he drank, he watched her hands and felt the frustration of the bandages around his own. He couldn't touch her, but perhaps that was better. Kinder.

Finn was losing his strength now, and a wave of tiredness washed over him. 'Be happy,' he whispered. There was so much more he wanted to say, but the pain was ebbing back and he had to click the medication control. The morphine seeped into his system and carried him off to a gentler place.

* * *

Rachel stared at her body in the bathroom mirror. There were burn marks, angry red patches, over her chest and waist. The doctor had told her they would fade in time. Her breathing was better today, and they were allowing her to leave. She put her jeans and jumper on, and brushed her hair back into a ponytail, wincing as the brush connected with the bruise on the back of her head, the legacy of her concussion.

Daniel was waiting for her in the ward. 'Ready to go?'

She nodded. 'I need to see Finn.' He'd had a bad couple of days with an infection and fever, so they'd had no more opportunities to talk.

'He's being transferred to a Burns Unit this afternoon. He's sedated.'

'Still – I want to say goodbye.'

Daniel picked up her bags and offered her his arm. They walked slowly along to Finn's ward. He was sleeping, Helen by his bedside as usual. She uncurled from her chair and gave Rachel a hug. 'All set? What time will you get to London?'

'About seven, I should think,' said Daniel.

'You'll take good care of her, won't you?' said Helen.

'I will.'

She left them alone with Finn while she went to get some coffee. Rachel dropped down into the chair by the bed and looked at him. He was still so pale, the long, thick eyelashes resting on his cheeks the only sign of colour. She stared at his bandaged hands. The knowledge of what he'd done for her was really too much to bear.

'Why did he do it, Daniel?'

'Because he loves you.'

'I told him it was all over.' Rachel's voice shook. 'He should have let me burn.'

'Rachel, don't.'

Daniel's hand was on her shoulder. She thought she saw Finn's eyelids flicker slightly, but his eyes remained closed.

'What about his TV show back in Australia?' fretted Rachel. 'It was his big break, but now he's injured.'

'Helen said they're postponing shooting for a few months. Apparently they really want him for the role.'

That was something, at least. He'd still have his work. Rachel was taking time off from her PhD. Her uncle had suggested a trip to Italy, to soak up some healing sun in Sicily ...

'Time to go,' said Daniel gently. 'We've got a plane to catch.'

'I know. Sophia's cooking up a storm. I'm warning you – she'll kill you with kindness.'

'I can't wait.'

'Just give me a moment with him, Daniel.'

'Okay.' He leaned down and kissed the top of her head.

Alone at Finn's bedside, Rachel took the envelope out of her pocket. It had taken her all morning to think of what to write. In the end, she hadn't been able to find her own words and so borrowed instead from Christina Rossetti's 'Remember Me':

Better by far you should forget and smile
Than that you should remember and be sad.'

Unclasping the Claddagh pendant from around her neck, Rachel pooled the chain in her hand, about to put it into the envelope, but it was too hard to part with the precious gift so she put it into her pocket. She loved Finn still. Maybe she always would. But with that love came too much pain. For both of them. The spectre of Ella would always be between them. Rachel couldn't imagine that she'd ever be able to not think of her sister when she looked at Finn – but even more in her thoughts now was that Finn needed to be away from her, even if he didn't realise it. He was still suffering from unnecessary guilt over Ethan's death – how much worse must he feel about Ella, and Rachel's presence in his life would only remind him of that. Rachel wanted to remember her sister on her birthday, at Christmas, at any given moment, but how could she share those moments with Finn, knowing that they would only torment him?

They'd only known each other a few weeks, and although

it would be hard in the beginning, they'd get over it, move on, find happiness elsewhere. She hoped he'd love again, but she wouldn't. Too much pain. She could never go through this again. There might be someone in the future that she could settle down with, someone she could like and respect, maybe even love. But it wouldn't be what she'd felt for Finn. That was a once in a lifetime love, and she was grateful she'd experienced it, but she'd never again leave her heart so exposed.

She stood up and placed the envelope on his bedside locker. Leaning over, she gently stroked Finn's hair and kissed his cheek.

'Thank you for saving me,' she whispered.

He didn't wake up, but perhaps somewhere in his subconscious, he'd heard her. Leaving the ward, Rachel wondered how long it would be for both of them until their pain healed.

* * *

Finn opened his eyes a fraction and watched Rachel leave the ward. He'd heard everything but hadn't wanted to make the parting more difficult for her. Or himself. Helen had told him Rachel had sat for hours by his bedside while his fever was raging. His aunt was still desperate for a happy ending, but Finn knew better.

In the hallway, through the glass, he saw Daniel put his arms round Rachel's shoulders and lead her away. Daniel Quinn was a good man, and anyone could see how he felt about Rachel. He'd be there for her through her sadness, and even though he'd once been a bully, she might grow to love him. Stranger things had happened.

Helen would be there to help Finn through, like she had after Ethan's death, but she couldn't mend his heart. He'd be giving up on love. Too much pain. Anyway, how could he settle for second-best? He'd had it all, but the magic had vanished all too quickly.

Epilogue

Rachel stood at the kitchen window, watching grown-ups and children alike having a fun snowball fight in the garden. The sun was shining brightly in a blue sky, so this unexpected winter wonderland would vanish soon and they'd all wanted to make the most of it.

She opened the fridge and took out the wedding anniversary cake, placing it on the counter. It was a huge iced monster, with a picture of the happy bride and groom on their special day – five years ago now. It didn't seem possible.

There was a knock at the window, and she turned to see little Dan pressing his nose against it, smudging the glass. His eyes were shining with the excitement of the day, and she blew him a kiss. He was sitting high on Daniel's shoulders, and pulling at the head of hair in front of him. Daniel gave a mock wince, but he loved Dan as much as the four-year-old loved him. Daniel had a real knack with children. She was glad he'd taken that life-changing decision years ago to give up the priesthood. Now he was doing what he was born to do – be a husband and father.

'Need a hand?' asked Sophia, coming from the living room. 'I'm craving cake.'

Rachel smiled at her cousin. 'If you get some plates and forks, I'll do the candles.'

The laughter outside drifted through to them in the kitchen, and Rachel marvelled again at how Daniel had managed to transform her life from desperate sadness to intense happiness. It was so much more than she had hoped for – and perhaps more than she deserved.

'Penny for them?' asked Sophia, taking up the candles and arranging them on the cake.

'Sorry,' Rachel said. 'I was watching everyone … and

thinking about Ella. The guilt comes back sometimes when I remember I married one of my sister's bullies.'

Sophia gave her a hug. 'If Ella's looking down right now, I think she understands. She knows you married a good man. Not the teenage bully she knew.'

It's what Rachel told her sister in those occasional imaginary conversations they had inside her head. Then she conjured up an Ella who was older, more experienced, no longer trapped for eternity at age fourteen. That Ella told her forgiveness was healing. 'You're right. He's the best husband.'

There was movement behind her. 'I'm glad to hear it.'

Rachel turned to see her husband holding little Dan, who was pointing hopefully at the cake. Smiling, she took the child into her arms and hugged him close, then blew a kiss to his daddy. Powerful feelings of love almost overwhelmed her, and she had to steady herself against the kitchen table, blinking the tears away.

'Come to Auntie Sophia, Dan,' her cousin said to the little boy. 'Let Mummy and Daddy have a moment together. We'll get you out of your coat and boots, and ready for some cake.'

After the two left, Rachel put her arms around the man she adored and said, 'I love you.'

They kissed until a snowball exploded against the kitchen window, Rachel reluctantly pulled away, remembering the dessert.

'I'd better take that cake through before I feel the need to take you upstairs,' she teased, and his smile made her long for the party to be over.

* * *

Rachel yawned as she closed the door behind the last guest. It had been a long day, starting at six with little Dan bouncing on their bed with excitement. She listened at the foot of the stairs. All was quiet. He was asleep now upstairs, after demanding one of Daniel's bedtime stories, which always featured a heroic four-year-old who saved the day.

Only one soft lamp was on in the living room, but the Christmas tree glowed brightly near the window, its red, green and white fairy lights reminding Rachel for a moment of that tree she'd watched being decorated years ago in the village square in Kilbrook. Then her life had been filled with thoughts of revenge. Now she only had room in her heart for love.

She smiled down at her husband sprawled on the sofa, their daughter fast asleep and burrowed into his jumper. Sitting down on the carpet and resting against the sofa, she watched the flames dancing in the grate as she thought about the road that had led her here, and how close she'd come to turning her back on this blissful existence ...

* * *

Eight months on from the trauma of Kilbrook, Rachel thought she was doing okay. Her thesis was almost done, she had a part-time job in an art gallery, and she was starting to socialise again. Daniel, who'd moved to London and was working with the homeless, was always there when she needed him, and sometimes that need was overwhelming. He'd managed to convince her to see a counsellor, and talking with the therapist about what had happened was helping Rachel work through her feelings.

Then one day she'd picked up one of those celebrity magazines in the gallery and saw that Finn was going to be filming in London. A willowy blonde was hanging on his arm, gazing at him adoringly. And who could blame her? It still hurt to see him, though, and she confessed as much in her next therapy session.

'You said that when you last saw him, he was unconscious,' said Ruth, her counsellor.

Rachel nodded.

'Then maybe you should see him while he's not.'

Rachel shook her head. 'He's with someone else now.' She tried to ignore that telltale sign of jealousy gnawing at her gut. 'And that's best for both of us.'

'What do you have to lose?' Ruth asked. 'If you're over him, it won't hurt. If you're not ... well, maybe you need to think again. Important decisions about your life should never be made during emotional upheaval, which is what you did.'

To Rachel's surprise, because she knew how he felt about her, Daniel had agreed with that suggestion, and during several late-night chats over bottles of wine, he persuaded her to meet with Finn. For that dreaded 'closure'. And so she found herself outside the South Bank Centre with its bookstalls and street performers. A busy place, where she could make an easy escape, if necessary.

She spotted Finn first, leaning against the embankment wall, watching the Thames drift by. For a moment, she just stood there, looking at him. He was surely a bit thinner than she remembered, but it was still Finn, even with the trendy brushed up hair and designer stubble. Very macho, but still boyish. He was wearing blue jeans and a tight white T-shirt, which accentuated his tan and his muscles. She smiled to herself, thinking he'd look good in a bin liner.

His sixth sense must have told him he was being watched because he turned and looked right at her, a nervous smile lighting up his face. For a moment, they said nothing, and Rachel was aware that it was like looking back in time, to another life. Or watching reruns of an old soap on TV, when you knew all the characters had moved on.

Over coffee later, she politely asked how he'd been, how Helen was, then brought up the question of his hands, which she'd always felt guilty about. He held them up. 'Good as new,' he said. 'Unless you get really close.' They parted as friends, agreeing to see each other again, 'for old time's sake.' He didn't mention the girl in the photo, and Rachel didn't asked. She had no right.

She met up with Finn several times after that, usually with Daniel present. It was easier that way. Initially, Rachel still felt confused, and at times doubted the wisdom of taking Ruth's – and Daniel's – advice, but slowly she began to regain confidence in herself, and in her future. And on a frosty November morning, she woke up and knew it was the start of her life. She was over the past. Her demons had been silenced and she was ready to take another chance on love. Slowly, they had crossed the space between them until the ghosts of the past had completely vanished. It wasn't a Hollywood movie, so there'd been no fireworks, or violins, or sudden passionate kisses. But it had been a beginning, and they'd taken careful steps, until they'd felt the stirrings of a need, the ignition of a fire that wasn't going to be extinguished.

* * *

'Our daughter wants Santa to come tomorrow.'

His voice was sleepy, and she turned to look at his flushed cheeks and sexy messed-up hair.

'Don't we all?' she smiled, and gently stroked his face.

'It was a great day, wasn't it?'

'The best,' she agreed. 'So good to see everyone again before we go back.'

'By the way, Santa came early for you.'

He pointed to a blue velvet box, tied onto the tree with a shiny red ribbon. When she opened it, Rachel gasped in delight at the ring of white gold, with tiny diamonds set into the band, clustered into the shape of tiny stars.

'An eternity ring,' he said. 'Together forever,' and he took it and placed it on her finger, next to her wedding band.

'It's beautiful,' she whispered. 'Thank you.'

As she leaned forward to kiss him, there was a whimper from the child caught between them.

'Time for bed, little Ella,' said Rachel, and she picked the toddler up, cuddling her close. Looking down at her hand, she saw the new ring wink at her in the lamplight. An arm went around her shoulder, holding her tight.

'Happy anniversary, Mrs MacKenzie,' said Finn.

* * *

Rachel didn't enjoy flying, especially at night. At least little Dan was sleeping soundly in the middle seat, as was Ella cuddled up in her mother's arms. Rachel looked at her watch. They'd only been in the air for two hours. She couldn't wait to get back to their home overlooking Sydney Harbour. Australia was their home now. It was what Rachel had dreamed about back in Kilbrook before all the revelations – that she and Finn would spend a lifetime together, raising children, loving each other.

Once again she raised a silent thank you to Daniel Quinn for the part he'd played in her happiness. He'd been such a great friend. As soon as he left the priesthood, he was like a child in a toyshop. He'd realised there were lots of other women just waiting to be wooed by a man who had a lot of catching up to do. Rachel had teased him that he may as well call his girlfriends by the months of the year instead of their names, but then he'd met Julie. The One. Rachel and Finn had already agreed to be godparents to their twins, due in four months. Daniel was overjoyed at the prospect of being a househusband – Julie would continue to work as an accountant, and he would look after the children. And write. Daniel had a talent for entertaining children, so planned to translate that talent into books.

'God,' Finn had said when Daniel told him. 'That all sounds too much like hard work.'

'I'm looking forward to it,' said Daniel.

'Wait till you change your first set of nappies,' Finn had teased.

It had been good to be back in London, and to catch up with friends and family. They'd spent six months – all paid for – there while Finn made his latest movie. He was a good actor, and Hollywood was beckoning. Rachel wondered what Marilyn made of that.

They'd taken a weekend trip to Toulouse and been the guests of honour in Henri's thriving restaurant. They hadn't gone back to Kilbrook – neither Finn nor Rachel ever wanted to go there again – but they'd met up with Molly in Galway for a day. She'd told them Jenny would be graduating from drama school in Dublin the following summer. Mel was miserable working for her father in his antiques emporium. And Jay was living with his parents in Westport and selling sporting goods.

Finn stirred from his nap, and glanced around, as though trying to remember where he was. He looked stressed.

'Are you okay?' she asked.

He nodded. 'I am now. I was dreaming I was back in Kilbrook, watching you and Daniel walk out of the hospital together.'

'When he flew with me to London for a couple of days, just to check I was okay. And you thought we were a couple …'

'I wasn't thinking clearly at the time.'

'None of us were.'

'I still feel guilty at times, you know – for hating him like I did. Especially when I think about everything he did for us. Talking you into seeing that counsellor – talking you into seeing me.'

Rachel laughed. 'And for staying in touch with Helen – the crafty pair! We didn't stand a chance really.' It would be good to see Helen again. She'd be waiting for them at the airport. She was always a regular visitor to their house. Along with Jim, a lovely widower who seemed to have designs on her, and who Helen certainly wasn't discouraging.

Later, Rachel slept, and when she woke, Finn had pulled up the blind and was looking out of the window. She took his hand, and he turned towards her, smiling.

'Look,' he said, pointing into the darkness. 'Maybe that's our star.'

'Yes,' Rachel whispered, holding his hand tightly. She could feel the Claddagh resting against her neck, as she gazed at the bright point of light, burning in the night sky, a reminder of their Irish promise to each other, all those years ago.

You won't ever lose me, no matter what happens.

About the Author

Isabella Connor is the pen name for
Liv Thomas and Valerie Olteanu.

www.facebook.com/isabella.connor.hartswood.hill
www.blog.isabellaconnor.com

Liv Thomas was born and raised in the South of England.
She always had the dream of becoming a writer, but never
had the confidence to pursue it completely. After positive
responses to Lord of the Rings fan-fiction, she decided it
was time to make the dream a reality. Wife and mum, Liv
works for the NHS, and is employed at the hospital which
first featured in Channel 4's One Born Every Minute. Liv
is a member of the Romantic Novelists' Association.

www.twitter.com/Livbet

Valerie Olteanu grew up in Scotland, and her childhood
ambitions were to travel and to be a writer. After studying
English and Art History at the University of Glasgow,
she moved to London where she worked in the Literature
Department of the Arts Council England. Some years
later, she decided to teach English and see the world.
She lived and worked in Croatia, the West Bank, and
Mexico, before settling with her husband in Canada. She is
currently an adult educator in Burnaby, British Columbia.

An Irish Promise is the authors' second novel with
Choc Lit. *Beneath an Irish Sky* was their debut.

More Choc Lit

From Isabella Connor

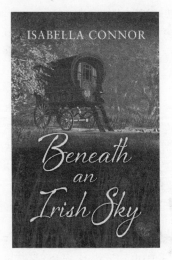

Beneath an Irish Sky

The past is never over ...

Jack Stewart thought he'd put the past behind him. On the surface, he has everything – success, money, a big house and he is never short of an attractive woman by his side, but a tragic road accident shatters his world.

Raised as an Irish Traveller, Luke Kiernan hasn't had it easy, and when he wakes in a Dublin hospital to find the man he's hated since childhood at his bedside, he's hungry for revenge.

Two very different worlds collide, bringing new dangers, exposing past deceits, and unearthing dark family secrets buried long ago. But from tragedy springs the promise of a fresh start with two women who are intent on helping Jack and Luke mend their lives.

Can new love heal old wounds, or are some scars there for good?

Visit www.choc-lit.com for more details, or simply scan barcode using your mobile phone QR reader.

An Excerpt from
Beneath an Irish Sky

CHAPTER ONE

'I'm here to identify the body of Annie Kiernan.' It was so long since Jack had spoken her name, the words almost stuck in his throat.

'And you are?'

The Guard was chewing a mouthful of sandwich. Jack caught the faint stink of onion through the gap in the security glass and his stomach turned. He shoved his passport into the tray and watched the police officer leaf through it.

'Are you next of kin?'

'Husband,' Jack replied, for want of a better word.

'Oh – sorry for your loss. Fill out this form, please.'

A paper and pen were pushed into the tray. The pen didn't work, so Jack took the Montblanc from his inside pocket. He pressed the words deep into the paper, a habit from years of signing contracts in triplicate, and passed back the completed paperwork. 'Where do I find the morgue?'

The man shook his head. 'It's in another building – only next door, but there needs to be a Guard with you to record the ID.'

Bloody bureaucracy. Jack would prefer to be alone when he saw Annie. He might do anything. Cry. Even slap her face. Better to have no witnesses to such loss of control.

'You came over from England?' the Guard asked.

'Yes.'

'Your wife lived in Ireland, though?'

'We were separated.'

Was that a flicker of interest? Or pity? That was worse. No one pitied Jack Stewart, least of all some desk sergeant in a crummy Dublin police station. He glanced at his Rolex. 'I'm booked on a return flight at two.'

'Right. Take a seat. Someone will be with you shortly.'

Jack wandered over to the decrepit waiting area with its rows of green plastic seats, where he joined the slouched bodies of the weary and the troubled.

'Shortly' was nearly thirty minutes.

'Jack Stewart?' A policeman scanned the waiting area.

'Yes.'

'I'm Sergeant Flynn.'

A handshake, as if Jack mattered. Christ, when did he become so cynical? But he knew the answer to that one. It was when she left him.

'Sorry for your loss.'

That platitude again. As if these people had any idea what he and Annie had shared, had lost. Of what he'd suffered because of her.

'If you'll come with me. We'll try to make it as quick as possible.'

Quick. Like her death. Alive one minute, driving her car, thinking of work or shopping or whatever she did these days, and then … gone. Wiped from the roll of the living. It was as much as he knew. As much as the police in Manchester knew. When they'd shown up in his office yesterday, telling him of an accident, he'd panicked and thought of his son, Matt, in Amsterdam on a stag night. That policewoman, oozing compassion, didn't know Jack had dropped down in his chair with relief, not grief. He'd refused to go to Dublin at first – Annie was firmly in the past – but then the police had pointed out he was still officially her next of kin. It wasn't until later the shock of having her reintroduced into his life hit him.

Flynn led Jack out of the police station and into the morgue next door. They were directed to a viewing room at the end of a corridor, but before they entered, Flynn said, 'The desk sergeant told me you and Mrs Stewart were separated. When did you last see her?'

Sod this. Weren't things bad enough without Jack having to

announce his failure as a husband to everyone he met? 'I last saw her over twenty years ago,' he said, quietly enough, yet the words seemed to echo down the long empty corridor.

Flynn raised an eyebrow. 'So there's a chance you might not recognise her?'

Jack thought about that. Annie would have changed. No longer the young girl he'd married. Forty now. Maybe a few wrinkles, some grey hair. That could be a blessing. Like looking at a stranger. 'I'll know her,' he said, with more certainty than he felt. 'Let's get it over with.'

The fluorescent strip lighting in the viewing room was harsh, its relentless blue-white glare attacking every corner. A clock registered almost midday. The body lay in the centre of the room, covered with a sheet. The hairs on the back of Jack's neck prickled, although he'd seen a dead body before. Just once. An asthma attack had taken his first wife when she was only twenty-four. Jack had cradled Caroline in his arms as if he could will some of his own warmth back into her. His tears had soaked her face and hair, the grief like a knife in his gut. And now his second wife had left him behind, although she'd actually discarded him years before.

'Ready?' asked Flynn.

Jack nodded. He was as ready as he'd ever be. The sheet was folded back, and he was looking at a heart-shaped face, wounds prominent on skin the colour of chalk. Dark silky hair, maybe the only part of her alive now. He'd read once about people opening a coffin and finding the corpse's hair still growing. Annie would be in a coffin soon. In the dark earth. God, he wanted to throw up.

Flynn was at his elbow. 'Is it …?'

Jack swallowed hard, attempting to make his voice normal. 'It's her.'

'I'll give you a moment.'

The door closed and Jack was alone with Annie. At least, Annie's shell. He didn't touch her. She'd feel like ice, not warm the way he remembered her. Was she watching him? Her spirit floating around, looking down, wondering why he was there? No chance now to find out why she'd left him. The dead don't talk.

'Why?' His voice surprised him. Thinking out loud. 'Why, Annie?'

The lights hummed, the second hand on the clock moved. Nothing else. No miraculous revelation, no gift of closure. Nothing for him here. Jack pulled the sheet back over the face still as familiar to him as his own, and walked away.

In the next room, Flynn had organised tea. Jack gulped it down, feeling the hot, sweet liquid revive him a bit. Almost done now, then back to Baronsmere and normality.

'Just sign here. It says you've formally identified the body.'

Jack scribbled his name, not even bothering to read the form.

'Do you need the name of an undertaker?' Flynn asked.

'Sorry?'

'I have a list of local undertakers.'

'Why would I need that?'

'Well ... for the funeral. We're releasing the body to you.'

'I can't take care of that! I only came here to identify her. I've got to get back to Manchester.'

'The body can't stay here, Mr Stewart.' Flynn spoke slowly, as if explaining something to a child.

'But what am I supposed to do with her?'

'The undertakers can move her to a funeral home. There's one – McBride's – near the hospital, which would be practical. They'll help you arrange the burial.'

Arrangements. Paperwork. Phone calls. Red tape. This was ridiculous. And why was a location near the hospital 'practical'?

'She has other family,' Jack protested. 'What about them?' Was he the only relative here? That seemed more than a bit strange given Travellers' strong family connections.

Flynn consulted his paperwork but shook his head. 'The car was registered to Joseph Kiernan, but no one seems to know where he is. He and his brother work away a lot, apparently.'

Useless bastards her brothers were, anyway. No-hopers, who never forgave Annie for marrying an outsider. 'And there's no one else?' Jack asked, not really wanting the answer. Even now, he preferred not to think about Annie in another relationship.

'Her father's dead, according to neighbours. Your son might be able to tell you where other relatives are.'

How the hell would Matt know that? Just how incompetent were these people? 'What are you talking about? My son hasn't seen Annie since he was four.'

Flynn flicked back through his paperwork. 'Your son, Luke, was in the car with your wife when the accident happened. He's in St Aidan's Hospital.'

Jack shouldn't have been surprised, but it still rankled that Annie had found happiness with someone else – started a family, even used the name they'd planned for their own son. His hand curled into a fist in his lap. 'No one told me she had a son,' he said, his voice hard. 'So why haven't you contacted the father, her … partner?' The Traveller. The one she'd shacked up with after leaving him and returning to her own people. 'He should be taking care of all this.'

'There is no partner, as far as we're aware,' Flynn told him. 'The birth certificate identifies her son as Luke Stewart, although he appears to be using the name Kiernan now, and you're named as his father. I'm sorry, I thought the Manchester police explained this to you.'

'How old is he?' Jack asked.

'Twenty.'

The walls of the room seemed to close in. Not enough air. Jack closed his eyes. A son he never knew about! Not possible. Why would Annie do that? It was monstrous. Cruel. If she weren't already dead, he'd probably have killed her.

'You okay?' Flynn poured more tea, but Jack couldn't drink it.

'He's not my son.'

'But the birth certificate …'

'It's not true.'

Flynn nodded. 'Well, perhaps you should still go and see him. He might be able to tell you who to contact to take charge of the funeral. We'll have to interview him about the accident at some point, but he's been in Intensive Care.' He handed Jack a sheet of paper. 'Here's the list of undertakers. They'll know what to do.'

That was good, because Jack didn't. All he could think about was what he'd just been told. A twenty-year-old son he'd known nothing about …

'Will you be okay? Do you want me to drive you anywhere?'

That look of pity again. Jack felt a flash of anger. He was no helpless victim. He was New Business Director at Stewart Enterprises. A successful man, renowned for coping with anything. He'd get through this. Somehow. 'I'll find my own way – thanks.'

The taxi dropped Jack at the entrance to St Aidan's Hospital. He stood next to a few furtive smokers. Should he go inside or just walk away? He could pay some local undertaker a hefty sum to take care of everything. What else was money for if not to ease the rough patches in your life?

Someone thrust an open pack of cigarettes in front of him. He looked down at an elderly woman, bent under the weight of her widow's hump. 'No … thanks.'

'Might take the edge off, son.'

So he looked like he felt. Gutted.

The old lady patted his arm. 'God'll take care of everything, y'know.'

'You don't happen to have his number, do you?'

The woman tutted and moved away. He was in one of the most Catholic countries in Europe. Insult God and it could be taken personally. Jack didn't believe in heavenly help or miracles, though. He was on his own. So he might as well talk to this young man who was supposed to be his son. Perhaps at last he was going to get answers.

'Good afternoon, Mr Kiernan.'

'My surname is Stewart. My wife and I were separated.' How many times would Jack have to repeat this?

The consultant, O'Meara, looked uncomfortable and glanced down at his notes. Probably preferred broken bodies to broken families. 'I'm sorry – my mistake. Luke's driving licence says Kiernan.'

'And his birth certificate says Stewart. Please just tell me about – my son.' This wasn't the place to voice doubts about Luke being his. The staff might get iffy if he wasn't a relative, and then he wouldn't be able to ask the kid any questions.

'Luke suffered concussion, bruised ribs and some torn knee ligaments.'

'But he's okay, yes?' That was all he needed to know. Why couldn't doctors just cut to the chase?

'Mr Stewart, Luke arrested at the scene. Luckily, a driver who came to help was familiar with CPR – resuscitation. Luke still needs to be monitored in case of complications, but he's stable. We moved him from Intensive Care this morning.'

'Does he know? About his mother?'

To Jack's dismay, the doctor shook his head. 'He's been on morphine so in and out of awareness. Not a good time to talk to him.'

Great. Jack would have to book into a hotel. This thing could take days.

'His leg will take a few weeks to heal, same with his ribs. He'll need crutches for a while.'

Jack wasn't going to be hanging around for a few weeks. Hopefully the Kiernans would show up soon and take over. 'When can I see him?'

'A nurse can take you now.'

Jack stood up.

'One more thing, Mr Stewart ... Luke has bruises on his face and body that weren't caused by the crash. The colouring suggests he got them some days earlier.'

Why was Jack being told this? Were they afraid he'd sue them for malpractice?

'Do you know anything about those bruises?'

God, O'Meara thought he'd done it. Beaten the kid up. Obviously had him pegged as a bad father. 'I haven't been near Luke in years,' he said. The truth, although twisted.

'Well, I'd guess some time recently he's been badly beaten. He'll need peace and quiet – and support – to heal. The past couple of weeks have obviously been very traumatic for him.'

So Luke was the kind of person who got into fights. Not surprising, really, with uncles like Joe and Liam Kiernan. Some start in life. Things would have been very different if Luke had grown up in Baronsmere. *But he's not my son.* It disturbed Jack that he'd forgotten this. He didn't want to get emotionally involved.

Thankfully, Luke was in a single room. No nosy fellow patients or visitors to worry about. Jack watched from the doorway as the nurse checked the IV.

'Why don't you sit with him for a while?' she suggested. 'I'll fix you a cup of tea.'

'Thanks.'

Jack slumped down into a chair, hoping the boy wasn't going to wake up just yet because he didn't have a clue what to say. The hospital bed made him look small and young, about seventeen, maybe eighteen. Unfortunately, the birth certificate said otherwise. He focused on Luke's face with its cuts and bruises, and tried but failed to find any resemblance to the Stewarts. Luke was his mother's son. With his long dark eyelashes and black hair, the kid was so like Annie that it actually hurt. Jack had thought he was over the pain, but all this was bringing it back.

What exactly had Annie told her son? Luke had probably seen his birth certificate yet he'd never tried to make contact, which seemed strange, especially given the Stewart's wealth. And if Annie wanted nothing more to do with him, not even financial help, why did she put Jack on the birth certificate at all? It didn't make sense.

A monitor beeped, and he flicked his attention back to Luke, whose eyes were now open. He looked confused, and Jack wished he'd gone to a hotel for the rest of the day because now he'd have to say something reassuring, and probably identify himself. Standing up, he moved towards the bed. 'Luke? You're in hospital, but don't worry, you're going to be okay.' He sounded and felt awkward. 'You don't know me, but …'

'I know who you are. I've seen your picture. You're my bastard father.'

Jack froze, his mind replaying the words.

'You threw my mother out because – what was it? – you didn't want a *gypo* kid!'

Luke was staring daggers at him. Annie must have said Jack had rejected *her,* instead of the other way round. 'What the hell are you talking about? I never even knew you existed before today.'

'Liar!' Luke's voice was raised and cracking with the strain. He struggled to sit up, winced, and sank back against the pillows. He looked exhausted but somehow found the strength to sweep a jug of water from the locker beside him towards Jack. It missed by inches, clattering against the wall, its contents flooding the floor.

A nurse hurried into the room. She spoke gently to Luke but it had no effect. He was obviously distressed and in pain. A male nurse appeared and frowned at Jack. 'If you don't mind, sir. We need to settle the patient.'

A firm hand on his shoulder steered Jack towards the door.

As if it were his fault. He flushed at the injustice. That was it. He was out of here, on a flight back to Manchester that afternoon.

'Where's my mother? I want to see my mother!'

Glancing back, the despair on Luke's face told Jack he already suspected the truth. Part of him was thankful he wouldn't have to be the one to tell the kid his mother was dead. The other part of him felt like a total shit, but what could he do? It wasn't his problem. It was all very sad but nothing to do with him. If he didn't go now, he'd miss the flight. Luke was not his son. But although his head said one thing, his heart said another. He couldn't walk out now and leave those terrible accusations unchallenged. 'I'll wait in the Relatives' Room,' he told the nurse.

Emer Sullivan sipped a strong black coffee and wished she still smoked. Five years without a cigarette and she was still waiting for those occasional cravings to disappear. They came when her in-tray was overflowing. Being a hospital counsellor was great, but to get through all the paperwork, you'd have to give up talking to the patients. One of life's little ironies.

She opened the file on her desk. A new case had just developed into a crisis. The details were sketchy: a woman killed in a car crash, her son badly injured. The father had just appeared on the scene and there'd been an argument. Emer had been asked to tell the son, Luke Kiernan, his mother was dead. She glanced at her watch. An hour since the incident. His tranquilliser would be wearing off but he should still be calm enough for her to talk to him. Emer left her office and reached Luke's side room at the same time as a nurse finished taking his blood pressure. His eyes were fixed on the ceiling.

To be continued ...

CLAIM YOUR FREE EBOOK

of

An Irish Promise

You may wish to have a choice of how you read
An Irish Promise. Perhaps you'd like a digital
version for when you're out and about, so that
you can read it on your ereader, iPad or even a
Smartphone. For a limited period, we're including
a **FREE** ebook version along with this paperback.

To claim, simply visit ebooks.choc-lit.com
or scan the QR Code.

You'll need to enter the following code:

Q221409

Introducing Choc Lit

We're an independent publisher creating
a delicious selection of fiction.
Where heroes are like chocolate – irresistible!
Quality stories with a romance at the heart.
See our selection here:
www.choc-lit.com

We'd love to hear how you enjoyed *An Irish Promise*.
Please visit our website and give your feedback.

Choc Lit novels are selected by genuine readers like yourself.
We only publish stories our Choc Lit Tasting Panel want to
see in print. Our reviews and awards speak for themselves.

Could you be a Star Selector and join our Tasting Panel?
Would you like to play a role in choosing which novels
we decide to publish? Do you enjoy reading romance
novels? Then you could be perfect for our Choc Lit
Tasting Panel. Visit our website for more details.

Keep in touch:
Sign up for our monthly newsletter Choc Lit Spread for
all the latest news and offers: www.spread.choc-lit.com.
Follow us on Twitter: @ChocLituk and Facebook: Choc Lit.

Or simply scan barcode using your mobile phone QR reader:

Choc Lit   *Twitter*   *Facebook*
Spread